LORDS OF THE FRONTIER

W. Bruce Kippen

LORDS OF THE FRONTIER

iUniverse books may be ordered through booksellers or by contacting:

iUniverse
1663 Liberty Drive
Bloomington, IN 47403
www.iuniverse.com
844-349-9409

Because of the dynamic nature of the Internet, any web addresses or links contained in this book may have changed since publication and may no longer be valid. The views expressed in this work are solely those of the author and do not necessarily reflect the views of the publisher, and the publisher hereby disclaims any responsibility for them.

Any people depicted in stock imagery provided by Getty Images are models, and such images are being used for illustrative purposes only. Certain stock imagery © Getty Images.

ISBN: 978-1-5320-7630-5 (sc)
ISBN: 978-1-5320-7633-6 (e)

Library of Congress Control Number: 2019906441

Print information available on the last page.

iUniverse rev. date: 04/29/2021

ACKNOWLEDGMENTS

Working all these years and all these hours to write this book, owes so much to so many, especially Emily Parson from Montreal who's editing and direction proved instrumental. I also want to thank my family, especially Alexander who encouraged me to keep writing and rewriting this story.

There is still so much more to rewrite and to improve before I could call this book finished. But my time is up and so this book is done. I hope you like reading it in a small way as much as I loved writing it. And maybe you will think of where this story can grow and become better.

My greatest hope is that you think of how three small town teens today might grow up to remake Canada in our century ahead. Because while this book is done, its story is endless.

W. Bruce Kippen
2019

CONTENTS

ATTACK ON CDR

Chapter 1

If you were to ask the average man to describe Ian MacLeod, here is what he most likely would have said: a charming, ambitious fellow with an appetite for the finer things in life.

If you were to ask his two best friends, Richard Benson or James MacTavish, here is what either might say: Oh, Ian! Real piss-and-vinegar type. Goodness, he's a cheeky little bastard, isn't he?

Physically, Ian was what a lot of middle-aged well-to-do men were: a little heavy in the gut and a little light in the hair, too much charm by far, and either too much or too little time on his hands. Certainly, he seemed inclined to idleness, spending time in the beds of women other than his wife.

Yet, he also devoted a great deal of time to managing his media empire. Ian controlled several companies, most of them newspaper companies, which was quite a feat for someone not born with a silver spoon.

In truth, Ian was, as most people were, a study of contradictions. At the moment, however, he was a host, preparing his study to receive his dear old friend, James.

James and he had been friends for over a dozen years at this point and business partners for about a decade. At this point, they were beyond the formalities reserved for lesser friends.

As such, Ian was not straightening his study to make it more presentable. No, Ian was pulling out his finest scotch and his expensive crystal tumblers. A sharp knock on the front door interrupted his final checks and he strolled on over, pulling the door open.

"James! How are you, old son?" Ian clapped his old friend on the arm, welcoming him inside.

"Ian! Fantastic! I have amazing news!" James grinned widely.

Now, Ian was not ugly, by far; he'd been a handsome youth and though his looks had gone soft with age, he was still on the better looking side of things. James, though, James was a handsome devil. Always had been and likely always would be.

"Oh?"

"Ian, I'm in love!"

1

"Oh? Well, come in then. Settle yourself down and tell me all about your lady love. Here, your favorite: double scotch."

"Thank you." James downed the drink in two sips and Ian topped it up obligingly. "Her name is Lady Jane Hampton Smith. She is stunning. Ian, I've never seen a more beautiful woman in my life."

"Don't just wax poetical. Give me some details, man."

"Ian, she's stunning. Her hair is the color of chocolate. She has the most amazing nightingale voice. I could listen to her talk for days. And her eyes! The deepest, darkest, calmest blue you've ever seen, Ian! And she carries herself like a queen. The sight of her sent shocks through my entire being."

"Like a lightning bolt? Or a *coup-de-foudre*, as the French say?"

"No mere lightning bolt, Ian! A storm's worth of lightning could not have struck me harder."

"James, you are a poet, and a hopeless one. Come, speak clearly. What you are really saying is that you felt a surge of blood to your erogenous zone, am I right?" Ian laughed.

"Don't be so crude," James rebuked, giggling into his third drink. "It wasn't like that."

"Pish. It's always like that. The male organ is the Achilles heel of any man. I know what it's like, same as any other man. It's an electric shock from the groin to the brain. It just sounds better to call it 'love at first sight'. Power of words, my friend. Works with and against a man. No, the challenge here is to combine the love of the body with the love of the head and the heart. So which is it, old boy? Do you love her with your head, your heart, or your bits?"

James paused, half way through refilling his glass. "I don't know, Ian. It feels like it must be all three."

"In that case, you must be a truly lucky man. Oh, don't look at me that way. It's rarer than you think."

"What about your wife? How do you love her?"

"With my head, mostly. She's a fine dame and a fox in the sheets but it's rare she joins me in bed these days and we both know I married her for her name. And speaking of names, it almost sounds to me like your Lady Jane might be married."

"She is, Ian. To a small-time London stockbroker. Ian, what am I to do? She has become my obsession, my muse!"

"James, let me give you some advice. And you are not to tell Richard I am repeating anything he's told me over the years. James, don't mess with married women. They're more trouble than they're worth. But, if this love does persist after a few months, I'll help you land her."

"Thank you, Ian. Richard told you all that?"

"God no! Richard told me to stay away from women, married women in particular."

"That does seem to be more in keeping with the man."

"So, what that what you came all this way to tell me? A wire would have worked just as well."

"True enough, but no, it isn't. I got a letter from Van Rennslleir the other day."

"Van Rennslleir? Our Van Rennslleir?"

"Do you know any other?"

"No, but it's been so long. I wasn't sure he was even still alive."

"Well, he does seem to be in poor health, according to his letter, at least. He talked about wanting to see us before it was too late."

"Sounds serious. What do think, James?"

James shrugged, blinking blearily as he tilted a little to the side. Ian sighed and plucked the bottle from his grip, capping it and returning it to its spot.

"Tell me more about the letter, James."

"Right. Right." He cleared his throat and drew himself up a little. "He'll be in town soon, likely by Tuesday, Wednesday at the latest. He wants to see us over at his hotel for drinks and lunch on Thursday."

"Thursday . . ." Ian pulled his day planner from the inside pocket of his jacket and flipped through. "I'm free for lunch. Where are you staying, James?"

"Got a hotel not far from here. Was gonna walk there once we were done catching up."

"You'll be wanting to take a taxi, old boy. Trust me on that."

"Yeah. I didn't bring any money."

Ian sighed. Digging out his wallet, he dropped some money on the table. "Meet me here Thursday and we'll head over together."

Sir William Van Rennslleir looked vastly different from the Van Rennslleir a younger Ian remembered meeting. He seemed shorter than before and he wasn't as big as he'd been when they'd met. However, where there'd been a muscular solidity to him before, that was obviously long gone, replaced with the softness of fat.

But that was not the biggest change. Van Rennslleir was still just as loud as he's always been but the exuberance was changed. It was a softer exuberance, one lacking the same bombastic energy as before.

"My boys! Welcome, welcome! Come, sit, tell me what I've missed since we last spoke."

"Mr. Van Rennslleir!" Ian greeted with a charming smile. "It is a true pleasure to see you. James, over here, old son."

James plopped himself down next to Ian. His eyes were a little glazed.

"Care for a drink, lads?"

James perked up, only to grunt a second later when Ian parked his elbow in the other's gut.

"Just a small one. James isn't much of a drinker," he emphasized subtly, "and I prefer not to drink before 5."

"Perfectly understandable. Scotch work for the both of you? I have a lovely aged scotch."

"Just a finger each."

"Wonderful." Van Rennslleir handed them each a beautiful crystal glass. When his back was turned, Ian cast James a warning glance. James grimaced but inclined his head in understanding. "So. I see you took my advice, Sir Ian."

Ian grinned. "A lordship is very useful in business. The number of doors that have opened to me since my knighting, it's incredible. I've had more opportunities in the year since my knighting than in the decade that proceeded it, not including you, sir."

"Well, I saw something in you and I invested. I'm sure you boys will find young'uns to do the same with in a few years. It's always worth investing in the youth. And speaking of youth, I heard you were married."

"Yes, sir. A wife and a son. I don't see them often though. I travel a lot."

"A pity," Van Rennslleir put forth. "Take some more advice from this old man: invest in them. You'll regret not doing so once you're my age."

Ian smiled, sipping at his drink. "My boy's in school and doing well. I imagine he'll join me in my business once he's old enough. There's time yet. But forgive me if I seem brusque, what did you call us here for? Judging by your letter to James, you seemed to have something urgent to say."

"Ah, yes! Well, it isn't too urgent, merely an idea, but one you would need to pounce on immediately if you want to benefit from it. Have you ever considered acquiring shares in a railroad?"

Ian leaned forth, intrigued. "Considered? Of course. I've simply been too busy to do so. James? What about you?"

James jolted, blinking blearily. "Yes, of course. Too busy." He cast a discrete glance at Ian, who mouthed 'railroad shares acquisition'. "My business has been expanding lately and I haven't had the chance to do much research into the issue."

"And a smart man always does his research before investing, a smart policy," Van Rennslleir agreed. "Well, let me present the both of you with a business opportunity. These days, my money comes from all over, but it used to be grounded in the railroad companies, specifically the Canada Dominion Railway. Have you heard of it?"

"Heard of it? I took it to Calgary way back when!" Ian exclaimed. "James too, I think." James nodded. "Bit rough back then but it must have been worth a fortune even then."

"Indeed. When I was a young man, I used to tell my fellows to sell their boots and buy shares in the railroad. Told them they'd eat diamonds in a few years if they did. But you know how young men are. They think with their bellies and the wrong head, almost focused on immediate pleasures instead of eventual success."

"Let me guess, you bought shares instead of buying beer."

"More than that, I bought the entire company! Ah, but that was a long time ago now. No more. The stock has since dispersed. Most of it is in England these days."

"And that's why you wanted to talk to us?"

"Yes. I have no horse in this race anymore. The stock I have is too small to do much with, though it still turns a profit. And the company president is someone I scarcely approve of. It would be a tough battle, I have no doubt, Sir Montgomery is a hard-headed man, but I have no doubt too strapping young lads like yourself would have too much trouble acquiring a controlling block in the company."

"And you would be willing to help in that regard?" Ian pushed, eyes sharp.

"I am but an old man, my boy." Van Rennslleir took a sip from his drink, eyes meeting Ian's over the rim of his glass. "What can an old man do? I would, perhaps, be willing to engage in a mutually beneficial arrangement, should one arise in the coming days."

Ian grinned and drained his glass.

He had a new project.

"That was interesting, now wasn't it? James?"

"Yes, interesting, very interesting." James' voice was frosty and his gaze was, if possible, even colder, the blue of his eyes chilled to a shade closer to ice.

"James," Ian sighed, melting into a free chair. He rolled his shoulders tiredly.

"What was that, Ian? I'm not a child. You had no right treating me like one."

"If you didn't drink like you were two decades younger than you are, I wouldn't have to," Ian snapped. "And if you hadn't shown up drunk, I wouldn't have had to in the first place."

"I wasn't drunk," James snapped, pacing.

"Hungover then. You obviously were not in the proper state of mind."

"You had no right!"

"James. James!" Ian barked. James whirled to face him. "I don't give a damn if you drink from nine to five every day of the week but I do care if you screw my business up. Van Rennslleir is still a powerful man. And if you had managed to make a poor showing of yourself, I doubt he would have tipped us off about CDR. Now, as far as I'm concerned, here's how things are going to go: you can work with me going forth, drink in your own time and all that, or I can continue as I have been. What will it be?"

James glared poisonously.

"Come on, James. Work with me. I need your help."

"My help?"

"Who's the better researcher between the two of us? It most definitely isn't me. And even Richard has complemented you on your method."

James scoffed, helping himself to a drink. He tossed it back, staring bitterly at the empty glass, and then slammed it down on the table. He glared at Ian, arms crossed, for a long moment.

"If you ever humiliate me like that again, we're done. Permanently."

"I won't have you messing up our business."

"We'll talk beforehand, plan things out. But that debacle will never happen again."

Ian paused, thinking it over. "Alright. I can work with that."

"Good," James snarled. He paused, took a deep breath, and continued, "So. You want me to do some research. CDR stock agreement and history, I presume?"

"Yes. Can you?"

"Of course," James scoffed.

"Thanks, old son. Say, pass me a drink?"

James poured them both a drink. The two toasted and drank quietly. It was a long moment before either spoke.

5

"James. How goes the research?"

James shrugged off his coat, folding it over the back of the armchair. "Good. It's a whole dreadful mess to sort through but I should have it done soon. I've also been working on a game plan for afterwards."

"Fantastic." Ian watched James for a second. The older man wasn't quite ignoring him but nor had their relationship been particularly warm for the past few weeks. "A drink?"

James looked up, opened his mouth, and paused. "In a moment." He reached into his coat and pulled out a crumpled telegram. "From Richard. Good news: he's Canada's Federal Minister of Justice. In a few years, he thinks he's liable to make Prime Minister."

"Wonderful! Good for him! Did he mention why he hasn't contacted me himself?"

James nodded. "He mentioned it a wire or two back, said he had a surprise and he didn't want to spoil it. He said you always could tell when he was keeping something from you. I imagine he thought it would work out better if he simply cut contact with you until he was ready to share."

"That makes sense. Oh, now I find myself impatient. Do you know what this mysterious surprise might be?"

James laughed. "No, I don't, and even if I did, I wouldn't tell you. Isn't the point of a surprise that you don't know what it is?"

"Ah, logic; my greatest ally and my most annoying enemy." Easy laughter filled the office. "What else does the wire say?"

James unfolded it, swiftly running through the contents. "He'll be visiting soon. In a few weeks. I wasn't planning on staying that long, I do have to get back, but I can extend my trip a little while. It's been too long since the last time we were all together."

"Now that I think about it, when was the last time?"

James paused. "You know, I haven't the faintest idea. Not Calgary, I don't think. Surely we've met in the days since."

"No, it might have actually been Calgary. Goodness, that was ten years ago. I know I've seen him since and I'm sure you have too but was that genuinely the last time all three of us were together?"

"What about for your wedding? I don't remember seeing him but surely he came?"

Ian shook his head. "An emergency arose. He showed up a week later with presents and stayed a few nights before heading back. What about for your grand party two years back?"

"If you're talking about my birthday gala, I invited him but his boat was delayed due to storms. We had a nice lunch when he finally arrived."

The two pondered in silence, but the answer to their question was clear. "It really has been since Calgary that we all three have been together. Good Lord, that is . . . an interesting truth."

"Well, at least we'll have a lot to talk about when he shows. I'll be finished with the research by then, all things permitting, and I'll have a plan of action ready to go."

"Oh?" Ian asked, intrigued. "Have you started on it already?"

James shrugged. "Only the basics. CDR is well-protected and its guard dog is . . . devoted, to say the least."

"Guard dog?"

James nodded. "The current president, Sir Edward Montgomery. The man is devoted to his job. A little too devoted, if you ask me: according to reports, he's practically rabid, not to mention obsessed, and he hates foreigners, especially Americans."

Ian frowned, puzzled. "But we're not foreigners."

"Yes, but I don't think he'll see it that way. He's very adamant about it. Here, read this."

Ian took the newspaper clipping James handed him and quickly skimmed the contents. His brow climbed steadily with each new word. By the time he'd finished reading, he was holding the clipping a good distance away, one eyebrow raised so high it had disappeared beneath his bangs.

"That . . . that was . . . interesting."

James nodded solemnly. "That's one word for it. Frenchmen, 'Yanks', basically anyone who isn't Canadian or British or Anglo. And he hates Canadian 'traitors' more than anything. He had a particular line in there about 'traitors', didn't he? A masterpiece of vitriol. What was it again?"

"Do you mean the line about 'traitors to the divine sanctity of the Dominion of Canada, turncoats driven by American greed and loose morals'?"

James laughed. "Yeah, that's the one. I don't think even Richard is as pro-Canadian as this guy. It's – honestly, it's impressive, but also more than a little concerning. If he gets wind of this scheme, he'll cause us no end of trouble."

Ian nodded, eyes fixated on the clipping. "Well, I suppose the only thing to do is to make sure he doesn't get wind of it."

Richard was, for the most part, a simple man with simple tastes and simple needs. He rarely let his pride get in the way of doing what he felt needed to be done, which was a large part of how and why he was so successful in his chosen field.

That being said, he did have very high standards, especially when it came to the places he frequented. As such, he chose a very particular establishment to host their little reunion: a private club's library, reserved with a dedicated drink service, on account of James' and Ian's personal appetites for booze.

It was comfortable, certainly, exuding a sense of casual wealth mixed with the common sense and practical tastes of the lower class. The three men took seats in soft leather armchairs, dark blue in colour and perfectly balanced between supreme cushioning and a certain amount of structural integrity. As such, each of them was perfectly comfortable while still retaining the posture befitting such men of power.

James was nursing his first drink in an engraved crystalline glass while Richard, a teetotaler, was sipping at a bright red sugary drink and Ian helped himself to a pint of beer in a brass mug.

"So, boys," Richard said, setting down his drink, "how are things? What's new in the lives of James MacTavish and Ian Macleod?"

"Well for starters, it's now Lord Ian."

"Lord Ian! Good Lord! Since when? Did I miss a letter?"

Ian laughed. "No, I was knighted not long ago. I figured we'd be seeing each other soon so

I wanted to keep it a surprise. Alas, we met sooner than I thought! I've only been a lord a few months now."

"You should have told me," Richard chided lightly. "I would have brought a gift. Well, you'll just have to wait now. Still, Lord Ian Macleod. Who would have thought it?"

"Actually," James piped up, grumbling slightly, "it's Lord Brandenbrooke." Richard cast a questioning look at Ian.

Ian shrugged. "It's much fancier than Macleod and I suspect people will be more willing to trade with an Englishman than with a Scotsman."

"You should be proud of your heritage," Richard scolded.

"I am! But I'm a businessman, first and foremost. If changing my name earns me more, I'm all for it."

Richard sneered into his drink but said nothing. Ian had heard it all before. If he hadn't listened then, it was highly unlikely he would listen now. "And what of you, James? Are you a lord too?"

James growled and drained his glass, slamming it down alarmingly hard. Richard jumped, turning a helpless gaze from the taciturn Irishman to Ian.

"He should be but he got muzzled out by a number of merchant princes who made money off the Great War."

Richard frowned. "The Great War's been over for a while now. Why wait so long to get a title?"

"It might have taken a while to consolidate funds or to get onto the list. There are plenty of possible reasons."

James snarled, "Goddamn it, Ian! Say it like it is: the PM doesn't want to knight me because I'm Irish. He's a prejudiced bastard, that's what he is!"

"Easy, James. No need to get the blood pumping. I'm not saying you're wrong. Besides, you're still on the list. It's coming. Might have to wait a year or two but you'll get that title, I promise you that."

"I'm gonna get another drink." Ian and Richard watched him stalk off.

"He's been a bit pithy since he found out," Ian offered.

"Do you think he's right? About the PM?"

Ian said nothing for a long moment. "I don't know. This is the second year he's been on the list. Last time, he was cut early on but it was close this time. It could be prejudice or it could be bad luck. The PM is a greedy man. It's entirely possible James wasn't the only one cut from the list due to someone richer wanting a title."

"He sounds pleasant."

"He is. For a politician." Richard glared playfully. "I kid, I kid. Mostly. He is pleasant enough, but, by that logic, so is a poisonous serpent so long as it hasn't gotten around to biting you yet. He's two-faced and greedy; not the type to tell you what he thinks of you to your face. Like I said, he's a politician."

"Now you're just being insulting. He sounds like a despicable character."

"Well, that's politicians for you."

"Be glad we aren't school boys anymore or I'd whoop you good."

"I'm as big as you now, Richard, and younger too. I doubt you'd be the winner in this scenario."

Richard looked Ian up and down. They had a good few years between them. Ian had been a boy when they'd met while Richard had been a young man. Back then, Richard would have won for sure. But time had passed. Richard was taller than Ian but slim by nature and thin due to his work. Meanwhile, Ian was the opposite, a solid frame turned soft by indulgence.

"If you won, it would have nothing to do with strength," Richard retorted, poking Ian in the gut.

"Nothing wrong with a little padding," Ian blustered.

"More like a lot of padding," James cackled, stalking back into the room. His crystal glass had been replaced with a brash mug.

"This is not 'pick on Ian' day, this is 'we haven't collectively seen each other in a good decade so let's catch up and celebrate' day," he protested.

"Well, by all means, let's catch up. Fun or business first?"

James looked down at his mug, thought for a moment, and then said, "Business." He set his drink down and took a seat. "What do you know about the Canada Dominion Railway, old boy?"

"Not a great deal, I confess. It's very rich."

"Indeed. It used to belong to our old mentor, Van Rennslleir. It's worth millions, Richard, and I have just the scheme to get our hands on it. I'll admit to being a bit light on the details, we will have to get back to them later, but I have the broad strokes down. Now, this scheme will, obviously, involve heavy financial commitment and bank loans. Even if we each borrowed our collective weight in gold, we wouldn't have enough. We'll need a syndicate."

"Don't look at me for help," Richard protested. "I'm a political figure now. I can't be tied to this."

"Don't worry, Richard," Ian placated. "Me and James do that. James, carry on."

"Ultimately, the goal will be to engender as much national interest as possible. We don't want to run the thing, we just want to make money off it. The better it does, the richer we'll be."

"Might make things harder in the short term."

James shrugged. "Extra difficulty is always worth a bigger payout. Besides, we do have some advantage. The stock's undervalued and the company has some substantial hidden values. The bank's are liable to go for a high loan-equity ratio."

"You'll be competing with the national debt, though."

Ian nodded sharply at Richard's words. "James, have you checked what the banks' limits are on a stock like C.D.R.?" James shook his head pensively. "Get on that quick. But be discrete about it, alright?"

James scoffed. "You don't need to tell me, Ian. I know what I'm doing. The trick will be to get bank support without tipping our hand. And we'll be wanting to avoid banks that are doing business with the company at all costs."

"Banks," Ian snarled, fighting back a strong urge to spit. "No sense of honour or business ethics. They're all two-faced."

James and Richard eyed him warily. "Sounds like there's a story there," Richard prompted cautiously.

"Oh, that there is. See, all the big chiefs of industry in the civilized world are tied to the banks. A few years back, I was in the middle of acquiring a well-known local company. Well, some powerful so-and-sos, directors from a whole mess of different companies, they tried to cut my line of credit in the middle of my deal."

Ian tipped back his drink, downing the remnants. Richard watched, aghast, while James whistled at the show. "Bastards all of them. Almost worked. But I was lucky; I had alternative lines of credit in other banks. But I would have been cooked without those." He laughed ruefully, sneering. "Those sons-of-whores directors never forgave me. They hate to be outfoxed, see?"

He motioned for another drink. "Still, they taught me a lot, including Rule One." He sipped at his drink. "Never get into a position where your banker has you over the credit barrel, 'specially not when the chips are down or when you're in conflict with other, bigger bank clients. There's not a banker out there that won't turn on you in a heartbeat in either scenario."

He snarled, rolling his glass in his hands. "See, they can tell when they've got you by the balls. Oh, they don't call it that. They'll mention analytical sessions, where they weigh the pros and cons of supporting one person over another, and they'll very politely tell you to go fuck yourself because the ultimate prize was too tempting to allow for things like loyalty and integrity."

"And what was the prize?" Richard asked. The story was tickling at his brain, familiar beats knocking against the dusty corners of his memory.

Ian shrugged. "The greatest of prizes, of course: one of Canada's largest and most prestigious enterprises. Shares listed in the London, New York, and Montreal stock markets, shareholders across Europe and North America. But the question for them was never 'if' they should go after it but rather how could they control it."

He set his drink down, leaning back in his chair. "They did their analysis, they examined all the data, asked and answered all kinds of crucial questions, and then they went for it. And I beat them back. All of them, the directors, the bankers, the whole rotten lot."

He was quiet for a long moment. "That time taught me a lot. Mostly, it taught me two things: don't trust bankers when the chips are down and don't overreach. Those bankers would have done better if they'd played their cards a little closer to the chest, that's for damn sure."

"Well, that's a story and a half. Come now, Ian, have a drink. We have much yet to talk about and this atmosphere does us no good," James cajoled.

"Bah!" Ian grouched playfully, picking up his drink again.

"There's the Ian I know. Now then, we'll be careful with the banks. We'll choose them carefully and we'll plan around the eventuality of a betrayal. But there are questions that need answering."

"Yes, such as the identities and locations of C.D.R.'s largest shareholders, its plans for future expansion and profit, the political risks, and anything that would attract government interference."

"Exactly. I don't have all the answers at the moment, but I will. Ian will lead the charge, I'll be in charge of any 'behind the curtain' things such as planning, and you'll—"

"I can't be involved in this!" Richard protested, looking shaken, an expression of disbelief and horror crossing his face. "I'm a politician! I can't go around wrestling control of a major Canadian corporation away from its current owners while also aspiring for party control and Prime Ministership! They aren't exactly compatible pursuits."

"That's fine," Ian placated. "You'll be a silent partner. All we need from you are funds."

Richard huffed. "Very well. I'll be with you boys in spirit but not one word of my involvement to anyone. I must be completely invisible."

"Of course," James nodded in agreement.

"You don't understand, James, Ian; think of my career. If anyone, and I do mean anyone, got word of my involvement in this sort of caper, my career would go up in smoke faster than Sibley Quarry! It would be a scandal to rival the Ames scandal!"

"Ames?" James questioned.

"Political and financial scandal, back in '72, wasn't it? Company ran a credit scam with the help of Congressman Oakes Ames. Setting the bar rather high, aren't you, Richard?"

"If I'm caught, that's what will happen to me."

"Ames only faced censure for his part. And the main problem is 'if' you're caught. Trust us, Rich. It's very simple: all you have to do is give out a loan to your dear old friends. That's it. You 'loan' us the necessary start-up funds and we 'pay it back' when the plan succeeds."

"But won't people talk?"

"Why would they? Well, why would they more than usual? It's just one man loaning two old friends some money in these trying times."

"Trying times?" Richard scoffed. "I'll loan you the money, on the condition you never try to convince them it's innocent. Please, you're liable to get me in *more* trouble, not less."

"Honestly, Richie, I don't know what you're so concerned about," James grumbled. "Surely you're allowed to have investments, aren't you? It isn't like we're going to be doing anything illegal."

"Illegal, no, but you two are far from the most moral people I know. Something will come up, you mark my words, and you'll respond as you always do. And while I can make investments – I do have an existing portfolio after all – it is strongly 'recommended' I not invest in anything I might have a direct influence on. Such as a railway company of significant importance to Canada's infrastructure."

"Well," James put forth, "you aren't technically investing in anything. You're just lending some money that may or may not go towards investing in such a company. All perfectly legal, old son, just . . . quiet."

Richard cast a look James' way and downed his water as if it were alcohol. He looked incredibly dissatisfied afterwards, glaring at his glass for having the audacity to remain water.

"I'll write you both a check. Now, let's talk about something else before I decide I prefer vodka to water."

Ian burst into uproarious laughter. "Don't say that, Richard! You'll make me curious." Richard grimaced while James cackled. "Jim, order us some good alcohol. Richard, have we got stories for you."

Richard growled under his breath but allowed Ian to manhandle him over to the couch. James came and went, returning with enough alcohol to drown a small battalion.

James wasted no time pouring himself two glasses of some particularly potent scotch and downing it like water.

"So, now that business is out of the way, what have I missed?"

With a grin, Ian began regaling Richard with a detailed account of recent times. Wine flowed like water and stories flowed like wine.

Before long, stories shifted from recent times, which mostly focused on epic retellings of Ian or James conquest of this or that company, to stories of older times.

"You remember old Belle?" Ian queried, a fond smile affixed upon his face.

James blinked blearily. "Belle? N-no, no Belle. Richie?"

Richard sighed. "Do you mean that harlot you took up with? Belle Leduc?"

Ian laughed. "That's the one! Ah, no finer a harlot in the world than old Belle Leduc. Though I could have sworn you met her, James."

James seemed to be thinking very hard. After a long moment, he shook his head decisively. "No, can't remember her."

"Well now, that is a true shame. Well, to make a long story short, I bumped into Belle the very day I arrived in Calgary. Ah, she was a real beauty, a fiery buxom redhead tough as nails and sweet as honeyed moonshine. She could give you a kiss and lay you out with a fist back to back."

"Sounds like my kind of woman!" James crowed.

"Well, I saw something in Belle. And when me and my old partner George Roberts got into the business of running a whorehouse, I could think of no one better to be den mother than old Belle. Best decision I ever made. She kept the girls in line and she kept the fellas in line too! And so creative. Half of the Pink House's appeal was Belle and whatever new game she'd come up with."

Richard sighed. "The two of you were nothing but trouble. Honestly, if I thought you were bad back in Chatham, it was nothing compared to how you were once she was in the picture."

Ian clapped Richard on the back, cackling heartily. "Me and Belle got on like a house on fire, ash and all. But the reason I bring her up isn't just for old times' sake. No. See, back when I was personally running the Pink House, me and Belle had a little agreement. Whenever she had special kinds of customers, the rich and influential kind, it was her job to ply them for information and then to report everything back to me."

"Ian!" Richard snapped, an affronted look plastered across his face.

"What? It's just good business, Richard, and it's an investment that's sure to pay off in coming days. I've used what she gave me, and still gives me, on occasion, to great effectiveness in the past. Plenty of well-to-do gentlemen frequent the Pink House, Richard. They spill their secrets into my girls' ears as easy as they–"

"Ian! I'll have none of that vulgarity in my presence!"

"Oh, honestly, Richard! You sound like an old woman! Are you not a man? Do you not understand the craving for soft flesh to hold and fuck? You may as well be a eunuch or a monk for all the interest you take in the matter! Well, let me tell you this, old friend: there's not a man in business who hasn't at some point availed himself of the Pink House or something like it and there's not a man who hasn't spilled more secrets in the ears of a whore than he's spilled money to bed her! And I'll not let that information pass me by because you're squeamish."

James leaned back in his chair, watching the two over the rim of his glass and taking slow sips. As he watched, Richard stood up, drawing himself up to his full height as his face progressively reddened. To James' inexpert eye, he looked mortified and enraged.

Ian did not stand. Ian stayed very deliberately seated and his gaze never wavered from Richard's own. And for several long, quiet, uncomfortable minutes, neither man moved. Richard stood in place, fuming silently, and Ian stared him down.

And then, with a deep exhalation, Richard sat back down. "Fine. But there'll be no more talk of such affairs in my presence. Please. You and James can discuss the matter all you like, but I would really rather not hear of it."

Ian sighed deeply. "Very well, but honestly, Richard, I weep for you. And for any wife you may have. How will you please her if you can't even talk about the act? And why any woman would want to be with someone so disinterested in sex – well, I know why, but it would still surprise me."

"Sex isn't the only thing in a relationship, Ian."

"No, but it is the most important."

Richard threw up his hands. "What of companionship or family or compatibility? Isn't that important?"

Ian waved him off. "Of course, of course," he said blithely, "but sex is why men marry and it's why they stay married. And a man who's good at sex is definitely a better catch than a man who derides it."

"I do not deride it. I simply don't believe it has any place in polite conversation."

"Fine," Ian sighed, feeling very put-upon. "We'll limit the talk to what's necessary."

"Thank you." Richard dipped his head gratefully and gracefully. Then, with a soft, unfamiliar smile tugging at his lips, he said, "I have some news for you."

"Oh?" Ian and James leaned in, intrigued. Richard's face was softer than either had ever seen it, with a gentle glow lightening his eyes.

Richard pulled himself up, puffing out his chest and sticking his chin as high in the air as he could manage, his lips quirking proudly. "There comes a time," he began, "when a young man's fancy turns to love. And my fancy, for the past little while, has been focused on a certain young lady." He sighed, lovestruck.

"Do tell us more, Richard!" Ian exclaimed, leaning closer. "Details, man! A name, at least!"

"Oh, do calm down, Ian, my boy. We have all night," Richard admonished. But even here he was more relaxed, more playfully, the retort lacking any bite. "Her name is Annabel, Annabel De Withers. And she is perfect. I have never before met a woman of such outstanding charm and intelligence in the entirety of my life on God's Green Earth."

"Of course he's interested in her mind," Ian teased, grinning as Richard flushed, babbling a flustered protest. James elbowed the older man playfully. "Surely there's more to it than just that, old boy?"

"There is nothing wrong with appreciating a woman for her mind. But, for such status and – physicality obsessed men such as yourselves, she is conventionally attractive and she does have some claim to status and wealth through her father, a lord or some such."

"Well, good for you, old chap! When's the wedding?" James ribbed.

"Summer." Ian and James' laughter cut off as the two turned to stare at Richard in blank astonishment. "Yes, unbelievable though it may be, Anna has agreed to put up with both my idiosyncrasies and my schedule. As such, I will be getting married in the not-so-distant future."

Ian stared, blinked, and kept staring. His jaw hung open. James, meanwhile, jolted; apparently, his hand had drifted in his shock, dumping most of the contents of his glass in his lap.

"Son of a–!" he snarled, leaping to his feet and shimmying in place. Ian snorted at the sight. "Ian! Stop laughing and start helping! This is an expensive suit!"

"Peace, James. What were you drinking again?"

"Scotch," James grumbled.

"Ah. Just go see the wait staff. A bit of water or soda should do the trick." Ian and Richard watched James stomp off. "Marriage, eh? Given half the things you've said to me about love and women, I am surprised."

Richard's cheeks flushed a dull, ruddy red. "Well, I still think people take the whole matter far too seriously. But . . . I suppose . . . it may not be as pointless as I originally thought. Nor as unimportant."

"Well, welcome to manhood, Richard, old boy! As a fair warning, from me to you, James and I will never let you live this down."

Richard pinched the bridge of his nose and sighed in resigned exasperation. "No, I didn't think you would."

Ian smiled quietly. "I'm happy for you, friend. I know you and I are very different beasts, but I am genuinely happy to see you find someone. Even if it took you four decades."

"Thank you, Ian."

"So, as a little gift from me to you, I'll forgo most of what I *want* to say and I'll just stick to congratulating you."

"Oh, thank the Lord," Richard sighed fervently.

"Since you're still a teetotaler, I'll raise a glass for you. Congratulations, my good man, on finding your one and only, and may your marriage be as fruitful as your political career. I – pray that your patience may reward you with sublime happiness."

"And," James cut in, returning in a cleaner and also slightly damp suit, "please advise two old roués. I need all the help I can get and the less said about Ian, the better."

"I say," Ian protested, affronted.

The *Empress of Scotland* was a grand ship. It weighed sixteen thousand tons, approximately, and was over 700 feet in length.

In truth, Ian had very little interest in ships. He knew little about them and desired to know little more beyond that. But the *Empress* was an exception for two reasons. First and least, it was the ship he was currently boarding for his return trip to London, and Ian, out of a perhaps misplaced sense of childish enthusiasm, always sought to know just a little bit about the vessels he boarded.

But secondly and most importantly, the *Empress* was owed by the Canada Dominion Railway Corporation. And that meant that at least one member of the 300+ crew had to something about the company.

It didn't have to be much but any information Ian could wrangle out of the crew over the course of the long journey would be worth it.

Which brought him back to the ship. From what he could gather, it was an impressive ship, though not quite as impressive now as it would have been two decades ago. In fact, twenty years prior, the *Empress* would have been either the largest or second largest ship in the world, depending on how it measured up to its – cousin? ancestor? inspiration? – inspiration, the RMS *Oceanic*.

Ian had never heard of the *Oceanic* but it was, he was told, a remarkably similar ship to the *Empress*, if a bit outdated in comparison and owned by a different company.

But the *Oceanic* had been a fine ship for a good portion of Ian's life and the *Empress*, while no record holder, was an even better ship. Not quite world class, one of the crew told him, but still impressive. And her 'little sisters' were apparently even better ships. The latest, the sailor told him, would be something else once she was in the water.

Ships were, rather obviously, not a primary concern of C.D.R.'s, to no one's surprise. The quality of C.D.R.'s ships, among other things, told Ian exactly what he wanted to know.

And with that, his information gathering was complete, meaning it was time for Ian to relax and enjoy himself.

In the short time since the ship had weighed anchor, he'd focused mostly on the sailors. Now, he could explore the ship.

Ian liked to think himself a practical man, a pragmatic man, the type who was prone to simple, common wisdom. In this case, he felt it best to perform some reconnaissance and familiarize himself with the ship. As with a new company, he wanted to know enough to not be unduly surprised or made to look foolish.

But a large part of it was merely a desire to explore, as he had in boyhood. In the wake of the Great War, in particular his part in the war, he had seen many of his childhood dreams tarnished by the blood and muck of reality.

He remembered playing soldier or spy back in school, remembered manning imaginary guns and 'killing' his schoolmates. Even just the memory sickened him now.

But it was only those specific dreams which had died harsh deaths. There were other fantasies he relished in indulging, dreams of being a cowboy like Buffalo Bill Cody, his old friend, or a rancher or a knight even.

If he had still wanted to play at being a spy, he might have snuck around the boat, dipping into hidey-holes and alcoves. If he'd still entertained dreams of soldiering, he might have marched the length and breadth of the ship.

But both dreams had died explosive deaths, the first in a tunnel in Norway and the second in a farm that no longer existed.

So instead, he walked. He pretended the ship was his, that he was the captain, and he strode with confidence, imagining what it might be like to actually be the captain.

And speaking of the captain, perhaps he should drop in on the man and establish himself.

Off he strode, on his newfound 'quest', but alas he didn't find the captain, who was presumably somewhere doing whatever it was ship captains did. Instead, he watched the passengers as he passed.

Some he recognized, by name, face, or reputation, and others were complete strangers. Regardless, there were some very interesting passengers aboard and he both expected and intended to know them better come journey's end.

His little adventure took him from bow to stern and back again. And while his search for the captain was fruitless, he did encounter the chief purser in his office.

The chief purser was a short and thin older man who would soon prove to be friendly enough, if a tad on the brusque side of things.

"Ian MacLeod," Ian introduced himself, puffing out his chest with pride and thrusting his hand forth, grinning winningly at the tiny man.

"Robert Spencer, Head Purser. What can I do for you, sir? I trust your suite is as expected."

"Well, I haven't it yet but I trust it will be perfect. I've no doubt you'll be seeing more of me once I'm settled in. No, I simply wanted to make a few enquiries. Familiarize myself with the ship and so on."

Mr. Spencer smiled understandingly. "Of course, sir. What do you need?"

"Oh, only a few little things," Ian dismissed. "I expect to be sending and receiving a multitude of telegrams so I'll be needing access to the wireless room."

"Of course," Mr. Spencer interrupted. "I'll have Mr. Hovington escort you there immediately." He motioned to a young man who was almost twice Mr. Spencer's height.

"Many thanks," Ian said, trying to bite back his irritation at the interruption. "But I will need one more thing before that. I would like a copy of the ship manifest, so that I might see if any friends are on this journey with me."

Requesting a copy of the ship manifest was an old custom, long fallen out of favour and not too well known in the modern climate.

"Of course, sir. I'll have Mr. Hovington deliver it to your room once he's shown you to the wireless room."

Ian grinned widely. "Thank you, good sir," he said, handing the purser a ten-pound note and allowing Mr. Hovington to direct him to the message rooms. There, he set about instructing the workers them, ensuring they knew to immediately send any received telegrams to his quarters, day or night.

"Thank you, sir," the head telegrapher said as Ian handed him a five-pound note. "We'll be on the lookout for your signals. I will personally assure prompt and immediate service. Call your steward when on deck, or whenever you wish to send a wire, we'll do the rest and advise you promptly of messages received."

With that done, the last dregs of the sense of adventure he'd boarded with left him. He felt . . . not tired, but settled, well-contained within his bones. He sighed mentally. It seemed it was time to do something else. Perhaps the list would be in his room already. He could get started on some social networking.

But before he could put into play a single plan, he was approached by a man. He was very tall and stocky, with a barrel chest and a beard that had obviously been hastily groomed.

"Good morning, sir. My name is William Travis, I am the ship's first mate. The captain has asked me to invite you to the bridge."

"Very kind of you, Travis. I'd be delighted. I've always enjoyed being on the bridge at sea, especially during heavy weather. It's exhilarating, don't you agree?"

"Quite so, sir."

"You know, I was just looking for the man not long ago."

"Were you, sir? Well, if you will come this way, I will lead you there. Was there a problem?"

"No, no problem. I prefer to meet with a ship's captain whenever possible. Who better to go to for the true scoop, yes?"

"Indeed, sir."

Travis led the way along the starboard side to the bow and then up the companionway to the bridge cabin. Inside, the captain greeted him with a firm handshake.

"Good morning, Captain. Your Mr. Travis here found me all right. I'm delighted to be here."

"A good morning to you too, sir. My name is Williamson. Allow me to introduce my second mate, Mr. Hamsen, and my navigation officer, Mr. Johnson."

Ian, never one to waste an opportunity, quickly took to grilling the captain and his officers on the *Empress* and on similar ships within the fleet, as well as the general state of the C.D.R. fleet and son.

Captain Williamson was very willing to share everything he knew with Ian, even giving Ian a detailed look at and explanation of the ship's compass bearing and navigation charts.

At the end of the delightful, if a bit too technical, conversation, Ian and Williamson shook hands again.

"You must join me for a little event I'm having tonight. I've invited several of the more interesting passengers aboard to join me in my cabin for supper. I imagine you would enjoy meeting some of them," he finished with a confident grin.

"Splendid!" Ian crowed. "Thank you, Captain! I look forward to it. 7:30, I expect?"

"Around then. 7:45 at the latest. Best to be a bit early. The best conversation is always before supper."

"True enough," Ian cackled, taking his leave.

Evening came quickly. Ian had spent much of the day looking over the ship's manifest, enjoying the ship's slow drifting down the mighty Saint Lawrence. However, as supper drew nearer, he began his prep.

First, he chose between his many suits for the perfect one to wear that night, settling on a less elaborate traditional piece, dull elegant brown with simple dark highlights and subtle dark buttons.

Once dressed, he strolled into the cocktail salon. He was early, of course, by a full half-hour, but he was not the only one. Already, the salon was half-full with guests, from distinguished gentlemen to the most elegant of ladies.

Ian was gripped with a fierce curious need to meet certain of his fellow passengers. One in particular, a Lady Sylvia Fox, had caught his eye. He'd noticed her name on the passenger list earlier, mostly because she happened to be rooming in Cabin 9A on the upper deck, not far from his own room.

And she happened to be travelling alone. As such, she was likely unmarried, though not necessarily unattached, and thus a potential conquest. Ian had never learned to restrain his libido and he'd never cared to try either.

His early days in the west had coincided with the creation of his first business, the Pink House brothel-in-all-but-literal-name. He'd frequently availed himself of the girls there and even after leaving the west, he was rarely without a female companion.

And when he was without, he was normally hard at work, focused to the point of neuroticism, or on the prowl for female distraction. He'd never found himself satisfied with more traditional pastimes, such as fishing and whatnot. No, women were his chosen outlet and it was a habit to which he was hopelessly, helplessly, eagerly addicted.

He pursued without even the faintest thought of restraint and his relationship with his wife Janice had and still did suffer for it.

Janice was a striking and gifted girl of unusual charm. A witty enough woman, in his estimate, and certainly pleasant in bed, but she was of such a different temperament and energy from him; they might as well be standing on the opposite ends of the Earth, for all the commonality of spirit they shared.

She could never keep up with him and even before her health began declining following the birth of his son and daughter, she'd never really tried. And between her weak health and his fast-paced life, the two had drifted apart, their marriage weakening under the strain of distant and alternative affections.

Ian blinked, wresting his thoughts back on target. The point of his mental diatribe, ultimately, was that though Ian was no glamour boy – he'd always been a bit scrappy and time had given him not height but a soft gut and a head woefully lacking in hair – he had a distinct interest in female companionship.

And he was good at acquiring it. Despite his appearance, he was energetic, bright-eyed and alarmingly charming. Many a woman had described him as magnetic, though none could quite pin down what attracted them so: his quick wit, perhaps, or his penetrating intellect? They called him hypnotic and left it there.

Lady Fox would be but one in a long string of partners and distractions.

Unfortunately, she was not one of the others currently present in the hall. His eyes wandered the length and breadth of the room, but to no avail.

But before he could feel too disappointed, the head waiter approached him. "Sir, we have a reserved table for you. This way, if you please."

Tucked in the corner of the salon, almost invisible from his angle, was a prominent corner table. It was positioned at just the right angle to allow him to survey the gathering and new entrants at a glance while also being invisible to new entrants until they had taken a few more steps into the room.

Ian ordered a drink while he waited and lit up a fine Cuban cigar, settling back into the soft chair. Only his eyes betrayed how alert he was, following every new entrant carefully.

It was strange, sometimes, to think back on how far he'd come since his youth. He remembered what life was like back then, breaking his back to earn a pittance, scheming and scamming his way into what he wanted.

And he remembered being an intrepid youth of nineteen, living a sometimes-glamourous life on the Canadian frontier with Richard and James.

He'd come so far, from lumber and journals to the bowling alley and the bordello and then back to journalism. A memory suddenly struck him and he nearly snorted into his drink.

Years ago, when he'd been a child of only maybe nine or ten, he'd acquired his first bank account. While this would not normally be some epic story, he'd had some difficulties acquiring that account.

To make a long story short, he had been trying to acquire it in secret from his father and had ended up a little over a dollar short of the minimum needed to open said account.

Luckily, he'd found a perfectly legal workaround to the problem: he'd borrowed the money he'd needed, opened his account, and then immediately paid back what he owed, ending up a little poorer than he'd started but with an active account.

And the only reason it held less than it ought to have was because the bank hadn't let him open the account otherwise.

He chortled quietly to himself. He'd been a brash pup, hadn't he? Brash then and brasher now, as Richard would put it. Although, if he was being perfectly frank, if they didn't want people pulling that trick, they really should have made a rule against it.

Actually, they may have done just that, after what he'd pulled.

He'd took another sip of his scotch and soda, putting the memory to rest. The last people had arrived while he was lost in thought and had begun taking their seats.

Dinner was about to commence.

In watched the people start to settle in and the waiters start to move about in preparation. However, his gaze was drawn to the door as a last-minute group managed to subtly and elegantly burst in.

Recognizing some of the passengers, he flagged down the head waiter and directed him to enlarge his table and invite them to sit. Of the five, he recognized four: Sir Montague Wentworth, Lord Mansfield of Scone Palace Scotland, and Lord and Lady Macmillan.

Wentworth was a well known City-of-London financier. He and Ian were not truly friends – only James and Richard really counted there – but they were close acquaintances and frequent business partners. The Macmillans, Lord Harold and Lady Dorothy, were a young couple he'd met in the past, back in Ottawa. At the time, Harold was aide-de-camp to the governor general.

Finally, Lord Mansfield was a preeminent Scottish peer and a staunch supporter of the

Commonwealth Express. He frequently advocated preferential commonwealth trade agreements, particularly with Canada.

The fifth member of the party was a very attractive young lady, perhaps even the most beautiful young woman Ian had ever seen. She was everything Ian looked for in a conquest: blond hair, somewhere between honey and Polish gold; blue eyes that sparkled with mischief and wit; and a charming, vivacious personality that shone through.

Ian stood to greet his guests and introductions were made. At the end, Harold introduced her as, "The Lady Sylvia Fox, a true star of the British Empire."

And then dinner commenced. It was a sedate affair, five courses, none of them heavy, and with plenty of time in between for good conversation.

Ian mostly talked with Sylvia, keen to both learn more about her and to begin his seduction.

She turned out to be even more interesting than he originally thought. She told him she was an old friend of Lady Dorothy's from school and also the daughter of the Duke of Devonshire. She had recently travelled to New York and Montreal, where she had met up with Dorothy for the return trip.

The more they spoke, the more intrigued Ian became. His mind was awhirl with questions – was she married? Divorced? A widow, with or without children? Who was her father, this Duke of Devonshire? Where did she live?

He was glad he'd had the forethought to sit her next to himself. It made it easy to simply lean in and ask to hear more.

"Lady Sylvia, I must hear more about these travels to New York and Canada."

Sylvia smiled back sweetly, eyes bright and knowing. "Of course, Mr. Ian, though I'm sure that between New York and London, or worlds must have crossed many times with many friends."

"By chance, Mr. Ian, do you know my ex-husband? Sir Gifford Fox. He's a partner in the London Brokerage firm of Butterworth, Samson, and Fox."

"I've had business dealings with him, though not many. I don't much remember the man, I'm afraid."

"Unsurprising. Gifford was a good man but not, I'm afraid, a very adventurous sort. He much preferred the simple, quiet life."

"Not you, My Lady?"

"No, not I. I wanted to see America, especially New York. My father told me such stories of New York. He visited it frequently, as it was home to many of his friends, and he would always bring back such gifts and tales. They were even more fantastical than your paper," she teased.

Ian grinned. "My paper may be fantastical but I assure you, its contents are purely factual."

Sylvia tittered and giggled. "Of course, good sir. How could I have assumed otherwise?"

"You tease me, my dear."

"I would never!" Her eyes danced merrily, belying her words.

"Well, if you have read my paper, you must hold a passing interest in politics, no?"

"More than passing, Mr. Ian. When I was twenty-four, I helped my father in an election. It was a wonderful experience. I learned so much more about England's politics than I could have ever guessed. In fact, that's when I heard about you and your paper. Your political campaigns are the stuff of legends amongst campaigners."

Ian was simply delighted with what he was hearing about his lovely dining companion, in particular about her marital status. With a gleam in his eyes and a flourish in his walk, he escorted her to the dance floor following dinner, to the strains of George Gershwin. Holding her to the rhythms of 'Lady Be Good' and 'Rhapsody in Blue', he was instantly conscious of her intense femininity: the softness of her body, her radiant complexion, and the graceful manner in which she danced and swayed to the rhythm of the music, as though she were dancing in a dream.

Her soft voice and accent, so attractive to North American men, soothed him. They dispelled all his anxieties and neuroses, stole his mind away from work and business, and soon he found himself melting into the charm of the moment. And she too melted into his arms, soft and sweet and yielding, shadowing his every step as though they were one.

As they danced, they spoke. They spoke of travelling the seas in summer. She seemed particularly excited. It was an adventure in her eyes. "A few days where nothing matters. It's as though time stands still, suspended – there are no cares, no worries, no responsibilities. The world stops when you're at sea," she whispered into his ear as they waltzed. Ian pressed her against him a little more firmly and took her acceptance for what it signified: the lovely Lady Sylvia was looking for the final piece to her adventure, a shipboard romance.

Still, it was best not to push too hard. They had time and she was young. He steered them back to their table and hoped she might take him up on his unspoken offer. There was a redness to his cheeks that had nothing to do with exertion and a lightness to his heart that had everything to do with how captivated he felt by her. Oh, she was a dangerous woman, to be able to so enthrall a man within such a short amount of time.

The two rejoined the other guests, who had begun a guessing game in their absence. They seemed to speculating at to the ship's precise location. A few were even taking bets on how many knots were to be traveled in the next twenty-four hours. Ian had been a great gambler in his youth but it was a habit he had been slowly falling out of as he had fallen into a different habit. He briefly debated betting but ultimately decided against it.

A short while later, Sir Montague and Lady Wentworth made excuses to leave, proclaiming a promenade on the upper deck would be the perfect end to their evening. Sylvia and Lady Dorothy Macmillan reminisced and reflected on their school days. Ian, engaging Lord Mansfield in discussion concerning the upcoming British election, overheard Sylvia recounting a naughty story concerning a song young ladies should definitely not know, or at least not sing. Captain Henderson, snorting quietly in response to the same story, bid them all goodnight. Apparently, he was required on the bridge one last time before he could retire for the night.

The evening sky was flooded with moonlight as the Empress leisurely plied her way down the river at twenty-nine knots. Dinner guests strolled on deck to the strains of music from the salon. Lady Sylvia expressed her curiosity about what she had read about early Canada and the Saint Lawrence Valley. She had many questions for Ian and she wasn't shy about asking. She seemed especially interested in France and its dominion of nearly half of the North American continent for over a hundred years. She knew a surprising amount about the whole affair, including Quebec

City's role as the capital of New France, as it had been at the time, and of the French explorers, the 'coureurs de bois', famous traders of fur and other goods.

Ian, as an amateur historian in his own right, was rather impressed with her knowledge of the river. He was more than willing to elaborate for her a brief history of the three hundred years of French-English history on the great river that was the cradle of the North American economy, in his humble opinion.

He spoke about its development following the British conquest in 1759. Led by young Scots in the fur trade, Canada's first entrepreneur capitalists, he identified two outstanding leaders, in particular, James McGill and, of course, Alexander Mackenzie, a pathfinder – the first explorer to cross the continent to the Pacific in 1793, by canoe and portage, exploring Canada's north-west in search of a passage to the fabled markets of Japan and China, leading Canada to what emerged as its Western Destiny.

Lady Dorothy, also conversant with Canadian history, joined in. She started by relating her father's perception of the Canadian story, something about how the river penetrating the continent had been pivotal in opening up the economies of Central and Western Canada and the U.S.A.

Following their promenade, they strolled to the cabin deck, bidding one another goodnight. As Sylvia and Ian continued to their cabins, 9A and 5A, he took her by the hand, hoping she might join him for a champagne nightcap before retiring. She seemed in such good humor that he suspected she really had adopted that carefree sea voyage attitude she had joked of on the dance floor and that she was indeed, as he had hoped, in search of a shipboard romance, being as she emphasized her awareness that, within a scant few days, they would return to, as she put it, 'the real world with the fleeting, enchanted moments at sea gone forever'.

"My dear, I can't remember enjoying an evening so much in years. We really must do this again."

"Of course, Mr. Ian," Sylvia teased. "Perhaps tomorrow?"

Ian flashed a blinding grin her way. "And perhaps every evening until our voyage ends?"

"Perhaps. We do have a few of those."

"Four days, five nights. I dare say we will be quite familiar come journey's end."

"I dare agree." Her answering grin was sly and sweet all at once.

"Shall we start with a little bubbly on my private deck as we enjoy a view of the moon over the river?"

"What a marvelous idea, Mr. Ian! Shall we away?"

Ian laughed and the two linked arms before strolling off.

"What a superb residence. It's like a London flat. Mine is not quite so big."

"No? Well, mine is a double cabin. All the better for entertaining guests. Now, would you prefer some Dom Perignon or a glass of brandy? I have a very nice one my friends gifted me before I set sail."

"Dom Perignon, if you please. I can't think of anything more delicious at the moment."

Ian popped the cork and poured them each a flute. They enjoyed a moment of companionable silence as they sipped their drinks and drank in the view.

"I am so very glad we got the chance to meet, my dear. You know, I very nearly delayed my trip at the last minute."

"That would have been a crying shame, Mr. Ian. Isn't it strange to think of how our lives can be changed by things like that? If you'd delayed your trip, would we have ever met?"

"A woman like you and a man like me? It's likely but it may not have happened for quite some time and we would likely have been very different people. But enough of this, shall we dance?"

Sylvia giggled. "To what music, dear sir?"

"Why, to a lovely little number I'm sure you've heard of before: *Give My Regards to Broadway.* Now there's a Broadway musical to dance to." He went over to the cabin gramophone and put it on, spinning around once he was done and offering her his hand.

Sylvia took it and folded into him exactly as she had on the dance floor. Her body pressed against him, a warm, solid weight that followed his every whim. On the dance floor, there had been a minute gap between the two of them, space enough to breathe, barely.

Space enough to maintain the illusion of propriety.

There was no such space now. Her body pressed so firmly against his that every breath brought them closer together. And where before she had behaved like a proper lady, now her body screamed her desire to be romanced and seduced, to be wooed into Ian's bed.

And Ian was more than happy to obey. Her body yielded to him easily as he turned the dance into a seduction, moving his hands from her waist up her back and sides to cup her face and draw her eager lips to his.

Over the years, Ian had cultivated sex into an artform. And he had done so, he had learned a thing or two. Young men were studs, unskilled but eager, making up for skill with talent and passion and vigour.

Young men had sex. They fucked. But Ian had learned to cultivate patience and practice seduction. He had learned how to be a lover rather than a stud and, in doing so, had learned how to bed a woman rather than how to simply better fuck one.

And he had learned that he preferred to bed and woo and tease. He had learned he loved the little noises women made when they were with him, the little hitches in their breath. But there was little he loved more, besides watching them come undone and wild beneath him, than watching women relax and laugh as they transitioned from the romance to the bed.

There was always this awkward little moment where they would bump into each other while trying to figure out which side of the bed to climb into.

And when they did, they laughed.

As did Sylvia now, giggling like a girl half her age, gently clutching at him and grinning slyly. "Shall we?"

"Well, my Lord, are you ready to receive her ladyship?"

Dawn broke over the horizon with a brilliant golden sunrise painted against the vast blue sky. Ian and Sylvia shared a gentle kiss before she departed, tiptoeing back to her quarters.

Not five minutes later, as Ian was settling back in to doze for a little longer, a deluge of telegrams were suddenly delivered.

Some he dealt with quickly. For example, one was from a reporter informing that Albert

Einstein had been awarded the Nobel Prize. He acknowledged and made a note to send it on to his company for printing once he was a little more awake.

Then came a telegram from James, updating him on the situation. Apparently, the Atlantic syndicate not had access to multiple credit lines totaling around $15,000,000. Good. Oh, and they'd also already managed to acquire 3,000 shares across Montreal, New York, and London, at $26 per in Montreal and New York and at £4.10 per in London. Not bad.

And alongside James' telegram was one final wire, from Richard in Ottawa. The wire was almost criminally short, consisting of three short sentences: major oil S. Alberta, national elections 2 years, and Ottawa Liberals no interference.

It was obviously written in Richard's famous, or infamous, shorthand. Treating it like a code to be cracked was often necessary just to understand the barest hints of what he was saying.

Luckily, this one wasn't too hard to decipher. Obviously, major oil deposits had been found in southern Alberta, which was good but not particularly relevant. National elections were likely to crop up in 2 years or so, maybe a bit less. And the Ottawa Liberals had no intention of addressing western economic problems.

That . . . that was news. Good or bad was a bit less clear.

Ian stared down at the missive, turning the thought over in his head for a long moment. He shook himself and tossed it aside. He'd think on it later. For now, it was a beautiful day and he had a lovely lady waiting on him.

The backbone of any good company lies in its paperwork. C.D.R. was no different. With a little digging, James managed to uncover a truly astonishing wealth of information on the company and its finances.

There were plenty of investment bankers and stockbrokers willing to weigh in for a small fee and it took even less effort than that to find records on the company's traffic volumes. A word to a friend delivered him similar findings from the government's railroad, which seemed to be C.D.R.'s biggest competition.

That allowed him to gage profitability and market trends but the other half of the endeavour lay with the shareholders. It was no hardship tracking down the names of the major, and a few more minor, shareholders, as well as share distribution, historic trading patterns, and technical characteristics.

Even for James, it was all highly technical and while he would never admit it to anyone, he could admit to himself that he had trouble understanding the sheer deluge of useful information available to him.

But, after a good amount of work, he had something useful. The syndicate's objective was to gain a major enough stock position to influence management policies, which would allow them to move C.D.R. towards profitable ventures without.

They wanted to accomplish this without moving the stock up beyond a level consisted with appraised values and earnings. If the stock grew too expensive, not only would it make it harder for them to buy, but it might also discourage investing.

Of course, it would be equally bad if it went too low, though for different reasons.

Either way, James was man enough to recognize this was beyond his expertise. They would need a professional, someone with the necessary skills, patience, and know-how.

Deciding to shelve the whole thing temporarily while he searched for an expert, he fired off a quick wire to Ian summing up the information.

Bernard Baruch was many things: a New Yorker, a Wall Street operator, a man of some fame and renown, a ruthless master of the stock market. But his most important trait, at least in relation to Ian and James, was his long-standing friendship with the two, though mostly with James.

Baruch was the best professional stock market speculator James knew of and the syndicate needed more partners, particularly partners like Baruch, brilliant people from outside of Canada.

And so it was that James called his old friend and arranged for dinner at a place called Delmonico's, an elite restaurant frequented by anyone of note on and around Wall Street. Baruch in particular maintained a permanently reserved table in a secluded corner.

"James!" Baruch greeted effusively. "Welcome! Come, sit. My goodness, it has been a long time."

"Not that long. It's only been, what, a year? Less? Either way, as much as I would like to just shoot the breeze with you, I have some business to clear out first."

"Of course. So, tell me about this 'Atlantic' of yours and what you need from me."

James wasted no time summarizing the events to date, finishing with, "Obviously, we now need a professional speculator, someone who knows all the players and all the plays. I could be wrong, but I think you fit that descriptor, yes?"

Baruch chuffed at James' teasing, applauding excitedly. "It seems a challenge to me, an excellent and exciting one. Reminds me of what Teddy Roosevelt used to say about stealing railroads."

"Something about a dumb man stealing from a train going to jail but a smart man stealing a railroad and running for president? I read it not long ago."

"Close enough, though he managed to make it sound witty as opposed to jumbled."

"Unlike you, I don't devote my time to memorizing quotes."

"Bah!" Baruch harrumphed. "Regardless. Let's steal a railroad. Now, you understand what I do, don't you?"

"Mostly. I'm no expert. From what I understand, you mostly judge values, market trends, the psychology of traders, that sort of thing."

"Indeed. Now, I haven't looked into C.D.R. too much, but here's something I do know: its asset value far exceeds its market capitalization. What's more, it is, currently at least, central to the Canadian economy, and likely to remain that way for some time yet."

James nodded thoughtfully. "That's most of why we chose to go after it."

"Good." Baruch nodded thoughtfully. "But that wasn't my point. Someday, the stock may be so widely bought that it could reach an overvalued situation. What happens then to your control block? How long do you and your associates expect to maintain a dominant position?"

"Five years. As far as my preliminary research has shown, the next five years are practically guaranteed to be fruitful for C.D.R. After that, it is a bit less certain. We've agreed to plan for five years and re-evaluate once we get closer to that point."

Baruch nodded. "Wise of you. Now, my profession isn't the only reason you've sought me out, now is it?"

"No, indeed. You worked there didn't you?"

"At C.D.R.? Yes, though that was almost two decades ago."

"Still, you were there. There are things you may know that others won't."

"Twenty or fifteen years is a long time, especially in the business world. There's very little I would know still of relevance. But if you're looking for a Hail Mary play, I do have two names for you: Morgan and Harriman. They both went after C.D.R. ages ago and they might be willing to play ball if you frame it right."

James pulled out his contact book and scribbled the two names in. "I've heard of them. Big names."

"Very big and very ruthless. Also persona non grata with C.D.R. You go to them, there will be consequences. I don't know exactly what kind, but there will be consequences. It might make the final fight harder."

James grinned. "If we have to go to them, it might be fair to assume we won't have many other options."

All good things must come to an end and Ian's trip was no exception. Before long, the last night of the journey had arrived. Tomorrow morning, the ship would pull into Southampton in the late morning.

Ian decided a small farewell party was in order; something that would allow him to say goodbye to his new friends and to the other prominent first-class passengers.

Of course, it must be understood that when Ian said small, he meant lavish. Very obviously, very blatantly lavish. Although, it was Sylvia who did most of the arranging. She was the one who spoke with the head steward and she was the one who took responsibility for the music.

Her tastes were a bit eclectic, running from modern pieces to the great classics, but she had a talent when it came to slotting the pieces into appropriate spots.

But while she did well with the music, she left the other aspects to those more qualified. She directed the ship chef to Ian and left the decorations to the head steward.

A wise decision, Ian later admitted, though he'd been angry at the time. The steward had thrown together a subtle marine theme that looked beautiful in both the light of the crimson sunset and in the light of the half-moon's iridescent silver ribbons.

The sea was calm, waves rippling hazily across the horizon. It was the perfect evening.

But Ian could scarcely focus on his evening, not when he had the most enchanting of creatures in his sights. Sylvia was a fox before a hound, a vixen out of mythos, cloaked in the reddest of fabrics.

For the two adventurers, this was the night of nights. The wind itself sang for them. They could not keep their eyes from each other. Ian felt weightless, suspended before a pit and eagerly awaiting the moment he fell.

For once, nothing went wrong. There were no unexpected occurrences. The supper was lavish. Ian delivered many witty speeches and he listened to and engaged in many complex conversations. Champagne was downed like air.

Through it all, his eyes never left hers.

As soon as possible, Ian swept Sylvia up and off to the dance floor, where they danced and they danced, for a good long while, until they danced away from the crowd and onto the empty deck.

The music faded into the distance, until only the faintest strains could be heard. And yet, not a word was spoken by either. They pressed close together, swaying in time with the music and each other's heartbeat.

The air felt electric. It clung to their skins, heavy with an unspoken question and their barely restrained passions.

Ian pulled back, a silent query in his eyes. At this stage, there were only two options: return to the party or retreat to his cabin.

Sylvia gazed back at him with molten eyes, her answer clear as day.

Ian swept them off to his cabin and he was certain they must have flown there so soon was their journey over. They paused at the door, silently confirming their decision, sealing it with a soft, impassioned kiss.

Ian lead his lady to bed. Finally, they could share in this. Finally, he could touch and taste. Finally.

Morning came quick, painting the night sky blue, yellow, and white with the rising sun.

After their encounter, they'd rushed back to the party. It was Ian's party, after all; he, at the very least, would be missed. They'd erased all evidence of their activities beforehand but Sylvia couldn't have hidden the radiant, vulpine delight emanating from her even if she'd wanted to.

Never had she looked more fox-like than in that moment, a smug, satisfied smile stretching her lips and eyes dancing with mischief and pleasant secrets.

And once the party had wrapped up, they'd retreated to Ian's cabin yet again, to enjoy their fifth and final night together.

Ian's good mood had lasted until the *Empress* was in the middle of docking. However, two wires arrived at that very moment, dashing his high spirits against the rocks of sour news.

Richard's wire brought a mix of good and bad news, mostly bad. On the one hand, Richard's greatest political rival and also one of the syndicate's biggest threats, Prime Minister King, had just made a couple big mistakes, refusing to support Great Britain and possibly enabling war with Turkey.

As such, King's other rival and Richard's superior, Meighen, seemed inclined to push for a vote of non-confidence, one that would likely bring the Conservatives, and Richard, back into a position of power.

None of it was really positive. Political upheaval, even potentially beneficial political upheaval, was never good for business.

The other wire, from James, was better, a bit. James had been in meetings with Kuhn-Loeb while Ian had been travelling, though it seemed nothing had yet come of it. It seemed he'd been leaving soon though, heading for Montreal come month's end.

The only piece of blatantly good news was a second-hand report from Baruch claiming that all the current syndicate players could be trusted.

In light of the grim news, Ian opted for a change of plans. His chauffeur met him at the boat and drove he and Sylvia to her house in Eaton Square.

The two lovers took time to enjoy one last encounter before bidding each other *au revoir*. As he left, Ian bowed low and kissed her knuckles. His eyes gleamed with a promise of a repeat performance.

Things quickly returned to their normal pace. Ian was back to his scheduled routine in no time, racing off at breakneck speeds to a Fleet Street meet with his editors or to a dinner at the Carleton Club with friends and potential syndicate members, like Winston Churchill, his old army buddy, and Andrew Bonar Law, a friend of Winston's.

He made calls and called in as many lesser favours as he could, drawing upon old contacts in search of new members or advisors. It was difficult, being discrete while recruiting so heavily, but it had to be done.

And meanwhile, James was in New York, meeting with Baruch, Herbert Hoover, and Jacob Schiff at the Union Club. He sent frequent reports to Ian and infrequent, faux-casual reports to Richard.

Each had something interesting to say. Hoover advised mostly on CONINC and the still-forming Pacific syndicate, Schiff had great advice concerning C.D.R. and how to avoid double-dealing from Wall Street bandits, and Baruch was just generally excellent.

James took notes.

At the end of their meetings, Schiff joined the Atlantic syndicate as a broker while Hoover stayed mostly unaffiliated. It wasn't a great victory but it was a victory, nonetheless.

And then it was off to Montreal for another meeting and then on to London.

James' ship of choice was *The Empress of Canada*, *The Empress of Scotland*'s little sister, only recently built and brought into transatlantic service. He booked himself the largest cabin suite on the sun deck overlooking the ship's swimming pool.

He bathed in luxury, never making excuses for what his critics called his pretentious extravagance. He relished his comforts as compensations for the austerity of his youth. Having been broke more than once, and now a successful merchant banker known in political and financial circles in London, New York, and Montreal, he wrapped himself in all the comforts money could buy.

On his first day, as The Empress slipped down the Saint Lawrence River, he commenced his reconnaissance of the ship, touring the decks and meeting members of the crew and passengers around the pool and salons.

He visited the bridge, meeting with Captain Hollings and his officers, and, taking Ian's advice, checked with the head purser's office for a look at the ship's first class passenger list. He recognized a number of names, and showed particular interest in the registration of Elizabeth, Duchess of Dunvegan, remembering their meeting a few years earlier in the royal enclosure during Ascot Race week with her husband the Duke.

"No doubt I will meet up with her," he thought, "on the deck or at dinner," as he continued roaming the ship, checking various sports activities and programs.

Returning to his cabin, he noted an invitation to the captain's table at 7:45 p.m.

While dressing that evening for dinner, he reflected on the extraordinary events of the past several months in Montreal and New York, his good fortune in meeting Bernard Baruch and the way the Atlantic Syndicate was developing.

'James MacTavish,' he thought to himself, 'you've lived forty-six years to date. You're in excellent physical shape and you have more energy than ever. Face facts, you have been lucky as hell in making a success of your life from humble beginnings, but what of the future? Do you think you'll continue to flourish under that lucky star? And what about that knighthood? What lies ahead as the universe unfolds?'

Changing his train of thought, he ordered himself a brandy and soda from the cabin steward and finished dressing before joining other guests for cocktails in the lounge adjoining the dining salon. It became quickly apparent, as he shook hands with Captain Hollings and glanced about the lounge, that a number of well-known personalities from England and Canada were among his sailing companions.

He spied several he had met in Montreal. He immediately spotted Sir Herbert Holt, President of the Royal Bank of Canada, and Sir Vincent Hennessy, former president of the Bank of Montreal. Over there was Percival Cowan, of MacDougall and Cowan, stockbrokers; and was that Sir Charles Hanson, the well-known London merchant banker and former Lord Mayor of London? He dare say it might be! He knew the man more through reputation; after all, it was his two younger brothers, William and Edwin, who had established Hanson Brothers and Company in 1885 in Montreal, the first real investment banking firm in Canada.

Mingling with the captain's guests, he was introduced to Lord and Lady Astor and a Broadway showman, Florenz Ziegfeld of 'Ziegfeld Follies' fame. Apparently, he was returning from a fishing camp in northern Quebec, en route back to England for stage reviews of aspiring young beauties dreaming of joining Broadway's 'Great White Way' and 'Ziegfeld Follies'.

It was indeed an eclectic group, and dinner promised to be anything but dull. As they gathered at the captain's table, he was seated between Lady Hennessy and Lady Nancy Astor, M.P., the first woman ever to sit as a member of the British House of Commons. Florenz Ziegfeld, seated opposite him, amused the table with tales of embarrassing incidents on stage and backstage with his beauty queens now so famous outperforming the Folies Bergère of Paris.

Following dinner, he enjoyed a chat over brandy with Sir Herbert Holt, an early Canadian entrepreneur and director of many Canadian corporations, including the Canada Dominion Railway Company. It was of considerable interest to hear his vision of the company's potential growth and that of the Canadian economy.

James had researched Holt's past. Upon arriving from Ireland as a young man, Holt had ventured west, joining up with a construction business contracted with the laying of hundreds of miles of track across the prairies to the rocky mountains. He'd worked long and hard for Sir William Van Rennslleir and the C.D.R., eventually amassing sufficient wealth to become a prominent shareholder of the Royal Bank of Canada. Ultimately, he had wound up its chairman and president.

"The stock is a buy in my opinion," he emphasized calmly. He seemed a very calm man, but also very intent on his goal. "James Ross and I are constantly in touch with management."

James responded, "Glad to hear your view, sir. I've bought a few shares of late, though wish I had more."

When the orchestra struck up and dancing got underway in the adjoining salon, James retired to his cabin to draft telegrams for the morning to London, New York, and Montreal. There were five nights ahead; plenty of time, he thought, to party and meet all of the passengers, but he was curious that Elizabeth, Duchess of Dun vegan, had not turned up for dinner, concluding he would meet her before long on his daily shipboard promenades.

The following morning, he was up bright and early for a fast constitutional on decks A, B, and C, enjoying the early sunrise and the taste of salty sea air before breakfast, as the ship moved into the Lower Saint Lawrence below Quebec City.

At breakfast in his suite, he reviewed telegrams from his London office requiring immediate attention. The headline in the Commonwealth Express read, 'Alexander Graham Bell dies at home in Canada', followed by a lengthy article on the world's first long-distance eight miles telephone message in 1876 from his home in Brantford to Paris, Ontario with a recitation from Macbeth – 'to be or not to be.'

On that bright, sunny morning, passengers gathered around the pool at about eleven a.m. as stewards arranged deckchairs and attended to their every whim. It was the place to see and be seen. The young ladies in exquisite bathing suits and chiffon dressing gowns provided an attractive ambiance.

FATEFUL ENCOUNTER

James arrived with his financial papers and a recent book by Somerset Maughan, prepared to spend a few hours in the sun before lunch. As the steward directed him to his deckchair at the end of the pool, he spotted a familiar woman: Elizabeth, an attractive Duchess he had met a few years earlier at Ascot. As he circled to her side of the pool, she waved him over.

"What a marvelous and pleasant surprise to see you again, James. It was at Ascot, wasn't it? Two years ago; I remember the party in Brook's tent so well, we had such fun."

"Absolutely right, my dear," said James, focusing on her with his twinkling blue eyes. "It was Ascot alright. You look as beautiful as ever. To tell the truth, I saw your name on the purser's list and have wondered where you were hiding."

"Oh, I've been around. Just getting my sea legs," said Elizabeth. "I'm traveling alone you know, and have been dining in my cabin."

He signaled the steward to rearrange their deckchairs side by side, and they relaxed in the sun, enjoying a soft, warm breeze while discussing their many mutual friends in England and Scotland. As she emerged from her dip in the pool, James studied her form from behind his dark sunglasses; her bathing suit clinging tantalizingly to her femininity; her long, slender California legs; her smiling indigo blue eyes, her honey-blond hair, and guessed she was no more than thirty years of age.

"Exquisite in every way," he mused aloud. "I feel younger by the minute." They ordered lunch together and sipped lemonades. Smalltalk quickly turned into a more serious discussion pertaining to her marital problems and subsequent divorce from the Duke.

"It was not a pleasant episode in my life," she confessed candidly. "My trip to California was a welcome relief, thought. I visited with friends in Hollywood and Santa Barbara, where my mother's family originated, before moving to England."

'Ah,' thought James. 'I was right about the California legs. They certainly are different from anything we ever see in England.'

A steward came by, interrupting the flow in order to deliver him a telegram fresh from the wire room. Although it wasn't uncommon for James to receive wires from various acquaintances and friends, he was surprised to find this one came from Jack D.G. Kippen.

31

Have bought 4500 C.D.R. at $25-3/4 - and 1550 at $25. Market 26-26-1/4 - our
Bid 26 until further notice - will advise. J.D.G.K.

He was pleased the stock had eased off and was prepared to stay on his bid price for the time being.

The pool atmosphere of brilliant sun with fleecy, white clouds floating over a rolling sea rendered him vulnerable to the charms and physical beauty of a young woman like Elizabeth; allowing his mind and body to relax, with early signs of flirtation in the air. He was clearly in his element and looking forward to the next few days with youthful enthusiasm as The Empress steamed towards the Gulf and the North Atlantic.

IAN'S FLEET STREET HARANGUE

In London, while being chauffeured from his house in Berkley Square along Piccadilly, through Trafalgar Square, and into the Strand for some important early morning meetings at his Fleet Street office, Ian scanned the morning papers of his competitors – the Daily Mail and the Daily Mirror, owned by Lords Rothermere and Northcliffe, and the Telegraph, owned by Lord Kemsley – in preparation for his morning harangue with his editors.

These same editors were waiting convened in his boardroom upon his arrival, called forth to account for his paper's morning headlines, articles, and editorials, and for those of his competitors. This was an almost daily occurrence.

"Headlines sell papers on Piccadilly Circus, never forget that!" he bellowed. "Now what do we have for tomorrow's headline? What is the subject of the editorial? If you haven't got dramatic stories, god damn it, get out and find one, or even create one if you have to. Don't ever forget, we are in the business of propaganda and entertainment!

"We are not the London Times with a few hundred thousand readers, and we don't want to be. Our market counts over three million readers, and they want entertainment, scandal, tragedy, human drama, political gossip; everything other than boring old news! That's what I want from you gentlemen. That's what you are paid for. Look at those political whores, the Telegraph and the Daily Mail, or maybe the Daily Mirror. These are the originators of the tabloid press and we've got to keep ahead of them if we want to stay relevant.

"I bought this paper when it was nearly broke ten years ago. Look how far we've come since then. We have garnered significant political influence in just these past ten years. One decade, that's it. That's why politicians seek my support, and a few of them get it," he grinned mischievously, thumping his desk, "providing they deliver. Don't forget, every political party has its public relations strategies, executed through its media manipulators, and that's where our editorials come in."

"This was Macleod's daily harangue," his editor-in-chief joked once he was out of the room.

"He's unrelenting," a junior editor grumbled to his co-worker. "Either we manage to produce enough copies and increase circulation or we're gone, we're history. He's a ruthless son of a bitch, that's what he is, a real take-no-prisoners bastard."

Following his morning session, he was on the phone to the city checking markets in Paris, New York, London, and Montreal. Calls flooded in from business associates and budding politicians seeking his attention. Then he was off to the House of Lords to a lunch date, where he would catch up with the landed gentry's views on the state of the nation and other world events.

His energy never flagged. Between journalism, business, and politics, he was active from early morning until well into the night, often using the early hours in the morning to author one of his many books.

The brokers of London, unofficially, formed a large part of the business information network. If there was information to be had, it could be found among their ranks.

So of course, when the syndicate needed more data, that was where Ian went looking for it. Historical data, earning trends, book values, dividend history, market highs and lows over the past twenty years: they had it all.

Ian went looking with two primary questions to answer: would four million shares be enough to meet their goal and how would they finance their equity margin if the stock dropped five or ten dollars?

The latter question was really the more important of the two. Every dollar of market value, up or down, would represent up to a four million dollar gain or loss.

But as he looked over the information available to him, he was relieved to see that the chances of C.D.R. stock dropping below twenty dollars a share were so low as to be hardly worth mentioning. Certainly, it was much more likely that they would grow to forty or fifty dollars over the long term, given the current climate.

Reassured, he returned his focus to his research. He still had the first question to answer.

James hadn't felt this good since he was in college. He hadn't realised how sedentary he'd become over the years. He hadn't felt lazy but he must have been. He'd been running about with Elizabeth this entire time, engaging in sports and events, talking and conversing the whole while.

It was the most active he'd been in years and he felt great. But more than merely feeling good physically, he felt light at heart. Every time he so much as glanced Elizabeth's way, his thoughts would become filled with her and his heart would soar.

Elizabeth was wonderful. She was everything he could have ever wanted and more besides. In just the short while they'd been together, she'd already expanded his mind.

Elizabeth was a drama school graduate and a consummate, though minor, actress. James had never had much of an interest in drama. He'd been too poor and too busy in his youth to develop an interest and he'd never really looked into theater in the years hence.

But listening to her stories of plays she'd been in or hearing her grill Ziegfeld about technique or his works, it was wonderful.

"Have you considered auditioning?" Ziegfeld asked one day. "Between your talent and your title, you could do great. And I would love to have you. I can just see the headlines now: Duchess Takes Broadway. Yes?"

"You're very flattering, Mr. Ziegfeld. I would be honored." But later that night, she told James, "It would be lovely, Jamesie, truly, but the theater is not so glamourous as people think. There's a lot of rough stuff behind the scenes. I'm not sure I'm cut out for that."

BARUCH AND HOOVER

Back in New York, Baruch met with Herbert Hoover in his office. Hoover had submitted for review his report on CONINC Corporation, the large base metal mine controlled by the C.D.R. in British Columbia. His report clearly outline the outstanding investment potential of the mine as well as a few other pros and cons.

Baruch, extremely pleased with the report, took to explaining the Atlantic syndication investment plan, "I am putting together a small syndicate, possibly as much as ten to fifteen million dollars, in New York. James MacTavish and Sir Ian Macleod are organizing an equivalent amount in Canada and Britain.

"We've set aside a war chest of over twenty-five million dollars and we expect to accumulate two and a half to three million shares, on a twenty-five percent margin, gaining between twenty-five to thirty percent of the company's outstanding shares.

"The stock sells at a considerable discount when compared to the true value of the underlying assets and earnings. It could move to over fifty or sixty dollars per share in a few years; wouldn't that yield a tidy profit to the syndicate?

"If we can get control of the board, we can initiate expansion south of the border. I'm inclined to think we could hold the position for a good long period of time. Why, by the time you're in the White House, Herbert, you could be the richest president we've ever had in Washington," he suggested with a smile and a chuckle.

Hoover thanked Bernard heartily and promising to look over and carefully examine his financial position and let him know in a few days. "As Secretary of Commerce under President Warren, I was required to withdraw from American investments to avoid conflicts of interest problems. However, in Canada, I may fall into a separate category, which I will have to examine."

"A good point, my friend. I'm afraid I hadn't considered that. Let me know as soon as possible. It would be grand if you could join me in this endeavour."

On the Empress of Japan, James and Elizabeth danced away their third night at sea. Elizabeth seemed more flirtatious than usual and James was having trouble resisting the charms of his delightful shipmate. 'A sea voyage is, after all, only a temporal interlude,' he mused to himself. 'Enjoy it, but rein in your impulsive nature, in spite of her charms.'

The band struck up the 'Merry Widow Waltz' and the two partners waltzed out onto the deck. The stars glittered dimly up above them, little pinpricks of lights against the black of the sky, and moonbeams danced across the waves.

James held Elizabeth close to him, in a firm and gentle embrace. Their rhythm slowed to a gentle sway keeping time with the distant music. Elizabeth tucked her head into the crook of his neck, pressing her lips gently against his throat and gently stroking the back of his head with one hand.

In the distance, the faint strains of 'Look for the Silver Lining' started up. She lifted her head to meet his gaze, eyes ablaze with a smoldering, irresistible look. He found himself staring into dark pools as she gaze him a look that both promised and anticipated pleasure.

He felt his breathing quicken as they stood in silence looking out over the endless rolling sea. Then after a thoughtful moment, he whispered, "We should slip back to the group, don't you think?"

"Lead on, Sir James," she giggled with uninhibited delight, clinging snugly under his arm as they sundered back to the dancing salon. He ordered a brandy for himself and a Drambuie for Elisabeth, but feeling flushed with romantic thoughts, he deliberately engaged Lady Astor for distraction.

The woman in question was amusing some of the others with quips of her recent election as a London Labor member and the first woman to sit in the House of Commons. She had been born Nancy Langhorn in West Virginia, a feisty socialist married to the eminent Lord Astor. She liked to say she was living true to her good husband's heritage. After all, the Astor line was descended from John Jacob Astor of New York fur-trading fame, Lord Astor's great-great-grandfather and a poor German immigrant who had made good money trading alcohol for beaver pelts from Indians in the Ohio Valley.

As James gazed at Elizabeth across the table, he felt overcome with amorous sensations, something he hadn't experienced since his adolescent years of blind, foolhardy infatuation. 'I certainly feel youthful when I'm with her,' he pondered to himself, 'but infatuation, that's for kids; perhaps, it's time to retire.' Being lost in contemplative thought, he excused himself from the conversation and, upon his return, suggested to Elizabeth that they take a quick promenade on deck before retiring.

"I must be up rather early with telegrams, my dear, but I'll see you safely to your cabin." As they strolled the deck, James rambled on about his work with Ian and partners. Then he gently kissed her goodnight at her cabin door, saying "À demain, cherie. If the weather holds true, we'll have another great day at the pool."

Strolling back to his cabin, James reflected deeply on his life. His thoughts turned to his wife and their two children. Steeling himself, he concluded that these last few days with Elizabeth, enchanting and captivating though they'd been, were little more than a brief interlude in his life, a welcome relief from his stressfully driven business life. They were like a dream and Southampton was the morning, the end of the dream.

He thought of Ian's words and decided he agreed. Infatuation was a trap chemistry set for youths and adolescents. A mature family man like James was safe so long as he remembered himself.

When they met up at the venerable Whites Club in Saint James' Street a few days later, the two had much to share. Ian updated James with research reports from his London brokers while James recounted his many productive meetings in New York with Bernard Baruch, Jacob Schiff, and Herbert Hoover. James' meeting with William MacDonnell was of particular interest.

Later that evening, over dinner and two bottles of Chateau La Fiet Rothchild, they exchanged tales of their romantic sojourns on the high seas with their seductive young femmes fatales, James confessing that 'it seemed like love at first sight, a sort of instant infatuation under the stars'.

"Dear God, James," exclaimed Ian incredulously. "That's precisely what I thought myself, but I sobered up. You sound like she really got to you. You're not twenty-one, you know; have you forgotten the old adage 'love 'em and leave 'em?' Or the one about 'infatuation is nature's trap', or that one the British poet said, 'romance is a love affair in other than domestic surroundings'?"

"I suspect you're right," James chuckled. "I guess it was just a case of ships passing in the night." He sighed and stretched in place. "I have to say, it is good to be back to the affairs of Atlantic. A romantic interlude may be a pleasant relief but it is only ever temporary; anything else would be far too disruptive to my life and my family.

"As you know, my marriage isn't perfect, but few are. And why should I replace one set of matrimonial problems with another? Besides, Janice is a wonderful mother." He paused, eyes far away. "I may joke about my life, but truly, I have it good. I'm happy, Ian. There's plenty yet to do, but I'm happy right now and that, that is a gift I think few are lucky enough to have, or realize."

TYCOON BARUCH SUPPORTS ATLANTIC

The next day, the pair got down to serious business. They met at James's office on Gresham Street, the designated headquarters of operation 'Atlantic' from which he would direct the buying and financing of the syndicate's investment activities. They agreed their initial objective was the purchase of up to two and a half million shares at thirty dollars per share or less. They wanted a total maximum capital cost of seventy-five million dollars, requiring twenty million in equity and commitments from banks and brokers for margin loans of up to fifty-five million dollars.

James reported with delight, "Good old Baruch has agreed to center the New York activities. He'll organize a minimum of ten million dollars from a few close Wall Street associates, of which he will put up the largest proportion himself. I've advised him that you and I have committed ten million dollars and that we expect him to bring in a London partner for no less than two million. That being said, I had planned to expand the syndicate if necessary to twenty-seven million dollars, subject to market trends and price fluctuations."

"It should still be possible," Ian offered. "We'll just have to see how it goes."

Montreal soon reported the purchases of an additional four thousand shares at twenty-six and a half, enhancing their position to forty thousand shares, for an investment of approximately 1.1 million dollars.

James wired to the Hanson Brothers in Montreal.

Buy 4,000 Atlantic 27 or better open." New York and London markets had been off slightly in the past week, alleviating the need to bid aggressively for stock. He placed another order in London, with Kitcat and Aiken in pounds sterling, at 5.2£. Baruch had alerted his own brokers on the floor in New York to report sizeable offers but placed no bids to reveal his interest to the floor traders.

Share accumulation continued throughout the fall months and into the New Year in the twenty-seven to twenty-eight-dollar range, resulting in an average price of approximately twenty-seven dollars.

By mid-1923, the syndicate held five hundred thousand shares, for a grand total cost of 13.25 million dollars. Company reports were encouraging, with earnings for the year projected at over twenty-nine million, up considerably from twenty-two million in 1922.

The New York market took a dive in August 1923 with the death of President Harding; the New York Times Industrial Average dropping ten percent, while the Dow Jones Industrial Average dropped almost nine percent. C.D.R. sold off in volume to a low of twenty-one dollars, allowing the Atlantic Syndicate to buy aggressively approximately two hundred and fifty thousand shares, over a three-week period, for a little over six million dollars, ending the year with nine hundred and twenty thousand, shares at a cost of approximately 27.6 million dollars, eight million dollars in equity, and margin loans of 19.6 million dollars.

Richard continued his dynamic activities in Western Canada combining his active law practice and directorships of companies he had founded with Ian twenty years earlier with speaking engagements, on behalf of the Conservative Party. He intended to run for re-election in Calgary at the first opportunity and return to the House of Commons in Ottawa. His net worth continued to increase as he prepared at fifty-three years of age for the party's leadership campaign.

Throughout 1924, the syndicate continued accumulating shares as opportunities occurred, and by year's end, it held 1.64 million, at a cost of approximately 49.2 million dollars, with C.D.R. trading in the twenty-nine-to-thirty range, and earnings anticipated at over three dollars per share for the year, supporting their judgment that the stock continued to be undervalued.

The syndicate's equity investment had reached eighteen million dollars, leaving a reserve of seven million dollars before additional equity funding would be required. Research reports and inside information from reliable sources indicated earnings could hit thirty-four million for the year 1925.

When James received a research report from Montreal brokers, MacDonnell Donaldson and Company, recommending C.D.R. stock, with an objective of up to fifty dollars, he again considered inviting MacDonnell into the syndicate to expand their buying power and consulted with Ian.

"It looks like we'll have to go for more than two and a half million shares; I understand management usually enjoys over three million shareholder and proxy votes; three and a half million would be more comfortable," he suggested. "MacDonnell could bring in others if necessary, he is a well-known trader and speculator, a bit like Baruch, he knows the Montreal market and all the players. Would he handle up to four hundred thousand shares? Would he support their slate at a shareholders meeting?"

Ian responded without hesitation. "Yes, I think he's a good bet; he'll play the game."

James sent MacDonnell a long confidential cable identifying the Atlantic Syndicate and its objectives and exchanged letters of confidentiality.

The stock was trading at thirty-two and a half by week's end, when MacDonnell confirmed his agreement to participate and advised he was already negotiating a large block, possibly twenty-five thousand shares or more. James wired, "Take it, but not above $32 per share."

The next day, a rumor swept through London that C.D.R. would be split three-for-one. The stock went wild, moving up to over thirty-four and a half per share on high volume. MacDonnell wired he had bought thirty thousand shares but had to reach for part of it at thirty-three dollars.

The group now controlled 1.86 million shares, a long way from their objective, but with the stock over-heating on rumors of increased earnings, and a possible stock split, James considered backing off the market for a time, letting things cool down but New York continued moving ahead with London and Montreal in phase. Baruch's advice was to secure their position without delay, anticipating stronger markets ahead. The stock-split rumor was denied by the president, easing the stock back to thirty-two dollars, allowing MacDonnell to buy another twenty-four thousand shares.

STUNNING HEADLINE

James was stunned when he received a cable the next day from Hanson Brothers Inc.

The Montreal Gazette carried a headline and article today as follows: "International group rumored seeking control of C.D.R." The article stated that it was rumored, "A group in New York and London have acquired a sizable position in the stock over a period of time and have been heavily in the market during the past several weeks. There is no indication who the group is, except it is understood some of the members are powerful Wall Street operators."

"Where the hell did The Montreal Gazette get the bloody information?" James bellowed over the phone to Ian, his voice rising with every word. "For Christ sake, what the hell's going on? Some son of a bitch is double-dealing us, but who? We've been so bloody careful to register shares in a variety of nominee names to avoid evidence of accumulation."

"Hold your fire," counseled Ian calmly. "I'll run it down, get a fix on it, and arrange for contra-newspaper reports to be printed, discrediting the Gazette's rumor. These newspaper scribblers get too fucking trigger-happy at times with sensational rumors."

Sir Edward Montgomerie, the excessively proud chairman and president of the company, convened a rushed meeting of his board, demanding from each director, in writing, any knowledge or rumor of a group marauding to take over the company. He prowled around in an almost comedic manner, telling several people, in a very loud voice, that he had received disturbing rumors himself and was checking them out.

Despite his paranoid showboating, the meeting adjourned without incident, though also without satisfactory explanations. Sir Edward snarled in parting, "No goddamned Yankee son of a bitch is going to get his hands on this jewel, gentlemen! I'll have the Prime Minister put through an order in council, if necessary; we'll limit foreign voting to ten percent, I swear to you. And if he won't respond, we'll provoke a national election issue! The railroad built this country to keep the Yanks below the forty-ninth parallel, and God damn it, that's where they're going to stay."

Rather unfortunately for the man, this little bit of vitriol leaked to the press; it made headlines from coast to coast, from London to New York: 'Montgomerie says Yankee Keep Out'.

Ian and James, on the other hand, felt amused, confused, and just a little concerned by the headlines, and the president's remarks. If none of the shares could be voted on by an American, or even by an Englishman, but by a Canadian, the play would fall to none other than James

MacTavish himself. In essence, the press may have done them a favor. At the very least, the hounds were on the wrong scent.

They decided to let the tempest blow itself out and allow Ian's planted news releases to cool the market before resuming their shopping spree. James remained perplexed, however, over the source of leaks. He reiterated, "Where the hell did this bloody rumor originate? Some son of a bitch is onto our game, Ian. Don't laugh! This could be costly."

At a private lunch in the midst of all the excitement over the rumors, the prime minister discussed with Ian in confidence the question of James's knighthood and his own thoughts regarding the peerage.

"James certainly deserves it, Prime Minister," agreed Ian and suggested. "Perhaps even a baronetcy."

"And what about you, Ian? We thought we might lift you into the peerage," said the prime minister with a hearty chuckle. "That is, of course, if you're agreeable."

"Well, Prime Minister, I might be persuaded," quipped Ian gleefully. "My Calgary friends will sure as hell be impressed, and it sells well in New York. What the hell do you think? Should I go for it?" Then they both broke out in shrieks of laughter. In a more serious vein, the prime minister cautioned, "But I can't do everything all at once. James will have his opportunity very soon. A knighthood will get him started. As long as we can continue to count on your generous financial and press support, we'll do our best."

When Ian related to James the magnitude of his brief interlude with the prime minister, James' response was to leap from his desk and run strutting around his office, arms up the air and waving madly.

In a deep, thunderous bellow, he sang out, "Great balls of thunder, we're going to make it after all! By God, when the boys in Calgary and New Brunswick hear about this, they'll know we've made it! Sir James MacTavish. I can't wait for the investiture at Buck House. And you, a bloody baron! What the hell will they call you? A lord? Lord Ian Macleod!"

He laughed himself sick and Ian had to catch him before he fell over. Almost giggling, James lay a heavy hand on Ian's should and roared even louder, joking, "That's a sort of godly handle, isn't it? Don't tell me you're going to get religion, too."

It was an ecstatic moment, as they released their pent-up ambitions to ascend into the stratosphere of the British establishment. "Damn right I am, Sir James, and I will have you know it will be Brandenbrooke, Lord Ian Brandenbrooke." He stuck his nose in the air and James laughed louder still. His voice cracked a little and he was clutching at his ribs, but the laughter didn't seem inclined to stop. Ian thumped him on the back helpfully.

"It will be submitted by the P.M. to the college of heralds. And as for you, old boy," he cautioned with his arm on James's shoulder, grinning from ear to ear, "as soon as you become a knight in shining armor, watch out for the ladies. They all love being called 'lady,' especially the ones who aren't."

With all the excitement, the fever pitch of business and the heavy heartbeat of politics, there was no time like the present for celebration and relaxation. "What do you say to a brief respite on my boat, The Idle Drift?" Ian suggested.

James had seen Elizabeth a few times for dinner and the theatre and had discussed their enchanting time together on the Empress, openly confessing how difficult it was when they said, "Au revoir," at dockside. He was sure she would jump at the thought of a cruise on the Mediterranean, but then what? Would he be compromised, or would it just be a brief dalliance without unintended consequences? With his approaching knighthood, a celebration was certainly in order – and tempting, as he thought of Elizabeth as his Mediterranean shipmate.

FROLIC ON THE *IDLE DRIFT*

The two friends reserved sleeping salons on a night train to Paris and onto the Cote d'Azur, aboard Le Train Bleu en route to Cannes and Ian's villa at Cap Ferra, near Monte Carlo, to board his yacht The Idle Drift.

Captain Harvey Sutherland was Ian's chosen captain as well as his trusted and discreet accomplice of many sojourns at sea with a variety of elegant women over the years. The man knew Ian well, his every want and need, and he had stocked the yacht in accordance, with only the best and finest vintages of wine, port, and brandy, as well as recordings of the latest musicals from Broadway and Drury Lane for their brief Mediterranean escape.

Arrangements were made for telegrams to be directed to the Hotel De Paris in Monte Carlo and delivered to his house at Cap Ferra, allowing them to phone from wherever they docked along the coast for reports, and as always, the morning headlines of the Commonwealth Express, in compliance with his standing order; failure of which unleashed the most unpleasant consequences.

Onboard The Idle Drift, they shed the pressures of business and basked in the warm glow of the Mediterranean sun and the charms of their Atlantic mermaids, with whom they reminisced about the parties and personalities on each of their transatlantic adventures.

Ian amused the girls with tales of cowboys and Indians on the western plains at the turn of the century, while James enthralled them with the story of his dangerous undercover engagement in Norway during the war.

They enjoyed beautifully appointed staterooms to which they retired, "*à deux*," whenever their respective lady friends saw that look in their eyes.

At Cap D'Antibes, they received a message that Baruch had bought an additional twenty-three thousand shares, between thirty-four and thirty-five dollars, and that the stock split rumor had surfaced again. The New York market continued strong, with the averages up almost four percent. From Montreal, MacDonnell reported news of further takeover rumors and advised they maintain their buying program up to thirty thousand shares at thirty-eight dollars or better.

The Idle Drift cruised westward along the coast to St. Tropez, slicing through azure-blue Mediterranean waters under sunny skies and brisk breezes. Swimming and sun-bathing occupied most sleepy mornings. Sometimes, they would take trips ashore for some shopping in the quaint

French harbors along the coast. One night, they harbored at the Nice Yacht Club on the way back to Monte Carlo and dined at the Negresco Hotel for an evening of excellent French cuisine.

The following afternoon saw them docked at the Monte Carlo Yacht Club. There were a vast assortment of other luxury yachts, each owned by an assortment of decadent European monarchs or their princelings or any number of nouveaux European merchant princes. Here, in the Monegasque fantasy world known to some as the 'Grasshopper Kingdom', James and Elizabeth would enjoy the Hotel de Paris and the famous casino.

The following day the happy foursome strolled about the Place du Casino and Le Boulevard des Moulin. The girls indulged themselves in the elegant boutiques and couturier shops. Each evening, they joined the gathering at the Hotel de Paris bar, where the 'Grasshopper' set convened for cocktails. Long days of sleepy luxury and aquatic play were followed by long nights of champagne, gourmet cuisine, and challenging gaming tables in 'Les Chambre Privées' at the illustrious and elegant casino.

It was easy to get lost in this Monegasque habit of living. Each night was spent enjoying the excitement and pleasures that might confine one to a noonday bed.

James was a veteran of games of chance, especially horse racing, poker, and backgammon. In his opinion, casinos were 'an idiot's delight'; he knew how heavily the odds were stacked against the players but the environment was contagious. And soon he too succumbed to the gambling spirit.

On their first night, James and Elizabeth toured the tables, stopping to check out games of Trente Quarante, Chemin de Fer, Roulette, and Blackjack. James made a quick assessment of the games with his usual mathematical approach of calculating odds. He smugly drew himself up, casting subtly disparaging glances at the other players in their smoking jackets with suntanned faces lurking behind dark glasses.

"These nouveaus are obviously from a different planet where there's no such thing as arithmetic," he joked. "If they could do simple mathematics, they would know they were pissing their money away."

"How can you figure it out so quickly?" Elizabeth inquired as the pair strolled over to a five-hundred-franc roulette table. Stony-faced players sat with faces hidden behind dark glasses and bodies cloaked in red velvet jackets. Flashy women many years younger than them draped over their arms, watching the men place bets of five hundred and one thousand franc chips on a variety of red and black numbers.

"See those two zeros on the wheel, Duchie? Well, those work for the house. If you count the numbers, out of a hundred spins one of those two zeros will come up more often than any other number. And that's why the house always wins over a given period. Now blackjack over here isn't so bad; you've got half a chance if you know your cards and don't overdraw."

He eased Elizabeth into a chair at the five-hundred-franc table and advised her, "Never draw when your cards total seventeen or more. If you hold to that rule, we might get out of here with a whole skin."

When she had placed her first five-hundred-franc bet on the table, along with the other players, the dealer dealt each of them two cards, face down. On the next go around, James whispered, "Draw; okay, you're okay. And again, once more. By god, you've got it, say 'Twenty-one, blackjack."

"Blackjack!" she sang out as she turned her cards face up. "Beginner's luck, I'm sure, but what fun!"

"Okay, Jamesie, you're my personal croupier. It's obvious you've been around the gaming houses a lot more then you let on. How much should I bet this time, and who gets the winnings?" she asked with a giggle, kissing him on his neck as he leaned over her.

They played the tables until 3:30 a.m. retiring to their suite for a very light snack and more champagne.

"Well, Ian, what's your damage, old boy? How much did they take you for?" inquired James humorously as he sipped his champagne. "Elizabeth and I beat the house," he boasted, "I started with five hundred pounds, lost most of it before two o'clock, but got it all back, plus three hundred. Not bad for an amateur, eh?"

Ian, slightly tipsy, and in a carefree mood after a night of champagne, confessed laughingly, "The house took Sylvia for about five hundred pounds, and I blew nearly a thousand more besides, but we had a great time. Nobody comes to Monte Carlo to break the bank or to make money – last fellow stupid enough to try that went broke and shot himself."

The next afternoon they were chauffeured over to Saint Jean-Cap-Ferra. They had decided to take lunch on the terrace of the exquisite Hotel De La Voile D'Or. One of Ian's favorite authors, Somerset Maugham, the author of The Razor's Edge, had shared that it had been one of his favorite haunts at the time of writing the book. They'd wanted to see it before they departed Monte Carlo, via the spectacular Grand Cornish to Cannes the following morning.

It had been a glorious few days, and all were in the best of humor and high spirits as they boarded their train for Paris. It was time to return to the battlefield and the faceless monster of the marketplace.

Before the year was up, the Conservative Party had regained power under the leadership of Stanley Baldwin, and stock markets advanced with confidence. The Atlantic Syndicate, now with 2.8 million shares to their name for a grand total of 28% of the company, was impressive by any standard. It now held a capital position, including collateralized debt of nearly 112 million dollars.

The syndicate had decided to leverage the equity they had gained from market appreciation. It was a dangerous tactic to be sure, but the stock still remained undervalued as earnings increased. Things were going according to plan: the banks were willing, interest rates were low, and the dividend was secure.

By the new year, the syndicate's equity investment totaled twenty-five million dollars, with a debt of eighty-seven million dollars. And with the stock at forty-seven dollars per share, their position was valued at 131 million dollars, providing an acceptable equity margin of nineteen million dollars, or fourteen percent.

After receiving the latest report from the syndicate, James sent word advising the syndicate members he would sail to Canada in early spring of the new year to prepare for the annual meeting, usually called for late April or May.

The king's New Year's honor list propelled the frontiersmen into orbit with the official announcement of their ascendance into the illustrious British elitist club. Ian and James laughed hysterically when the news reached them.

"Great streaks of lightning!" crowed James, strutting about like a peacock. He looked more than a little ridiculous but Ian, currently doing a strange little jig, didn't notice. "They've finally crowned me with a knighthood. Well, I'll be damned.

"Tell you what though, this will make good copy in the Canadian papers, and we certainly won't underplay it here in England. Let's crack out the champagne and throw away the cork! We'll wire the news to Richard, and update our letterheads," he jested, striding about his office, waving his arms in the air. "You, a real live lord and me, a bloody knight! What will those goddamn Limey snobs in London have to say when they hear the colonials are moving in?"

"I know the type you're referring to," laughed Ian, dropping happily into an armchair. "I overheard that pompous Lord Hewarth at White's just the other day sneering about a 'colonial' he thought was, and I quote, 'posing as a proper English gentleman, suede shoes and all' and commenting that 'that colonial bastard ought to be taken down a peg or two'." James laughed at Ian's overblown impression of the stuffy, arrogant, and thoroughly dislikeable lord.

Richard, upon hearing the great news, wired his congratulations.

> I'm sure knights need shining armor at times to protect them from the ambitious ladies. Letter following re: another important oil discovery known as Royalite No. 4 in Turner Valley.

The market continued its bullish trend into the new year, with C.D.R. hitting a high of forty-nine dollars, despite continual denials of a stock split and a possible takeover by a foreign group.

MARKET EXUBERANCE AND CRISIS

Baruch was a man who always kept a critical eye on the market and he was becoming concerned with its excessive exuberance. The New York Times Industrial Average had gained nearly fifty points, approximately thirty-four percent, in the past twelve months. He wired James the news.

Market too frothy, optimism is burying fear, anticipate a pause or a market correction near term. Baruch

As spring approached, England suffered the consequences of the Chancellor of the Exchequer Mr. Winston Churchill's ill-timed legislative folly. It seemed the decision to revert to the prewar gold standard, fixing the pound at $4.86 U.S., had been ill-advised; it was playing played havoc with exports while simultaneously encouraging imports. In time, this decision would precipitate the great general strike of 1926 and sharp market sell-off.

The Times Industrial Average in New York lost over forty points, twenty-two percent, through March and April. Montreal and London markets followed close behind. C.D.R., being inter-listed, was hit hard. It fell from its forty-nine-and-three-quarters high like a boulder, eroding the syndicate's equity position by 16.8 million dollars.

The fact that there were research reports forecasting potential earnings of over four dollars per share was not enough to stem the slow slide activated by persistent margin calls from banks and brokers. Baruch reported his discussions with the Chase Bank and the Bank of Manhattan, who were collectively holding almost six hundred thousand shares. Macleod was focused on the Westminster Bank and Lloyds Bank in London, while James took care of wiring the Royal Bank in Montreal requesting accommodation loans in an effort to relieve brokers' margin calls.

Many stock market pundits forecasted the slide would run its course by early May, but, as with many forecasts, that wasn't what happened. June brought more disturbing economic news of strikes and unemployment as the averages continued to fall and C.D.R. traded down to thirty-nine dollars per share. Street rumors flew of brokers liquidating margin accounts. The volume of shares being traded grew daily as the stock continued slipping, losing another ten percent by late June, to a new low of thirty-five and a half.

It was heard on the street that Sir Edward had remarked, "This shakeout won't last long, but at least it might clean out those goddamned raiders, whoever they are. They've got to be long on credit and short on brains." The company's annual report, when issued, was expected to be encouraging, and brokers continued advising that the sell-off was a healthy market correction from overbought margined positions.

The problem was staying power. Where were they going to get the bridging to buy the time until recovery? The Atlantic Syndicate was under severe pressure, requiring a minimum of twelve million dollars of equity to restore its minimum margin requirement.

Richard, over in Calgary, sent a wire out to his closest compatriots.

> Understand the problem. Wiring $2,000,000 bank draft (Bank of Montreal). Waterloo Place, London for account Atlantic c/o Sir James MacTavish. Hold the fort. Best, Richard.

At the exact same time, Baruch also sent out a telegram, ironically to these same persons.

> Arranged $3,500,000 credit at Chase and $3,500,000 at Manhattan which will hold the position temporarily. Awaiting further funds. Will advises. Bernard

Ian and James arranged together to borrow a total of 6.5 million dollars against their personal portfolios, providing the syndicate with a total of twelve million dollars, enough to hold the position for a limited time, but anticipating the possibility of further declines in the immediate future, they steeled themselves to face the crisis, feverishly searching for additional back-stop support if required.

James wired funds to demanding margin accounts, keeping track of the syndicate members' various proportions, and awaiting word from MacDonnell, in Montreal, and Baruch, in New York, who advised he was consulting with Kuhn-Loeb.

The market rallied on July 5 and 6, with C.D.R. moving up to thirty-eight dollars on unconvincing light volume.

In the last week of July, another selling wave hit with news of the collapse of the Florida land boom. The Times Industrial Index took another hit and fell down another five percent to 137. C.D.R. joined it at 35 dollars, reducing the syndicate's margin by an additional 3.5 million dollars.

It was their blackest hour. If the stock broke thirty-five dollars, their margin position would face forced liquidation at distress prices, for a potential loss of up to thirty-seven million dollars. This was a prospect too desperate for even the stalwart frontier twins to contemplate. "We may be out of credit, James, but the challenge reminds me of what Napoleon meant by 'Two o'clock in the morning courage'."

"Courage is a currency that will always pay off," reassured Ian. "We stand firm."

While wrestling with their dilemma, Baruch wired he had made some progress with Kuhn-Loeb, but it was expensive. They would wire James directly.

The next day, the wire arrived addressed Sir James MacTavish, care of Lord Brandenbrooke, Fleet Street, London.

> Will endorse bank loan of $12,000,000 to syndicate against guarantee joint and several from all members and option to buy 400,000 shares from Syndicate at $35 for 12 months. K.L.

James, dining that night with Ian at Brooke's Club in Saint James Street, reviewed their options. The Kuhn-Loeb offer was at least a backstop, but expensive, requiring the agreement of all syndicate members.

"Goddamn it! It's too bloody rich! An option on four hundred thousand shares for a guarantee backed by all of us. Those boys sure as hell know how to make money and exploit a market opportunity. I'll try to defer our decision for a week," exclaimed James with tension in his voice as he ordered another scotch and soda.

"If the market holds above the thirty-five-dollar level we can buy time, negotiate Kuhn's proposal and wait for the upsides. Where the hell is that goddamned annual report," he asked anxiously, "it's expected to be bullish, but what's the delay?"

He wired Baruch to advise Kuhn-Loeb they appreciated the proposal and would require a week to respond. Was the offer firm for seven days? Baruch wired back: "Offer open and good for seven days, providing no further downside in stock."

They wired MacDonnell details of Kuhn's offer, requesting his comments. His response came within the hour and provided some much-needed insight.

> Market sell off about completed. Expect recovery over summer months. Will endorse nine million five hundred-thousand-dollar loan to syndicate from Chase New York against guarantees joint and several and option on 300,000 shares at $36 for eighteen months. WM.

There was no time to consult further with banks and brokers. Pressing for margin, they decided to accept MacDonnell's proposal, recognizing he was a shrewd professional speculator who seldom lost and judged the odds were in their favor.

MacDonnell arranged the credit on the Syndicate's behalf, accrediting them a grand total of 9.5 million dollars and dispensing the funds as required to deficient margin accounts. To ensure haste, he had to allow James to complete the transaction at the bank's London office, which turned out to be le problematic than he originally thought.

The next few weeks continued to be anxiety-ridden as the stock oscillated in the thirty-five to thirty-six range before suddenly dipping to thirty-four dollars, three weeks after their 9.5 million dollar capital injection.

"This goddamned roller coaster is bloody lethal," shouted James over the phone. "What the hell do we do before this tidal wave hits our beach? And where is that fucking annual report? That arrogant fool Montgomerie must be deliberately delaying it.

"Ian, do you think he knows our position? I'm still haunted by those rumors of the Yankee assault, and I'm sure it haunts Montgomerie; there's a missing link in this bloody puzzle, Ian, we've got to smoke it out!"

"You're too far into the booze, old boy," Ian cautioned. His tone came out a little sharper than intended, but James had worn down his patience over the past hour. "Lighten up, they haven't got us yet," cautioned Ian. "This is no time to go off the rails." He paused as his words caught up to him and laughed. "What a joke when we almost own all the track."

James simmered down, admitting, "I'm just blowing off steam, but my god, those rumors haunt me; they're being planted, and we don't know where the hell they're originating. Some goddamn son of a bitch is sure as hell double-dealing us."

"At thirty-four dollars, another two million, eight hundred thousand dollars of equity has evaporated; we're so close to the wind, another four points and the banks will be all over us again, in cold blood."

"If we hit thirty dollars," Ian admitted stoically, his voice pitched high, "we'll surely have to take up religion or start a new bordello for a living." He smiled grimly. "Not a fate I'd wish on my worst enemy." And then, as an afterthought, "Well, at least not the religion bit." He gave a nervous laugh. "We'll need to reach out to every person we have connections to. We need every ounce of support imaginable, even if we have to steal it, James, or all the sirs and lordships won't be worth a goddamn. There's nothing more pathetic than an impecunious peer."

James gave a nervous chuckle and offered up a slightly sickly-looking grin. "How much did you say peerages are selling for these days?" Ian swatted him on the shoulder.

Reports indicated the selling was coming again from under-margined short-term trading accounts. Ian estimated it would take buy orders for at least two hundred fifty thousand shares to clean up the market overhang. While this wasn't impossible, it was certainly a difficult challenge.

He decided to bring his old partner, Paul Wallenstein, into his confidence, presenting him with the C.D.R. situation and its potential value. If Wallenstein, a true genius of a financier, couldn't find a way to fix this, no one alive could. The man's placing power, spread throughout the capital centers of all of Europe, could easily generate substantial investment interest in a company like C.D.R.

Wallenstein, a market operator and shrewd judge of value, was intrigued, seeing the picture instantly and agreeing that thirty-four dollars a share for C.D.R. was cheap and better value than a lot of blue chips on the London and New York market.

While they frantically schemed a defensive action with Wallenstein and others, a disturbing wire arrived from MacDonnell.

> Re annual report understand delayed. Annual meeting to be held in June. Suspect president has motive. Connected with Atlantic Syndicate. Writing confidential letter today with details. Stock closed at 34-1/2. Looks like more margin selling. Working on large buying order. Will advise. WM.

While they were discussing MacDonnell's disturbing wire about the president and possible motives, another wire arrived from the Empress of Britain, off the coast of Ireland, from James Roswell, a prominent director of the Canada Dominion Railway Company.

The message was short, simple, and offered up some potentially good news in these trying times.

LORDS OF THE FRONTIER

Lord Brandenbrooke

Fleet Street, London

Arriving South Hampton en route Paris, at Claridges for two days. Look forward
to seeing you and Sir James. Will advise upon arrival. James Roswell

Roswell was a wealthy and prominent Montreal investor with a reputation to match Ian's
back in his bordello days. His father had made his fortune contracting the laying of C.D.R. track
across the prairies west of Winnipeg, Manitoba, between 1880 and 1885. Roswell had been one
of the people James and Ian had scouted out and thus he was well-known to the both of them.

The two entrepreneurs were happy to hear from him and they were quick to send him a short
wire confirming their excitement.

Looking forward to seeing you at Claridges, advise on arrival.

Wallenstein advised that he was willing to play. He asked James to wire his terms for him.

I think you'd better work that out with his lordship, Paul, but I know damn well,
you can make a big score on this one. Just don't get too greedy. James

"Wallenstein will play," he advised Ian. "You'll be hearing from him," as he tripped over his
words, sipping his scotch.

Ian, sensing James was going on one of his liquid diet tears again, insisted that he be on deck
when Wallenstein arrived in the morning.

"Oh, sure, I'll be there, old boy," he said, slurring his words, "Tipsy or sober, Paul will understand."

Wallenstein arrived in London the next day, finding Ian under pressure, and in a belligerent and
black mood. while emphasizing that C.D.R. would be over sixty dollars a share within a year. "When
you buy C.D.R., you buy Canada, Paul, which one day will be the center of the British Empire," he
stated dogmatically with his usual air of authority. "And sooner than most people realize."

"Zat's great, my Lord, but where's zee dough? You're looking for millions, no? What's for me?"
said Wallenstein in his French-Jewish dialect.

"Wallenstein, you take fifty to one hundred thousand shares, or whatever you can generate up
to two hundred and fifty thousand shares out of the market. The syndicate will compensate you
with an option to buy our shares at $37.50 for a year on the basis of ten percent of your purchases
or your clients' purchases, executed within the next thirty days. Now, how's that for a deal?"

Wallenstein chuckled, pointing his pencil at Ian, "Look here." He scratched a few numbers on
an envelope. "Deal, zat's no fuckin' deal. You want me to buy fifty thousand shares for $1,750,000
and you give me a call on five thousand shares at thirty-seven and one-half a share; pah! Hell, even
at fifty dollars a share, zat's only a bagatelle of sixty-two thousand five hundred. Your Lordship can
do better, yes? Here's my offer: you give me a deal, I'll make da stock fly. You know what I mean."

Wallenstein left, saying he'd work it out with James and would get back to him. "Very well,

Wallenstein, you do that. If you can find him; I'm afraid Jamie is having one of his bouts with the bottle."

"Zat's no problem, my lord, we've done deals zat way before," he chuckled, "Sometimes he's sharper wiz da booze than dry."

As Ian was driven along the embankment into the Strand to meet James Roswell at Claridges, his driver stopped briefly at the Savoy Hotel to pick up the evening papers. Jumping out of the headlines was more bad news about the general strike. It was beginning to paralyze the British economy and was seriously impacting the stock market. The headline provoked in him a desire to rethink his meeting with Wallenstein. He had the sudden urge to have a long talk with James concerning how they should respond to his demands.

At Claridges, Roswell welcomed him to his suite. The two businessmen had met last year at the Montreal Hunt Club, though it had been a less than exemplary encounter. As such, he was quite relieved when James turned up ten minutes later, dead sober and in fine form.

Ian decided to let James take the lead this time, a wise decision apparently as Roswell took to the Scotsman quite warmly, letting him lead the conversation around to C.D.R. and the forthcoming meeting, once the pleasantries were out of the way.

"I'm glad you ask," Roswell posited, pouring the three of them drinks. He was a remarkably friendly man, with a disarming countenance. "As you know, I've been a large shareholder for many years, on account of father, and I keep pretty close to what's going on as a member of the board.

"The stock looks pretty cheap to many of us on the street, but Sir Edward is up in arms about some international group making a play for a dominant position. He's been deliberately delaying the mailing of the annual report and the calling of the annual meeting.

"There's been heavy liquidation in the market, you see, and I understand he'd like to see the market squeeze those double-dealing 'interlopers', as he calls them, out so he is in no rush to put out a report. He's quite paranoid about the potential American influence; always has been. He simply can't tolerate the idea of anybody south of the border getting their clutches on what he calls Canada's jewel."

Roswell's remarks were a sorely needed welcome relief and a glimmer of light in the vast gloom, encouraging further discussion. "My god, Jim!" exclaimed Ian. "Who in God's name are they anyway?"

"Well, we don't know exactly, but I have heard that Kuhn Loeb in New York may be involved. Schiff's always been a big railroad speculator, you know."

"Well, I'll be damned!" said James with a poker face. "Maybe we should buy a few shares at these levels."

"We've heard the rumor of a stock split over here in London," commented Ian, "but I understand the president has denied it."

"Well, I've heard him say he wants to clean those sons of bitches out before he hands out any goodies," replied Roswell. "I would guess there is a good possibility of something developing before the year's out, which would give the stock quite a lift."

"By the way, where did the stock close today in London?"

"Oh, about thirty-three and a half," replied Ian with indifference. "Off about a point since yesterday, I think. We'll get the Montreal close in a few hours."

As they finished their drinks, James asked Roswell where he would like to dine. There were plenty of interesting clubs nearby, or maybe he'd prefer something a little more amusing. "You know, James, there's this place, the Carleton Club; I used to go there quite frequently. Bastion of Conservative power in England, in my estimation. I haven't been there in forever. I've always enjoyed my time there. It would be the perfect place for dinner and business. But later on, if you have any exotic ideas, I'm always game for a little sport on London Town."

"I hear you," said Ian with a grin. "I know just the place."

The chauffeur was quick to come collect them and the drive was filled with discussion centered on CONINC, the huge base metal mine controlled by C.D.R.

"A good friend of mine, Graham Watson, is a director at the company and a major shareholder. His father's fortune was founded on the discovery of the mine at Kimberley, British Columbia. I don't know too much about his business practices, but I do know he's very bullish on the stock," Roswell volunteered, confirming what Herbert Hoover had turned up in his research several months earlier in New York.

At the club, they ran into Winston Churchill and former Prime Minister David Lloyd George, both of whom enquired, with interest, about the Conservative Party of Canada, asking whether Richard Benson might lead the party to power in the next election.

With their stock hovering perilously close to the disaster level, they welcomed Roswell's positive remarks. They were more than happy to chat and entertain him into the early hours of the morning. After the club, they moved on to a private theatre club in SoHo. Ian and some of his old roué friends used to visit the place on special occasions. It had been a very treat, subject to one special club caveat.

"Members are required on joining to take a pledge never to divulge by word, deed, or inference the names of attendees or what transpires between them with non-members, particularly with their wives," Ian explained gleefully. "You'll soon see why when we get settled in."

The club, named 'The Clandestine Club', provided exotic hostesses trained and well-versed in all the techniques of guile and seduction known to man. They were joined at their table by three of Ian's favorites and entertained by an exquisite floorshow of provocative dancing girls into the early hours of the morning. Ian, a long-time customer at this exotic hideaway of pleasure, was offered only the best, the royal treatment so-to-speak, as he was known to tip rather handsomely, sober or once he was deep in his cups.

The next morning, while on the phone to James, reviewing the evening, on what they had learned from James Roswell, Ian inquired about Wallenstein.

"Yes, I've just seen him," replied James faux calmly. Nothing betrayed his anxiety, but it was there, tying a knot in his guts. "He will play, but he wants a call on twenty-five thousand shares. He says your offer, considering what he can do for us, was pretty bloody thin. You know, it's becoming clear to me, particularly after last night with Roswell, that Monsieur Montgomerie thinks he owns the company.

"There is a lot of good news though: earnings, dividends, maybe a stock split, and at thirty-three dollars a share, you're getting CONINC for practically nothing. But that goddamn son of a bitch, Sir Edward, he is deliberately delaying the release of good news. Damn fool thinks he can sweat out the so-called power players by delaying the meeting as the stock keeps dropping. I'll bet the little bastard doesn't own twenty-five thousand shares on his own.

"The shareholders' list records eighteen thousand shares in his name and I can't find a director with more than fifty thousand shares on the list. He can't hold up the annual report indefinitely, but he could probably delay it by a month, maybe longer, and we can't afford to wait that long. The stock closed in Montreal last night at thirty-three and a quarter on volume. It's still under liquidation pressure.

"Thank God it's not us yet, but how much longer do you think we can hold out, Ian? Atlantic will be busted if we can't hold the line. What's the code breaker? We've got to break the bloody code! If I ever get to that goddamned meeting in Montreal alive, you can bet your ass there'll be to be hell to pay over this train wreck," he sneered, "and we'll back it with a block of stock ten times bigger than all those fucking belligerent director toads have in total."

Ian had rarely heard his partner in such a state. His volatile temperament was erupting to its limit; he had his Irish up, fighting mad, and out to win, continuing with, "Let's settle with Wallenstein, I know he can perform. He'll go to work instantly on a handshake of our joint commitment to him. We've got to move fast; we're too close to the bloody wind. So, he makes a million, so what? Who gives a shit? Let's do it!"

"I'll go along with you," replied Ian. "Tell him from me he's got an option on twenty-five thousand shares at thirty-seven and a half for every fifty thousand bought, and I don't want to see the bloody stock near thirty-five dollars ever again, or I'll have his head for it. The one good thing about this crisis is that when the stock selling dries up, and the news comes out, there is going to be one hell of a rally. It will be a gravy train if we're still onboard when it happens."

They met with Wallenstein and shook on their deal, agreeing to confirm the details in writing. James emphasized, "Get at it, Paul. Get two hundred and fifty thousand shares of buying into that goddamned market, and fast. Go! Go! Go! The ball is in your court."

The Gold Dust twins had been bloodied, but so far were not bowed. The next few weeks would be critical, but they could see a glimmer of light at the end of a long dark tunnel, if they could hold the fort until the gale blew itself out.

The next evening, as James Roswell was leaving on the boat train to Paris, he inquired casually whether they had picked up any stock. James replied, "Yes, indeed. I've put a few bids in, but haven't heard from my broker."

"Well," said Roswell, "you can't go wrong, boys, C.D.R. and CONINC both look like excellent investments to me, and when that report comes out, you'll be pleasantly surprised."

Ian and James were veterans of this jungle of capitalism. They'd fought and endured many a battle, suffered exposure to the vicissitudes of the marketplace. His remarks were music to their ears. This trial had been testing every ounce of strength and skill they could muster just to try to maintain an even keel.

"It's like Rich always used to say, right? 'The faceless monster of the market knows no compassion and once in its grip, the victim must draw on his deepest resources of mind and spirit in the struggle to survive. He must extricate himself and maintain control of his own destiny. Courage becomes the number one priority. If that fails, all is lost.'

"I remember Richard expounding on the qualities of survival some years ago," replied James. "When he was extolling our virtues rather dramatically, he said, 'If you two boys ever go down, you're the kind who would find a way to climb out of the slimy jagged vertical walls of the deepest darkest snake pit, to the heavenly blue skies and warm breezes of financial independence once again.'"

"By God, I hope he's right, we've all been there," lamented Ian. "I'm still haunted by my financial crisis before the war when my partner nearly put me in bankruptcy, and I certainly remember your close call, James. So what's new? It's the same old jungle: a battle of wits and stamina; a new tune but the same refrain."

James in a somber mood while imbibing his whiskey, ruminated, "Have we lowered our guard too much, giving fate a chance to strike a deadly blow? Is it the lust for power and glory that drives us to take such risks? We all have to rationalize our actions and judgments, but in the final analysis, the cold, bloodless verdict of the market will tell the tale, vindicating our judgment or sending us swirling down the drain into the cesspool of history."

"Come, come, James, old boy, it is not quite so bad," ventured Ian, drawing deeply on his cigar. "Where's that fighting Irish blood of yours? The glass sure as hell ain't full, but neither is it half-empty. That damn stock is a steal if ever there was one; it's just a matter of time."

The Frontier Boys were smart men; they could see it was high time they left, withdrew from the fray, if only for a few days, now that they had shored up their defenses.

They departed London, exhausted, but in good spirits, buoyed by a sense of cautious optimism. James continued to be bewitched by the enchanting Elizabeth; he easily succumbed to her invitation to her secluded country estate near Torquay in Cornwall.

Ian and his wife went off to the highlands of Scotland to stay with friends in Argyllshire. He took the time to reflect on alternative syndicate support, should Wallenstein fall short of his boastful intentions and additional liquidation continue to hit the market.

London was magnificent, a sight for sore eyes, and scarcely an hour had they been there before James turned to business. He told Ian about wiring MacDonnell and J.D.G. Kippen concerning Wallenstein's support and intended buying program and about the surprise 'Confidential' letter he had received from MacDonnell.

The letter had painted a grim picture detailing the shareholders' meeting and the strategy in delaying the mailing of the annual report. The letter did not divulge his sources, but it contained was shocking enough. It seemed good Sir Montgomerie, the president, was aware of the syndicate's buying scheme and estimated they held over four hundred thousand shares on thin margin.

"Ian, I can't believe this! I can't bloody well believe this! Goddamn it!" barked James vehemently. "MacDonnell reports Sir Edward's onto our syndicate operation. I'll be damned if I can put my finger on where the son of a bitch is getting his information. This isn't the first time we've heard of the president's inside information.

"There's a fucking con in every deal, we both know that; we've got to outfox him and head him off at the pass. But, what the hell can Sir Edward do anyway when he sees our hand holding a royal flush?"

"I'll tell you what he can do!" exclaimed Ian in a burst of frustration. "If he's half-smart, the son of a bitch will try to flush us out by hammering the bloody market down on the short side again, unless MacDonnell, Smithers, Kippen, and Wallenstein can hold the line with their buying power to absorb a barrage of selling."

Ian had been a major client and a close friend to Mr. Smithers during his early days in Montreal and had often joined him on the night train to New York, sometimes with another heavy stock market player from Toronto, Sir Henry Pellet. They'd go off in pursuit of a boozy weekend and the pleasures of a few Broadway damsels might afford them, obtained on short notice through his connection with Florenz A. Ziegfeld.

They had spoken often and Ian had grown to trust Smithers more than most people. As such, there was no one Ian trusted more to investigate the syndicate leak, other than Richard or James, and they were both busy elsewhere, than MacDonnell, as the provider of the information, and dear old Smithers. Who else could ferret it out than them?

They exchanged wires at length over the next few days, coordinating the coming hunt. They were confident they could not only stay active in the market but that they could simultaneously dig up important information on the company's year-end financials and the syndicate leak.

The market sold down to thirty-two and a half before their arrangements for market support became operative. Wallenstein was still only beginning to accumulate shares. He advised them daily of orders placed and executed, picking anywhere from as few as one thousand shares per trade to as many as five thousand. Sometimes, his notes included mention of blocks of shares here and there, blocks between five and ten thousand shares.

Wallenstein was probably the savior of the syndicate. The stock ticked back up, recovering by two points over the next two weeks, bolstered by the constant influx of volume.

Every point up added 2.8 million dollars to the margin of equity and edged the syndicate back from the precipice that had loomed a few short weeks ago. MacDonnell wired that he was in the market for eight thousand shares while Baruch advised that Kuhn-Loeb and Hayden Stone had both put out bullish research reports on railroad companies, including C.D.R., which he expected would generate considerable buying.

But just as they thought they had stabilized the market, all hell broke loose yet again. Within the week, at the opening bell on the London Exchange, calls flooded James' office, calls primarily from the brokers he had watching the market.

Someone had put large shares of C.D.R. on the market. Thankfully, New York and Montreal were both still five hours from opening, but the brokers reported that overnight sell orders from Canada and the U.S.A. were being executed by several large London firms. Some of the firms taking part in this debacle included Casanove and Company, not one he was too familiar with, and North Cote and Company, this one a little more known to him. The stock was off one and a half points by 10:30 a.m., to thirty-two and a half.

"This is no ordinary market action." James paced. An observer might have thought he looked the part of a caged animal, were anyone there. "It has all the signs of a deliberate raid to bust the market. Who else could it be," he snarled, "but that thrice-damned C.D.R. gang. I'll bet they're deliberately attempting to force a liquidation of the syndicate position. They're engineering this bloody raid, that they are, but they won't get what they're after."

He picked up the phone and bellowed into it, exasperated, "I can't get a fix on the size, but it's offered at thirty-one dollars. The floor tells me it's a goddamned market order from Canada, and there's more behind it! We could see thirty and a half, or thirty dollars even before New York or Montreal opens. Those fucking bloodhounds must think they're on point and smell blood."

He fired off wires to Baruch and the Montreal group, trying to coordinate the plan he and Ian had come up with to personally buy any stock offered at thirty-one dollars. By 11:30 a.m., they had been hit with ten thousand shares, and there were another twenty thousand were being offered at thirty and a half. They convened over at James's office in search of a solution to the renewed crisis, all the while frantically taking calls from brokers in Brussels and London, mustering all their strength for the inevitable pushback.

"I'm convinced," asserted Ian, lighting his cigar, "that this is a deliberate raid on the short side, that son of a bitch Sir Edward and his paranoid gang are behind the tactic."

"The question is, whose fucking stock is being sold?" fumed James, "They're giving it away, or if it's a short-selling exercise, at what price will they buy it back, and who takes the loss?"

"By God, the more I think of it," interjected Ian, "you're right. Sir Edward could easily have set up this shorting scheme. So, it costs them a few million! They're so goddamned paranoid, they'd think it was worth it, especially If our margin positions were liquidated, and the stock took a dive; they'd cover by a wide margin. The bastards! That's what this raid is all about. They think they've got us over a barrel!"

"By the gods of war, we'll call their goddamned bluff with heavy buying," he asserted pounding his desk, and when they're forced to cover, we'll have them by the balls, driving the bloody stock up until they scream with pain. It reminds me of your Baruch story of the Northern Pacific battle between Harriman and Morgan."

While they schemed and released their venom, New York and Montreal opened with more offerings, with the stock trading down to thirty dollars.

And at the end on that fateful day, a total of sixty-seven thousand shares had traded between Montreal, London and New York, closing at thirty and a quarter, putting the syndicate within a whisker of disaster.

Baruch, after receiving a short wire from Ian, sent his reply back post-haste.

> Agree with your analysis. It's deliberate. Tape is telling story. They will back off if they see that they can't crack it, but the bigger their short position, the bigger the rally when they have to cover. Talking to Kuhn-Loeb and you know who. He loves this kind of game. He says it's vintage wall street. B.B.

This was truly a strange but exhilarating time to be alive.

HOLD THE FORT AT $30 OR BUST

It was late in the evening after another hectic day. James sipped his whiskey, scheming. He needed a new plot to finance additional buying power. This strategy of absorbing short sales would lead to victory, in time, and it would put Sir Edward and his financial nouveaus up the proverbial creek, but how much defense money would it take? Who would provide it? And at what cost?

And those weren't the only questions that needed answers. How much did Sir Edward's gang know about the syndicate or the size of its position? Certainly, 2.8 million shares would be threatening, but too large to be liquidated without driving the stock back to perhaps as low as twenty-five or even lower, inflicting great losses on all shareholders. James tried to reason it out from Montgomerie's perspective. 'My guess is they're guessing and they don't know the true position.'

"But we can't be sure," expounded Ian when James informed him of his thoughts later on. "We've got to soak up all their goddamned stock until they're forced to cover. It's a test of wills; it's a war of attrition. With Bernie's help in New York, we can hopefully outgun the bastards and clean up at their enormous expense. It's called 'staying power,' or going for broke. Bernie knows the game; as he says, 'It's vintage Wall Street.'"

They wired all members of the syndicate, marshaling resources in preparation for the onslaught the next day. Ian's wire was perhaps the most inspiring.

> When the enemy opens fire, we'll turn the heavy cannons on the bastards. So, load up, my boys. With our backs to the wall, it's a shootout. There ain't no daylight at thirty dollars per share. We either turn the tide with all cannons blazing, with Kuhn-Loeb, Baruch, standing shoulder to shoulder, or Sir Edward's scheme will be mortally wounding. Ian.

Baruch's was cautionary.

> It will be the Alamo all over again. Only this time, we'll hold the fort with the line drawn at thirty and not a bloody nickel less, damn the torpedoes, full speed ahead.

James's message was, as James himself, powerful and a little wild; a call to riot more than a call to arms.

> Bring the bastards on. We'll catch them with their fucking pants down and when they cover in a hell of a panic, it will be a donnybrook and a payday of paydays for us.

The following morning in London, share offerings continued to hammer the market; one thousand shares, five thousand shares, seven thousand shares. Montreal and New York opened five hours later, giving the arbitragers a shock.

It was madness on an intercontinental scale. Brokers in London were trying to cover in New York, but the market held solidly at thirty U.S. dollars, absorbing thirty-five thousand shares in the first three hours of trading. There was a brief but thoroughly welcome respite as offerings dried up after two p.m. and short-term traders moved in buying twelve thousand shares before the close at thirty and a quarter.

At the end of the day, totally exhausted, Ian groaned. "I feel like the Duke of Wellington at Waterloo, fearing all was lost with Napoleon close to victory. His famous words, 'Give me darkness or give me Blucher.' He got Blucher and won. Bloody hell, where is our Blucher?" he called out in a desperate tone of anguish. "This is our last stand, but if we can outgun 'em, it will be Sir Edward's Waterloo."

As their last task of the business day, they prepared for tomorrow's market offerings. They arranged solid bids again at thirty dollars on the London, New York, and Montreal exchanges.

London was hit at the opening with an offering of five thousand shares but held firm. The stock then traded lightly for several hours until New York opened with another block offering. Again, the bids were firm, taking every share on the floor. Baruch reported that he sensed the worst was over.

> The raiders are running out of steam! I estimate their short position at over eighty thousand shares, wow! The short covering is going to be a classic; one for the books. They'll be called for delivery soon. It will be the sport of kings. When they come charging in to cover, we'll squeeze 'em by the balls! I can't wait.

James wired back immediately.

> I hope you're right, Bernie, but they better be called for delivery soon, before we're called for margin. The banks are on my tail, breathing fire.

Sir Edward was a lawyer by profession. From his earliest days with C.D.R., he had used his professional expertise to accomplish his goals. Now, many years since his youth, he engaged a prominent Montreal law firm, one he had once been intimately familiar with, to review

C.D.R.'s charter, bylaws, and all matters relating to the casting of votes in person, or by proxy, at shareholder meetings.

He particularly wanted them to explore the possibility of having someone from the government intervene and restrict the voting of foreign-owned shares to ten percent.

Sir Edward told the board he was taking these precautions due to continuing rumors of an American syndicate that was becoming, or trying to become, a major shareholder in the company. According to rumor, they had already accumulated as many as nine hundred thousand shares.

"I do not know for certain who is heading the group, but I have my suspicions, and we have to be prepared to head them off, whoever they are. There may be a way to force a liquidation of their position that would send them home, back to Yankee land with their tails between their goddamned legs. As of right now, we are pursuing a number of strategies."

His financial advisors, men who had monitored the stock as it rose to forty-nine then slid back to thirty, were of the opinion that a lot of forced margin-selling had already occurred during the market slump and short-selling barrage. Given time, they said, and further liquidation, these 'raiders' or 'market operators', whatever one wished to call them, would be squeezed out for lack of sufficient credit.

The infuriated chairman, however, was taking no chances. I don't give a goddamn, one way or another," he thundered. "We'll beat 'em back or bust 'em, and I have no scruples as to the weapons we choose, or what it costs."

George Smithers knew most of the C.D.R. directors on a personal, or at least professional, basis and made discreet inquiries into the American raiders rumor, in response to Ian's request. He diligently pursued any leads that might potentially shed light on Atlantic's security leak. To date, he hadn't much luck.

One day, one of his biggest long-time clients, William MacDonnell, now also an active member of the syndicate, asked him if he had heard about their friend, Ian, and his romance aboard the Empress of Scotland.

"No," said Smithers, "but you know old Mac, he just can't leave the ladies alone; especially the exotic femme fatale type. Who was his latest victim, and where did he meet her?"

"Well, I'll admit I don't know a great deal about her, but apparently she's a well-traveled English gal, visited America and Canada a lot. According to rumor, she's a knockout in all the right ways, charming and talented. And she's a lady."

"A lady? Lady what?"

"Lady . . . Lady Fox! Yes, that's right, Lady Fox. She's a divorced lady, with a London stockbroker ex-husband. From what I gather, Ian's having quite a time with her. Hope he doesn't overdo it." He waggled his eyebrows in a most unbefitting manner and Smithers choked down an undignified giggle. "That old letch isn't as young as he thinks he is; trouble is when he's with a voluptuous woman his libido often gets the better of him."

"Well, I'll be dammed," laughed George. "The old bugger must be having a ball. I'm envious just hearing about it." But MacDonnell's comments roused his curiosity. Who were these friends with information on Ian MacLeod's love life? Where would they ever hear about an affair on the high seas, unless they had been on the Empress of Scotland themselves?

Smithers was the type of man who enjoyed horse-racing and he was prone to a little philandering himself at times. In fact, his proclivities had earned him a bit of a reputation, that between his slow horses and fast women he might very well go broke, a costly combination that has snared many a playboy. In many ways, he was sympathetic to Ian's infatuation.

A few days later, in a wire to James confirming stock purchases and advice on the market, he added, "I hear big things about a Lady Sylvia Fox. Any relation to Sir Gifford, the London stockbroker I used to know? Check with Ian. Best, George."

Ian was astounded when he heard of Smithers' comment and query, "How in the hell did my relationship with Sylvia cross the Atlantic?" he exclaimed.

He wired Smithers immediately in jest.

> Yes, 'Sherlock,' she was married to Sir Gifford. Am I being followed? Curious about your sources.

Smithers replied, a few days later, astonished Ian.

> Oh, just a casual comment from some of the boys at the club.

Ian knew most of the members of that elitist Montreal group. "Who the devil are these friends that Smithers referred to? I wonder if Sylvia would know some of them," he pondered, realizing they had seldom discussed her Montreal friends.

Sylvia being in Switzerland at Saint Moritz, and with his heavy agenda; including a meeting with his editors on Fleet Street, a lunch at which Prime Minister Stanley Baldwin was the guest speaker, and meetings in the afternoon with his bankers concerning the possible purchase of another newspaper, he deferred the matter until her return.

James continued working frantically to stabilize the C.D.R. market with the support of this friend, Paul Wallenstein. He focused his buying interest on and around Europe, while Baruch and Kuhn-Loeb stuck to New York and MacDonnell active in Montreal.

All the while, the stock traded in modest volume, creeping up to thirty-three and thirty-four dollars, providing slight relief, at least for the moment. He pondered what other surprises lay ahead, with the syndicate being so vulnerable and still under-margined.

James had observed the social anatomy of Britain for nearly twenty years. It was a complex, fascinating dynamic, chock full of complex and occasionally baffling social idiosyncrasies. Some days, he could scarcely fathom how the bizarre caste system functioned.

While he was now 'Sir James', he was still recognized as a nouveau Irish colonial adventurer in some circles, and therefore he relished a woman of Elizabeth's standing to crown his financial success with broad acceptance in the hierarchy of British and Scottish society.

James loved Elizabeth, he truly did, but he was a man of business, of political intrigue and affluence, and his love affair with Elizabeth also happened to be well-suited to that side of him. Just being with her unlocked doors he never could have unlocked himself.

As an example, James and Elizabeth were invited to dine with the Earl and Countess of DunDonald at the Savoy. Before the meal, they enjoyed a lovely play at the Haymarket Theatre. As a consequence of this dinner, they were invited to the Earl's Scottish seat in Argyllshire the following weekend.

The DunDonald family was of particular interest to James. The earl's father, Lord DunDonald, was a Scotsman had served as the general commanding officer of the Canadian militia during the Boer War in 1901. As such, the earl seemed far more receptive and welcoming than many other members of the peerage, particularly the more British members.

James admired that. He also admired the many other Scottish peers who were equally welcoming and accepting of successful, self-made Canadians. After some delicate prying, the earl confessed it was mainly because of how many Scottish immigrants had been so successful and instrumental in building Canada's economic infrastructure. It was admirable; more than that, it was useful.

The house-party was a new and welcome experience, but it was the other guests who were of special interest, in particular one Lord Coleville of the Coleville Scottish Investment Trust. The Coleville Trust had headquarters in Charlotte Square in Edenborough and it held one of the larger founding positions in C.D.R., similarly to several other Scottish trusts.

After approaching the man about it, Lord Colville readily acknowledged their position in the company and discussed its future in glowing terms. "Would you ever consider selling your position, sir?" asked James.

"Oh, I should think not," said His Lordship. "We've had the stock now for thirty-six years. I bought some at the issue price of ten dollars and some around thirty dollars before a stock split. It was a good investment; solid.

"No, we would not consider selling it, certainly not at these low prices. Unless, of course, we got into a vastly overvalued market, say around seventy-five dollars a share or thereabouts." He stroked his chin thoughtfully. "The stock could get there, you know, if it sold at twenty-five times earnings.

"Now, I think the stock is oversold at its current prices. Looks like there was heavy liquidation recently. Maybe forced selling, hard to say. You, of course, must know the management pretty well in Montreal, Sir James. What's your view?"

"Oh, they're first-rate, but conservative, highly conservative. They ought to be thinking about expansion into the United States as an offset to the government's competing national railroad."

DunDonald's estate was located in the highlands of Scotland, not far from the Firth of Lorne. James had always loved the highlands in the spring. He took a deep breath and let the Atlantic breeze fill his lungs. Elizabeth seemed to share his love for the land. She had spent a good deal of her youth near Sterling and Loch Lomond, and she'd confessed to him she always hoped that she might someday live in this part of the country.

Truly, she was a tower of strength through these trying days. She was more than he could have possibly hoped to ask for had he even thought to do so. On top of being talented musically and theatrically, she had a good head for business. She was perception, gifted with a remarkable understanding of markets and finance.

He often found himself thinking out loud when he was around her, begging her attention to matters he could not solve alone. A brilliant man James might think himself, a personification of Horatio Alger in his humble estimate, but he could not do it alone and he was glad to have her at his side.

He remembered the last time he had spoken to her of Alger; he had drawn comparison between himself and the twentieth century personality. She had laughed quietly and smiled and reminded him of Mark Twain's words on illusions.

"Hang on to your illusions, because when they're gone, you'll have nothing to live for," she'd said, patting him on the arm with a sly little grin. "And let's not forget the words of Abraham Lincoln concerning leadership: Give me a man with his mind in the sky and long enough legs to keep his feet on the ground."

"Timely maxims to consider in my present predicament, don't you think, my dear," confessing that he was a dreamer all right, but with his feet on the ground, and had never let his dreams be his master.

Their weekend with the Earl and Countess and other house guests had been a welcome respite from the fray, to which they returned on the night train from Glasgow, arriving in London early Monday morning, refreshed and rested.

Interesting news from Ian awaited James's arrival at his Gresham Street office. It was a confidential letter from Richard, concerning the customs and excise scandal that had been brewing for some time in Ottawa. Apparently, it was blowing up into a king-sized embarrassment for the government.

Richard, as a leading member of the select committee carrying out the investigation, had indicated in his letter that there could be some fireworks if the evidence continued to mount against the government.

Reading between the lines, Ian guessed the days of Mackenzie King's Liberal government might be numbered. If so, Richard could be back in Ottawa on a full-time basis again before year-end, not to mention well on his way to becoming leader of the Party as well as one step closer to achieving his lifelong ambition. He wrote to congratulate Richard immediately, wishing him the best of luck and including a concise update on the Atlantic market crisis.

SHOCKING REVELATIONS

Sylvia had been in Saint Moritz until just the other day but now newly back in London, she invited Ian over to dine with her at her home in Eaton Square. They had great fun gossiping about the well-known London personalities staying at the Palace Hotel.

There were currently a number of athletic guests present for the Cresta Bob Sled Run being hosted at the British Cresta Club on the outskirts of Saint Moritz. It was a very famous event.

Sylvia had visited the Cresta Club as an extension of her interest in cross-country skiing but confessed that the only time she challenged the mountains was by the funicular to the exclusive Corvilla Club for lunch each day.

Ian, relaxing with his cigar and savoring his brandy in her library following dinner, quietly turned the conversation to Canada and Montreal, tossing out a few well-known names. "My dear girl, you must have met some of my friends while you were there," he suggested. "You know, I don't think I've ever asked you who you stayed with in Montreal."

"Oh, Ian, I thought I had. I stayed with the Bishops. You know them: I'm sure. Billy Bishop, the famous Canadian Flying Ace who shot down seventy-two German fighters aircraft and won the Victoria Cross."

"Oh, of course, I do know them. As a matter of fact, years ago for his company. I think it was called The Bishop Barker Flying Company. I really couldn't do much for him, but indeed he was quite the hero. Where in the world did you two meet?" he asked quizzically.

"Well, it's a long story, but Billy was in the Royal Flying Corps with my husband, Gifford. So, we saw a lot of him in England after the war."

"Well, well, how interesting for you; you must have been well looked after and met many Montrealers."

"I certainly was, my darling. In fact, Billy and his wife, Margaret, gave several marvelous dinner parties for me."

"I had no idea, my dear!" responded Ian. "I am surprised we never met around town before our romantic rendezvous at sea." Being an impatient man, and hoping to put to rest some of his suspicions concerning the Atlantic Syndicate leak, he asked, "Sylvia, my dear, have you ever met someone called William J. MacDonnell or some of his friends?"

She seemed a little tense when MacDonnell's name was mentioned; a little defensive and then a little irritated. "Why are we going into such a quiz all of a sudden on Montreal?" she questioned with a surprised look. "I guess I've heard of William MacDonnell, one meets so many people while traveling."

"What about friends of his? Can you recall meeting some of his friends?" asked Ian impatiently.

"Ian, you really are in one of your moods. Let's have a brandy. Oh wait, I'll put on the gramophone. I have new Broadway songs, which you'll love, from Jerome Kern's musical 'Show Boat'."

He stood and walked about the room, puffing on his cigar, and then he turned and fired one of his blunt, to-the-point questions. "Sylvie, my dear, have you ever had a love affaire in Montreal?"

"Ian, I love you dearly, but that's a rather personal question." Then she burst out laughing, asking, "Why? I've never counted them up, but I'm sure I'd never be in your league. Anyway, does it really matter as long as you and I are together?"

"Well, it does in a way, my dear, which I shall explain later," he said, pacing up and down the room blowing puffs of smoke from his cigar. Then, suddenly looking serious as she handed him a brandy, he asked impatiently, "Have you ever heard of a Senator Olivier De Rolland? A sort of tall, dark, handsome fellow; a French Canadian, I think. I understand he's quite the charmer."

Sylvia nodded shyly, quiet for a long moment, before saying, "Well yes, I guess he is, but he's a charming bastard. You know the kind. Words like sugar and a smile like a trap.

"I thought they were all in England, but I guess they are over there as well. He's very English, in many ways, despite his French name. Very sure of himself. I was wild about him, at one time." She paused, sipping her drink, her gaze distant and introspective. "We met on my first trip to Montreal and corresponded for over a year. He asked me to marry him. Actually, I went up to Montreal from New York because of him on my last trip."

Ian, gulping his brandy and drawing harder on his cigar, sat down, then stood up in a state of consternation, asking, "When did you end the relationship? I mean when did you last communicate with this fellow?"

"Oh, it doesn't matter, Ian, darling. It's over, and I have no regrets."

"I know," he said, "but when did you actually stop writing? I am not jealous. I don't give a damn about this Frenchy senator. I just want to know when you really broke it off."

"Well, all right. Actually, it was last year, probably mid autumn, I think," she replied casually.

Ian knew more about Olivier De Rolland than he let on. He knew about his business affairs, and that he was on the board of several well-known Canadian companies, being one of those rare wealthy and eligible French Canadians very much at home in the English establishment of Montreal.

Ian had only one more telling question. "Did you break it off, Sylvia, or did he?"

"Well, I guess I did," she said with a sigh. "It got to be such a bore, I just couldn't see it from here and wrote to him less and less. I knew he was continuing to have affairs around Montreal and I just lost interest. He got very nasty when I didn't answer his letters, and he started sending me wires saying that he was coming over. I had to tell him, 'Please don't, c'est fini.' I know he was pretty chagrined."

Ian interrupted again, "Well, Sylvia, my dear, would he know anything about me?"

"When we first met on The Empress," she replied reluctantly, "I guess I wrote to him about the interesting group on board. Of course, he knew your name. I think that might have even made him jealous." She added with a giggle, "And so it should have."

Getting more and more agitated as he got closer and closer to what he hoped was not the truth, he fired off again, hoping for a negative answer. "Well, you probably made some references to my business activities. You saw all those wires in my cabin, and God knows you've often been with James and I when we talked business, particularly about the railroad."

"You know how little I know about business, Ian darling." She seemed to be catching on to his panic now. She looked ill at ease and watched him with a sort of anxious confusion. "I wrote to him a few times, told you were involved in an arrangement with some New York financiers about the railroad, and that I thought you might be buying stock. I thought I was doing him a favor so he could make some money on the market with the information. Of course, that was before we broke off."

"My God, my worst fear!" exclaimed Ian, his face ashen white. "Does he go fishing a lot?"

"Fishing! Fishing! Well yes, I think he is rather big on that sort of thing. Fishes with a few friends, a senator named Beique and Edward something. I can't think of his last name, but Olivier has mentioned him occasionally."

The remark struck Ian like a bolt of lightning, sending shivers through his body. "Goddamn it, Sylvia!" he raged. It took considerable effort not to throw either his brandy or his cigar at something. "You have no idea what all this means, what the consequences are for me and James and all our syndicate friends!" he thundered in exasperation. "Your 'bastard', as you called him, has done his level best to use your information to feather his nest all right! Beique, goddamn it, is a director of the bloody railroad and this Edward fellow you refer to just happens to be Sir Edward, the bloody president of the railroad! Now they are hot on our trail and trying to bust us."

"Bust you!" she cried, "But how?" She burst into tears observing Ian's rage, explaining between sobs that she never realized the connection. "Oh, Ian, I've been such a bloody fool, I can't believe it! Are you sure? How do you know?"

Strutting about the room, he lit another cigar. growling. "I've had all I can take for one night of this bloody disaster," he said as he stormed out of her house in a fury. It was 10:30 p.m. when his driver pulled up to Whites Club in Saint James Street. Rushing in, he ordered a scotch and soda and phoned James at his country property in Kent.

James's Irish temper flared hot as hellfire and expletives spewed forth from his mouth as oil gushes from the ground. He went outside with a chair and threw it around until it was little more than kindling. And when he was panting and tired and a minor weakness had settled in his limbs, he came back in and plopped down into his softest chair.

He groaned, "What in the hell do we do about it? They've got us over a barrel, Ian. They've been trying to nail us through this whole bloody bear market with their bear raids on the short side. Do you think it possible the president has the bitch on the payroll and De Rolland is only a decoy? Bloody hell, if that's the case, I will do horrible things to that woman!"

"Who knows? I'll have to flush her out and see who's using who." Ian ran his hand over his face despondently. "She's blown our cover, old boy. I'm truly sorry, James, this is sure as hell my gaff as much as anyone's, but rest assured, I'll find a remedy."

James and Ian met for breakfast the next morning, tired and drawn, at the Berkeley Buttery in Berkeley Square. The food there was some of the best breakfast food in the world, in their opinions, and the atmosphere was a balm on their stressed souls.

It was easy enough for them to conclude that the entire railroad board probably had been informed of the syndicate's activities thanks to the playboy senator and his vindictiveness over being jilted by Sylvia for Ian. Sylvia's part in this was a little harder to pin down and it was a thought to be shelved for a later date.

"I think it's clear what we must do now, what our only viable strategy has become: Sylvia will have to act as a mole, a double agent. She'll have to mislead that damn senator and make it known that the syndicate has failed and is being dissolved."

"Can she be trusted to do this?"

Ian tried to hide what he thought of that. "She knows nothing of finance and business. She was misled and confused. That will have to be enough. Anyway, the plan is that, apparently, a number of members have been sold out at big losses, and Lord Brandenbrooke is on the outs with the Americans, who have also been selling stock. I'll bet you a hundred to one; information like this will be wired immediately by the lover boy Senator to the boys on the Board."

"The ploy might work, yes, goddamn it!" reasoned James. "It just might. We'll give it a shot."

"Sylvia will have to concoct a long letter to lover boy, something sweet and enticing and believable enough to fool him," continued Ian. "It will have to rekindle his interest in her and convince him not only of her renewed interest in him but also of the demise of her relationship with Lord Brandenbrooke and his syndicate's reverses and liquidation. See what you can draft up."

James had a talent for manipulation when the need arose, though it wasn't a talent he made frequent use of. Knowing of Sylvia's intense infatuation with Ian, he was sure she would do anything he demanded to resolve the problem. As such, it was no hard task to draft the propaganda letter in time for their meeting that evening.

Sylvia, still in a state, and visibly upset as she joined them in her library, confessed, "It has been one of the most horrible days of my life, as I kept thinking what has happened and what I could do now to help."

James opened, saying, "Sylvia, you can do a hell of a lot. There's no use worrying about the past. But we all damn well better do something about the future, and fast. You are going to follow my instructions to the letter, and hopefully we can tame this raging crisis. I don't want tears, my dear, I just want action."

"How, James? How?" she sighed. "I'm so glad you think there's a way out of this mess."

James went through the plan and showed Sylvia a draft of the letter she was to write to Olivier De Rolland.

Ian, in a more cheerful tone, advised her not to worry about the part that referred to their relationship. "That's just to hook that jackass De Rolland," he said with a cynical smile. "You and

I aren't going to change anything between us, unless it turns out you're playing a double game. And frankly, my dear, I think your talents are better expressed in other pursuits."

She started crying again. Then, drying her tears, she laughed a watery, hiccup of a laugh. "It is sure to be a fantastic ruse, Mr. James, but how am I going to get Edward all fired up again?"

"You'll ask him over for Ascot week in June," advised James. "He'll love the idea of being in the Royal Enclosure with the king and the Prince of Wales. That's big time for a social-climbing Frenchy from Quebec. You can always write a letter with an excuse to change your plans later on."

"My God! You two really are a pair, aren't you?" she mused aloud.

"You've been used in spades, my dear, and we are over a barrel," growled James. "You have to fix it, god dammit. It is so bloody important. If we don't get this Canadian clown off our trail, it could cost us millions of dollars, even ruin us; do you understand?"

They started to relax a little as the tension subsided, with Sylvia asking who would like a drink. "I know I would," she said. "One of those ultra-dry American martinis, I think, would be the right medicine."

Ian attended to the cocktail while she and James went over the letter, with comments here and there. "Well, I hope this will excite him, and that he'll respond the way you expect him to. That Ascot caper will whet his appetite, if I know Olivier," she said with a giggle.

"Don't you worry, He'll take the bait, hook, line, and sinker," insisted Ian. "You get it off to him tomorrow.

Come to think of it, we'll send him a wire saying you are mailing a very important letter to him about the demise of Brandenbrooke's financial scheme. This charade has to get into high gear immediately."

"Yes, that's for sure," James emphasized. "Get the little Frenchy son of a bitch started right away, take the heat off the stock, and eliminate the shorting."

The die was cast as they drank to the success of the ruse. Ian rushed off to a meeting in Fleet Street while James went off to meet Elizabeth and friends at the Savoy for dinner.

The syndicate was a stubborn beast and it found a way to claw its way back to a modest equity position. Prices gradually improved to the thirty-five-dollar level on improved volume, helped by Wallenstein, Kuhn-Loeb, and the MacDonnell-Smithers duet.

But they remained vulnerable. Another downswing in the general market or selling pressure from the raiders could spell disaster for the syndicate, perhaps even bring about their end. Their objective now was a minimum of forty-two dollars per share before they could feel reasonably secure.

With the annual meeting to be held at the end of June and fast approaching, James arranged passage on the Montcalm, with arrival in Montreal scheduled for June 2.

Several weeks following Sylvia's concocted letter to Senator De Rolland, Smithers wired the Frontier Boys something of a breather.

The president thinks he's let the syndicate hang itself. He is reported to have said, "I gave those pirates a long rope and I think they're swinging." Meeting will have to be called soon and report mailed. George

"What a relief," exclaimed James, "We've hit a bull's eye at last."
"Looks like De Rolland took the bait all right," chuckled Ian. "Sylvia will be amused."
The boys were smiling again when more good news arrived by wire from Ottawa. It was from Richard.

Have just gained control of a small paper company from an estate. Committee evidence condemning. Bound to be a showdown soon. R.B.

Ian knew what that was all about, knowing the estate Richard represented, and he expected that the showdown meant a national election during the summer. Things were looking up.

RICHARD, MINISTER OF FINANCE

It wasn't long before the latest political scandal hit the headlines: 'Custom Committee Indictment of the King Administration.' It set off the wildest turmoil ever witnessed in the history of Canadian parliaments.

The government fell on a vote of non-confidence. The Conservatives under Arthur Meighen formed a government at the request of the governor general and Richard B. Benson, already in the shadow cabinet of the party, was sworn in as Minister of Finance.

The partners celebrated with prominent members of the British Conservative Party at the Carleton Club. Many guests of great importance were in attendance, including many faces from their past. There was Andrew Bonar Law, former prime minister, as well as Harold Macmillan and Winston Churchill. Even the infamous wartime prime minister, David Lloyd George, was in attendance to toast to the future of Richard B. Benson and the Conservative Party of Canada.

It was a memorable evening for the two colonial boys from New Brunswick. To hear leading members of the political power structure of England drink toasts to the third member of the New Brunswick trio, their oldest friend and mentor . . . well, it was truly momentous

A gathering of such an elite core afforded James the opportunity to engage former Prime Minister David Lloyd George on the subtleties and tactics employed by politicians during election campaigns. He was astonished by the candid admission that fell from the lips of the famous and eloquent Welshman.

"In the heat of political campaigns, it's too often the skill of what the French call 'double entendre', or double meaning, that provides escape routes from broken promises and outright lies. You could also call it double-talk," he joked lightly. "Your Canadian Indians had it right when they claimed, 'White man speak with forked tongue'.

"All politicians lie and so do most good businessmen. Intellectual honesty and political campaigning are strange bedfellows; hardly compatible. Lying by omission, I'm afraid, is also far too common; we have all, from time to time, needed to stretch the truth or hide certain facts in order to present a situation in the best light.

"Your friend Winston here once uttered in jest an amusing definition of a politician: 'He is asked to stand; he wants to sit; he is expected to lie'. It is quite true, for a given definition of truth."

"Isn't what some journalists call 'planted propaganda'?" suggested James in amusement.

Lloyd George's response was suffused with an uncharacteristic candor. "Well, yes; after all, what is propaganda but a deliberate attempt to obfuscate the truth? The spinning of truth and fact has been a concern of democracy since Athenian times. Plato rightfully despaired of this democratic falling, of the focus politicians place on presentation to get elected rather than on the bare, unvarnished truth as expressed in his 'The Republic', the elevation of appearance over ability or integrity.

"It was his suggestion that, in a democracy, politicians unfortunately cannot be confined to truth and justice alone, that they instead have to sense the whims of the fickle and willful electorate and slave themselves to it, telling them what they want to hear rather than what they need to hear."

It was an astonishing confession, particularly coming from the mouth of the formidable, and in the eyes of many quixotic, wartime leader. There was no doubt such a comment was only made possible due to his being out of office and retired.

"To contradict Plato's criticism, sir, I'm sure you'd agree that our democracy, in spite of its, admittedly many, shortcomings, has proven to be a great deal more productive than Plutocracy," James put forth.

"Yes, of course," he chuckled, "and we will always have to fight to preserve it."

A new wire arrived from Richard, carrying with it fantastic, and somewhat unbelievable, news.

> It's time a young man's fancy turns to love. And my fancy has been focused on
> the outstanding charm and intelligence of Annabel De Withers, who has agreed
> to put up with my idiosyncrasies and strenuous schedule. Yes, boys, believe it or
> not, I'm getting married. Signed: Richard.

James and Ian, remembering many a comment on love and women from their third compatriot, spent a very long moment collapsed in breathless laughter.

"Can you believe it?" exclaimed James when they had caught their breath. "Our boy Richard is getting married. I can't believe it. Richard! Serious, 'ignore the ladies' Richard! Why didn't he tell us beforehand?

"Marriage is the single most important and most difficult decision a man ever makes in his life, unless, of course, he's blinded by the chemistry of infatuation and can't wait to walk the aisle – nature's trap, her ingenious sexual ambush. I wonder which one it is? His head, his heart, or that mysterious thing we call infatuation?"

James laughed and shook his head, pouring himself a large whiskey and soda. He raised his glass with a toast to Richard, "I really thought he was a confirmed bachelor. I'm delighted! Let's fire off some fatherly advice," he joked to Ian. "This is one time we can play mentor to him, what with us being married men ourselves: in estranged marriages, with advice to the smitten bachelor. Say, who was that British poet who wrote, 'Romance is a love affair in other than domestic surroundings'?"

Ian shrugged helplessly. Between the drink and the mad cackling, he was in no fit state to talk.

The news was a timely relief from the tensions of the past months and they proposed to celebrate with a party in his honor at the Carleton Club with senior members of the British Conservative Party.

They wired Richard their support, and also their amusement.

Congratulations on finding the one and only. May your patience reward you with sublime happiness. Please advise two old roués.

re the most difficult decision a man ever makes. Is it blind love or temperamental compatibility? Signed: The Frontier Boys

THE ROARING TWENTIES

As the spring wore on, visions of boundless hope and optimism continued to bubble in the United States. The second year of Calvin Coolidge's presidency was going strong and the general aura of hope, faith, and goodwill was spreading across the civilized world to England, Canada, and throughout Europe.

Unfettered American capitalism was entering a brand new phase of industrial expansion. Automobile production was on the threshold of increasing a whole 25% from 4.3 million units in 1926 to over 5.4 million in 1929. It would be a new record high, one that wouldn't be surpassed again until 1953.

It was the roaring 1920s, as it was so aptly and colorfully described by F. Scott Fitzgerald, the man who polarized the emerging attitudes of immoral liberalism among wealthy Americans with his immortal novel The Great Gatsby. It was an age of relaxed inhibitions, a reflex brought back from the tragedies of war-torn Europe. It was a new era of optimism and economic expansion – coupled with prohibition, speakeasies, and bathtub gin – as Americans everywhere flocked to the get-rich-quick schemes of Wall Street and the roller-coaster carousels of pleasure, led by a parade of clowns dancing the Charleston.

The Times Industrial Average had recovered from its 143 low to reach 162 while the Dow Jones Industrial Average reached 140. Industrial stocks on the Montreal Stock Exchange, reflecting Wall Street's sweet, beckoning music and the Conservative government in Ottawa, were trending up with increasing volume.

The Canada Dominion Railway Company common stock continued to improve, with a little help from short-covering, moving up to thirty-six dollars and providing the syndicate with a modest equity margin for the first time in a little while. Every dollar of enhanced market value lightened James's burden of anxiety and he felt he could finally breathe a little. Still, he continued orchestrating his market operators patiently awaiting the issuance of the company's annual report.

They were in the home stretch now. James prepared for his trip to Canada and the inevitable confrontation with the board of C.D.R., his major priority being the collection of proxies from bankers, brokers, and new investors in support of the syndicate's objectives. He expected to vote over three million shares at the meeting, challenging the board as never before in the company's forty-two-year history.

A stream of transatlantic wires continued to keep him both informed and amused. They reported leaks of the president's indiscreet remarks over the supposed impossibility of how a group of, and they quoted, "goddamned upstart buccaneers from outside of the country" had fumbled the ball and had gone bust in attempting to gain control of the company. James liked to share the funniest of these wires with his friends and with Elizabeth. It was always a source of good humor.

One of his favorites was a long wire, almost a letter in length, reporting of how the president's great exuberance prompted him to go so far as to speculate that the group had lost millions of dollars and would have to liquidate more shares in the future.

"This might be somewhat of a depressant on the stock in the short term," he was reported to have said in warning to his board. Ian, in particular, had found that especially hilarious. And speaking of Ian, Sylvia was proving to be incredibly useful. She was eager to erase her mishaps and was now again in communication with her former lover.

He had, in turn, eagerly accepted her letter and invitation to Ascot for a week in late June. As such, the syndicate now had a direct channel to the president's office through his director friend, Senator Beique, who continued to pass on the indiscreet comments of board members. It seemed far too ironic to be getting information directly from the horse's mouth while the horse in question was likely laughing at them.

"I wonder how his credibility will rate when it becomes known that he has been set up and is being played like a trout on a three-ounce rod by his former mistress working on behalf of the tycoon press baron," mused James gleefully.

The high-wire act of the power play fascinated Sylvia as she observed the schemers discussing tactics. "Power works like an aphrodisiac on Sylvia," remarked Ian. "It is a common female frailty, of course, but she does pick up an occasional gem from the enemy camp."

She confided at times to Elizabeth about her discussions with Ian concerning his marital problems and his admission that reconciliation with his wife seemed more and more difficult but that he had been reluctant to discuss divorce. "When this financial deal is completed," she fanaticized, "perhaps we'll find a way to get together."

Elizabeth would discretely shake her head and offer comfort. It was obvious to her how little Sylvia knew the real Ian Macleod. Ian was magnetic, but he was self-centered.

In fact, only a few months earlier, he had written Richard on the subject of marriage, confessing, "To love a woman unconditionally, she must be as important to you as you are to yourself so far in my life, I must confess, I plead guilty, I have totally failed that test. I'm too self-centered, too egocentric and narcissistic; but I've seldom met many self-made men who weren't also guilty."

James was greatly looking forward to his voyage on the high seas. His duchess was joining him and the trip had to be as close to perfect as possible.

He reserved a stateroom on the HMS Montcalm to act as a sort of interim honeymoon to celebrate the relationship they'd formed in the time since their earlier shipboard flirtations. A quick review of the ship's first-class passenger list presented a few interesting names, people they might enjoy interacting with during their time on board.

One name, however, presented something else: the Right Honorable Reginald McKenna. He was a British director of the Canada Dominion Railroad Corporation and, whether he knew it or not, a clear indication that the shareholders' meeting must surely be occurring in late June or early July.

On May 27, after being chauffeured to Southampton for a noon departure, they settled themselves in their double sized stateroom with their own small sitting room and deck as the Montcalm cast off in a dense fog and choppy seas, steaming out into the North Atlantic.

From the moment they boarded the ship, James was in high spirits. He guided Elizabeth up to the rail to watch the water and the horizon. It was a beautiful sight, both the woman in his arms and the exquisite view.

"My darling Elizabeth," James declared gleefully, "I have crossed the Atlantic more times than I can count, but I dare say this trip will prove to be the greatest adventure of my life. Why, it might even surpass my exploits in Norway during the war!

"The meeting in Montreal will crystallize the Atlantic syndicate's challenge to this Canadian titan. It will obliterate the status quo that has so long ruled such a powerful and prestigious company. It will most assuredly be an undertaking of epic proportions, a magnificent endeavor, a feat beyond compare, unsurpassed in the annals of Canadian corporate history. What do you say to that, my love; it calls for a toast?" Then looking deeply into her sparkling eyes, he kissed her, saying "Here's to you, Duchie; without you, my dear, I'm afraid it would only be a hollow victory."

The five days at sea provided an excellent opportunity to slow down, review issues requiring his serious consideration, and process what was happening. There were so many questions, so many details.

When would he alert the president of his mighty proxy position? What number of outside shareholders would support management's slate? What legal roadblocks could the board conjure up?

More importantly, could these powerful industrialists instigate legislation to block his voting trust? Could they precipitate another raid on the stock, driving the price down far enough to actually force the syndicate into liquidation and possible financial ruin?

The voyage would give him time to weigh these and other matters of strategy and tactics, together with his proposed list of new directors that he had discussed with Ian before sailing. To date, this list included himself, Baruch, and Ian, as well as Sir Henry Pellet, for Toronto, William J. MacDonnell for Montreal, and a senator named Lougheed, a suggestion of Richard's to handle Calgary.

He expected to add additional names, subject to discussions with the president, but anticipating a battle royal, he knew that proxy voting power would be the ultimate weapon. He had retained Mr. John MacArthur, of the prominent law firm of MacArther, Ward, and La Flamme, as counsel to fend off directors whose wrath and legal maneuvers he anticipated would be formidable.

On his first promenade of the ship's upper deck, he met several shipmates of varying levels of importance, including Reginald McKenna, the C.D.R. director, as well as another director, Mr. E.R. Peacock. Truthfully, their meeting amused him; he spent the entire time contemplating their surprise at the shareholders' meeting when his stock and proxy voting position was revealed. But for now, he deliberately avoided company discussions or even any form of corporate topics, engaging them mainly in political talk, focusing primarily on the new Conservative government in Ottawa and the impending election in the United Kingdom.

LIFE AND MARRIAGE

As the days at sea blended one into the other, James and Elizabeth spent many hours in their chaises longues, ensconced with their books. They lounged, they drank, they enjoyed soft, quiet, intimate moments, and they spoke of their relationship.

Elizabeth enjoyed probing James' innermost thoughts and internal persona. She wanted to know him, James MacTavish, as fully as possible. 'What was it that really drove him?' she often wondered. 'How had his early life shaped his ambitions and beliefs? Had he ever experienced unconditional love and romance before?'

The idyllic days drifted by in such a manner, as serene as a dream, replete with candid conversations and easy discussions of dreams and ambitions. They bared their souls to one another.

"James, why does a man who has made so much money drive himself the way you do and take such horrendous risks? What is it you are pursuing that you haven't already got?" she asked thoughtfully as they stared out over the expansive ocean to the distant horizon.

James, smiling as he pondered her question, replied slowly and thoughtfully, "I've asked myself that question many times, Duchie, especially when I've been in a financial jam; down and out, in dire financial straits, the whole nine yards. I suppose, when you've been the only child of a single mother with no father and no money to speak of, with just your poor, hard-working mother to call your own, you develop a burning, relentless drive to overcome your deficiencies and insecurities."

He chuckled, "It's like how you get pearls, isn't it? You get something hard and painful stuck in your craw and it stays there until it becomes something beautiful or it makes you into something beautiful. Sometimes we refer to it as a 'fire in your belly'. I had to work my way through school and college, did whatever I had to do to get through, and to my everlasting regret, my dear mother died before I could do anything to make her more comfortable in her old age."

He paused, gazing out upon the rolling sea, "You know, money is the great insulator. It's not unlike a moat to surround your castle, a wall built between you and the world. It's comforting, in a way, so money and the influences attached to it become your aim, your priority, your passion; and it drives you at times, so hard, like a bullwhip to a recalcitrant beast's back, that you wish you could turn it off; but it's relentless.

"It's like a drug, a drug made from success and power. And when you become hooked on it;

oh, there is little you can do to put out the fire. The small and simple achievements which sated you once leave you feeling empty and hollow, cheated. You keep rising to more challenges and climbing more mountains in pursuit of the elusive satisfaction of security. Ian and I are the same in this way; perhaps that is why we have been partners for so long. But I've found him to be even more driven than I am. I suppose we'll be pursuing new challenges until our last days, hammering out our dreams and fantasies on the ringing anvil of achievement and recognition.

"Trouble is, you miss a lot. You pay for wealth and success with time, the time you'd otherwise take to enjoy what you're earning. Your family life is impacted rather severely. Or at least, mine certainly has been," he confessed. "Janice has often accused me of being narcissistic and self-centered. And my answer to her has always been, 'I plead guilty, but there are few men who start with nothing who manage to succeed and take the lead in this capitalist jungle without total focus and that, I guess, often means self-centeredness.'

"In my early days at university, I experienced what I believe was the first, and perhaps only, deep-rooted love affair of my life. I thought her my true soulmate, a kindred spirit. I was young, ambitious, penniless; I hadn't even met Ian and Richard by that point. I loved her dearly, but I knew she was unable to bring anything but herself to a marriage. If I wanted her, I had to accept that she would give me nothing but herself. Alas, I dreamt of a girl like her, but of one having additional attributes, in vain.

"I was coming from behind and so was she. I wanted a lift in my marriage, an advantage, not just love. Was I wrong? Who knows? Should a young man marry for love or passion alone? That was the dilemma my young self faced." He paused, eyes fixed on some distant point. "In the end, the choice was taken out of my hands; as I struggled with my emotions and my ambitions, she lost her life in a tragic accident.

"When I met Janice, I was attracted to her beauty, her elegance, and her voice, but I have to admit that her social background and her father's position also attracted me like a magnet. After our marriage, though, we discovered that our temperaments, our aims, our ambitions, were starkly at odds.

"We couldn't make music in harmony, and try as we have, we've never been able to reconcile those fundamental differences. I admire her a great deal and her character is beyond reproach. I was infatuated with her when we married, and for good reason, but my dear Elizabeth, we both know a marriage requires more than mere infatuation. You need to be in tune temperamentally as well as physically, your life's goals must align, or a marriage grows and falls apart.

"I'm sorry to admit it, but we've been out of tune for many years. Successfully married young couples have to know what they want in life, where they want to go, what their respective ambitions are, what price they are prepared to pay to achieve those ambitions. If they don't have some sort of cohesive commonality, the world will tear them apart, no matter how much romance initiated the marriage."

"How right you are," responded Elizabeth. "Many of my contemporaries have learned that lesson the hard way, I'm afraid."

James continued rambling on thoughtfully. "The very young are often driven by a variety of motives. They are greedy and ambitious, but untampered. Their agendas corrupt the essence of pure romance in the name of 'treasure'; be it money, security, social position, connections to advance their careers, it's all treasure. When you reach my age," he chuckled, "it is sure as hell much easier, or maybe that's just a triumph of optimism over experience talking. Who knows?" He burst out laughing, taking her hand, "All I know is that when I'm with you, my dear, I'm complete."

Elizabeth's sign was more than a little wistful. "You are ever so right, dearest; the young, particularly the very young, are often motivated by powerful fantasies and imaginings. They strive for recognition, especially recognition of the name.

"I'm a living example of such folly. How many girls could resist becoming a duchess? Not I. It's the vanity game, I know; I sprung the trap freely and willingly." She laughed, her voice lighter now, as she said, "That's why we have so many songs about how romance is better the second time around, when our values, needs, and priorities are so much clearer and cleaner."

The waves rolled in the distance, lapping at the horizon as surely as they did the same to the bow down below. Light danced across their seafoam crests and even sometimes shown through the deep blue water. James breathed deep and smiled, his head bobbing in peaceful agreement.

He paused, taking her hand in his and rubbing her knuckles, and with another chuckle, he continued in a jocular vein, "You know the old paradox about how the rich old man, fat and lecherous, attracts a young and beautiful seductress? We've all heard this story: she gets the dough, and he gets the sex until he's old and dead. She gets more dough from his estate and can afford to seduce a handsome young lover she can dominate with her wealth and lead around with a ring in his nose.

"Those superficial relationships, they deserve one another; they're bust! But my love, I have always believed a marvelous relationship could form between a happy couple that could be rooted in a blending of their minds and spirits rather than merely in their flesh; a relationship built on intellectuality, emotional support, compatible temperaments. And such a relationship, should it exist, it would have to be nurtured physically; a rare combination, perhaps, but what a symphony it must be!"

Once again deep in thought, he continued, "Intellectual and temperamental harmony are powerful catalysts, the perfect elements needed to properly sustain a healthy relationship. Sex, I believe, is the icing on the cake, but first, you should be soul mates before being sexual mates. The trouble is, as young males, we tend to reverse the order. Our libidos are so in overdrive, we prefer infatuation, the desire for an appealing sexual mate, to romance, the need for a partner of the soul.

"Indeed, young men are often completely oblivious to the second; and then we wonder why the relationship soon goes off the rails. Passionate love alone, devoid of anything more substantial, will ultimately lead to nothing else than romantic disaster, I'm afraid. It seems to me that the emotion of love, in spite of what the romantics say, is not self-sustaining unless the lovers love many things in common."

Elizabeth gazed at James with simmering love in her eyes. "Oh, I know what you mean, James, dear, it is so rare and can be so beautiful. I love the way you think about life, love, and ambition. You're not really as one-track as you think you are. You know, You've certainly taught me a lot about things beyond my realm since that lucky day at the pool."

"Well, I hope you're right, my darling, but right now, I want a lot more of these things in my life, while I still have time left to enjoy them. And you, my dear, are the one person in the world who can give them to me." He laughed, putting his arm around her and gently pulling her in close. "Maybe we each have what the other is looking for. Are we soulmates, kindred spirits? I don't fully know.

"All I know is that when we're together, I feel a profound sense of serenity and peace. This is something quite rare in my experience. When I look at you in conversation, I find myself sinking deep into your mind; meshing with your thoughts and emotions. It's the harmony we have together that draws me to you, the ability to converse, to exchange thoughts and communicate complex opinions and notions. And you know, my darling, how the feeling consumes me and is finally expressed dramatically in passion."

Elizabeth shivered a little, sensing exactly what he meant.

They continued their conversation into the late afternoon, with Elizabeth discussing his children.

"But your children, James. Those wonderful pictures in your cabin of your daughter and son, Sheila and Matthew."

"Yes, Sheila is ten now, and Matthew is seven. They're wonderful kids and they're doing well at school. I really have been lucky, so far, playing what I call genetic roulette. Time will tell. I must say that Janice is a wonderful mother and has done a lot more than I have in bringing them up."

The air became chilly, with the sun sinking lower in the western sky, as they strolled, arm in arm, to the grand salon at the tea hour before changing for dinner and evening activities. As they walked in from the deck, Reginald McKenna waved them over, asking if they would join him for a spot of tea.

"We must get along, Reg, I have some business to look after, but what about a cocktail in my stateroom 2A anytime after 6:15? And do bring Edward along."

"Very kind of you," replied Reg. "Sounds splendid. Look forward to seeing you in about an hour's time."

When McKenna and Peacock arrived, James walked them out on his little deck, casually discussing their trip and the C.D.R. meeting. "I've had a position in the stock for several years; don't think I'd ever want to sell it," said James. "I presume you're going to the meeting."

"Yes, of course," said Edward Peacock. "Should be an active meeting. I understand it's a long agenda. Haven't seen it yet, but the report should be out by the time we dock."

"Do you think the majority of the stock is held in the United Kingdom, Reg?" asked James.

"Oh, yes, I believe about fifty-two percent of the shares are owned in the United Kingdom, but it's wildly spread, you know. Not too many very large blocks left, except perhaps Lord Stonehaven's estate, and the family of Lord Elgin in Scotland, both very early shareholders, founders really. Then, of course, there is the Royal family. I'm really surprised more stock isn't held by Canadians. I understand it's only about nineteen percent. Canadians aren't the greatest risk-takers in the world, are they?"

"Well, maybe the Brits will sell as the stock moves higher," suggested Peacock. "Sir Edward worries about control, you know. He says the stock is too bloody cheap, and some group from the States might be tempted to take a run at it. I think he's got a plan to block any attempt if it ever occurred. In fact, we did know something big was going on a few months ago, but we think they ran out of steam."

"Oh, really," said James. "Who were they?"

"No idea," said Peacock. "But they're busted, we think."

"Well, maybe we'll have some excitement with the Conservative Party back in power. That should lift the stock," said James.

"I think the annual report will make good reading with earnings up which should help the stock," commented Reg. They stepped back into the stateroom joining Elizabeth and other guests, as the steward served hors d'oeuvres and mixed dry American Martinis, currently the rage, especially with the Brits.

At the captain's table later that evening, James struck up a conversation with a young Mr. Morgan, the founder of a new investment bank in New York, Morgan Stanley and Company, an offshoot of the famous J.P. Morgan and Company, allowing him to get an outside perspective on Wall Street activities and particularly about his two Wall Street tycoon syndicate partners.

After dinner, as the band struck up, they decided to make it in an early evening, and danced quietly out onto the deck, to the popular love song, "They'll Never Believe Me."

With James whispering in her ear with a chuckle, "Oh, yes they will when I tell them." Then following a short stroll, they were off to the bliss and quietness of stateroom 2A.

In the morning, stateroom 2A served as James's office again. There, he handled the usual flood of telegrams from London, New York, and Montreal, providing market information and comments on C.D.R. activity.

Richard wired some interesting news their way.

> Between being Minister of Finance and engaged to be married, my schedule is heavy. Please advise developments re Atlantic. Richard

Ian wired back the next day with a progress report.

> Forwarding proxies from friends at North Cote and Company, Vickers Da Casta and Company, and Casenove and Company. Baruch reports that efforts with many large Wall Street firms bearing fruit, not only in market action.

> Stock now trading around the thirty-seven-dollar level. Additional committed proxies from Lee Higginson and Company, Inc., Clark, Dodge and Company, and of course, Kuhn-Loeb and Company. Ian

Paul Wallenstein continued to report progress, having executed orders for over ninety-two thousand shares, and he was constantly in the London or New York market bidding for stock.

Time was running short as purchases had to be registered with the company's transfer agencies in either London, New York or Montreal a number of days before the meeting, to be valid for voting.

Later that morning, as they sunned in their deckchairs, the steward handed him a telegram just received from Ottawa, Canada. Knowing a wire from Ottawa could only be from one person, he tore it open impatiently.

> P.M. has been asked by president of Atlantic to consider order in council re maximum number of shares voted at meetings of certain Canadian companies by foreign shareholders. He's still on the trail. Don't worry. Have advised London and Annabel sends greetings. Richard

"My God!" exclaimed James. "He's still paranoid about a takeover. Well, thank God there isn't enough time now for legislation to be effective for this year's meeting, but the threat of it sure as hell complicates things."

Wanting to head off any major surprises at the meeting, he anticipated his opponent's tactics and prepared for their heavy guns. He fired off a telegram to MacDonnell in Montreal, asking him to ferret out leaks from the president's office regarding voting restrictions.

> Understand Ottawa been asked to consider order in council Re foreign share position. Can you assess president's attitude? I am sure De Rolland would be helpful. J.M.

He relied more and more on Elizabeth to handle a myriad of details. And found her judgment to be remarkable, considering her limited business experience. She was fascinated by the Atlantic Venture and the talented people involved, as James explained the complexities of finance and the backgrounds of the personalities with whom he was associated in the syndicate.

He repeated to Ian one of her perceptive questions with amusement: 'In business,' she asked, 'How in the world do you learn to separate the wheat from the chaff, the truth from the blarney, the con artists, from the committed, when you're dealing with such Con Artists, an eclectic gang of greedy egocentric ambitious players?'

"An astute question," replied Ian. "She was amused when I used the analogy of her own theatrical background, likening it to Shakespeare's observation, 'All the world is a stage, we are but the players on it'.

"She's a very smart woman. When I pointed out that, in business, we are all actors, that it's just a matter of learning how to identify and separate the bad actors, the poseurs, and the charlatans from the good actors, she understand my point. 'Oh, yes,' she said, 'Just like showbiz'. Of course, the real difficulty is that often the really bad actors were sometimes very good actors. She roared with laughter when I told her this."

"James, you've got a jewel in that gal, you're hung with horseshoes. I should be so lucky. She's got it all. Never let her go," responded Ian emphatically. "Your roving days are over. How many men do you think are lucky enough to combine a wife, a soulmate, and a mistress, all wrapped up in the same beautiful woman?"

As the Montcalm sailed into the gulf of the mighty Saint Lawrence River on a sunny, windswept day in early May, a strange and beautiful sight greeted the passengers. The lonely coast of the awakening continent was blanketed in a fresh bed of snow and a chilly current of Arctic air swept the snow into drifts and snow devils.

The ship plied a steady path to the northwest, passing through the Cabot Strait and revealing for anyone topside the tiny coastal hamlets in the distance and the smattering of green patches of cleared Newfoundland farmlands.

As she sailed into the Saint Lawrence Valley, the inspiring scenery provided a vision of boundless opportunity and potential. This was a young land, vast and still a little wild. The future beckoned, a promising future surpassing anything ever imagined by its early explorers. And through this land cut the mightiest of all rivers, the Saint Lawrence, so wide at some points a person might be forgiven for mistaking it for a lake or a sea.

James and Elizabeth were enjoying a stroll on the desks, eyes affixed upon the distant land. Elizabeth confessed to being curious about the river. It was different from any other river she'd ever seen and she asked if he knew anything about its early history.

"This river valley was really the cradle of the North American economy," explained James, "from the earliest settlements in 1608 through the great fur trading era of the seventeenth and eighteenth centuries and onto the logging and lumbering eras.

"The Saint Lawrence has always served as the great commercial highway of North America, cutting straight through into the heart of the continent. Several of the past invasions, or attempted invasions in most cases, have centered along this river valley; the British invasion of Quebec in 1759, the attempted invasions of 1775 and 1812 by the Americans, and a few others I'm sure."

He spoke of the monarchists, the Empire Loyalist migration to the maritime provinces when Richard's family arrived, and to Quebec and Ontario in the late eighteenth century following the American Revolution, which initiated the early development of industry and commerce in Halifax, Quebec City, and Montreal, and westward to the Great Lakes all of which centered on the great river.

It was a revelation to Elizabeth, a history little known, and seldom taught in British schools. "Everything seems to be on such a grand scale compared with tidy neat little England," she exclaimed. James pointing out that England together with the North American continent, had led the industrial revolution of the western world, accounting for over half of total world trade for nearly half a century.

The light of the setting faded slowly, painting the sky at first shades of dull red and burning orange. But as the light retreated, the bleeding sky faded to a soft pink and then to faint shades of purple shot through with dark blue and vague hints of almost-gone red. Elizabeth tucked her head into his shoulder, breathing out in awe, "What a beautiful sky! I hope it's a good omen for your trip to Canada." And then laughing, and with a burst of enthusiasm, she shouted, "A toast to your success, my darling Jamsie." Throwing back her champagne and tossing her glass, into the swirling sea.

LOVE À LA CASBAH

"Come with me, my dear, to my Casbah. It's time for you to teach an old dog new tricks," James chuckled, as he carried her back to his stateroom. He stood her before the mirror and she watched his reflection as he slipped off her blouse and bra and kissed her shoulder. Her heart beat slow and loud in her breast as she drank in the soft look of intense focus painted across his face.

His hands splayed across her shoulders, he moved her body as effortlessly as if she were a puppet on a string. He reached one hand to the side to pick up her dressing gown and he draped her form in it, silently guiding her arms into position. His hands repositioned themselves on her hips and he guided her to his bed, gently laying her down beneath the covers and soothing them into place.

"You'll have to await your prince, my Duchie, but not for long," he chuckled as he slipped into his dressing room, emerging in his blue, silk dressing gown. The intense man had disappeared back inside him, replaced by an excitable boy instead. He wriggled about, watching her as though he were 10 again, anticipating opening presents on Christmas morning.

That she was the present in this case need not be said.

He joined her in bed, sitting beside her and taking her hand gently into his own. He pressed a kiss first to her knuckles; then her palm, then her pulse, and then her lips. Smiling sweetly down at her, he slid under the sheets and drew her body close to his in a moment of blissful anticipation.

"It feels like a dream, James, we seem to be floating on air again. Will it always be like this? Oh, it must, it must, I do l love you so."

"Elizabeth, my darling," he said romantically, "When we get back to London, we're going to get things moving on our marriage; that is, if you're willing to forego being a Duchess, becoming just a plain, young 'Lady MacTavish'," he chuckled.

"Oh, Jamsie, who cares! Mrs., Lady, Countess, or Duchess; what's the difference, as long as I'm with you?"

"Well, don't be so cavalier, my darling. A duchess is a duchess is a duchess, you know," he emphasized with a deep laugh. "How many are there? Only twenty, I think. And on Broadway or Drury lane, my dear; Wow, it's a big ticket, but perhaps I'll become a viscount or a baron like Ian someday," he joked. "Trouble is, dukedoms can't be bought."

They giggled together as he slipped off her gown and caressed her bosom, mumbling, "I'm very inexperienced in the boudoir, my darling, you'll have to direct me."

She broke out into rapturous laughter. "My God, you do tease me, Jamsie! I'm the neophyte, only twenty-eight, but you, my darling, how many women have you known? At least I'm the prime beneficiary of all your experiences, but you won't be needing additional practice, not if I have anything to do with it."

MONTREAL AND INTO THE FRAY

The Montcalm docked at Montreal on a beautiful, breezy June morning, with James and Elizabeth in the pink of health and vitality. They checked into their suite at the Ritz Carleton Hotel on Sherbrooke Street, to be his business headquarters for the next six weeks.

The following morning, he convened his first meeting, inviting William MacDonnell, George Smithers, and Jack D. Kippen to his suite to be updated on the market and street gossip concerning the president's plans for the annual meeting.

MacDonnell reported he'd heard of the board's ongoing concern of a hostile group of investors showing up at the meeting with a sizable stock position, and that the president continued to seriously explore the possibility of government legislation to limit foreign voting to ten percent.

"We understand," said George Smithers, "that Sir Edward watches the transfer sheets from the trust company like a hawk and is aware that heavy transfers were occurring, but with no clear pattern of concentrations."

Jack Kippen reported, "Substantial New York buying in recent days by Wall Street firms."

James had been skillful in masking the syndicate's operations. Nobody, except Ian and himself, knew the exact number of shares or proxies the syndicate controlled, which at the last tally they calculated was approximately 2.8 million.

A call came from Baruch, with a report concerning rather unusual volume in the stock, moving it up to thirty-nine and a half, but he could not identify the buyer, advising, "None of our crowd are in the market at the moment, but we are watching things carefully. It could be more short-covering, but I doubt it at these prices.

"There's been an odd rumor circulating about Goldman Sachs and Company being a big buyer for some time. I'm trying to track it down. You never know, we might find an ally who could strengthen our hand."

"We've heard that Sir Edward continues to be extremely sensitive to any trend of accumulation," James cautioned. "Is it possible this is just the company buying its own stock, perhaps through a subsidiary company, to shore up votes for the meeting? He knows goddamned well how vulnerable he is; he's been jumping at every shadow he sees, even his own. He's even attempting to gain protection from the prime minister's office. Look, I'm here in Montreal at the hotel; call me, day or night, whenever it's important."

The following day, MacDonnell reported a rumor that Sir Edward suspected one of the big American railroad titans might be after the company. Some members of the board reported his sounding off about "That son of a bitch Harriman or J.P. Morgan". Harriman was a giant from Union Pacific and J.P. Morgan hailed from the Great Northern Gang, both definitive candidates and easily capable of what he was accusing them of. He was unable to pin the rumor down and his call reflected his anxiety and frustration in rare outbursts of temper.

James had mixed reactions to these reports. He was, of course, delighted to see the stock up from the dreaded thirty dollar mark – the 'wipe out' level as the gang had taken to calling it – but on the other hand, the syndicate was fresh out of both money and credit from the bust. They were in no position, financial at least, to add to their holdings.

No, they would have to make their stand with their current, disadvantageous position. The question remained, however, how many votes management could bring to muster. Would it be necessary to keep an ongoing search running for new investors to support of the syndicate's initiative?

A wire from Ian provided some direction.

> Stock active here today. Rumor New York buying by major Rail Group. Get Bernie on the case.

James had deliberately maintained a low profile following his arrival in Montreal, confining himself to his suite, and seeing only his closest advisors from the street who knew all the leading lights of the small, compact business establishment. He guessed that James Roswell, who he and Ian had entertained so well in London, had returned from Europe, but deferred calling him, preferring to run into him casually around the hotel or at one of the clubs.

He continued inquiring about the shareholders' meeting, but he always got the same reply. Sir Edward hasn't decided yet. "Perhaps," thought James, "he's still working on the prime minister about the ten-percent rule as an insurance policy."

As each day passed, C.D.R. continued trading actively, moving ahead in all markets to the forty-four-dollar level, providing an equity margin of over twenty-two million dollars to the syndicate, less what had been assigned in options during the crises.

"Sorry to wake you, sir, but a telegram marked 'urgent' has just been received from London," said the concierge.

"Bring it up, bring it up, immediately," directed James, somewhat nervous, it being only four o'clock in the morning. "Slip it under my door." Within minutes, he read the shocking contents.

> Wallenstein fatally shot early this AM. Am pursuing circumstances. Rumored was heavily indebted to Swiss Banking Syndicate. Ian

"My God, Elizabeth, Paul's been shot! What in the hell is this all about? Ian suggests heavy indebtedness – no, not Paul; it can't be." He woke Baruch with the news and fired back a telegram off to Ian.

Advise market opening and your assessment situation. Check Paul's associates.
James

Ian's response was delivered to him at 5:30 a.m.

Market opened down with heavy offerings. Trading $42-1/2. Somebody being liquidated. Will advise. Ian.

James was in a state over the shocking news. Elizabeth watched him as he paced, wild-eyed and frantic. She'd already tried to calm him, to no avail; it seemed this was one time where he needed to simply get it out of his system on his own. She wasn't surprised. Paul Wallenstein was a dear friend of James'; not as close as Ian or Richard, no, but closer than most. And he'd been a trusted partner as well.

"I can't fathom this, Elizabeth, I can't. It just doesn't add up; sure Paul had his share of enemies, who doesn't in this business, but assassination? Who could want him dead that badly? Who the devil was it had him over a barrel? Perhaps it was an act of desperation, a suicide; but I can't believe that either." His mind raced ahead, discounting possibilities and envisioning various ramifications of the event, including heavy selling and a precipitous fall in the market.

Baruch was back on the line. James had zoned out for a moment and the words that greeted his return were questions relating to the sizable debt Ian had reported. "I understand your friend Paul had generated orders for over two hundred thousand shares – approximately seven million dollars worth. Do you think it could have been for his own account?"

"I . . . I don't know." James' voice failed him. Baruch waited for a moment but took back control of the conversation when it was clear James had nothing else to say at the moment.

"I expect we'll witness some heavy selling. If my hunch is right, the mystery buyers will be on the bid side; let's hope so at least. I suspect Goldman Sachs and Hayden Stone were acting for one of the rail syndicates for some time. If we think it's such a steal, James, it's not surprising that some of the pros down here wouldn't see the light as well."

"I hope you're right, Bernie, but goddamn it, we're out of buying power to absorb what looks like urgent European selling; a buying opportunity for sure."

William Hanson of Hanson Brothers, the oldest investment banking firm in Canada, and Jack D. Kippen, his son-in-law and a former banker turned stockbroker, invited James and Elizabeth to join them for dinner at the Saint James Club, together with the famous war ace, Colonel Billy Bishop, and his wife. The invitation was a welcome relief from the day's unsettling news.

While walking up the long, winding staircase of the venerable club, James spotted James Roswell with a party of two, as they entered the dining room. Roswell greeted him with enthusiasm. "How wonderful to see you again, James! I just docked today on the Duchess of Bedford. We must get together. Where do I get in touch with you, James, at the Ritz or . . . ?"

"Yes, I'm at the Ritz and would be delighted to see you."

"Good, I'll call you in the morning."

The head waitress escorted Roswell and his friends to the other side of the dining room to a large table, at which other guests were already seated. Glancing towards them, James instantly recognized the one and only Sir Edward, the ruling knight of the largest transportation company in the world, his nemesis, the chairman and president of The Canada Dominion Railroad Corporation.

Ian had known Sir Edward back in his Montreal days, but James had only met him briefly at the club a year earlier. His host, William Hanson, and of course Billy Bishop, knew the railway tycoon well, making it likely that they would get together before the evening was over, probably after dinner downstairs when they convened for coffee, brandy, and cigars.

Throughout dinner, Hanson and Kippen dominated the conversation with talk about the growth potential of the company. They cast speculations of potential earnings; Hanson was convinced they could exceed forty-five million dollars' worth of shares, assuming approximately four and a half dollars per share.

Following dinner in the members' lounge, James Roswell approached their table, accompanied by good Sir Edward whom he introduced. The man extended a hearty handshake. James had to bite his cheek to keep from laughing as he greeted the man, "Well, Sir Edward, I've heard so much about you, I'm delighted to say hello. Our old friend, Brandenbrooke in England, will be happy to hear that we've met."

Sir Edward replied with a smile as he puffed on his cigar, "I've heard a great deal over the years about your exploits, Sir James, and please give my warmest regards to Ian. He is one of Canada's great ambassadors abroad, and his commonwealth trade preference efforts are good for my business. How long are you in town?"

"Well, quite a while, I expect," said James enthusiastically, "As a matter of fact, I'm hoping to be here for your annual meeting. I've been a shareholder for quite some time."

"Splendid, splendid, I hope you're here for it," said Sir Edward. "We haven't set a date yet, but it shouldn't be too long."

"A group I represent in London," replied James, "has recently bought a few shares and asked me to be sure to attend the meeting if I was in Montreal."

"Oh," replied Sir Edward, laughing and drawing on his cigar. "So, you're the big buyers in the market. We've been wondering who it was. Well, well, good luck! I think the enterprise is in pretty good shape. We might even pay our dividend again this year if everything holds up."

It was a bit of a charade, but an amusing and timely meeting. The two future adversaries, both about the same age, had finally met formally for the first time; but by no means would it be the last.

As they shook hands, saying goodnight, James's parting remark was, "I shall look forward to the meeting, Sir Edward, and I hope it won't be too long."

As James Roswell departed, he reminded James that he would call him in the morning at the Ritz about meeting for lunch or dinner in the next day or two.

Upon returning to his host's table, Colonel Bishop remarked, "Sir Edward is perhaps the most eligible bachelor I've heard of in modern times. It truly is a mystery that a man of his good looks and distinction has never married, in spite of the legion of women who have made every effort to lasso him," he chuckled. "One of Margaret's friends from England probably came closest to graduating than anyone that I know of, but I gather he Bared off when things got too hot and heavy."

"Anybody I know?" asked James.

"Oh, you may have met her or heard of her in England. A beautiful girl, with the most stunning golden hair and green eyes, called Lady Sylvia Fox."

James froze in his chair, looking bemused. He was thunderstruck. It didn't add up. "Quite impossible," he thought, "How many love affairs had this girl had in Montreal?" When he recovered his composure, he casually asked the Bishops if they knew a Montrealer called Olivier De Rolland.

Margaret Bishop responded with amusement, blurting in a gossipy tone, "Oh, my goodness, of course, Olivier, I certainly do. He's quite the ladies' man about town; very good looking. He was pretty keen on Sylvia too, as I understand it, and still is. She met him through Sir Edward, I think."

James returned to his hotel, dumbfounded by the evening's revelations and in a quandary as he confided to Elizabeth his suspicions about Sylvia.

"Do you suppose Sylvia has revealed her affair with Ian to Sir Edward, directly?" he asked. He didn't wait for her answer adding, "Probably not. We know she told Olivier De Rolland about meeting Ian on the Empress of Scotland and about New York brokers who were interested in C.D.R., but we thought that leak was taken care of by Sylvia's contrived letter at Ian's insistence and direction."

He continued thinking out loud. "At least that was our conclusion from the feedback we got. Sir Edward never let on to knowing anything of our interest when we met tonight. He obviously has his own agenda, and he's playing for time. He put on as good an act as I did, but perhaps now he's written us off; thinks we've been liquidated maybe and only an American syndicate is his adversary. The joke of it is he may be half right."

He wired Ian details of the evening dramatics, carefully disguised to maintain security, but ended with a specific request.

> Please check with 'S' about Sir E. How long is it since she has had any correspondence
> with him, and has he any knowledge of her present relationship with you. James

Reports flooded in the next day. C.D.R. had opened in New York down again on volume and it had remained active throughout the trading session, closing at thirty-six and a half.

"A tape reader, you think?" James suggested to Jack.

Kippen observed the stock's strength over the past month and sudden sell-off, thinking hard before concluding, "It was deliberate liquidation under duress. Can we track down the selling and the size of the offerings? This is critical, Jack, in view of the many stories surrounding Wallenstein's death."

Roswell telephoned, as promised, inviting James to lunch with a few friends at the Mount Royal Club whose membership was composed of every banker and industrialist of consequence in Canada. It was a bastion of the nation's wealthy establishment, a club with limited membership and a long waiting list.

The morning was spent on the telephone with Baruch in New York and Richard in Ottawa, who advised that he was taking the afternoon train to Montreal, as important developments required their having a private meeting immediately.

Baruch expressed his suspicions concerning the identity of the rail syndicate who might be buying C.D.R., and he indicated that he would have something specific to report in the next few days.

Things were moving swiftly as he left to meet Roswell for lunch, speculating who might be of interest around the club, and looking forward to seeing Richard that evening, with the benefit of his judgment in accessing the present situation.

James Roswell was already at the club when he arrived. "I was delighted to see you last night. It's been too long. I'm glad we could get together," said Roswell. "Come, let's go upstairs and have a drink while we wait for the others. I've reserved a private room for lunch."

After casually instructing the head steward to alert Sir Vincent Hennessy and Mr. Watson to their location once they arrived, he led James upstairs. James, after so long dealing with C.D.R., easily recognized both names as company directors.

He mused to himself, 'This is going to be an interesting lunch. Perhaps they intend to give me the third degree.' The thought was one part amusing and the other part nerve-wracking. 'Sir Edward must have had an afterthought following our meeting at the club and had Watson and Hennessy do a little research."

As they settled into a private dining room, Roswell took off on a brief tangent about his father's career as a contractor, laying rails across the prairies forty years earlier. In the next two minutes, James learned more about laying track than he'd ever known before and he was surprised to find himself almost disappointed when they were interrupted by the arrival of Mr. Watson and Sir Hennessy.

Roswell was quick to introduce the two. Graham Watson was a director of C.D.R. whose father had been an early investor in both the company and CONINC. Sir Vincent, a fellow company director, was a former president of the Bank of Montreal. BMO had been the prime financial institution originally responsible for funding the building of the railroad between 1880 and 1885 when George MacAlpine was president.

"Gentlemen," James greeted enthusiastically. "It is an honor. I have heard so much about you. You are the directors of a great enterprise, the people behind the success story. I can remember the early days in Calgary, at the turn of the century, when the company was just getting underway. It is truly spectacular how far you've taken it since those early days. Why, you could liken C.D.R. with the young nation of Canada; a young upstart new to the scene rising to prominence and prosperity!"

Talk quickly turned to Western growth and the future of Canada, C.D.R., and the West. Richard, as the rising Calgary star of the Conservative Party, was a surprisingly popular topic of conversation. Both Watson and Sire Vincent expressed high hopes for James' friend's success in his political endeavors and ambitions, and especially his goal of becoming the Canadian Prime Minister.

From Richard, their talk turned to Lord Brandenbrooke. Apparently, they had met Ian years earlier during one of his early Montreal stays back when he was in the middle of developing his investment firm, Macleod and Company, Inc., oh so many years ago. They hadn't seen him since he'd returned to England in 1912 and were happy for any tidbits they could scrounge up.

James, who was rapidly becoming impatient with the need to know why Roswell had invited these two prominent directors to lunch with him, used the annual meeting as an opener, commenting, "I hope I will be here for your shareholders' meeting. Gentlemen, will it be soon?" There was no response, merely a long, almost eerie silence as looks were exchanged.

After nearly a full minute of awkward silence, Sir Vincent turned to address him, fixing James with an impassible, unreadable look, "We understand, Sir James, that there may be a group in New York which represents one of several prominent railroad corporations. We understand that this hypothetical group may have taken an interest in C.D.R. and we understand that you and Lord Brandenbrooke may in some way be involved.

"Now, could you perhaps clarify this rumor in any way? Our president, Sir Edward, is . . . 'curious' about the behavior of the stock, not to mention the persistent rumors which have been floating around for a good many months." Sir Vincent steepled his fingers and James met his gaze full on. Out of the corner of his eye, he could see Mr. Watson watching them with a gimlet eye as Roswell sat back, sipping a drink, as motionless as a statue.

The air sat heavy in the room, an almost physical weight pressing down on everyone present. The two gentlemen were obviously not as oblivious or ignorant as they had portrayed themselves. James quickly mulled over his options. He wasn't quite ready to let the cat out of the bag, but it might be a timely opportunity to take some risks and explore some unexpected options.

Choosing his words carefully, he replied, "Gentlemen, Ian and I, as you may know, have been shareholders of C.D.R. for some time. Like most, we've heard these rumors of American interest in the railroad. That being said, we haven't any direct evidence of whether it's true, and if so, who it could be.

"I personally would have thought your transfer agents and registers could, perhaps, provide important information on the subject. After all, these shares must surely be being transferred into various names. I've no doubt your lawyers have been watching this carefully. What seems to be the great concern here, Sir Vincent?

"Isn't it true that the largest stock position was and is still held in England? I gathered that the Stonehaven estate and Lord Elgin's family in Scotland, both among the original founding shareholders, are still holding large positions. Am I wrong? Has something happened? I've often been asked in London how much stock the board of directors own."

"The point is," Sir Vincent replied sharply, "that Yanks have viewed our line with envy for a very long time. Back in 1905, our company serviced an important part of the central and western markets of the continent. And while we were doing that, James Hill and his Great Northern Railroad gang got support from J.P. Morgan and decided the best use of that power was to give us a rough time fighting a control battle. We blocked them then, on the railroad chess board, and we kept them south of the 49th Parallel.

"The Great Northern, the Northern Pacific, and the Union Pacific have been vicious competitors ever since, fighting over our border markets all the way down to the Pacific. We have to watch them like hawks; otherwise, they'll make like hawks and steal our stock out from under us. You may have heard of Sir Edward's paranoia; amusing it might seem, but it is justified. Yanks have been trying to muscle their way into our exclusive preserve for ages now. The company is the passion of his life; he'll fight for it as much as he has to. And as far as he's concerned, the Yanks belong below the 49th parallel."

James smiled in complete agreement. "Of course, of course, keep the Yanks out." He paused, contemplating. He'd long had an idea when it came to western transportation and he wondered what the board might make of it. "If I was running the operation, I'd go the other way. I'd look for control of tracks and markets on the other side of the border. I think that strategy could drastically accelerate growth by dominating the Pacific Northwestern and Canadian markets. Do you think one of these U.S. railroads is after C.D.R. as a protective measure?"

"That's why we're asking you," responded Sir Vincent, somewhat abruptly. He looked a little taken aback; James wondered why. Had his idea been somehow shocking to them? "I rather thought you might know more than I do about such things. A lot of stock has changed hands in the past year, and we know there is currently constant buying from Wall Street."

"Surely," said James, "management is well supported at annual meetings. How much would a foreign railroad have to own to be a threat?"

Sir Vincent evaded the question, commenting that what they were looking for was a clue as to who Wall Street was representing.

"I can assure you," James reiterated calmly, "I know of no one group in particular, though I'm sure many exist. My people do feel the stock could go a lot higher, and we are certainly interested in a substantial trading profit. We have a sizable block. If we can be of help to your board at the meeting — against a hostile foreign group, per se — we would most certainly be willing to cooperate."

If James was fooling anyone, it would be too good to be true. The verbal dance continued through lunch, no one seeming willing to admit to what they knew. It only ended, finally, when Roswell, looking torn between amusement and frustration, suggested a subsequent meeting, perhaps with the president himself.

James left the club walking on air, foreseeing the possibility of a deal of a lifetime. Circumstances were rapidly evolving that could put him in the 'Catbird Seat' – the power seat - where he could call the shots and write his own ticket, particularly if he could unravel the mysterious Wallenstein assassination, and Bernie could identify the New York group.

RICHARD AND IAN RE: ELECTION

Richard, the proud Minister of Finance of the newly appointed Conservative government, arrived from Ottawa for one of their late-night powwows at the hotel. They poured some drinks, lit some cigars, and put their heads together. The first item on today's agenda was the government. The Conservative administration had only just barely managed to eke out a majority and it was only a majority is the most technical of terms.

The big question here was when should they risk going to the country for a working majority? And then came the question of Sir Edward's discussions with the Prime Minister concerning Canadian control of the Canadian Dominion Railway Corporation.

Richard, pleased as punch, reported, "The P.M.'s been reluctant to introduce restrictions on foreign ownership. The Liberal government under King probably would have gone for it, but Meighen feels – and I support him on this – that it would set a bad precedent in our capital markets."

"My god, that's a relief," exclaimed James. "At least that's one threat we can scratch from the list for the time being."

James then related his lunch conversation with Roswell and Sir Vincent Hennessy. It all tied in with what Richard was reporting. Sir Edward had apparently been deferring the annual meeting hoping to get some support from Ottawa.

"We need to identify which American group has accumulated a large block of stock. Once we know who it is, we can play both ends against the middle. If they have, say, one million shares, and they join us, we could vote over four million shares. I'm damned sure that would rule the meeting. We could also vote with management under certain circumstances – that is to say, presuming they cooperated with us – or against them, depending on their attitude; but we would hold the whip hand." James looked positively smug.

"James, you old conniver," said Richard, breaking into a broad, boyish grin. He reached over and clapped his friend on the shoulder. "You'd have a heyday with this, wouldn't you? And if the board refused to cooperate; well, there would be blood on the floor in no time, mark my words." He paused, rubbing his chin in thought. "I'm guessing the board will split, the meeting will adjourn, and serious negotiation could commence immediately. Do you think you should just present all of this to Sir Edward before the meeting, or wait and take the board by surprise?"

"That's the important tactical question. We'll have to weigh it carefully; I'm not sure yet. What do you think?"

"Well, I tend to think you might do better with a private meeting before the annual. You know, there will be a hell of a crowd at that meeting; if you take them by surprise, all hell could break out, and the president, under the circumstances would probably have to adjourn. You'll end up with a group of lawyers in a private room, all putting on an act to support their fees. But let's think about it."

They composed a long wire to Ian and settled down with Elizabeth for dinner in the suite, during which Richard was updated concerning the Wallenstein tragedy and possible ramifications. "I can't contribute much to that mystery, James, but keep me up on developments.

"Having said that, if the government falls on a vote of confidence, Meighen might resign as leader. I've already contributed over $350K to the party's financial fund."

"Well on your way to ultimate party leadership, I say," James ribbed.

"Indeed." He puffed out his chest, trying to look pompous and 'dignified'. "I will have you know I am now a major pillar of influence in the Conservative party." On top of his ridiculous air, he affected a truly horrendous accent of unknown origins and some absurd mannerisms. Not one person could keep a straight face by the end of his little performance, especially not Richard himself.

Once everyone had stopped laughing enough to start breathing again, James, in an optimistic mood, assured him that the way things looked with C.D.R., there would be plenty of money to support his leadership campaign; and ultimately an election campaign.

Richard waved him off. "Enough about politics. Let's talk business. What do you remember about George Getty?"

James shrugged. "Old friend and correspondent from Oklahoma, if I recall correctly. Working with oil? It's been so long."

"He's got a company now, 'Minnehoma'. I've acquired some oil leases and I've also subscribed to a few shares. It seemed worth exploring the epic oil rush of California. I really have enjoyed corresponding with Getty, even though we've never met; he obviously is a frontier lawyer like me, seeking opportunity in the west. He's got a young son, Paul, about your age James, who is also dealing in leases and hopes to drill a few wildcats quite soon."

"I'm not that young, Richard."

They met up again the following evening for supper at the club. James told himself he'd been patient up until now and he took it upon himself to interrogate his old friend on a topic that had long fascinated him: Richard's love life.

And for the first time in James's experience, he got to see a spectacular sight: Richard, serious, studious, no-nonsense Richard B. Benson, became exuberant and even emotional. He extolled the charms of his bride-to-be, waxed poetic and sang her praises.

"I've known Annabel for years now, both professionally and socially," he confessed sheepishly. James resisted the urge to smack him upside the head for not telling anyone; he and Ian had been worried about him. The last thing they wanted was for the third member of the triad to grow old alone. "She really is my soulmate, James – she can practically read my thoughts and moods. It's been bliss having her support and comfort in the political jungle of sycophants and hypocrites I live in. It's taken me a long time to find her, but I believe my patience has been rewarded."

"When we got your news in London, Ian and I opened a bottle of champagne, being delighted to hear it, but you never took us up as the two old roués offering matrimonial advice," chuckled James. "It sure sounds like you've got it right, and your Annabel is a winner."

The stock markets in London, New York, and Montreal continued their merry uptrend, with the Dow Jones Industrial Averages reaching one hundred and seventy, but C.D.R. continued its decline trading in the thirty-four- to thirty-five-dollar range on increasing volume, reducing the syndicate's equity again by fourteen million.

Baruch, in constant touch from New York, was more convinced than ever that a powerful Wall Street railroad syndicate was a major buyer of the stock, but was alarmed at the selling pressure from Europe.

"We are approaching the crisis level again if we can't stem the tide," wired Ian. "Am pursuing selling sources but so far no luck."

James speculated that Wallenstein must have become seriously compromised with obligations he couldn't meet, but to whom? And why? He was at a loss to guess.

"We are back to the precipice, Bernie, if we can't dry up the selling or identify the new buyers."

"Could be anyone, James. There's more than a few that could and more than a few that would." Baruch rattled off a few potential suspects, familiar names for the most part. "Some would want money, some territory, and some connections. I don't know what to think about this, James.

"Still, I've got this to say: if, and that's a big if, if these phantoms were aware of the Atlantic Syndicate," he reported, "they might want to discuss a joint deal of mutual interest to serve both of our objectives. Someone will talk sooner or later. That's just how people work. Until then, we're in the dark." The crisis fuse was short as he anxiously stalked the street, looking for the signal that would give him the clue.

THE CONTROL CHARADE BEGINS

James Roswell called asking to see James at the hotel, agreeing to meet at six o'clock p.m., but emphasizing that the meeting was to be completely private and off the record.

Upon his arrival, James ordered drinks to be served as they got down to business. Roswell reviewing their lunch, reported, "Sir Edward feels that you and Brandenbrooke know a great deal more than you're revealing and senses you represent a substantial block of stock."

"How much?" asked James wryly.

"Well, over five hundred thousand shares," replied Roswell.

"Well, that's not so much," laughed James. A mere eighteen million dollars at the day's market. What could anybody do with that number of shares? The board of directors must have much more than that themselves."

"There is no secret about the board's stock position," said Roswell. "Any shareholder is entitled to have that information. The fact is collectively they don't have that amount of stock. That is one of the problems, and is why Sir Edward gets so agitated when he hears about outside groups buying heavily into the company."

James knew what Roswell was coming to. The mere thought of it quickened his pulse. "Well, what the hell has Sir Edward got in mind?" he quipped impatiently. "I told you at lunch that we could help out if it got to a battle royal, but I'll be goddamned if I know who the hell has been buying in New York. If I knew, I'd tell you. But god bless them. I hope they bid the bloody stock up to the sky, the last few days certainly have not been encouraging with the stock at thirty-four dollars."

"Trouble is," Roswell drawled nervously, a bite of desperation echoing in his voice, "if it is a rail group, we might be facing a takeover offer on a share exchange basis. That would set up the biggest anti-American reaction since the War of 1812." He picked up a cigar and bit into the end nervously. He pulled not lighter nor match from his pocket and nor did he ask for one. "Sir Edward thinks he knows who the New York players are now and that's why I'm here. The stock closed at thirty-four and a half today. For some unknown reason, it's down six dollars in the last few days."

"Well, if he knows who's been buying, does he know who's selling? And if so, does he have any idea how much they have? Or if they're still in the market?"

"No, not precisely. But we suspect they have accumulated a large block; larger than any blocks in Canada or England," replied Roswell.

"Tell me, what's a reasonable number of shares to turn up at an annual meeting in person and by proxy?" asked James casually, containing his excitement as he poured himself another drink.

"Oh, I don't know. I think last year it was about three million, but that's without any special proxy solicitation,' answered Roswell.

James, seeing the picture clearly and maintaining his poker face, asked, "By the way, with all this excitement, where and when is the annual meeting going to be held?"

Roswell answered, "I don't know exactly, but Sir Edward said he'd call it as soon as he was satisfied he could control the meeting. That's why he wants your support, James. Frankly, he thinks that the Harriman Gang and Union Pacific are hot on your trail."

"My God!" exclaimed James. "Not that Union Pacific gang! I can't believe it, but then I guess it would make a great marriage of territories, wouldn't it? But goddamn it, Canada's not going to put up with a coup like that. We'll have to head those double-dealing buccaneers off at the pass. Tell Sir Edward that Ian and I are available if he thinks we can be of assistance."

James grabbed the phone the minute Roswell had left his suite and got Baruch at his Fifth Avenue penthouse. "Bernie, it looks like Union Pacific with Harriman. That's what the president thinks. How does that grab you?"

"It's possible, but if they have been the heavy buyers, and I'm not saying that is the case, then what in blazes are they up to now?" Baruch scowled furiously. "The stock is being hammered again. Could be a deliberate shake-out to buy it cheaper; it's a well-known tactic in Wall Street and it makes sense if it is U.P. and Harriman.

"Those Wall Street players have got the ball in their court. And if the stock dips another few points down, they'll be buying under thirty dollars." He clicked his tongue, infuriated. "Oh, can't Ian solve the Wallenstein mystery? That's your code-breaker right there, I tell you."

Ian, frantically scouring the behind the scenes of the Wallenstein maze of intrigue, was making some headway, which he wired to Baruch.

> Am advised Paul heavy buyer personally CDR. Perhaps 340,000 shares, collateralized by his holdings of Belgian public utility company suddenly under investigation, fraud charge and bankruptcy. Will advise soonest. Sherlock

Baruch responded to the news with alarm. "That's a hell of a block, James. In a debacle like this, the creditors must be dumping stock at any price. They could break thirty dollars in no time."

"The bloody irony of it is, Sir Edward thinks it's the marauding gang being squeezed out," said James. "What a joke; if it's really that rail gang in the market and we get clobbered, they'll have control on a silver platter. Bernie, we've got to meet with that rail group, whoever they are, or we're cooked. Ian is tracking the sellers. The damn stock just traded at thirty-two and a half. I can hear the margin calls already."

As he hung up, a call came from Richard down the hall, "I'll be right over, Richard. The scene is intense."

Richard was a man inclined to look for the positives in a situation; as such, upon hearing the news, his reaction was to say, "Talk about lucky; you're hung with horseshoes, my boy. If Ol' Bernie can get confirmation of Union's buying, all you'll need is a little time, like 'Gene Tunney' in the long count, being saved by the bell and beating Dempsey. Get Union on your team, negotiate the Wallenstein liquidation to their advantage, and you'll hit a home run, Babe Ruth style."

A bolt of electrical optimism shot through James and he grabbed at the phone. "It may be a long shot, Richard, but by God, you could be dead right; let's bounce it off Bernie."

"Great strikes of lightning! It's a natural," Baruch shouted into the phone. "I had pretty well come to the same conclusion!"

"Really?" James wondered if he looked as pleasantly confused and astonished as he felt.

"Yes! I was going to call you tomorrow. If that's the play, you've got a hot hand, my friend, a royal flush in the business world. I'll check and verify it before getting back to you. By the way, I love that Tunney analogy, boys," he joked with a snicker. "I was at the fight; what a scene it was, the long count! 'Tunney was saved by the bell!' Ah, what fun. But yes, if Union is our big buyer, it's a godsend.

"I'll meet with Averell Harriman tomorrow. I know him well; as you know, I knew his father, E.H., from the Northern Pacific battle I told you about. He was the little broker who took on J.P. Morgan, remember? The man built the Union Pacific's sixty thousand miles of western rail years back. Averell has since become a major shareholder of Union and, of course, a director in turn.

"I'm thinking we can have a frank discussion. After all, if Union is seriously in the market for C.D.R., there's no doubt he'll want to consult with his superiors, specifically his president and chairman. Presuming we can get the brackets on their position and they realize our own position, a lot of options become available to us, not least probably being able to buy out the Belgian block and stabilize the market."

"I'm guessing you saw the stock today."

"Oh yes, I saw. I can't believe it's still opening so low; just thirty-one and a half today, not much better than the past little while and still way too damn close to the precipice for comfort."

Sir Edward's directors, now very used to being summoned to urgent meetings by good Sir Edward, trailed into the room. Sir Edward, of course, was already there, quietly ranting to a junior about wild, and often conflicting, rumors and market action.

As soon as everyone was present and seated, he presented today's topic, which amounted to a rehash of his views and the various countermeasures currently under consideration. There was little new, though he had put a new spin on some old ideas. Still, the moment he moved away from his ideas and back into his frequent reminders to the board of the company shareholders' 1914 resolution, their minds started to discretely wander again.

There wasn't a single man on the board who couldn't recite the resolution forward and backward. It was essentially a sanction permitting the issuance of up to seven hundred and fifty thousand shares of capital stock during difficult times, and upon such terms as the directors deemed appropriate. However, just as the board members were starting to genuinely drift off, Sir Edward brought forth something new. It was enough to recapture their flagging attention.

"Gentlemen, I am considering recording this resolution in our agenda at the annual meeting," Sir Edward advised, drawing himself up to his full height. "My only reservation is that the announcement may reduce the price of stock even further, allowing those Yankee bandits to buy more at advantageous prices. We could, on the other hand, consider a rights issue, thusly allowing all shareholders to acquire additional shares at a discount to the market. If I knew how much those barracudas owned, it would help; rumor has it possibly as much as nine hundred and fifty thousand shares, but we can only guess at the moment."

"What's the position of Lord Brandenbrooke and Sir James MacTavish?" asked Senator Beique deliberately, providing an opportunity for the president to convey his awareness of Brandenbrooke and MacTavish's involvement.

Sir Edward paused and responded with a quizzical look, "We don't know exactly, Senator. We know they were forced to liquidate in that down market in January and February, but Sir James has said they would assist us with whatever they have left, if necessary."

"Have you had any encouragement from the prime minister's office?" asked Sir Vincent Hennessy. "He could block these Yankee carpetbaggers with the stroke of a pen, if he so wished, couldn't he, through the passing of an order in council?"

"Gentlemen, the Prime Minister hasn't got the guts. That fool Meighen thinks it would be political dynamite. He thinks it would set a bad precedent; limiting capital flows and share ownership across our mutual border." The president's tone was biting and mocking. "Goddamn it, if King were in office, he'd move to kick the bastards out. That's what we did back in 1775 when that highwayman, Benedict Arnold, thought he could take Montreal for George Washington and that's what we've done since!

"But this government," he sneered, "it's hanging by a thread. A majority too weak to do anything. They're so vulnerable to a vote of non-confidence, they haven't got the balls to take on anything as controversial as this." He looked like he either wanted to spit or to curse. "I'm going to talk with Minister Benson, but I doubt he'll get seriously involved. He is known to be pretty foxy."

"How do we account for recent market action?" asked James Roswell, "It sure as hell looks like liquidation, not accumulation, it contradicts, everything we've been discussing."

"There's a joker in the pack somewhere, James, and we may be on his trail," answered Sir Edward as he stood and began pacing restlessly about his board table drawing on his cigar in his usual fashion when under tension. "You know, gentlemen," he expounded, "my greatest concern has always been that old bogey of government nationalization.

"You know damn well that if a Yankee railroad like Union Pacific or any other foreign group threatened control of C.D.R., there would be hell to pay up in Ottawa. The nationalists would campaign to the government for them to take their privately-owned National Railway and expropriate our company in the name of patriotism and on the grounds of national security.

"And worse, that monster of a mountebank chairman, the ever-honorable Sir Henry Thornton, would certainly gloat over that. He could even be behind the scenes in this whole bloody scheme, plotting and pontificating." Every syllable dripped with disdain and scorn. "Everything would play right into his greedy, grubby little hands.

"That man has been secretly working towards a merger for years now, as all you good men know. I want you gentlemen to give this issue your full concentration, your most serious consideration. I want you to report your private, unvarnished views in writing unequivocally here at 10 a.m. sharp tomorrow morning. I've been advised by counsel that we can't delay the annual meeting much longer, so we must make vitally important decisions and we must do so quickly.

"I am determined to beat off these buccaneers, but I'm going to need your help," he emphasized, waving his arms and pointing to each of them. "I'm swearing you all to secrecy concerning our discussions. I don't want to hear one goddamned rumor floating around the street about the Union Pacific or any other goddamned group. Not one! Nothing goes out of this room. Agreed?

"Tomorrow is the day we beat back these rapscallions, these Americans. They are intruders, invaders! And we will not tolerate their continued presence, not in our company."

Graham Watson stood, accepting the pledge of secrecy, and moved a motion that it be included in the minutes. Sir Herbert Holt seconded the motion, which passed unanimously, then moved the meeting be adjourned.

The market for C.D.R. common broke thirty-one dollars the morning Bernard Baruch was ushered into the palatial private office of the young multimillionaire, Averell Harriman, heir to the giant Union Pacific railroad fortune. Harriman, a man of great charm, greeted Baruch warmly. "What a great honor it was to receive your call, Bernard. Delighted to see you again."

Baruch recounted knowing his father and how he had acted for him as a broker in a number of large speculative railroad deals at the turn of the century, back when he was a very young man starting out in Wall Street.

"Your father liked betting on horses, prize fights, and elections, as I did. I do recall his giving me the odd tip," joked Baruch.

They talked about the early days of Union Pacific and reviewed how his father had wrestled control from J.P. Morgan, one of the classic proxy battles in Wall Street history.

Baruch then initiated the subject prompting his call, "Averell, I'm part of a syndicate, with friends from Canada and England, which holds a very large position in the Canada Dominion Railway Corporation, the flagship of the Canadian economy."

He walked about the office as he spoke catching a view, in the distance, up Wall Street of Trinity Church. "I don't expect you to divulge anything you feel is classified, but we have heard that Union is interested in the company; and looking at a map of the two railroads' western territories, it wouldn't surprise me one bit."

Harriman made no comment, nor did he express any sign of interest as he listened intently.

"I'm here only to say that if your board has an interest in the company and is looking for a major partner or ally, I think we can do business together. I can tell you we own over twenty-five percent of the company, and can give you details of our objectives and syndicate members, some of whom I'm sure you'll know."

"Bernie," Averell soothed, "that's a mighty big stake. I do know a little about C.D.R., and it sure is a big prize. It's got a good future, a great future, and you could do awfully well. I just want you to be careful. I can't comment on Union's position, assuming there even is a position to comment upon. Frankly, you know we're always looking around for expansion opportunities, but I'll have to check with the chairman about any specific interest. Can you tell me who is with you in this syndicate you refer to?"

"Well, yes, of course," replied Bernie. "The two biggest investors are Sir Ian Macleod, the Lord Brandenbrooke of London, and Sir James MacTavish of London and Montreal."

"How interesting," said Harriman, his eyes alight with interest. "I don't know MacTavish, but I do remember Brandenbrooke; we met in London just after the war. I understand he has become a prominent press lord in recent years. I often read his paper's editorials when I'm in London; but back to Union, let me have a chat with my chairman and get back to you."

Baruch, not wanting to overstay his welcome, owing to the delicacy of the subject under discussion, thanked Averell, advising that he would be in his office, should he require further information.

They shook hands as Harriman expressed his pleasure at seeing him again and advised, "I'll make some inquiries and let you know if we have any interest in that particular situation, as soon as possible."

"He didn't blink, James," reported Baruch immediately upon returning to his office. "I haven't seen such an excellent poker face in ages; couldn't read him worth a damn bloody thing. But he did ask a few very astute questions about the syndicate and he indicated that he would have to check with his chairman. You know as well as I do what that means; he just wants a little time to think it out before he shows his hand. They may want a bigger position before they share their plans with anybody else. We would do exactly the same thing in similar circumstances."

"That's hot news, Bernie. Sounds like you'll hear back very soon and we hear Sir Edward has called another urgent board meeting for tomorrow. I don't know what's transpired, but I'm sure they've got the wind-up."

"I'd like to be a fly on that wall, wouldn't you?" joked Baruch. "We'll see what tomorrow brings. Hold onto your hat."

James was feeling the tension as the drama unfolded. The money on the table was awesome, the stakes were high, with stock breaking thirty dollars again was haunting. Having Elizabeth, his soulmate companion, with him was indeed his good fortune; she always relieved his tensions as they dined together each evening following his frantic days on telephones and at meetings.

Ian sent out a wire the next morning.

> Have identified the liquidation account. 110,000 shares, remaining to be sold forthwith. will entertain a bid all or none. Advise today.
>
> Ian

"Well, there's the challenge, Bernie: a hundred and ten thousand shares. It's Harriman to the rescue, he's our Blucher," stated James cautiously. "It's a break for them, something to head off the looming train wreck. The banks are on me again."

"Hold the fort, James, I'm on top of it. We'll find a buyer; the stock's a steal at thirty dollars."

"The stock has just opened on big volume," Sir Edward snarled at his board, "at thirty and a half, with sell orders from London." He paced the floor, looking the part of a freshly caged lion. This was, admittedly, not a new, or even particularly unusual, sight.

Looks were exchanged throughout the room. A sense of urgency gripped the meeting. Sir Edward puffed away at his cigar, mentally damning his invisible enemy. Then he gathered himself and called the meeting to order, requesting each member's written opinion concerning the problem they faced.

"Gentlemen, here's the situation as it stands: if Union Pacific is after our ass and is accumulating a significant position, and they probably are, this market is as close to made in heaven for them as can be. What's your reaction and advice? Sir Herbert, why don't you lead off?"

"Mr. Chairman," Sir Herbert replied, "I doubt they have enough of a position to be a threat on their own. They would have to partner with a sizable shareholder to be effective."

Each of the directors varied in their analysis, but all were of the opinion they should mail the annual report with a specific request encouraging all shareholders to send in their proxies promptly.

Lord Stonehaven reminded the board, "Our management proxies and shareholders, voting at previous meetings, have usually accounted for over three and a half million shares. I doubt Union can match that position," he asserted smugly."

"Well, suppose they set up a joint account and team up with other major shareholders," queried Sir Edward skeptically.

"Who are the largest shareholders registered?" asked James Roswell.

"Are there any with over two hundred thousand shares? That doesn't mean anything if a group wants to disguise their position," answered the company's counsel John McGillvary. "There's a hell of a lot of stock in brokers and trust company names."

Senator Beique deliberately asked, "Do we know the position of Brandenbrooke and his group?"

"That's the question, Senator," growled Sir Edward. "That's the bloody question, and I'll be goddamned if I know the answer, but I'm betting it's bigger than Sir James has implied, unless the recent liquidation was theirs. I have reasonably reliable and confidential sources of information on that subject, and I'm checking further."

The chairman adjourned the meeting, to be reconvened the following morning at ten a.m. for further discussion.

SYLVIA, DOUBLE AGENT

James,

Yes, she knew Sir Edward. Yes, she had been infatuated with him; but when she met Olivier De Rolland, she claims she lost interest. In any event, he was single, unattached, a confirmed bachelor. She maintains she hasn't seen or heard from him since.

I admit I was livid. I exploded. She felt the sting of my tongue.

Ian

The letter, a response to an inquiry James had sent on a little while ago, was electrifying. It produced a jolt of unease which ran from his crown to his heel and back again. More than that, it confirmed something he had senses in his gut in the days following his many meetings with Roswell and Hennessy.

For the past little while, a thought had been ruminating in the back of his head, quietly lurking, fed by suspicions and tidbits, things that didn't add up. The final nail in the coffin had been Sir Edward's suspicions of Union Pacific, his idea that they seemed to know things they shouldn't about the syndicate, certainly much more than they should know.

There could only be one source, he concluded, and if his gut feeling was right, they would have to turn it to their advantage. He cabled Ian his suspicions, hoping he was wrong.

The president is getting his information from some mysterious source. Time to put 'S' to the acid test. Let her know we have control of over 4,600,000 shares. The bigger the exaggeration, the better.

If the president receives this information, which I suspect he will, I will sense it immediately, and we can write our own ticket. We'll have turned 'S' from a liability into an asset. Advise setting her up quickly. She may be the one-hundred-million-dollar Mata Hari of the Canada British Axis, but we won't make her face a firing squad at least not yet. J.

James carefully considered the strategy he planned on adopting at his meeting with Sir Edward. The stakes had never felt higher. He only realized how fast his heart was beating when he reached for a drink of water and found his hand shaking and his head spinning. He decided then and there to confer with Baruch last minute. He wanted his plan neat and nailed down before the actual event.

"When he and I come out of our corners with the gloves off for round one, it's going to be a titanic confrontation, Bernie," James blustered loudly into the phone, trying to sound more confident than he felt. "My plan is to have a nice, clear-cut proposal for his board and an arsenal of weaponry that will shiver his timbers!"

"Yes, yes," Baruch chuckled absentmindedly. He was in full support of the outlined plot, but he was also anxiously awaiting a call from Harriman and his eyes kept drifting back to the clock. "Look, I can't talk much right now so here's what I can tell you. People on the street are talking. They're saying C.D.R. is ripe for a takeover or merger. So damn the torpedoes, James. Full speed ahead!" he shouted into the phone. "I'll call you in the morning."

When James revealed to Elizabeth, that evening, his suspicions concerning Sylvia, she was astonished and couldn't bring herself to believe it being even half-true.

"Are you suggesting she's what is called a 'courtesan,' a sort of professional? "she asked in disbelief, "Is Sylvia that sort of person. I know she's really wild about Ian but is she smart enough to play such a double game? I doubt it."

"Don't be so sure, my dear. She's might even be wilder about Sir Edward," suggested James. "Don't forget: he's a rich, eligible bachelor, probably the best catch in Canada, from a woman's point of view. Ian is older, he's not free, and she must know by now, not the marrying type."

TITANS NEGOTIATE

The next morning, Baruch received his call from Averell Harriman. "Just calling to see if you're going to be in your office this morning, Bernie. If so, I'll drop over for a chat."

"Delighted to see you again, Averell. What about 11:30? You know my office: #5, Wall Street, Thirty-Fifth Floor," replied Baruch.

"Great, I'll be there, and I look forward to seeing you."

Baruch was elated sensing Harriman must have a proposal, or he would have just chatted on the phone in generalities. He sensed he and James had been right about Union and put a call in to him immediately.

"James, Harriman is on his way to my office for a chat. Thought you'd get a kick out of hearing the news."

There was a long silence as James absorbed the significance of the call. "Well, by God! Congratulations, Bernie. I won't tell you how to handle your meeting. You're a master at it. I'm sure you'll hit the jackpot. Just keep your powder dry. I'll wait for your call."

Harriman arrived with Mr. Jonathan Fairbanks, of Wentworth, Levittson, and Fairbanks, a prestigious law firm that worked as corporate counsel to Union Pacific. "I hope you don't mind I've brought Jonathan along, Bernie. He's a senior partner in a law firm and has been truly indispensable. Given what we are about to discuss, I felt his presence necessary.

"He signed a non-disclosure agreement with me and we took the liberty of drafting a near-identical contract in advance for you to examine and sign as you wish. It is simply that the contents of this meeting are of great importance and I understand they mustn't go beyond these walls. Why don't you both just review it and excuse me for a minute? I'm afraid I'm scheduled for a brief call to the White House."

Baruch and Fairbanks reviewed the confidentiality commitment, and being in agreement, signed it, binding himself, James, and Ian.

Harriman rejoined them, following his call to the capital, commenting, "I told the president I was meeting with you here in your office. Bernie, he sends his best regards."

"Oh, great," smiled Baruch, "I've been on a number of his advisory commissions. I think Calvin is doing a fine job."

"All right, Jonathan," said Harriman. "Can we open our discussion with Mr. Baruch? Have we dispensed with all the necessary formalities?"

"Yes, indeed, Mr. Harriman, everything is in order."

Harriman then opened the discussion, saying how timely Baruch's visit had been, in view of Union's current investment policies, which the board had been developing over the last several years.

"I will admit, Bernie; we have been in the market for C.D.R. stock off and on for over two years now. While I cannot divulge our exact position at the moment, we do believe we have made a sound investment at very attractive prices, and the recent sell-off continues to attract our attention.

"We've been following the same policy with a number of railroads, in fact; we've managed to collect a sizable portfolio in doing so. C.D.R. is our single non-American holding. Now, I'm curious; has your syndicate bought for investment? Or are you perhaps going for a heavy position sufficient to restructure the board?"

Baruch's reply was measured, "We are open, but if we had enough stock, we would alter the board somewhat and look at possibilities of expansion in the northern border states, mainly by acquisition or joint venture agreements with smaller lines like Northern Pacific or the Great Northern Railway."

Harriman's eyes lit up as he fired a straight question, revealing his degree of interest. "Your position, Bernie, I think you said, was approximately 2.8 million, or twenty-eight percent of the company shares. What would you think of a bid for the whole bloody block at current markets; that is, thirty dollars per share, or eighty-four million dollars?"

Baruch held his breath, managing to maintain his composure and poker face. "Frankly, Averell, we might do much better combining forces with your company and making broad policy changes which could move the stock considerably higher. Of course, that depends on the size of your position.'

"To do that," Harriman replied, "My board would probably ask for a voting trust agreement in favor of Union, and your syndicate would have to let Union call the tune as the railroad partner in the deal."

"We might have a problem going that way with the Canadian government, cautioned Baruch." They would kick like steers if the road was openly run by an American company such as Union Pacific. Whereas if Union gave us their proxies, the syndicate would present as a Canadian entity, and I believe we could accomplish our joint objectives. Then, at a later date, perhaps Union could buy out the syndicate position".

"Yes," smiled Harriman. "But at what price? We might consider an option arrangement. What would you think of that?" And then, as he thought further, he said, "How many votes do you and Brandenbrooke think you need to gain control of the board?"

Baruch replied with candor. "We calculate approximately 4.1 to 4.3 million shares, which means you would have to vote nearly 1.5 million shares less, what we will pick up from private investors who have bought stock in the past six months, probably around a two hundred thousand shares."

"Well, then," said Harriman. "You're saying we would need a minimum of approximately 1.3

million shares to put us in the driver's seat; possibly a little less. That's really not so bad. What do you think of that, Jonathan?"

"Sounds all right, Mr. Harriman. Financially, we can certainly afford it."

Baruch interjected, "I understand your position, Averell, but I really think we'll have to put all our cards on the table in order to make an intelligent decision. Can you disclose Union's position? If you are in for more than just an investment, you must have a sizable holding."

"Ah, Bernie," sighed Harriman in response, "the truth of the matter is that the Union board has been taking their time accumulating stock. We were never in a great hurry. Our interest lay in acquiring enough stock over time to negotiate market-sharing policies, particularly those in the Pacific Northwest, where we compete so intensely with one another.

"Your entry into the picture has changed our focus somewhat. Together, our two groups might be able to force the issue, especially if we bought a few more shares. We currently have one million, forty thousand shares, so let's say we picked up, oh, another three hundred and forty thousand shares; maybe a little more, maybe a little less, we're adaptable. If we had that, we would collectively hold a total of 4,120,000 shares, not counting outside proxies. That's a heavy position; about forty-one percent, I think, if my figures are correct. They would have to hustle every shareholder to beat it, wouldn't they?"

"Indeed, but I'm not dismissing the possibility," cautioned Baruch. "Averell, we've got 2.64 million shares outright, and another hundred thousand by proxy. You've got one million, forty thousand. That's a combined total of 3.68 million shares, before additions.

"Now, from there, there are several things to consider. One, do we throw our proxies in with you and you vote the block? Two, do you throw your proxies in with us, and we vote the block? Three, you buy us out and then you own and vote the entire block, plus the one hundred thousand share proxies we could direct to you.

"Or four, we option our position to you but we vote the block for political reasons I have already cited. Now as a matter of immediate interest, we are in touch with a sizeable block of a hundred and ten shares in Europe that's up for grabs. I suggest you advise your boys to communicate with Ian in London."

"That is of definite interest," confirmed Harriman. "Now can we distill your summation even further? It seems to me time is of the essence, and I am going to have to take something definite to my board before we can consider an agreement."

"Let me report our discussion to Sir James and Sir Brandenbrooke," Baruch insisted. "They'll both have some very interesting thoughts and ideas to contribute. I'll get at it tonight and call you in a day or two; just remember Sir James has to be the one twisting the tail of the tiger, so he will require some latitude in his discussions with the president and members of his board.

"They already suspect Union's interest, but of course, they don't realize just how sizeable our positions are yet. We'll have to handle that one with some delicacy." He paused, considering. "I'll confer with you constantly as the picture becomes clear."

He spent most of the evening on the telephone with James, reporting the day's events and revelations. He felt tired but ultimately enthused. They were in the very envious position of having several viable and preferential options.

James was confident he held a royal flush and equally confident Sir Edward's hand wasn't stacked with aces. But as he admitted to Elizabeth, "I learned long ago never underestimate your enemy or his ability to make an end run. What you see ain't always all that's there. It's what you don't see that you have to anticipate that counts."

Before heading to bed for the night, he cabled Ian a quick report.

> They're already in for size but want more. Would buy us out or join forces if we granted option for a take out later. Combined position is impressive, but they are continuing to accumulate. Have advised re: 110,000 shares, expect wire bid from Union. Letter following. No doubt 'S' is reporting. James

The next day, James met with MacDonnell and Jack Kippen for lunch at the Saint James Club. His dinner companions brought with them a report of street-level rumors, most conflicting, outrageous, or downright confusing. More worryingly, the stock was trading at twenty-nine and a half.

MacDonnell and Kippen were both unaware of Union Pacific's interest, but they had continued to observe the Wall Street antics each morning at the opening from London. MacDonnell claimed to have it on good authority that the board was divided over what tactic to adopt.

Apparently, Sir Edward suspected his archenemy, Sir Henry Thornton, who was chairman and president of the government-owned and -funded National Railway Corporation, of engineering a conspiracy to provoke the Canadian government to intervene and take over C.D.R. in a defensive measure, keeping it from the clutches of a U.S. corporation.

James discounted the report as a product of the rumor mill; he knew the board was divided, and that Sir Edward would use it to beat the tom-toms of a war dance.

Late in the afternoon, Harriman called. He seemed in a hurry, opening the conversation with a brusque, "Regarding that 110,000 share block; James, they'll take it. They're going to contact London. The consensus is that you should vote the whole block of stock, combined with any proxies that can be picked up on the street. But Union wants an option on the syndicate's position in exchange for their support. So the question now is to determine the terms, price, and expiration date of this little venue."

"That's a tough one, Averell." James considered the options. He mused aloud for Harriman's sake, "Our block is key to control. You have to put a value on that from Union's perspective, and an option period would have to be very short, by that, I mean six months to one year, maximum." He paused. "I'll talk it through with Lord Brandenbrooke, but he's a bullish sort; he won't want to sell at all. I'll get back to you in the morning, or as soon as I hear from London."

He conferred with Baruch concerning Harriman's proposal, who reacted with some reservations but commentated positively on two counts. "You've got leverage with Sir Edward, James, and you've got leverage with Union. Looks to me like you're in the catbird seat. I think it's time you saw big Eddie alone. I'll have further discussion with Averell and aim for a middle ground we can all live with."

Gordon Howard was a specialist, an expert when it came to the many rules of corporate procedure at shareholders meetings and proxy battles. A partner of Ogilvie Howard, Fraser, and Casgrain, one of Canada's largest law firms, he was kept on by James as a retainer, there to act as counsel to the syndicate.

Howard arrived at James' hotel earlier than expected, which was actually quite alright as far as James was concerned. It gave them more time for a briefing and strategy session. James wanted Howard's opinion on Union's position and the C.D.R. board's initiatives regarding foreign ownership. He kept coming back to the analogy of Wellington's strategy sessions in Brussels prior to riding out on the fields of Waterloo to meet his nemesis, Napoleon Bonaparte.

"I want you to be so bloody well-informed, Gordon, that when we meet the chief on the field of battle, there won't be any guessing about what we can or can't do, or what he can or can't do. I intend this meeting to be decisive, and knowing Sir Edward by reputation, we have to be precise and uncompromising. We have to put that bloody fool back in his bloody cage when he comes out swinging.

"You know what people have been saying about him for years now? There is no life in the C.D.R. without Sir Edward, and no life in Sir Edward without C.D.R. I want you to remember that. I want you to keep that thought buried in your head and plan accordingly."

"The syndicate's voting position," James continued. "Assuming support from Union Pacific and other shareholders, will be an impressive 4.14 million shares, and when we play that card, I know he's is going to explode, accusing us of being monstrous frauds, traitors, et cetera; selling Canada down the river to 'Yankee revolutionaries'. He'll threaten every roadblock his lawyers can devise."

They reviewed in depth a variety of other reactions they might encounter and a variety of countermeasures they could evoke to maintain their dominance of the meeting.

Each day that passed brought fresh hope to syndicate as they watched the stock market averages inching their way up, each day higher than the last. C.D.R. was, at last, starting to recover from the madness of before.

James had thought that would mean the meeting was about to start, but with each passing day, he received no call, not from the president's office or Roswell. He tried to be patient, but just two days saw his temper beginning to boil. His pride demanded the president make the first move and so he kept waiting.

Finally, while heading out to dinner, he was rewarded when he ran into Sir Edward and his predecessor, Lord Stonehaven, in the Ritz Carleton Hotel lobby.

"I'm so glad to see you again, Sir James," said the president. "Your name came up today, and I had intended to call you tomorrow."

"I'll be here most of the morning," replied James, "and look forward to hearing from you."

James returned to his suite on springs, almost hopping with excitement. He swept Elizabeth into arms the moment he saw her, exclaiming, "It's happening tomorrow. Oh, I can hardly wait. Tomorrow's scene is going to be a classic."

He fully anticipated that the first day in the ring of round one would focus on the establishing of battle lines and the unveiling of alliances. Presumably, good Sir Edward would try to wrap himself up in the flag of nationalism and play high-and-mighty with him.

Elizabeth was his savior, as usual, as they retired; knowing the importance of the meeting and preparing him psychologically for the storm ahead.

Early the next morning, he called Baruch, "Bernie, old boy, it's happening. I've no doubt I'll be meeting the big chief very soon." Their conversation dipped into rapid-fire back and forth examinations of a great many potential possibilities and countermeasures.

Baruch, apparently in a rush as James could hear the frantic rustling of paper and cloth over the phone, ended his side of the conversation with, "Don't let him bluff you, old boy. You've got the heavy guns. You've got him outgunned and you can outmaneuver him if you need to." James' ear was suddenly assaulted by the sound of crinkling paper in the receiver. "Sorry about that; dropped the phone. As I was saying, don't forget your friend Richard's advice regarding Disraeli's dictum: exploit his blind spot, his Achilles heel, his arrogance and vanity, his false pride, his insecurities. I'll update Averell. Good luck!"

"Thanks for reminding me, Bernie. Good luck, my friend." He hung up and let his thoughts turn to Richard. Rich had been a great admirer of 'Dizzy', as he and Ian sometimes liked to call him, for years now. He always claimed to have found his dictums to be useful weapons in the cutthroat world of political confrontations and machinations.

James had never been as taken with Dizzy but he had always been fond of one particular tale involving the man. Apparently, Disraeli had been faced with his nemesis, a man named Gladstone, in the House of Commons. Gladstone had been in vehement opposition to Dizzy's bill and had eventually been frustrated enough to threaten his opponent by saying, "You will die either by hanging or of some vile disease if you persist with this legislation."

Dizzy, master of wit, had simply responded, "That all depends, sir, on whether I embrace your principals or your mistress."

James often wished he'd been present to see the response to that comment.

At 10:30 a.m., Elizabeth answered the phone. It was Sir Edward's secretary asking for Sir James.

"My name is Mary MacNeice, sir, calling for Sir Edward, who had to rush out to a meeting and asked me to call you to arrange a convenient time for a meeting here at the office."

"Thank you very much," said James. "Will you ask Sir Edward to call me personally when he returns from his meeting. I may be off to New York tonight, so I suggest he call me as soon as possible."

"Yes, sir. I'll convey that message to him, thank you, Goodbye."

BATTLE ROYAL

"Who the hell does that little 'knight' think he is, having his secretary call a 'baronet' to make an appointment?" James sneered. His cadence was joking but his tone was too sharp, too cold, for his humor to be genuine. "The son of a bitch doesn't seem to realize he's working for me. We control forty-two percent of the company goddamn it!" He paced the floor, every step clipped as he tried not to let the full extent of his frustration escape.

"He'll soon learn," he said to Elizabeth with cutting sarcasm and a vicious grin. His voice cooled and he crooned to her, half in jest, "But don't take me seriously my dear, I'm just revving up for the bell in round one."

He kissed her, lit a cigar, and settled back with his morning paper awaiting the call to arms he had looked forward to since arriving in Montreal.

Gordon Howard called from the lobby, advising he was on his way up with documents to examine.

"Glad you're coming, I was going to call you to stand by for a meeting with the president. Come on up."

He arrived with shareholders' lists and other corporate information on C.D.R.'s charter and by-laws, so he could have a bearing on procedures to be followed at a shareholders' meeting. As they exchanged documents, the call came in from the president's office.

"Sir James, this is Mary MacNeice again. Please hold on, sir, Sir Edward will be with you in a minute," she said.

"Good morning, Sir James," said Sir Edward. His deep authoritative voice had a commanding quality as he apologized for calling so late in the morning.

"I'm glad to have caught you before lunch. Would you do me the honor of meeting me this afternoon? I think we may have important matters of joint interest to discuss."

"What have you got in mind, sir? Do you want me to join your board of directors?" responded James, with a chuckle.

"Well, now that's a thought, isn't it, how would you like to come to my office or meet somewhere else? What do you suggest?"

"I'll be right over Mr. President. I'm anxious to see your inner sanctum, the nerve center of your great empire."

"What about four p.m.?" said James.

"That's fine with me, and I'm sure you know how to find me."

"See you then. Goodbye."

He turned to Elizabeth and Gordon, announcing gleefully, "Now for the sport. The mating dance is on. Now we'll see how the big chief beats the tom-toms. Wouldn't it be great to have access to his boardroom deliberations; you know, from someone on the inside?"

Then with a big twinkle in his eye, he said jokingly, "I've got a great idea, Gordon. We'll get Elizabeth to romance someone in the inner sanctum and report back to us. They'd all fall for a beautiful duchess. Wouldn't that be a coup? What you think, my dear?"

"Great idea, dear Jamsie," giggled Elizabeth, "Except I'd be a disaster at such antics. I may be an actress, darling, but a double agent!? That would give me real stage fright, maybe you need a pro, like Sylvia."

"Oh my god! No!" laughed James. "Not Sylvia, she may be working the other side of the street! A double agent, who knows?"

They arrived at the company's head office precisely as scheduled and were quickly ushered into the boardroom to await the president. James didn't expect they would have long to wait, but he took the opportunity to really get a good look at the room. It was massive and stately, the ceiling a few feet above his head. The walls were paneled hardwood, dark and soothing, and the floor was made up of large grey tiles.

In the center of the room was a long wooden table. The top was thick green glass and the legs were beautifully, elegantly curved. Spaced evenly on either side were identical rolling chairs, black in color with a simple but professional, elegant design. The two chairs at either end were slightly more elaborate, obviously sturdier and of higher quality, even in the design wasn't too different.

The president chose that moment to burst into the room, throwing open the beautifully carved double doors and strutting into place with all the confidence of a peacock and a readily apparent aura of impatience.

"Make yourself comfortable, gentlemen," he gestured, taking a seat in one of the rolling chairs at the head of the table, obviously the chairman's seat. "I'm delighted that you could come down on such short notice; I particularly wanted to discuss the forthcoming annual meeting."

James had been well-briefed on his opponent's egocentricity and autocratic personality. He knew all about his intolerance to challenges of his authority; his intense competitiveness, his worshipping of power, his inability to contain his arrogance. His critics stated that, even when defeat stared him in the face, he was incapable of changing course, at times allowing destructive tenaciousness to lead him into battle.

He opened their discussions laconically, directing his first question rather bluntly to James. "I take it, you're expecting to be at our annual meeting, Sir James. Do you intend to vote for management's agenda?"

"I don't know," responded James quietly, "that depends on what's on your agenda. I haven't received your annual report; I have no idea what resolutions are being proposed."

"Let me rephrase my question, sir," replied Sir Edward impatiently, with unquestioned formality, while peering intently at James. "You know our board of directors. We propose to re-elect the same slate. Do you have any other ideas?"

"That's a good question, sir," responded James, poker faced, as a matter of fact, Lord Brandenbrooke and I have considered a few other nominees to your board including ourselves and have looked forward to discussing the matter with you."

"We have considered other candidates as well," he replied, "but have decided to stick with our present slate."

"Well, then, we may have a conflict," suggested James smugly, and with a flicker of a smile. "I guess it's a matter of votes."

The president's eyes flashed, reflecting his resentment of the suggestion of a voting contest as he eyeballed James. "How many shares do you think it would take to overrule management's proxies?" he snapped with a scowl, his jaw set as he drummed his fingers impatiently on his desk.

"You'd know that better than I, Sir Edward. You tell me what you expect, and I'll tell you if we can match it or not."

"Look, let's cut the 'sir' business. I'm Eddie and you're Jimmy," said the president impatiently. "We might as well get down to nut-cracking and cut the shadow-boxing bull shit. I've heard wild reports that you Brandenbrooke control over 2.7 million shares of my company, but frankly, the evidence isn't convincing. I think it is blarney."

"My god," James thought to himself "Sylvia is on Sir Edward's team or payroll as I suspected." He shot back sarcastically, knowing it would strike a nerve, "That's a pretty round number, Eddie. Sounds big. Hope your sources are reliable. A man in your position needs to be careful about rumors."

"Don't lecture me, goddamn it. I'll be the judge of my sources," he snapped, his eyes flashing again with hostility.

"Well I'm delighted to hear that," replied James with a twist of sarcasm. "So how much stock do you think we have if your sources are so bloody good?"

Sir Edward's face froze and went ashen-white as he answered, "I have no interest in this kind of Hollywood bullshit. Do you want to talk turkey, or shall we pack it in?'

"We can talk all the turkey you like, but I think talking proxies would be more to the point, Eddie. I represent a substantial investor group, and we want to make changes. The enterprise has great potential, and the stock should sell at twice the current price."

'Great balls of thunder!' he bellowed, "You're just a bunch of goddamn financial manipulators and stock market promoters! You don't know a goddamned thing about running a railroad. You wouldn't know a cow catcher from a caboose!"

"I guess you're right about the caboose; that's at the tail end, isn't it?" laughed James. "But cowcatchers? Now that I like; that's saying, 'I'm out in front, ahead of the game, and we're going to catch you by the balls if you don't smarten up'. We have associates who are rail experts and the shareholders will benefit from their expertise. Furthermore, we have unlimited capital resources to commit for expansion purposes."

The president jumped up in a rage. He looked ten times bigger and he prowled around the boardroom with the intensity of a poked bear. His arms were in the air, waving, moving, gesticulating wildly as he scoffed and snarled, "We don't need capital for expansion. You're a goddamned bluffer, Jimmie, and so is your wheeler-dealer friend in London. He's been getting away with murder for years and no more, I tell you. I know him; I know his kind and I knew him years ago in Montreal.

"Oh, he was well-known for his fucking financial skullduggery, especially with that infamous Dominion Cement deal, when he watered the goddamned stock so heavily, the shareholders all nearly drowned." Every word was biting, dripping poison. He spat and snarled; James was not impressed. "Well, not this time; this time, that son of a bitch has bitten off more than he can chew.

"Do you realize the kind of power this corporation has at its disposal, the kind of power its board of directors has? The largest banks listen to us and we've beaten off pirates like you before. Your little gang isn't the first, and you won't be the last. I'm sure whoever is holding shares carry them on credit." He grinned, wide and toothy and full of malicious intent. "That makes them vulnerable as hell to the types of pressures we can bring to bear."

James had to laugh and he had the distinct pleasure of watching Sir Edward's toxic grin slip off his face. Slowly, sarcastically, he drawled out, "You don't mean to tell me that fine, upstanding Canadian banks would ever be party to such unethical or unprincipled dealings at the request of a powerful account like yours, now do you? Surely you wouldn't cast such aspirations on the good men of the Canadian banking system." He couldn't help how patronizing he sounded. If Sir Edward wanted to play this game, he deserved what he got.

"And besides," here his words turned sharp again, "those financial wizards of yours have already tried playing that card, I'm sure to as much success as your attempt. I wonder, how much did your raid on the stock cost you? Look, Eddie, I'll level with you; we ain't amateurs. We know the game and we deliberately decided to leave out any Canadian banks in our deal. There's no one you can buy off since we decided to go with the backing of American and British banks and an American corporation instead.

"So you can forget about your goddamned threats of intimidation and credit squeezes. We're beyond your reach of influence. You can blackmail us, or dirty pool. We've got you by the balls, Eddie, not the other way around. So wise up, or we'll put the squeeze on."

The remarks hit Sir Edward in the solar plexus, rocketing his adrenaline and blood pressure to new levels, rendering him momentarily speechless, but he quickly composed himself, calmly asking, "So who are these bloody sycophant partners? What's the size of their position?" It was obvious he had serious concerns, and James played him out with plenty of line, as he would a twenty-pound salmon who wouldn't give up.

"Eddie, let's be realistic here. We've got a major investment bank and a major railroad corporation with us. Are we going to get down to nut-cracking or not? I mean, do you want to wait for me to throw my cards on the table at the annual meeting? I'm more than willing to so, I can assure you, and you know the effect that would have; it would rock the government and the country to its foundation.

"Who knows? It might even open the door for a certain Mr. Henry Thornton to persuade the government to nationalize C.D.R. for reasons of national security. Wouldn't that be the kiss of death for you?"

Sir Edward exploded again in a burst of anger, "All right, goddamned it! Enough of this bloody charade, Jimmie! Let's hear what you've got and kept that son of a bitch Thornton out of it. I'll be having a board meeting tomorrow, and my directors will know how to handle him and your nefarious scheme. I only want facts. Now, you understand? No bluff and no bullshit, okay? Let's have it."

James sat back, reviewing the opulence of the boardroom, and eyeballing the president before responding casually, "You may be interested to know, Sir Edward, that the Union Pacific Railroad has been buying your stock for over two years. So, has Kuhn-Loeb and Company and Baruch and Company of New York."

Sir Edward remained stony-faced, without emotion, commenting only that he had heard a rumor that Union had an interest, but didn't know their size.

"Well, I know exactly how much they have, and its size, Eddie, my boy; real size. I am unable to divulge details, but it's big-league stuff and growing."

"Goddamn it! How much do these bastards own?" he asked with anguish in his voice, "Our shareholders' list doesn't show them at all. What the hell do they want with a minority interest in C.D.R., anyway, except perhaps for trading purposes?"

"The fact is," responded James, "they don't have a minority position, not when they combine their holdings with ours and other interested parties."

"You mean to tell me you would sell the railroad down the goddamn Hudson River to a bunch of fucking Yankee doodles?" roared Sir Edward in exasperation. He was breathing heavy. The note of ill-concealed desperation in a voice was likely meant to come across as determined, but his trembling jaw did enough on its own to crush his confident image.

He stalked the length of the boardroom, fists clenching, eyes flashing, voice thundering, "Do you and Brandenbrooke have any principles at all? Come on, tell me; tell what it is you think you have on me that will make me roll over for you. What is the magic number your den of thieves has managed to gather up that makes you think you can steal the railroad from me?"

James sat passively, staring the man down in silence with a steely gaze. It was a look Sir Edward would not forget for some time. James' lips curled slowly into a disturbing smirk as he very quietly said, "How does four million, one hundred and forty thousand, and climbing, grab you, Mr. President? Don't you think that position is entitled to a say a few things about how to run this bloody railroad? You'd better face it, Eddie. You're working for us, and we can hire you or fire you and ship you out by express or slow freight. Take your choice."

Sir Edward glared at him venomously, puffing on his cigar like a steam engine. He turned and continued his impatient striding about the boardroom in a silence that would have made stones seem loud. James caught him glancing up at the illustrious portraits of the company's founding shareholders.

In their day, back before the turn of the century, those same people would have been the buccaneer entrepreneurs of Canada, just like James and Ian. He wondered what Sir Edward thought of that. 'They, too, would have played my game with relish if the opportunity had presented itself,' James thought. 'I wonder how they would have played in Sir Edward's position?'

As he regained his composure, he shot back, "So what's this bullshit about Baruch and Kuhn-Loeb? Are they bedmates with Union Pacific?"

"As a matter of fact," replied James with deliberation, "Bernard Baruch, an old friend of mine and Ian's, has known of Union's long-standing interest in C.D.R. for some time. I have had meetings with Mr. Averell Harriman and have heard of the company's plans for expansion in the west."

"By God, I'll see you in hell before that son of a bitch Harriman lays a hand, on our road, it's out of the question, Jimmie, do you hear me? Out of the fucking question! You're a bunch of whores. My board won't stand for it, the government won't stand for it, the country won't stand for it."

James couldn't resist putting the knife in. "Maybe the chairman of the government's National Railroad would be delighted to stand for it. He's had his eye on taking you over for some time, I understand."

"By God, MacTavish," he thundered, again spewing out uncharacteristically, a string of expletives in a towering rage. "Are you telling me this whole bloody charade was engineered to steal the company on behalf of the government railroad, with you and your unscrupulous accomplice acting as hired pimps in a national whorehouse? By god, you'll both surely die of a dreadful disease."

James, never one to let an opportunity pass him by, couldn't resist a colorful, if moderately tasteless, response. He doubted Sir Edward would believe him if he told him it was just an attempt to relieve the high-tension atmosphere. "Well since you've elected to refer to bordellos, Eddie, you ought to know that when you've got the best girls in town, you don't need pimps to bring in the business." He snickered at the scandalized expression on Sir Edward's face, frozen in shock. "We can set our own terms because we own the bloody house – get it? And we intend to double the business and the stock."

The stunned silence stretched on in an endless minute. James could hear the annoying ticking of the only clock in the room. Trying to cute the silence, he added, "Everyone should love that, including my dolls."

Sir Edward's pulse continued racing as he strode about his boardroom again, in a fit of fury and then charging out, he blurted, "You bastards! You're lower than a snake's belly! The meeting is terminated."

James broke out in a fit of laughter. "By god, Gordon, wasn't that a class act? Let's let him cool down. He'll be back, so let's have a cigar and relax."

Sir Edward was surprised to find his antagonists still at the boardroom table when he returned.

"I thought I was clear. The meeting's over," he announced sternly, waving them out.

James, raising his hand, said slowly and rather quietly, "Why don't we just cool things down, Eddie? We both have important business at hand, and substantial profit potential for all shareholders."

"What do you mean by 'profit potential for all shareholders'?" Sir Edward sneered. "We don't need your gang to show us how to maximize profits."

Sensing a possible moment of calmness between them, James pointed out, "We do have a very positive plan for the company, which I'm sure will appeal to your board, when they know the whole picture. Our big stake is your protection – anything we make, your shareholders make."

Gordon Howard volunteered that he had verified the syndicate's position, and also the positions of Union Pacific and other major shareholders. "It's a minimum of 4.14 million shares, sir, and Union is adding to this position whenever reasonable-sized offerings are available," he advised.

"The question, Eddie, and I repeat, is do you really want a knockdown, drag-out proxy fight? We could do it; the whole nine yards, with newspaper ads, editorials, accusations against management, et cetera, et cetera. There'd be blood on the streets. Or do we construct a pact before the meeting, something everyone will benefit from?"

"Now that's the question, Mr. President," said James in a conciliatory tone, flashing a disarming smile. "I believe we can hammer out a deal with Baruch and myself; and of course Brandenbrooke will join us, if he can catch the next boat and be in Montreal within a few weeks."

"I'm going to meet with my board tomorrow. I will advise you accordingly," Sir Edward growled, barely restraining his temper. He took a deep breath, obviously trying to choke back the anger in order to actually finish this conversation. "We have number of options to consider, which I'm sure will come as a complete surprise to you bandits."

He huffed, taking a long drag of his cigar. "Perhaps we'll talk again in a few days, but you can tell your friend Harriman that he'll never get his greedy little mitts on C.D.R, not while I'm around. That's written in stone, gentlemen," he sneered the word, "and the same goes for your upstart Calgary cowboy robber baron." His pulse rose again as he spat out, "Does anybody know how he made his first dollar? Well, I do. How would he like that story spread around England, especially around the House of Lords? How to make it into the peerage?" he tittered mockingly. "Start a bloody brothel, that's how one of your peers got started. You might ask him, Jimmie, and let me know."

"Forget it, Eddie," James laughed, waving his hand dismissively. "That would be the height of British hypocrisy and Ian wouldn't even give a good goddamn; he'd just laugh it down with the Commons. Let's face facts, there's many a highbrow Lord in the house who's whored in his time, and there's not one who doesn't know it.

"As a matter of fact," here, James' grin turned devious, "for many years, Ian kept a list of all the prominent directors and executives of C.D.R. who enjoyed his famous little prairie palace of pleasure, the Pink House. Lucky for you, it was a little before your time. He always said it might come in handy some day. Sounds like he was dead right, doesn't it?" Sir Edward's face flushed an unbecoming shade of puce that told him that whether or not the man agreed with him, he would never admit it. "Ian could give some of your older, stuffy English poseur directors a few juicy and embarrassing, not to mention scandalous, headlines. Wouldn't that be the sport of kings?"

Sir Edward jumped up in a rage and strode out of the boardroom, a cloud of cigar smoke, throwing over his shoulder, "I have another engagement. Good day to you, you son of a bitch."

While reviewing the drama with great amusement when they returned to the hotel, James, in high spirits, asked Gordon, "What's next? How do you read the bluffing?" On reflection, they concluded the big chief would call back immediately following his board meeting having reviewed their options and strategies.

James later recounted the entirety of the colorful, overly dramatic episode to Baruch. Neither man would likely ever admit to giggling like madmen, but that was exactly what they did. Wiping away mirthful tears, Baruch exclaimed, "It sounds to me like you adopted the 'Dizzy' approach and got him in his Achilles heel." He clapped James on the shoulder.

A few humorous hiccups escaped them yet. Baruch sniffed, his face snuck in a manic grin. His voice was serious when he spoke. "Union has agreed, in principle, to support you at the meeting, in return for assurances of board representation and support of specific resolutions. They have also confirmed purchase of that European block of stock and they are now back in the market. The heat is off, James. We've been saved by the bell. Anyway, they've sent over their list demands; here take a look."

Union's list of demands were fairly simple, neatly laid out for their perusing. One, the board was to agree to pass a resolution splitting the stock of the company, three for one. Two, four directors were to be retired, forcibly if necessary, and then replaced by four of James's appointees who would include Lord Brandenbrooke, Averell Harriman, Bernard Baruch and James himself.

Three, the annual dividend on common stock would be increased by no less than ten percent. And finally, four was a resolution that no further stock would be issued from the treasury for a minimum of one year, unless sanctioned by James and two-thirds of the board of directors.

Baruch and James went over each item in preparation for James' next meeting with Sir Edward – or with Harriman, whichever came first. James excused himself after a few hours of perusal. He needed rest before tomorrow's events and Baruch had a phone call planned with Harriman.

As soon as James was gone, Baruch dialed up the American business and opened the conversation by relaying the tale of James's encounter with Sir Edward. As with James before, the two men enjoyed themselves at Sir Edward's expense, but Baruch cautioned the other; it was quite possible Sir Edward would call to question Union's objectives.

"If he calls you, Averell, it might be best if you were to invite him to New York for a meeting with yourself and your chairman. He'll probably refuse, but it would be a good gesture. I will be available if you need me, but let's see how the big chief reacts when James presents his conditions."

Harriman thanked him, agreeing that a meeting certainly would be extremely enlightening. "Though, from what I hear of him, I doubt he will show his hand."

Back at company headquarters the next morning, the big chief conferred with his executive committee. He spent much of the early minutes of the meeting reporting in startling, vivid detail his off-color encounter with Sir James. Each word tasted like ashes and fell from lips like shards of glass. Needless to say, the committee was a mixture of shocked, appalled, and apprehensive of the alleged voting block of 4.14 million shares. They all but urged him to get in touch with Harriman immediately for a frank discussion.

"Impossible!" he snapped. "Harriman's father was one of the Wall Street's greatest railway vultures in his time. He and J.P. Morgan locked horns, the J.P. Morgan! I've no doubt his son is no better than him. What the hell are we going to do with that son of a bitch on our board? They only want insight to our operation for competitive advantages out west; that's what it's all about.

"He hasn't got enough stock to influence us. It's only when those international whores, and philanderers," he spat the words, looking very close to literally spitting, "Brandenbrooke and MacTavish, get in the act that Harriman has any leverage. He's riding their coattails, and they're prostituting themselves out for his support." The sheer amount of vitriol coating his words was, admittedly, impressive. "Bastards, the lot of them! It's a contrived wholesale sell-out, in typical Brandenbrooke fashion and skullduggery."

After he had blown off steam, however, he reluctantly agreed to talk with Harriman, bending to the board's persuasion.

James Roswell added, "Eddie, just hold your nose, bite your tongue, and pick up the phone. At least you'll know their real intent and stock position, getting it direct from the horse's mouth."

As the drama unfolded, C.D.R. stock continued recovering back to the thirty-five-dollar level, with the street awash with rumors of a proxy battle or an American takeover.

IAN – SYLVIA

Back in London, Ian was, in turn, fascinated and angered to hear news of Sylvia's antics. The confirmation of Sylvia playing the role of an international Mata Hari of finance did funny things to his gut, simultaneously sickening and amusing him; but it suited him to continue exploiting her channel to the president's office.

It would seem they were both playing Machiavellian roles in and out of the boudoir. Ian deliberately fed Sir Edward specific tidbits of propaganda and false news via Sylvia, designed to unnerve him enough to make a deal with James or face a fate he could not counter.

Admittedly, this whole ruse was starting to wear on him. He'd never thought he'd be playing a game of corporate spying with a mistress he'd once happily taken to bed. But by maintaining his relationship with her, he was able to play his adversary in a unique way and that was certainly a role he relished, had always relished, as he was a ruthless man when it came to a major confrontation with an adversary.

In a letter, he admitted to James that, while he had mastered many things in life – journalism, finance, and politics – he had never been a good judge of either women or horses. Ian smiled sardonically as he reread a particular excerpt.

I lose my bets with both. And that bitch, Sylvia, is living proof of my blind spot.

But he couldn't seem to get over the twist of fate that had placed this attractive, seductive, adventurous woman in the center of the biggest corporate control battle in Canadian history. He was sure, however, that when the smoke cleared, and it was known how he and Sir Edward had both exploited her talents and emotions in and out of her boudoir, she would not graduate with either in marriage.

SIR EDWARD AND HARRIMAN

It was only a matter of time before Sir Edward would have to call Harriman and James and Baruch were both tickled pink imagining the ensuing conversation. They amused themselves by speculating which questions might come up.

What was Union's stock position? What was Union's long-term objective in owning stock in C.D.R.? Were they contemplating having Union representatives on the board? Would they vote their proxies with MacTavish, or with management? Would a discussion of respective freight rates be of interest?

There were certainly plenty of possible questions, more than either of them could conceivably guess. But after coming up with a few plausible questions, their conversation turned to plausible responses to those same questions. One thing that became immediately clear was that Harriman could not commit his board, but he and his chairman likely had a clear idea of board policy, some of which would no doubt be very diplomatically discussed over the course of the conversation.

"I hear my company is rather popular down there on Wall Street, Mr. Harriman, and how is Union Pacific doing these days?" asked Sir Edward when Harriman picked up the phone.

"Yes, a number of us on the street are high on C.D.R. and its future, including my own board. I am happy to say we acquired a few shares some time ago at considerably lower prices. We feel very comfortable with our investment," responded Harriman cheerfully. "I'm delighted you called!"

Sir Edward then got down to business concerning the forthcoming annual meeting. "I don't know how much stock Union holds, Mr. Harriman, but I'm told by Sir James MacTavish that it's rather large; not a few shares as you imply. What exactly is your long-term interest in my company?"

"Union has been interested in your company for several years, sir," replied Harriman. "We've been buying continuously, if intermittently, for ages now. Our objective over the medium term has always been to slowly accumulate enough stock to be represented on your board. We've simply never been in any great hurry.

"However, when Mr. Baruch and Lord Brandenbrooke approached us, we agreed to support them, seeing as they had considerably more stock than we did. Combined, I believe we have something in the order of four million, one hundred and sixty thousand shares." Sir Edward could practically hear the vicious grin in Harriman's voice. "My chairman and president would be delighted to see you in New York, if you expect to be in the city in the near future. It is obvious we have some important joint interests to discuss."

Sir Edward shuddered in silence for a long moment upon hearing Harriman's share estimate; that was not a number someone in his position ever wanted to hear, especially when it was in someone else's hands. He growled coolly, enunciating each word with slow deliberation, "That's not control, Harriman. What the hell do you think you're playing at?

"I'll discuss your call with my board, but I can tell you straight out, we have no interest in sharing our company and its competitive secrets with a foreign-owned railroad, especially one like Union Pacific. You will no doubt understand why. I'm sure we'll see you at the shareholders' meeting. Good day to you, sir." Though his tone was civil, it would take a deaf man to think it genuine. "Enough is enough!"

He slammed the phone down into its cradle in a fit of fury where it made a distressed clunking sound. He ignored the phone and shouted to his secretary, "Get my chairman of the executive committee on the line immediately!"

The phone rang not a minute later. In a way, that was probably a good thing. He felt calmer now, having moved passed burning rage into simmering indignation and righteous fury. He picked up the phone slightly less violently than he'd slammed it down and reported, in a voice like roiling thunder, "Sir James and Brandenbrooke have locked up Union Pacific on their team; to beat them we'll have to launch a proxy battle royal. What other strategies are we considering?" he demanded. "Call the board together for an emergency meeting; my office, at five p.m."

It wasn't long before James received a call from Baruch. The other man had managed to gather details of Averell's telephone exchange with Sir Edward and his thinking concerning proxy support. "I'm confident now that Averell, after that exchange with Sir Edward, is more disposed to giving you Union's backing. Here, listen to what he told me earlier."

Quoting the man in question, he said, "'Whatever the syndicate does to enhance the management and stock value will accrue to the benefit of the Union. If Union wanted to take over the whole deal at a later date, it could be exceedingly profitable for the syndicate. Sir Edward's reactions to our conversation was dead cold; he stonewalled me. There is no way he's coming to New York; we might as well prepare for a battle royal.' I'm paraphrasing a little, but that was the gist of it."

It was obvious that the time had come to cut a deal or prepare the troops for battle. He held a hot hand - some would say a royal flush- and he guessed the C.D.R. boys knew it, even though it was not outright control. He exchanged cables with Ian in London, who concurred, "Put their feet to the fire, James, and force that egomaniac to a decision; exploit his fear of nationalization."

He called the president's office and was surprised at how quickly he got through to the big chief. "I understand you've had a chat with Averell Harriman," James began. "He's looking forward to seeing you in New York, and he feels the two giant continental railways have a lot in common and complement each other in many ways."

"Is that so?" growled Sir Edward. "It's the lack of what we have in common that worries me. There is absolutely no basis for a marriage or even a flirtation; not even a corporate relationship, from our perspective. It's the camel trying to get his big fat nose in my tent. Tell him to put me on his goddamned board and see what he says," he demanded.

"Eddie," replied James calmly, "Harriman, Baruch, and Brandenbrooke have suggested I see you again. I think we should clarify a number of important items. In short, it's time we got to 'nut-cracking'."

There was a long, and slightly incredulous, pause on the telephone, followed by, "Well I'll be goddamned. Nut-cracking; cracking what? You know our position; there ain't nothing to crack, and I'll have my executive committee on hand if you want proof."

"That's great, let's set a time and place. Wherever and whenever you suggest. You assemble your committee, and I'll be there with Gordon Howard," responded James authoritatively.

"Well, all right, goddammit, be here tomorrow at ten o'clock a.m.," he snapped abruptly, then clunked down the phone.

BATTLE ROYAL

As James walked into the illustrious boardroom the next morning, there was a chill in the air, as if he'd entered a giant refrigerator. The stony faces and glassy eyes of the executive committee members painted a very clear picture of what had happened. James could see it in his mind, all these fine gentlemen assembling at an early hour to speak, convening around the boardroom table with Sir Edward in his chairman's seat overlooking them like a Roman emperor.

And now they maintained that position, deliberately staged; an effort to throw him off-balance, to take his power away. These men presented a façade, likely a true one, of being in no mood for banalities and pleasantries. There was not a handshake offered or even a courtesy nod; they remained seated while he was briskly introduced to the gathering.

The president's opening salvo was curt, "Well, MacTavish, you asked for a meeting. What are you peddling, and how much are you asking?" he asked in a condescending tone.

James's adrenaline surged, the arrogance of the chairman's opening remark grating against his skin. He stared down the long table, steely-blue eyes meeting the gaze of each director in deathly silence, before he responded.

"Peddling. Peddling! Peddling what?" he demanded, indignantly. "Trust me, gentlemen, I'm peddling anything. On the contrary, Mr. Chairman, you must be suffering from some sort of a delusion. I am not here to peddle a goddamned thing; nor am I here to buy anything, and you know it. I ain't askin' for nothin'," he spat out in his best Cockney accent. In line with his intent, he watched the humorless men fluff up with insult like birds before a fox. "It's more a question of what you and your board are prepared to offer. You've spoken to Harriman. You know the cards in our collective hands. It's your move, Mr. Chairman. What's your offer?"

This put the ball back in the president's court, provoking him to fire back, "No, goddamn it! We did not invite you here to make you an offer, but we do have a bottom line. We will not be manipulated by that goddamn Yankee Harriman or his gang."

"You don't have to be manipulated by them," counseled James. "Just give them representation on your board with us and agree to a few policy changes, and we will all carry on
together."

Sir Edward, fearful of being outwitted before his committee members, took the offensive, exploding with, "Look, MacTavish, you and your little parvenu baron, 'the Pink House whore', can do what you bloody well like. We're not dealing with a proprietor of brothels. This board is calling our loyal shareholders together, and we'll see who really owns this great Canadian enterprise. You buccaneers are talking a big game, but we haven't seen any evidence to confirm your so-called position. I will tell you this though: whatever your position is, it ain't control. We have our own plans, which you will learn about at the meeting, in no uncertain terms.

"Very well, gentlemen, the battle lines are drawn," asserted James, slowly eyeballing each member of the committee, one by one. "I look forward to seeing you all again on the battlefield in a few weeks. It promises to be a hot and bloody meeting. Frankly, I love a good fight; it's my Irish blood. But I warn you, you're making a big mistake. Your president will end up in a caboose on a slow freight to Timbuktu."

The remark incensed committee members into a barrage of quips and curses, with one-member sneering, "This little upstart Irishman sure as hell has kissed the blarney stone; who does the little son of a bitch think he's fooling?"

"Goddamn it, Jimmie!" retorted Sir Edward. "You cocky little bastard! You run your bloody blackmail business, and I'll run my railroad. That's final. The meeting is terminated."

James refused to leave without firing one more salvo. "You gentlemen are great actors. You should be on Broadway, instead of being directors of a great Canadian enterprise. I fear you're miscast in the wrong profession; wasting your talents."

Another member of the committee, responding to the insult with contempt, snapped, "Your charade, sir, wouldn't even survive opening night! They'd bring the fucking curtain down on you in act one."

James let loose a hearty laugh and quipped, "That will be just fine, sir, because this is a one-act play and you, sir, are out." He stood to leave, grinning to himself; while not the desired outcome, this was certainly a fun alternative, in his eyes. He turned back and fired a final volley to the table, "And don't count too heavily on your legal beagles running us off the track. They may sweet-talk you with a forked tongue, of course, but remember what is said about lawyers: 'they're like whores; the one profession in the world that can't afford to dislike their clients'."

"Shocking," muttered a member in the steely silence of the boardroom, as they filed out in disgust, grunting and murmuring to one another.

One was heard reminding the others, "I dare say these rogues know more about whores than we do." James rushed back to the Ritz on springs, and in high spirits, to telephone Baruch and Harriman and wire Brandenbrooke with a vivid description of the great charade.

"He wants to fight, Bernie," said James. "He doesn't believe our stock position and is very anti-Union Pacific, but it's all a gigantic bluff; I can see it, he's obviously over a barrel. The committee was a comedy act; totally impotent, trying to appear defiant."

"Well, hot damn!" cried Baruch. "Now we're free to use any tactic available. It's open season, and I'm sure Union will add to their position at these prices, if necessary."

ANNUAL REPORT

Union stepped up their buying, while Baruch attracted a number of other large investors whose proxies he could count on.

The stock moved up through the forty-one-dollar mark, and within a few days, was at forty-four and gaining. Ian continued generating buying from London, aiming to register as much stock as possible before the transfer books closed.

It was a frantic few weeks for syndicate members. They could smell victory at last on paper, but what could C.D.R. do to foil their objectives? It was well known in all markets that a major fight for control was in the making. The die was cast, and as Baruch had observed, "Sir Edward has crossed the Rubicon and will have to abide by the consequences."

The annual report was, at long last, finally mailed. It reported profits for the year, ending December 31, at forty-one million dollars, $4.12 per share, for a total increase of nine-and-a-half percent over the previous year.

James took note something the president wrote in the report, a reference to a foreign group who had acquired an unknown number of shares in recent months and who might be trying to assert themselves at the annual meeting. He was encouraging all shareholders to make a particular effort to return their proxies as soon as possible or to attend the meeting in person to cast their votes. James was, personally, a little impressed, despite himself, with the president's restraint. The wording was serious, formal, and nowhere near as insulting as the man had been in person or in rumor.

When Union Pacific received the report, on the other hand, they decided to up their bid to acquire any stock offered up to fifty dollars per share. They weren't going to be sandbagged on the last day, at the last minute, losing the battle for want of a few shares. They vowed they wouldn't be left twisting in the wind, as speculators unloaded short-term trading positions if they were outvoted. They were in the home stretch in a winner-takes-all gladiatorial battle of titans, and both sides knew there would be blood.

THE MOLE

When James had teased Elizabeth about infiltrating Sir Edward's inner sanctum, he was really musing out loud about his best-kept secret weapon. Not long ago, he had met an attractive and talented young woman who was not only willing and able, but was actually already in the inner sanctum of the president's office and privy to his daily deliberations. The cost of this subversive operation, dubbed 'Atlantic II', was minuscule in comparison with the priceless information he was receiving. Already it was beginning to pay dividends.

As the stock continued climbing, he could almost chart the President's anxiety curve, thanks to her reporting promptly the growing chorus of dissension among his directors.

Sir Edward's executive committee members, she reported, apparently took him on, following their heated and vitriolic meeting with James. "The committee is divided," his informant reported. "Several members were critical of his tactics, and in exasperation, he advised them he was going to the prime minister."

Ian was ecstatic upon hearing details of James's secret initiative. Although no stranger to corporate espionage, putting a mole on the payroll in the enemy's camp was the ultimate ploy; and the mole in question, a woman who James had described as 'a beauty with a legal mind', was perfect. He composed a telegram immediately to convey his congratulations.

> Excellent tactics, James. When the gloves come off, there are no rules. Anything goes, and winner takes all. Hit them where they ain't. The president is a one-man band. The rest of them with a few exceptions are yes-men. Keep up the heat until he folds, and remember all is fair in love, war, and corporate raiding.

Not too long after hiring her, James received an insightful report from his mole. Sir Edward was intending to lobby the prime minister's office in support of legislation that would, among other things, limit foreign investors' voting rights to a maximum of ten percent. Richard confirmed this and reported in turn his many discussions with the prime minister. He advised that he didn't think the PM would go for it, although the possibility remained a distinct threat, especially if the politics became inflamed. Such a thing would deal a deadly blow to the syndicate's capital position, as Union Pacific would likely become a net seller.

While James continued monitoring the deliberations in the president's office, Ian concocted a truly devious scheme, a masterful plot of mischievous, misleading propaganda to be relayed from Sylvia to Sir Edward. He stayed up all night detailing the ploy which would highlight the existence of a secret agreement between Union Pacific and the syndicate, wherein Union had committed to buy their entire position for sixty-two dollars per share, a grand and terrifying total of 173.6 million dollars, if the C.D.R. board did not come to terms with James.

He called James up to tell him that he was releasing this vital information to Sylvia at an appropriate moment of pillow talk. After that, the only thing to do was wait, impatiently. They would only know if the scheme had worked once James' mole reported back.

They entertained themselves imagining, anticipating, Sir Edward's impending explosion. If they knew the man at all; hell, if they knew his board at all, it would be a truly epic blow-out. There wasn't a man there who didn't abhor the idea of Union becoming the largest shareholder, of control slipping to the Yankees. Perhaps the only thing they hated more was the notion of C.D.R. being nationalized by Canada's government.

GOVERNMENT FALLS

The Conservative government's life under Prime Minister Arthur Meighan was scarcely one hundred days old when 'treachery dealt the party a deadly blow', reported Richard to James over the telephone, his temper boiling.

The first vote of confidence in the House was defeated by a single vote, cast by the member from Nelson, British Columbia, who had been paired with the absent Richard B. Benson and was honor-bound not to vote in his absence. By breaking his commitment and double-crossing Mr. Benson, he brought down the government, threatening to destroy Meighan's political future.

James, both awed and a smidgen alarmed by the bloodthirsty politics, was prompted to exclaim, "What a jungle the political landscape is! It's a bloody ruthless business and we call it political science."

"Political science be damned," scoffed Richard. "What's that? Political games may be political art or political mania, but science, there ain't no science in my profession. You're dead right, at times it sure as hell is a jungle.

RICHARD MEETING JAMES RE: UNION

Sir Edward was delighted with the news of an impending election. He firmly believed the Conservatives would return with a stronger majority and the 10% voting limit legislation could be introduced to greater effect.

During the campaign, the antagonists preparing for corporate battle were at least in agreement from a political standpoint. Lord Brandenbrooke, Sir James, the Atlantic Syndicate, and Sir Edward, they backed and funded the same cause: the election of the Conservative Party with a healthy majority. They provided funds on a grand scale, the C.D.R. and aspiring leader Richard Benson, each contributing one hundred and fifty thousand dollars.

James and Ian had never once wavered in their commitment to support their old friend on his quest to become prime minister. The bond they had forged long ago had kept them united until now, but in the midst of a pending election campaign, Richard's position in the syndicate was extremely delicate. If word got out about his involvement in the C.D.R. scheme, it could even be lethal from a political stance.

They both knew how best to turn Union Pacific's perceived threat to great advantage with a skillful propaganda spin, gaining praise for rescuing Canada's national jewel from the clutches of Yankee predators, by wrapping themselves in the flag, and covering themselves with glory, while enhancing the syndicate's profit potential.

The question as always was: Could Sir Edward be made to play? "He's got to be maneuvered into a position of no choice. It is that old Jesuit conundrum; 'the lesser of two evils,'" advised Richard by phone. "And the Yankee buyout ruse might do it. I have spoken to him briefly; I'll be in Montreal tomorrow, see you then."

Upon arrival, he recounted details of his talks with Sir Edward. "He's very concerned about Union," he said, relaying some of Sir Edward's notes and remarks. "Richard, as an old friend of those two international pirates, Brandenbrooke and Sir James, you've got to prevail upon them not to consider a deal with that Union Pacific gang. It would constitute an act of high treason.

"You've got to block it, man. We've contributed two hundred thousand dollars to your campaign, we expect your support in this; we want action and we want it now. We know they've had an offer for their entire position and those unscrupulous bastards might be tempted to sell out if the price is high enough. They've greed for blood, they wouldn't think twice about it.

Brandenbrooke in particular isn't exactly known for his high principles. My advisors have been telling me that, on a combined basis, they own the biggest single block of company shares.

"I'll go public with this if I need to, I swear by God; if I need to cause a major election issue, a political crisis of the first order, in order to do what's right, I will. What a donnybrook that will be, don't you think? The country will support us for our righteous actions and any perceived opposition will hit a brick wall. Don't fight me on this.

"We both know how the Liberals and King will make political capital out of the threat; none of us want that little toad in office, but if I don't get you and your party's support, I'll have no choice. I'll go to King, and damn the consequences, because he'll probably threaten nationalization. This is a fight for the independence of Canada's greatest enterprise."

Richard's account of the president's demands was, to say the least, portrayed in a very dramatic fashion. "He's got a hell of a strong argument, James," continued Richard, "and he'll play into the King camp if he has to. He's got the bit in his teeth, I'm afraid."

"Did you tell him you were in full agreement with his concerns?"

"Of course I told him! And I told him I would talk to you and Ian at the first opportunity. He didn't believe me of course but that's why I'm here tonight. We've got to put together a plan immediately."

James was all smiles, and all ears, as he listened to Richard. "That is precisely what I wanted to hear. My friend, you have brought me the best of news. Why, it is music to my ears. I can't tell you why, not now and maybe not ever, and it's probably for the best, but this is good.

"Someday, maybe, I'll tell you the whole story, but in the meantime, we must keep you at arm's length. There must be the illusion of distance between us. Anyway, the point is, if the president is that concerned about the buy-out rumor, he'll bend to our demands. I'll have a chat with Baruch and I'll wire Ian immediately. I think we can engineer a subtle scheme; maybe even manage to simultaneously wrap ourselves in the flag, make the Conservative Party look great, and turn Richard Benson into a budding statesman. What do you think of that scenario, old boy?" he asked, roaring with laughter.

"You don't have to tell me what you're going to do, James. Just do it. I'll keep out of it as long as you, save for advising Sir Edward that I have acted on his behalf and used my best efforts to influence the 'Buccaneers', as he calls you. The last thing I need is having the chairman of the largest corporation in Canada mounting a campaign against us. The election is tough enough as it is. If King wins, my bet is he'd move on the ten-percent rule."

James immediately dialed up Baruch. The two men spoke at length, their talk dragging out for hours. He relayed his conversations with Richard, commenting on how paradoxical the circumstances surrounding the election might be, how easily they could become a blessing in disguise, one that could play into their hands.

"If we feign resistance to selling to Union, Bernie, we can get a higher price in the long run by voting the Union stock at the meeting. Here, explain the situation to Harriman; see if you can't persuade him to confirm our Union proxy. I'll get him on the board, the dividend increased, and the stock split. They can't lose and we win no matter how you cut it. What the hell, it's a 'blackjack'," he laughed. Baruch had to agree; the plan was genius and it should appeal to Union.

James's informant took that moment to report invaluable information from the executive suite: the president was putting the heat on Benson and the Conservative Party, fearing a sellout by Brandenbrooke and his group to the States, confirming that James' trap was ready to be sprung. The time was ripe for another meeting with the big chief.

"Call Sir Edward back, Richard," James directed, looking pleased as punch, "and advise him you've pressured me to hold off making any deals with the U.S. until he meets me again."

EDDIE AND RICHARD

"First class, I'll call him in the morning," agreed Richard. "But be sure you've got Union's proxy tied up before you make your proposal."

"Don't worry, Baruch will get that in the bag."

Sir Edward expressed his appreciation when Richard called, suggesting a meeting with James. "Goddamn it, Richard, of course I'll see the 'Little Baronet', but the son of a bitch better not try to hijack me or my board, or we'll play our political aces, and you know what that can mean to your party."

"Eddie, I'm sure we can hold him off making any sellout deals," replied Richard in a tone of confidence. "See what you can do and keep me informed. I may be able to play the honest broker role on your behalf I am sure the boys would rather make a deal with you than with the Americans. They're more patriotic than you think."

"I doubt that," retorted Sir Edward curtly, "but we'll bloody soon find out."

Richard reported back to James, adding he felt the president's bark was much worse than his bite, and that this time, he might see reason. "Have your stock and proxy position up to date, talk precise numbers, then turn up the heat," he advised.

James soon heard again from his informant, confirming the president's discussions with Richard and that some of his directors were strongly urging him to negotiate a deal with James; while others, including the company's prestigious team of lawyers, were of the view that he should call his bluff and fight it out at the meeting.

The prospect of a control shift in C.D.R. had finally leaked out and become more than just market gossip and rumor. It had been picked up by the press, and both political parties began exploiting it as the election campaign heated up.

Sir Henry Thornton, chairman of the government-owned National Railroad Corporation and Sir Edward's stated nemesis, exploited the topic with relish. He had lobbied for years to have the government expropriate the private railroad company, on the grounds that Canada should be served by one government-owned national railroad, providing maximum efficiency at minimum costs to Canadian taxpayers.

Both political parties began endorsing the importance of Canadian ownership of Canada's transportation facilities. If there was the slightest chance of C.D.R.'s control slipping to the U.S.A., both parties would support National Railway Corporation buying out the foreigners, or failing that, expropriating the entire corporation. It was a heaven-sent issue for political exploitation.

Sir Edward's office was bombarded with calls from the press, politicians, and candidates, together with policy consultants to both parties and their leaders. The message was clear: the country would pay anything to keep C.D.R. Canadian-owned, if not privately then by the public sector.

The flamboyant chairman of the National Railway Corporation campaigned publicly for a thorough investigation of the company's ownership. He gave speeches and held press conferences, calling out for control to remain in Canadian hands instead of falling to Americans as rumored. He demanded confirmation of Canadian control, even going so far as to suggest that his own company would buy any foreign stock holders position at any price, if necessary.

Sir Edward knew that if the National acquired a stock position in C.D.R., it would be the thin end of the wedge, leading to a complete takeover and merger of the two transcontinental lines, similar to the government's takeover of the Grand Trunk and the Canadian Northern Railroads ten years earlier.

"This goddamned election couldn't have come at a worse time!" he lamented loudly to his board. "These unprincipled politicians are exploiting nationalism for political gain – and what's worse, they're playing into the hands of that fraud, Thornton. Everyone knows he's been after our company for years! If King forms the government, they could contrive a scheme to nationalize if there was the slightest prospect of control slipping out of the country."

He called Richard again in Ottawa, asserting, "This insidious propaganda being spread by Thornton has to be smothered in its cradle. The press is already full of irresponsible statements about the National taking us over because of these goddamned Yankee rumors. I tell you, Richard, it will not happen; I will not let it happen. I want the Conservative party to stand and be counted. We've got to get rid of Union Pacific, to eclipse Thornton – they're both a goddamned menace to me, my board, and my country."

"Take it easy, Eddie," counseled Richard. "You know the old saw: 'Slowly, slowly, catchee monkey'. I've told you before, your man is James MacTavish. I've told you I think he can skate the deal on side. You boys must get together. I know he is expecting your call."

"Suppose I had a large Canadian institution, Richard, to buy out Union Pacific. Where would that leave those two-little title-mongers from England?" snickered Sir Edward. "They would be alone twisting in the wind; they'd be up the well-known creek, dying of the stink, wouldn't they? You're goddamned right they would, and the banks would have them by their balls," he emphasized, raising his voice.

"That sounds like one solution, Eddie, buy out Union, get our company back to Canada. You've got the money, why not? I wish you luck!" agreed Richard. "But be sure to check with James first."

When James heard from Richard of the president's wild scheme to head the syndicate off at the pass where they would be left twisting in the wind, he responded with wild laughter, "What's wrong with that turkey; doesn't he know a new buyer would want to saddle up with us? And besides, Baruch and Union both know that if they maintain their position, they'll do much better than selling out at these levels.

"Well, he's obvious gone round the bend. It seems we may have pushed him too far. Oh well." He shook his head and carried on thinking aloud. "According to Baruch, Union will support us with their proxies or buy us out if we want to sell, so our bets are hedged both ways. I've already send out memos to all members of the syndicate and to all allies asking for a tally of their proxies to have in hand when I meet the big ogre to back him into his cage."

Turning back to Richard's report, he called up his informant to ask her to track down the president's attempts to find a Canadian buyer that could rival Union's position. No sooner had he finished the call, now contemplating his good fortune in having this privileged source of information, that a disturbing telegram arrived from Ian.

Suspect some direct communication between your informant and 'S'. We may be being set up. Am testing the scheme. Will Advise, Ian

UNION STANDS FIRM

Baruch called, reporting further discussions with Harriman concerning the Canadian election and the widespread rumors over company control, advising that Union had acquired additional stock, and that the board had formally agreed to the syndicate voting their proxies at the meeting.

He also confirmed for James that Union had received a strong bid from an investment firm in Toronto; $58 per share for their entire position. Union had turned them down in writing, being quoted as saying that they had no interest in disposing of their position now or at any point in the neat future. He relayed Union's long-term objectives and continuing interest in buying out the syndicate in spite of recognized political implications.

Baruch ended his report with a warning tone, "I strongly suggest, James, that you have another chat with Harriman before you meet your big ogre." James nodded absently before catching himself and humming his agreement. He hung up with a quick farewell and dialed Harriman in the same breath.

Harriman picked up and opened the conversation with a very short greeting before moving on to, "I understand we've stirred up a hornet's nest in Canada over the national icon. The last thing we needed was an election occurring in the middle of this deal, but that's the luck of the draw. The storm will pass, my friend. The press boys always stir up a tempest whenever possible, it does wonders for sale, but I'm not concerned. I've been through a lot of them by now.

"The latest news is more important: we were approached by a Canadian dealer offering to buy our block. We turned them down, as I told Bernie. 'Thanks for the complement,' we said, 'But no thanks: we're not for sale.' In fact, we've been in the market again. After the election, we would still like to buy your position. But I know you're not interested at these levels."

And then, obviously joking, he added, "I guess we'll all have to hang together, James or we'll wind up, as Benjamin Franklin put it, 'hanging apart'."

James smiled hearing his views. "What's the size of your position now, Averell?" he asked.

"I can tell you now, James. It's exactly 1,374,350, shares as of yesterday."

"And what about your proxy; when do we get it in our hot little hands?"

"Yes, that's been agreed," confirmed Harriman, "You'll have our proxy, providing you can assure the board elections, and the stock split."

"I think we've got the leverage to deliver," answered James. "I think I've got that egomaniac boxed in," he chuckled. "His options are limited. Time will tell, we should know in a few days.

"That's great," enthused Harriman. "We understand each other. You've got a pretty strong hand, James, you can outgun those boys. It's just a matter of out-gutting Sir Edward, that prima donna. I hear he's a real tiger."

"He's a stubborn son of a bitch, all right," quipped James, "and a vain bastard; that's his weak point, and we're going to exploit it. We shall prevail, have no fear."

James was elated by the news. He wasted no time in phoning Gordon Howard and reporting Union's 1,374,350-share position and proxy commitment. "Could you send over an update on the syndicate's overall position, including the positions of everyone from England, Brussels, Paris, et cetera, as well as those from brokers, bankers, and trust companies who are holding shares for clients?"

"Of course," Howard reassured him, promising an update within the day.

His first call the next morning came while he was out having breakfast with Elizabeth; it was his secret informant. She told him about the president's fury over Union's rejection of the Toronto dealers' bid; about him having advised the members of his executive committee to up the price to $62 per share. She also relayed, word for word, his reaction: "I want that goddamned block of stock. It's the key between us and that whoremaster from Calgary. With that block in hand, we'll leave those cutthroats hanging by their balls at the mercy of their creditors."

"Wow," exclaimed James, grinning sharply. He could practically taste the panic in Sir Edward's words. He related the story to Elizabeth over the course of breakfast and afterwards, he called up Baruch to let him in on Act Three of the charade.

He concluded with, "Sir Edward will have to come across soon if he wants to avoid confrontation and a political calamity at the meeting. His nemesis, Thornton, is intensifying his campaign. He keeps telling anyone that will listen that if C.D.R. was in even the slightest danger of being taken over by American interests, it would be the government's patriotic duty to intervene and nationalize the company for the sake of national security.

"What's worse is that though Sir Edward may despise Thornton, not even he can deny he has a plausible case. If the flames of nationalism are fanned enough, the government would have a hard time resisting social pressure to merge the company with the government-owned railway corporation."

Sir Edward convened a meeting of his directors and laid before them the gory details of his dilemma, his options, and other possibilities. The board agreed unanimously that under no circumstances should they allow Sir Henry Thornton further ammunition to stir up political passions in favor of nationalizing the railroad.

"The American threat must be put to rest," insisted Sir Vincent Hennessy. "Either we buy them out or we make a deal so that the shareholders meeting will enjoy unanimous support for management resolutions. As you have indicated, Mr. Chairman, this will require the cooperation of Sir James and Company, and since his terms and conditions are still unknown to us, I suggest we'd better lock horns and get down to bedrock with this maverick manipulator."

As soon as the news made its way to his ears, James fired off a cable at Ian.

Now have commitment proxy from Union and open offer to purchase our entire position. My informant reports pressure on the chief to settle with me, but on what terms? It's great to have so many profitable options. Check if 'S' is getting info from you-know-who. James

From Ottawa, Richard again expressed his apprehension over the election. "It looks like the Liberals have the edge," he reported, sounding sullen. "Fortunately the election won't occur until after your shareholders' meeting." He sighed into the phone. "One way or the other, Eddy is going to have to hedge his bets; he knows if the Liberals form the government, there's a good chance the railroad would be nationalized if Union takes the driver's seat, and that's exactly where they'll be if you sell out to them. Just keep Eddy-boy guessing a little longer."

"Sure thing, Rich. Are you doing good? You sound tired."

"It's a madhouse up here. I'll be happy when the whole thing's done with and we can all get back to the usual amounts of stress and chaos."

The date of the meeting was rapidly approaching, leaving little time for the president and his board to maneuver. On the other, the trio of buccaneers were all prepper and ready approaching their moment of truth. They had all their files and folders in order, they'd called in every single person they could think of, and they'd consolidated as much stock as possible.

Still, the cautious person leaves nothing to chance when victory is on the line. The trio took to reviewing their options and speculating on the board's decision. They didn't have long left to decide and as they were right now, they could go any which way.

Would they gamble or bluff their way to the end? James's channel to the lion's den was invaluable, but he wasn't privy to the entirety of the board's thinking. He exercised his imagination and his analytical capabilities, running through countless mental simulations in anticipation of every possibility. Meanwhile, the stock sat at a new, sustained high of $58 with a majority of the buying continuing to originate from New York.

THORNTON RE: NATIONALIZATION OF CANADIAN RAILWAY

"Our transcontinental railway networks – those ribbons of steel that link our federation from sea to gleaming sea – the very backbone of our political body, have been and must always be owned and operated by Canadian hands. They are the vital infrastructure of our economy," preached Sir Henry to the popular Canadian Club luncheon. "Canada welcomes foreign capital in all areas of business, but not this one, not in the railroad business.

"Let that be known, far and wide, in the capital markets of the world: not the railroad, not at any price. The Canadian government would rather nationalize our railways before allowing them to be owned by foreign capital," he thundered.

Many a canny listener in the crowd would turn these words over in their hear, deciphering the things that went unsaid, the inference that Canada's C.D.R. was a tempting target to American rail companies serving the border states and the Pacific Northwest markets. Whether it was meant this way or not, his words would give rise to further rumors of Wall Street buying.

The Montreal Star, one of the Canada's largest English language newspapers, carried a startling headline: "N.R.C. chief recommends nationalization of C.D.R. to Liberals."

Sir Edward was aghast and furious when he heard the news and he wasted no time calling on the Star's press baron, Hugh Graham, known as Lord Atholstan, to very dramatically protest the irresponsibility of printing such misleading headlines. "That mountebank Sir Henry is playing politics, Hugh, stirring up nationalism for the bloody Liberals and his friend Mackenzie King. He's using your paper for his own aggrandizement and political agenda, Hugh.

"You're being suckered, my lord," he urged. "Where the hell did you get such misleading garbage? It's irresponsible bullshit journalism and you bloody well. It's a sham, Hugh, a fraud. I demand a retraction!" he snarled. Graham sat quietly on the other end of the phone. If Sir Edward could see the man, he would see a man who had sat through a great many of these sorts of phone calls and was thoroughly unimpressed.

"And let me tell you, sir, there is no goddamned way the Yanks are going to get their greedy little tentacles into my company. It's Sir Henry who wants to get his greedy little hands on us; we'll put that flannel mouth son of a bitch back in his cage for trying to hijack our enterprise. He's trying to exploit" – succeeding, in Graham's opinion – "the rumor mill deliberately to promote nationalization and your paper is dancing to his tune. We ought to ship him back on a slow freight to where he came from!"

Henry Thornton hailed from a small town in Indiana, U.S.A.

His thundering tirade resulted in the paper printing a mild retraction, but without the same commanding display as the headline story. The damage had been done. The election and the shareholders meeting were now inexplicably linked, and the heat was on Sir Edward and his board.

Following the speech and the headlines, James was in high spirits, expecting to hear momentarily from the president, and was amused when he came on the line, breathing fire and cursing his nemesis, Thornton.

"I presume you've seen the papers," he growled. "Who's the son of a bitch putting out this garbage? It better not be who I think it is, or there will be hell to pay. We better get together, fast; today or tomorrow. When will it be?"

"Any time you say, Mr. Chairman," chimed James in a condescending tone. "You're still the chairman, at least for now. I'm open. Meet me here at the hotel at ten o'clock. I'll book a private meeting room."

A long silence followed.

"Well, I'd prefer the office, James. More facilities, you know."

"Sorry, Eddie, I've been there twice. This time it's here, on my turf."

There was along silence again, before Sir Edward responded that his secretary would call back to confirm whether or not that was suitable.

"Very well, I'll be waiting," replied James curtly. "Good day, sir."

When he advised Baruch of Sir Edward's call and proposed meeting, Baruch joked, "You're in the fifteenth round; he's punchy, go for the jugular."

No sooner had he hung up that his phone rang again; his informant, reporting that Sir Edward believed he had planted the rumor. James had thanked her for the information, hung up, and sat there for a long minute. He hiccupped. He choked. He burst out into barks of wild laugher.

He laughed long and loud. He laughed until he was crying. He laughed until his lungs burned, his sides ached, and his face hurt. He laughed until his breath was weak and shallow, until it came in sharp, rasping, painful bursts, and Elizabeth burst into the room for fear of his life.

"Can you believe it?" he asked her. Distantly, he was aware he likely sounded hysterical, but he could hardly help it. The ridiculousness of the situation had to be seen to be believed. "They think I'm behind the wild rumors of nationalization. It shows how paranoid they all are, including the irresponsible press, by God, why not keep them that way? The real question is, who's informing him of this large American position, and what's their motive? I'll answer that one later."

"That's all very good," Elizabeth told him, "but are you well?"

THE ROYAL BRAWL

The president's secretary called to confirm that Sir Edward would be at the hotel at ten a.m. the following morning with his company counsel and some members of his executive committee.

Upon their arrival, James welcomed the entourage and wasted no time seating them at a board table, with himself at one end, intending to chair the meeting and control the agenda; and with Sir Edward at the other.

"Gentlemen," he began, "you've requested this meeting for one very important reason, which I hope you all understand. It's a question of who is going to control the future destiny of this great national enterprise, and whether that group is to be Canadian or American."

Sir Edward jumped in, saying, "I'm not prepared to discuss–"

"Excuse me, Eddie," interrupted James, smiling charmingly at the president. "I believe I have the floor." A nerve jumped in Sir Edward's jaw and a few committee members whispered disapprovingly, but he conceded the floor with good enough grace. "Let me give you the whole picture before we get into a pissing match." The whispers grew louder as scandalized expressions joined them. "As you may, or may not, know, my colleagues and I own a very large number of shares to be voted at the meeting next week. Gordon Howard, who is here with us today," he gestured to the man, "has had each of the trust companies, banks, and brokers report their accurate up-to-date positions.

"In a few moments, I will ask him to give you a complete tally of our voting power, as precise as possible, as of a few days ago. However, let me assure you: our position is formidable and our agenda is demanding. We aren't to play. I want you all to know that I, personally, hold a blank check to vote all of the proxies of our group. In other words, gentlemen, you're dealing with me, James MacTavish, and me alone. If we can agree, you can rely upon my commitment."

Sir Edward, face flushing a deep shade of red as his adrenalin surged, spoke civilly, though he looked like someone had dipped a lemon slice in salt and shoved in down his throat while he was looking away, "Look, James, I want to say . . ."

"Hold it, Eddie; when I've finished, okay? Now for some hard facts," James continued. "Union Pacific has acquired over 1,375,000 shares over the past several years. My syndicate has 2,800,000 shares and change. We also have a number of proxies representing various accounts; trust companies, brokers, individuals, and the like." He waved a hand dismissively. "I will therefore vote a minimum amount of 4,175,000 shares; nearly 43% of the company's share capital.

"In casting my votes, I have three options. He held up three fingers and slowly lowered them again one at a time as he counted down. "One, I can vote this entire block for your management on an agreed-upon basis. Two, I can cast my vote independently of management for my own agenda and board. And three, I can sell the syndicate's position to Union, realizing a very substantial gain, and in no time, Union will be running the show." He shrugged slyly before adding, looking at ease and unconcerned, "Unless, of course, the Canadian government nationalizes the company."

A stunning silence ensued at the table. Sir Edward, drawing heavily on his cigar as usual, glared at James and finally broke the silence, "Well, MacTavish, which bloody card are you playing today?"

James remained motionless and poker-faced as the silence continued. Not a sound came from anyone, except for the occasional shuffling of papers. Finally, Sir Edward broke the silence again, while straining to maintain his composure. He sneered, "You say you have options. If that's so, then what options?"

"I think we now know each other well enough from our many meetings that it is time I asked you the question again: do you want my support? Or would you rather fight it out in public at the annual meeting for the whole country to witness? We could take our little dispute before everyone, including the politicians who will blow it up into a grand event. You know as well as I do what they're like. They'll take our business and turn it into a major political issue. So tell me, Eddie. Shall we come to an agreement now before the meeting or should we start counting ballots and seal C.D.R.'s destiny in Yankee land?"

"How many bloody votes and proxies do you think management enjoys at our annual meetings?" responded Sir Edward scornfully.

"I don't know, Eddie, and I don't give a goddamn. If we don't outvote you this time, Union will outvote you very soon, because we'll sell them our position and they will acquire more stock, putting them well over the fifty-percent mark."

Sir Edward exploded, thundering the loudest he ever had before, in James' experience at least, "Nothing has changed! It's the same goddamn con game it's always been, Jimmie! You have exploited the press, you've encouraged Thornton and the government railroad, you've flirted with Union and Harriman."

He looked so genuinely ready to spit, it was a surprise when he carried on, "Everything you've done has been designed to blackmail and manipulate us. You and those unscrupulous bandits of yours will rue the day you embarked on your little power-play. And as for Brandenbrooke, he's scum, the worst of the worst and that's saying something when every other nouveau riche scoundrel is worse than the last. That son of a bitch would sell his grandmother for a dollar and sell Canada down the Hudson River to Yankee land without shedding a tear!"

James quietly enjoying the vitriolic outburst, judged it was time to fire his proposition while he had the president on the ropes in the presence of his committee members. "Why go for a knockout when he could win while they were both still standing in the ring?" he thought.

"I think we are running off the track, Eddie. Let's park this train on a siding and discuss an equitable solution?" he chuckled, waving a sheet of paper with his conditions.

"What the hell is equitable? Macleod wouldn't know how to spell the fucking word," growled a member of the board.

"Mister Chairman," blurted another member, "The majority of our loyal shareholders will support you and management; they always have and always will. Let's ship this little Irishman back to Cork, where he must have kissed the Blarney stone."

"Hear, hear," responded the others.

"Let's take option number one," continued James calmly, ignoring the insinuation. "We can vote together, provided your board passes certain resolutions before the meeting."

"All right," growled Sir Edward. "What are your nefarious resolutions about? Let's hear them."

James paused again, slowly scanning the table, then quietly he cited his terms. "One: the following individuals are to be elected to your board as replacements for five retirees of your choosing: Lord Brandenbrooke, Sir James MacTavish, Mr. Bernard Baruch, Mr. Averell Harriman, and one more Canadian yet to be named.

"Two: you are to pass a resolution, to be ratified at the meeting, splitting the shares on a three-for-one basis. The current stock is way too high for the ordinary public investor. It should be trading in the $20 to $25 range. Three: the board is to declare an increase of 10% in the dividend rate. Last year's earnings were much higher and the company can easily afford a more generous payout.

"Four: no additional treasury shares will be issued without the permission of two thirds of the board of directors, including myself, Sir James MacTavish. And there you have it, Mr. Chairman, pure and simple. I look forward to your response."

James leaned back in his seat, eyes roaming the room, taking in the heavy, stony atmosphere, drinking in the silence, the climactic lull. Soon though, the dark, almost oppressive silence, so complete a man could hear his own heart pounding in his ears, began to lift as the silence was broken by whispers, whispers that felt so loud they hurt.

James excused him, pushing back his chair and standing tall. He strolled casually into the adjoining room to contact Baruch, fully aware of the multitude of eyes fixed upon his retreating back. He could hear the shuffling of paper, whispers so quiet they would pass unheard in any other situations. He picked up the phone and dialed, leaving them to the contemplation of the consequences of the various alternatives and awaiting the chairman's remarks.

The president scribbled notes and conferred in low tones with the company's counsel while several members of the executive committee, including James Roswell and Sir Vincent Hennessy, requested a private room and telephone.

The proposal had come as a shock to several members who had not attended previous meetings between James and the president, but no one wanted to express a personal opinion at the table until Sir Edward had taken time to consider the resolutions, and they all had exchanged views between themselves.

When they reconvened and everyone was seated, James began by emphasizing his preference.

"We don't seek outright control of your company gentlemen, as you can see. Although that is within our reach."

"We'll see about that, young man," asserted the eldest member with a crotchety voice, "By God, the shareholders will rally to the cause when they hear of your nefarious scheme with Union."

"Excuse me, sir, as I was saying," interjected James, "what we want is a more dynamic board controlled by Canadians, building for Canada, and the making of money for all shareholders."

James was starting to think people didn't like what he had to say, since, once again, silence fell as soon as he stopped talking. It was quickly broken again, by Sir Edward, but the fact remained it was becoming a bit of a constant. "This whole god-be-damned matter will be discussed by our full board, gentlemen." He seemed to be in a better mood now, or at least in a calmer mood. "I will say, however, I am not in favor of a dividend increase or Americans on my board." Never mind; calmer he may be but happier he was not. "We'll reconvene immediately and determine our company's response to these matters." Then, tersely, he said, "I think we've got your message, Mr. MacTavish, loud and clear, and I don't believe there's really anything more to add. What do you say, gentlemen?"

"Quite right, Mr. Chairman," piper up Mr. Peacock. "As far as I'm concerned, we'll take it to our shareholders." There was a moment of hesitant silence as the board members looked back at forth, gesturing questioningly. However, no one else seemed to have anything to say, at the moment or possibly in general, and so the meeting was terminated.

James personally felt invigorated. He was convinced that the time for Richard to play his political hand had arrived. C.D.R. and its president were large financial supporters of the party and well aware of his position as next in line. He made a mental note reminding him to suggest to Richard that he engage in another subtle consultation with Sir Edward. If Richard could put the right spin on things, maybe tell Sir Edward about the escalating attitudes prevailing in the capital, about the growing concern of American domination over the company, it would be a synch getting the ornery president on his side.

His faithful informant called again from head office, reporting a wild and heated discussion between directors: a major split between the members of the executive committee and the board, and that Sir Edward intended to confer with the leaders of both parties, namely King and Meighen, to size up their political attitudes before making his final recommendation to his board.

When James received a call from the president's office the next day, suggesting another meeting with the full executive committee and board members, he responded with alacrity. "Wow!" he exclaimed to Elizabeth excitedly. "This will be command performance, fourteen actors on stage, taking shots at the little baronet; better get my shiny armor out."

He strutted into the large paneled boardroom, admired the walls adorned with historic paintings of Western scenes by Russell and Remington, of the buccaneers of the late nineteenth century who had gambled a hundred million dollars to build the railroad across the empty continent that had literally secured Canada as a sovereign nation. There was a sense of historical admiration in their layout.

But beyond the paintings, the room exuded an atmosphere of opulence and power. It framed this moment as one to remember, James thought, staring down the length and breadth of the room and the stately twenty-foot boardroom table. His eyes burrowed into those of his adversary, pinning Sir Edward to his seat. The man sat, as he always had, in his elaborate chair at the far end of the table.

But where before the chair had seemed a throne and Sir Edward a king, his court of powerful Canadian businessmen flanking him on either side, now the very air seemed different. Sir Edward's court of humorless, fish-eyed, pompous directors, fourteen strong and powerful with wealth and connections, looked the part of guards rather than court officials and Sir Edward sat like a general.

For a single moment, James forgot that Sir Edward's board consisted of the worst kind of Canadians, the ones he liked to mock for their efforts to emulate the mannerisms and the vernacular of the British establishment. He could hardly link such an image with their current selves.

But the moment passed and the fight resumed.

BATTLE ROYAL

"Sir James, I have called my full board together today and asked you to join us for the express purpose of reviewing our previous meetings and advising you of our decisions," declared Sir Edward authoritatively and deliberately. The first salvos were the most important of any confrontation. After James' last showing, Sir Edward would have a tough time establishing himself enough to impress the board. Much of it would be, by necessity, a bluff. If he faltered, even the most loyal, most trusted members of the board would drop him.

"Would you like to address the board before I respond to what we discussed yesterday?" he asked condescendingly.

"Yes indeed, sir! I sure as hell would!" snapped James. The easy confidence of his earlier forays was slowly making way to arrogance and his tone reflected that. "As I stated at the last meeting, Mr. Chairman, our group owns nearly one-half of this corporation, and we want rapid growth. We won't ask for outright control unless, of course, you give us no choice.

"And we don't disagree with you about maintaining Canadian control. Both Brandenbrooke and I are Canadians, so there would only have to be two Americans on the board, two out of fourteen. That seems to me a very reasonable proposition, considering our other options, of which I believe you are completely aware."

Sir Edward interrupted, "Yesterday, you mentioned four resolutions you and your gang wanted put in place. Here is our answer. To the first: we will accept you and Brandenbrooke on the board, but that's the limit. Secondly: we'll agree to a stock split of three for one. Thirdly: we do not propose to increase the dividend. The board agrees that the company needs the funds for operations and future expansions. And fourthly: we cannot restrict the issuance of stock, as capital needs may necessitate financing at any time."

James smiled mentally. One of Ian's earliest lessons to him had been about the code of business, how the key to success was to crack the code. Well, that was precisely what had just happened. He had cracked the code. Admittedly, he didn't think the battle was won and done yet. They had come this far and the directors had plenty of fight left in them.

Rather than let them carry on and potentially set him back, he interjected swiftly, "Mr. Chairman, I'm afraid we object to your first point. If we don't have five members of this board, including Mr. Baruch and Mr. Harriman, we'll have the whole bloody board." Sir Edward tried to silently glare him into submission. James ignored him cheerfully. "And it's about time you had some French members, as well.

"As for the other resolutions, the only one there won't be an issue with is number two. Concerning number three, a dividend increase of ten percent is long overdue. We aren't willing to compromise on this point. And as for number four; with all due respect to capital needs, if there is a capital requirement, a two-third majority of the board will be required. We would probably insist it be a rights issue in order to be fair to all shareholders."

Knowing these salvos would provoke controversy and leave them in a state of confusion, he added, "Now, gentlemen, do we all understand my group's position? Have I made it dear? Mr. Howard and I, if you don't mind, will retire from the meeting while you deliberate."

A member of the executive committee interjected, "What's this reference to Frenchmen on our board; are you suggesting someone from Paris?"

"Paris? Paris! Certainly not, "James fired back, "From right here in Montreal, a French Canadian; it's about time, don't you think? After all, Quebec is French Canada, I believe."

"Preposterous!" blurted a director. "A Frenchy frog Catholic on our board, contributing what? Religion and decrees from the pope? Or ten commandments?"

"Hear, hear!" was the response, the remark relieving the tension somewhat.

"Take your leave," grunted Sir Edward.

They were shown into a private office, leaving the directors to confer among themselves.

"What did you think of that charade, Gordon?" asked James in a jubilant mood.

"Quel affaire," Gordon sighed, sounding both tired and elated. "I think it was a grand slam. You could leave a few crumbs on the table, but they know they're over a barrel. They're all going to make money on the deal, so it's a win-win situation for everyone. The problem is Sir Edward, specifically his ego and pride. He is so used to ruling his empire, he doesn't want to give that up; and he knows that with your people onboard, that's over. But their dilemma when you played the French card was capital; that really got their juices flowing. They're a board of WASPs, if ever there was one."

"I meant it, Gordon. It's high time this racist town got with the program and brought some talented French Canadians onto the boards of not just C.D.R. but of all national companies. I have several potential names in mind. I knew how much they would want to resist me so I included it in my conditions deliberately, in order to assert my authority. Next time I may play the Jewish card; now tell me that wouldn't get the adrenalin flowing," he laughed.

When they returned to the boardroom, the directors looked much the same, with their cold stares of frustration, but there was a degree of decorum as Sir Edward led off. "We'll recommend to the board the appointments of Harriman and Baruch as additions, together with yourself and the Calgary Baron," he said facetiously. "but we can't retire more than two members at the moment.

"As for number two, we will agree on the stock split of three-to-one. We'll also recommend a divided increase of ten percent, but the stock issue, restriction, is impossible. It would fly against all precedent. We can't have one board member controlling the future financing of a corporation this size."

James knew that if they ever tried to outvote his group with a private sale of treasury stock, he could block it and call a special general meeting of shareholders to force a rights issue, and he was therefore prepared to compromise on this item. It was one he had expected he might leave on the table anyway.

"I said five new appointees, Mr. Chairman, not four; the fifth will be named in a few days," stated James emphatically. "He'll be a well-known French Canadian from Quebec City."

"I say, what is this French-Canadian business all about?" interrupted Sir Ramsay Butterworth from England. "The French Canadians didn't build this railroad, I dare say there are precious few shares held by any of them here in Quebec."

"Here, here!" was heard loudly around the table. "Maybe so, but isn't it time they did?" asserted James. "You British think the sun never sets on the British Empire, but I'll tell you, it'll set on Canada someday if a quarter of the population isn't recognized by les anglais here at home."

Comments flew fast and furiously around the table before Sir Edward pounded his gavel, calling, "Gentlemen, gentlemen, the chair, the chair, one at a time, please!" And then, addressing James directly, he stated, "You're pushing your luck, young man, it will never fly!"

James, amused by the board's behavior, fired off again sarcastically, "No doubt you Anglo-Protestants would prefer a prominent Parisian on your board, a real foreigner; or maybe one of my wealthy Jewish friends in London. I know one who's a major shareholder.

"Both perfectly valid options. That being said, Mr. Chairman, our company's head office is in Quebec, French Canada, and that calls for French Canadian representation. So you can take that ostrich head of yours out of the sand. Now, onto our other conditions; you say you'll recommend them to your board, but I can only presume that's a mere formality.

"I imagine we'll require a resolution voted on and signed before the meeting on items one through three as well as one relating to a fifth director, to be decided upon in the future. In other words, the resolutions are to be written in stone. We will, however, agree to wave item four under the circumstances."

"And why should we agree to these resolutions? Let the shareholders decide at the meeting," said a member of the board, throwing up a hand in vague dismissal, "when we count the proxies."

James gave the man a slightly incredulous and disgusted look before turning his attention back to Sir Edward and summarily ignoring the member. "Well then, Mr. President, when can I expect to hear from you? There really isn't a great deal of time. I would advise you to remember that if I don't receive those resolutions approved and signed in a day or two, you'll find a raft of proxies ganged up on you at the meeting, voting for a completely new board of directors and control in the hands of Union Pacific the next day."

"Yes, yes, we all know about that bloody act of yours," he responded in exasperation. "We'll see you on the twelfth. I move we terminate the meeting. All in favor?"

James strode out into the sunlight with a spring in his step, tasting his first moments of glory in months, and realizing that he could win the biggest prize of his career, combining a large stock market gain, with a corporate victory of a lifetime. He couldn't wait to get back to Elizabeth to share his enthusiasm and relate the drama of the meeting.

Baruch, normally a serious, stoic man, was as ecstatic and excitable as a boy when he heard the news. "The stock will hit $70 a share as soon as the news is out," he predicted happily, "following the three-for-one split; that's a mighty score, even in Wall Street. The syndicate will have access to an unprecedented gain of nearly ninety-eight million dollars." He swallowed audibly; that was an impressive amount of money. "And with the 10% increase in dividends, the shares will yield almost 5%. What's more, with the general market in a bull trend, there are considerably higher prices in the offing."

Richard was equally elated when James called him up to tell him all about the meetings and agreements. He was in Ottawa at present, enjoying the Rideau Club, a local center of political power in the nation's capital.

"Thank God for some good news, James. The campaign is proving tougher than ever; things aren't going well for the Party in the West or in Quebec. I'm glad your deal is coming together before the election. If the Liberals form the government, they surely would come to Sir Edward's rescue and threaten to negate Union's vote," he groaned. "This turned out to be a very close call! We are damned lucky in our timing."

"Timing's everything, Rich. Any half-way decent businessman knows that, and we're better than decent, right? Well, timing and luck; God knows you need luck too. Cheer up, Rich; we're getting there, slowly but surely, and your share will put you on top of the world. Baruch thinks $25 per share is quite feasible following the split, and maybe even higher prices in the not-too-distant future. We just need to tidy up the loose ends on this deal and then we can work on your leadership of the party. I guess if Meighan doesn't make it this time, he'll resign; am I right?"

"I can't comment," Richard verbally shrugged. "We'll just have to see, won't we? It won't be long now. Anyway, keep me posted, won't you?"

The next morning, a cable arrived from Ian in London.

> Congratulations, Jimmy. Sounds fine. You've lassoed a whale. Wish I could be there for the party. I'll send a message to the president and congratulate him on having such an illustrious group of new directors to sit on his board. My friends in London are still buying the stock. Ian

In preparation for the meeting, Gordon Howard continued mobilizing proxies to insure their ability to head off any surprise shareholder group, including management, who might be tempted to top their vote in a last-ditch stand. He waited anxiously for the signed resolutions, knowing of the board's dissension with the dismissals of five members.

Ian cabled a follow-up to his congratulatory message, "What are the odds these boys are playing for time and talking cooperation while scheming a proxy roadblock. I'm sure money is no object. They'd pay any price to knock us out.

James wasn't quite willing to open a bottle of champagne and throw away the cork in celebration; not until he had concrete evidence of the signed resolutions. Ian's cable had merit; the deal wasn't in the bag until the ink was dry, but he was in high spirits in spite of the tension, and was in need of relaxation as he dined with Elizabeth and planned a brief respite.

LAURENTIAN ROMANCE

The following afternoon, they were picked up at the Ritz Carleton Hotel by a Rolls Royce touring car. The car was comfortable, the driver a tall, thin man with a severe face and a professional demeanor; it was a comfortable drive and there was always something pleasant about being chauffeured.

They were dropped off at a mountain lake inn, almost fifty-five miles north of Montreal, near Saint Marguerite. There, in the cool air and gentle beauty of a late summer evening, they enjoyed a swim in a crystal-clear lake. They dined on smoked salmon and champagne and danced until the sun was halfway set, their backdrop the popular rhythms of the day. It was the first evening they had been able to spend just the two of them together for weeks and they took full advantage, allowing Elizabeth a chance, and an excuse, to exercise her charms of tender loving care.

Following dinner, the pair took to the lake in a beautiful old-fashioned birch bark canoe. They paddled slowly and watched the sun paint the sky. It was lovely but James couldn't help but ruminate over the personalities involved in this dramatic corporate power struggle.

"What's wrong, my love? Elizabeth asked him, obviously noticing how his mind was drifting. He smiled and reached over to pat her on the hand.

"Elizabeth my dear, I have a very serious and very dire question to ask you." He waited for her to ready herself before asking, "Whose side do you really think Sylvia is on? There are so many possibilities, I don't know which is the correct one. And what about that Frenchy fellow, De Rolland, and my secret source at head office?"

"I don't really know the answer to that, Jamsie, but I do know it often helps to say things aloud. Talk to me. Tell me what is happening. Even if I can't help, it might be that hearing it said out loud will help you make sense of it all." James gave her a sweet smile. He was willing to try and besides, he loved talking to her. So he talked. He told her about every person he'd met in this little drama and he outlined everything that was happening, encouraged by Elizabeth's intuitive responses.

"Of the three go-betweens in this battle of wits," he thought out loud, "who can be trusted? De Rolland can be bought, I'm sure of that. Sylvia's allegiance would be governed by her lust for love and financial security. And my delightful informant; what are her undeclared personal motives?

"Ah, there is yet more to this web of intrigue and deception than has surfaced to date." He bit the inside of his cheek in thought; a lengthy moment later, he added "The biggest player of all, of course is Sir Edward, but where exactly does he fit into the Sylvia puzzle? I've wondered for some time now if he has a secret agenda. Who knows, he might be a better actor than I give him credit for."

Elizabeth laughed lightly. "Jamsie, I love you dearly, but there is a time and a place for business. Look, the sun has set and the stars are out. No more business talk." She patted him lightly on the cheek and laid back to rest her head in his lap.

It was romantic, it was serene, it was beautiful. James petted her hair as she pointed out the Big Dipper and the North Star. The canoe drifted sleepily through the water as moonlight bounced off the mirrored waters of the lake.

In the distance, they could hear the faint, shrill calls of loons cutting through the silence. Looking up, James could see the wharf looming in the distance. Using the oar, he corrected their course, allowing them to easily drift back to the dock.

He helped her out of the canoe and secured it for the night. They linked arms and he escorted her up the dark path in silence. They wasted no time in retiring for the night themselves. James had a few last things to do before bed so Elizabeth headed up first.

She slipped on her pink silken nightgown, dimmed the light, and curled up in bed. Looking out the window, she had a perfect view of the lake, the moon's silvery shine casting ribbons of light over the lake. The water sparkled slightly, a reflection of the night sky perhaps even more mysterious than the starry sky itself.

James joined her a moment later, settling himself next to her. "What a view," he breathed. "And the lake is beautiful as well." She tittered, giving his shoulder a light, embarrassed shove. He caught her hands and lifted them to his lips, pressing a firm kiss to her palms and knuckles.

"You know," he commented slyly, "if the next few days go well, we can plan a trip to the west. We could go see the foothills of Alberta and the Canadian Rockies where Ian and I made our first dollar nearly twenty eight years ago. It's beautiful country, just the sort of place you'd love, and I haven't been there in so long."

As he leaned over, kissing her gently, her arms extended eagerly, drawing him to her bosom, as he slid in beside her.

"I'll never forget that enchanted evening when we first danced on the high seas," he whispered. "It was, without a doubt, the luckiest night of my life. I couldn't stand this guerilla warfare I'm engaged in without you, my darling. It means so much to have you near me, and I know it always will.'

As they lay together, with moonlight flooding the room, he felt the warmth of her thighs pressed against his body. Sleep came easily to him that night. He drifted off listening to the slow rhythm of Elizabeth's breaths and the shrill call of loons and the gentle melody of cricket chirps.

THE POWER STRUGGLE

Back at the hotel the following morning, James' phone kept ringing as both Baruch and Harriman directed urgent queries his way. They mostly focused on his stated resolutions which needed to be passed by the board of C.D.R.

What was his strategy if they rejected or amended certain of the conditions, agreeing to a dividend increase, but refusing to split the stock? Or might they agree to two new Canadians on the board, but oppose Baruch and Harriman. "What's your back-up tactic?" they asked. "And what about your Monsieur Maurice Lachance as your French nominee director."

"You both know damn well what my tactic will be; I'm going to hold his damn feet over the fire. We won't give an inch, gentlemen. We've fought too long and too hard to let them win. No, it has to be all or nothing," he asserted firmly, straightening his shoulders. "And by nothing, I mean we vote our block for a totally new slate of directors; we wipe them out, giving Union control of the board. I'm bloody sure Sir Edward won't risk that scene. Can't you just picture it? A full-blown proxy brawl, with the press and political support chanting in favor of nationalization; he loves the company too much to let it happen."

"We can't underestimate the management or its ability to gather support in defense of itself," cautioned Baruch. "We haven't got 51% yet and that's the only way we'll ever truly be 100% in control. We don't even the exact count and we won't until we hear the scrutineers' report at the meeting. You know the old rule, James: Never underestimate your opponent's secret weapons. Or how about that famous German general's war axiom: Always anticipate and prepare for the unexpected tactic."

"Which German general?"

"Uh . . . I think it was . . . von Moltke, maybe? Anyways, that's not important!"

Harriman then reported that Union had increased their position by over two hundred thousand shares, while Baruch reported associates had acquired an additional twenty-six thousand shares. "Could management match our numbers?" he asked again. "They may try, but the count would be too close to risk a public brawl. I'll bet they throw in the towel before there's a bloodbath," responded James.

"You're assuming common sense will prevail James, but in my experience on the street, common sense is uncommon when passions are aroused, big money is on the table, and in this case, a combination of nationalism and patriotism spells poison," asserted Baruch. "Let's make sure we don't get ambushed."

"The big risk, gentlemen," James reminded them, "is the same thing it has been since the start: Sir Edward's ego and his stubbornness. He may try to bulldoze the board and gamble. I can't put odds on that; he's unpredictable like no other. But if he does, we can always demand a special general meeting of shareholders later. I'm confident we have, or will have, enough votes to throw the rascals out if we need to." He glanced up, checking the hanging clock. "It won't be long. We'll know the answer concerning the resolutions following their directors' meeting."

A knock on the door claimed his attention as a man came bearing a cable from London.

Hell, hath no fury like a board of directors under siege. I have it from a reliable source; She's officially a double agent. There's no accounting for a woman in love. Maybe she's been jilted by the president wouldn't that be a twist of fate. Ian

"By God, Elizabeth," exclaimed James, "What in hell is Ian onto now?"

The phone suddenly rang. It was Richard. James waved Elizabeth out as he reported the situation. Richard made a noncommittal noise.

"I have some news, off the record," he said. "The president is continuing to harangue Meighen as to how to insulate the company if he wins the election. The man has been refusing to commit to anything concrete. I've tried advising that the 10%-limitation would establish a bad precedent, possibly one that could negatively impact the future of trade between Canada and the U.S.A., but Sir Edward continues to desperately explore every possibility.

"I understand he has received some encouragement from the Liberals, but he can't bank on it; it will be too late, anyway, following the shareholders' meeting. I personally think you've got a watertight case, unless they really want to go down to the wire with all guns blazing and top us on the vote." He sighed. "Some people are willing to do that. I have to admit, I don't like this situation, James. The situation is very precarious. If it goes the wrong way, it could have a horrible affect on the future of this country.

At the opening of the exchange the following morning, Jack Kippen came on the line excitedly. "What in hell is going on, James?" he shouted over the phone. "The stock has just gapped three dollars a share at the opening, trading at seventy-seven dollars on volume, somebody is dead serious, and in a hell of a hurry."

James reacted with alarm, "My god, was the buying in New York, Montreal, or London? Who were the brokers?" he demanded. "Some son of a bitch is out to blockade the meeting. I'll get on to Bernie and call you back."

Baruch's reaction was cool and measured. "Those C.D.R. bastards have been trying to buy time while they organize a heavy buying program to even out the votes with us. We might have to head them off at the pass."

"You think so?"

He shrugged, growling, "It all depends on the extent of their resources. What does Gordon Howard have today on our total share position? I'll call Harriman and Schiff immediately."

A call came the next morning from the trading desk at Jack Kippen's company, a company oddly enough called Kippen and Company, Incorporated. The first caller was a trade manager at the company, a soft-spoken fellow whose name slipped his mind the second he heard it. He laid out the specifics of the morning's trading in the markets of Montreal and New York. Soon though, it was passed to Jack himself. The man seemed busier than usual; he picked up the phone and nearly shouted into it.

Jack stayed on the line for only a minute, long enough to quote James a stock figure of seventy-eight and a half to seventy-nine. James, thoroughly taken aback, burst out, "They're buying votes at any price, Jack. Bloody hell, it's a train wreck in the making; we'll have to beat 'em to the punch, size up the market; I'll get back to you."

He hung up a moment later, Jack apparently rushing off to try to contain this latest forest fire. He turned to Elizabeth, his face flushed with fury. "That son of a bitch," he snarled. "That pompous, weaselly, stuck-up, prejudiced fox and his stupid little gang of huffy, bigoted toads have been conning me for weeks.

"Bernie was dead to rights. The bastards are going for a showdown, a gory, bloody, no-holds-barred, drag-down showdown. We'll have to play down and dirty now to sink them. That jumped-up knight is high on pride and low on brains. He's trying to top up his last-minute voting power with shareholders' money to challenge our position and defeat the resolutions.

Baruch called, following discussions with Harriman and Schiff. "If the C.D.R. gang are in this market, you sure as hell are going to hear from the chief – he's going to play hardball with a show of strength and independence. Just tell him Kuhn-Loeb and Company are in the market and will top every goddamned bid. See how he sings to that tune."

"You're right, Bernie, fight fire with fire, I'll get back to you."

Late in the afternoon the expected call came from the president's office.

"Hello, Sir James," said the voice. It was Sir Edward's secretary. "Would you hold on a moment? Sir Edward would like to have a word with you, sir."

"Hello, James. Eddie here. I'm meeting with my board at 9:00 a.m. tomorrow. You would be wise to have a drink with me later today here at the office, just the two of us," he said rather formally.

"Just the two of us alone, what's up?" queried James.

"We'll talk when I see you; say about six o'clock," answered Sir Edward.

"That was quite a show your gang put on today, Mr. President," James fired off. "Driving the stock to eighty-one at the close. Why didn't you tell me you wanted a ton of stock in such a hurry? We probably could have helped you out."

"As if—" Sir Edward tried to interrupt, blustering and bristling.

James carried on as if he hadn't spoken up, "If you're that worried about your management proxies, we happen to have more than we need for our purposes. We could lend you a few shares." A stony silence ensued as James smiled to himself, licking his lips, awaiting a response.

Sir Edward broke the silence abruptly. "Will I see you at six o'clock, yes or no?"

"I'll be there. Good day, Mr. President," answered James cheerfully, biting down on a chuckle only semi-successfully.

When he hung up, he turned to Elizabeth quizzically, "What do you suppose that actor has up his sleeve? I'll be damned if I know. Is he going for broke? Maybe, as I have speculated, he is a better actor than I've given him credit for."

He called Gordon Howard immediately. "Gordon, how do we look on the proxies and shareholder votes tally, as of today?"

"James, they've been coming in nicely. We are now over the four-million-four-hundred-eighty-five-thousand-shares mark; not quite 50%, but getting there."

"Good, I'm off to see the big chief again later today." He tossed on his coat, checked over his supplies. He was quite certain he was ready for another round in the ring with Sir Edward but a rogue thought prompted him to call up Baruch.

"Bernie, hey. Listen, I don't have a lot of time; I'm off to fight Sir Eddie again. I just need you to do me a little favor. Can you get Schiff to call me at Sir Edward's office in thirty minutes, at exactly 6:05? He'll probably guess the script we'll follow concerning the shares. When he hears my question, just tell him I'll take the call in the presence of the chief; he'll know the script," he joked.

"Of course, James. Best of luck."

At Sir Edward's office, he was beckoned right on through by the man's private secretary, a stern, no-nonsense middle-aged woman who formally greeted him with, "The president awaits you in his private suite." The two businessmen exchanged handshakes coolly but civilly as the secretary offered him a sherry.

The atmosphere was tense. The two opponents took deep drags of their cigars. They sipped at their sherry. They locked eyes and bantered back and forth, small talk and doublespeak, verbally circling around the topic at hand like a couple of veteran prizefighters in the early rounds of a world championship.

They sat across from one another at a small boardroom table. Sir Edward was puffing his chest so far out he looked like a swollen pigeon while James kept trying to use his height to his advantage, trying futile to sit a little straighter, to eke just another inch out his form. James's blue eyes flashed with confidence as Richard's credo came to mind: In business, politics, or in the jungle, your choices are limited; you're either predator or prey, and predator is sure as hell preferable.

He led off the conversation with a casual reference to expecting a call from Kuhn-Loeb in New York, "Hope you won't mind me taking it here, Eddie, it will only take a minute," he advised nonchalantly. "Now, what's your problem? Or are you going to bluff your way to a national fiasco?"

Sir Edward reeled with the insinuation, but maintained his composure, responding, "I don't have a problem, James, my boy, but you may have one, a bloody big one when the votes are counted at the meeting."

"Oh really, but I thought we had a deal," replied James, quizzically. "Or was that a great charade? You must have rounded up a ton of stock."

"Yes, indeed," he quipped, "Many of our shareholders are rallying in favor of management; they resent, like hell, Yankee marauding."

Sir Edward's secretary excused herself, advising that she had a call for Sir James from New York.

"Ah yes, my dear," responded James. "Could I take it here? There's no need for me to be private. Excuse me, Eddie, this will only take a minute, it's probably Jacob Schiff of Kuhn Loeb on the line, one of our New York Partners."

"Hello, hello, Jacob? Oh, you're with Bernie? Good, good. Oh, that's fine, just fine, Jake; just checking on our position. Yes, good. How much have we bought today? Good, excellent. I'd say that, plus another two hundred and forty thousand shares between eighty and eight five dollars would put us over the top; I'll be guided by you and Bernie. Use your best judgment, keeping in mind our timeframe. Keep me posted after the opening in the morning.

"Yes, of course. I'll talk to you then, thanks." James, with his eye on Sir Edward as he hung up, observed his countenance of fury and desperate frustration, as he recoiled from the overheard conversation.

James donned his poker face and returned to the previous conversation. "As you were saying, Eddie, before we were interrupted by my phone call, I may have a problem; rather, I do indeed have a problem, in the form of you and your goddamned board. The lot of you are a bunch of loose cannons on my deck and now I've got to spend a few more million to put you boys overboard. Oh, dear, oh, my, you'll be like Bleigh on the Bounty as you float off into the sunset," he mocked.

Sir Edward had reached his boiling point, exclaiming in a booming voice, "You expect me to buy it that blarney bullshit, that goddamned rehearsed charade with the Kuhn-Loeb gang; your act is so goddamned transparent. What the hell are you pirates trying to do; provoke the government to nationalize the railroad?"

"No way, Eddie; we're businessmen. So long as you try to head us off, we're going to head you off. We can't trust you and your board." He made it sound like a simple statement of fact rather than a slight directed their way. "You're all suffering from the arrogance of power. It's a very dangerous disease, you know, and common, especially among men such as you and I. You see, I thought we had a deal. I thought you understood the position you were in. I thought you were smart.

"And instead, you start accumulating stock like crazy for a proxy fight. Well if that's what you want, by god, we'll take you on, share for share. But I hope you're aware of the consequences this will have: the press will have a heyday, Sir Henry Thornton will lick his lips, and if you lose, the railroad will be nationalized. You, my fine, feathered friend, will have your wings clipped; more than likely, you'll be out of a job. And my syndicate will sell out at a hell of a price.

"Am I right, Eddie? You're goddamned right I'm right. All of this just for that morose ending. So what's your best bet? What gets you out as close to on top as you can get? I'll tell you: you have two choices. You can either buy my syndicate out, at one hundred dollars a share, or go for my proposal with the four resolutions. I think I know your answer." His sinister smile, omnipresent so far, dropped as his cool and collected demeanor was shed like an old coat. Instead of his cool, jovial charm was rage and force. "So do we put this train back on the rails or do we go for a wreck?" he thundered.

Sir Edward was aghast and speechless following James's diatribe. The silence was icy, interrupted only by a call on his phone. He picked it up while waving his hands, gesturing that the meeting was over. "I will consult my board; good day, Mr. MacTavish."

James began to relax as he returned to his hotel headquarters convinced that, this time, he was in the driver's seat. The implied buying power of Schiff and Baruch had been awesome, and Sir Edward couldn't be sure it was a charade.

When Baruch got a blow-by-blow description of the encounter, he counseled, "Sounds like he's seen the light, but we'll keep the buying up. When his board witnesses the share volume, they'll feel it in the gut, and your nemesis will be back to you in no time."

"You're right, Bernie, it was pretty brutal; we'll sure as hell hear from him, and soon, I predict."

Soon after C.D.R. opened the following morning, at eighty-three and a half, eighty-four in heavy volume, James's informant reported another stormy meeting of the board was in progress, a very different beast from the last ones though. This time, the president was under siege by the board to settle with the syndicate, but he was quoted as telling them, "If we can't beat them off with a majority of proxies, then we'll hold them to their present stock position by agreement."

As expected, Sir Edward called, coming on the line abruptly with, "My board and I have set our conditions, come on over."

"I'd prefer to meet you here, Eddie. I have to stay on top of this market, no doubt you've noticed the volume. I'd be glad to see you any time, but I can't leave my phone."

The usual silence prevailed when Sir Edward was being compromised, but he capitulated, growling, "I'll be there at 3:30," clanging down the phone.

As Sir Edward entered his suite, James hung up his phone, commenting casually, "The market seemed rather firm today closing at eighty-six to eighty-seven on good volume; the way I read it, Eddie, we seem to have been the big buyer, how did your gang make out?"

Ignoring the sarcasm, Sir Edward launched into his presentation abruptly. It range with a single-minded note of repetition; he'd likely practiced it over and over again. "Let's talk realities: my board knows your bottom line. Your little band of buccaneers, Brandenbrooke in particular, as well as yourself and Baruch, are well-known stock market promoters. You don't build companies, you buy and sell them.

"What you want is appreciation, market profits, and we can give you both in spades; my price isn't high. You'll be interested to know we are anticipating profits for the current year to be the highest in company history, possibly reaching forty-eight million, up from last year's forty-two million dollars."

James responded with an exacerbated sigh and a broad grin. "Why in hell do you think we bought so much goddamned stock, Eddie? We knew the earnings were on a growth trend, but I'm glad to hear you confirm it."

Sir Edward continued, acting as though James hadn't interrupted him, "It is obvious that Union is piggybacking off of your stock position to gain a foothold in Canada with the company. You say they've got approximately twelve percent of the stock, but without your support, they couldn't get to first base, and neither could you without them."

"So, what? For Christ sake, what are you driving at, Eddie? Let's have it!" snapped James impatiently.

"All right," he replied. "Here it is. I want Union to agree to freeze their stock position for two years; no further purchases. They do this in exchange for your support and getting them on the board."

"Why the hell would they do that?" snickered James. "They'll do it as a condition for you putting Baruch and Harriman on the board, that's why. We know damned well they haven't got a chance without your support."

Because of how paranoid Sir Edward was about Union's long term agenda for control, James knew he was the only one who could protect him. There was a well-concealed sense of desperation in the air. He mentally grinned; Sir Edward acted large and in charge, but he could sense it was possible, easily possible, to extract additional considerations.

He also guessed that the C.D.R. board was betting the syndicate's position would be reduced by year's end, owing to sales of stock at bull market prices. It was a logical scheme; depending on who won the coming election, there was a chance they might get legislative protection.

The proposition might make some sense, but there was one sticking point: the prize. What did the syndicate and Union stand to gain here?

"I see what you're driving at, Eddie, but frankly, we can't hold Union off just like that. Why should they? What's in it for them?" he replied with a poker face.

"I'm only talking about two years, James, they're going to do very well on their stock position in that timeframe."

He leant forward, eyeballing James. He sneered sarcastically, "Now tell me, why did you include a stock split of three-for-one and a dividend increase of ten percent in your conditions? Was this to give the public a break or are there other motives?" James fixed him with a calm, placid gaze. Sir Edward slammed his fist down, rattling the table. "You know bloody well what I mean! Your game here is the stock market, not the public interest, not the railroad; they're just red herrings. You boys are just looking for a big score and you're using Union to get it."

James laughed, quipping, "Oh, sure, Eddie, we think C.D.R. should be owned by small investors and the share price is too goddamned high for them. So we split it; with earnings up, why not pay out more to the shareholders? They deserve it, and lot of people can invest and live off the dividends. So what's the big revelation?"

"Well, that's all very altruistic, high and mighty stuff," he countered. "But let's face it, you buccaneers are corporate operators; you want the price up so you can pay down your debt. We know you've got pretty hefty loans outstanding and are bloody vulnerable should anything happen to the market or the economy."

James laughed, amusement coursing through him. He had always guessed the board would consider their ace in the hole, their secret weapon, to be the syndicate's loan vulnerability, but he hadn't considered how stupid they could be. "Don't you remember, Eddie? You've played that card before, and contrary to any expectations you might have, you failed." The amusement was starting to fade. "Oh, you sure as hell hit us hard, but ultimately it didn't matter.

"It won't work again; we're not worried about debt, damnit!" he snarled. "Our position is just fine; but sure, the stock should move ahead. It's worth a hell of a lot more than eighty-six dollars in our view. So what's in your scheme for the syndicate? Let's have it."

Sir Edward, swallowing discretely, offered two considerations, "If you get a freeze commitment out of Union, two years from signing, and appoint four directors, not five, we'll agree to split the stock at four-for-one instead of three-for-one, and we'll increase the dividend, by twelve-and-a-half percent instead of ten. That will simultaneously enhance your market profits and encourage more Canadians to invest in the company."

James had to smile at the way his opponent was presenting the scheme. This was quickly proving more amusing than he'd ever expected. "Not bad, Eddie, not bad. "Your corporate boys can come up with a good idea once in a while. It might satisfy everyone and it'll buy you a couple years of protection from the big bad wolf down south. I like it; it serves me well enough. But I can't say how Harriman or his company will react. What are you going to do if they tell you to shove it?"

Sir Edward eyeballed him again with a deadly serious look, growling, "Then it will be war, Jimmie; outright bloody war, and we've got aces you've never dreamt of. I'm making you a very fair proposition. There's no one on the board or in the government who won't give you and Brandenbrooke a lot of credit for holding Union at bay. You'll stand tall as patriots, wrapping your selves in the flag and profiting at the same time. How can you beat that for a combination? By God, it's a 'blackjack'," he shouted as he pounded his desk.

"Yeah, if the croupier deals from an honest deck," retorted James with a smirk before drawling, "You ain't going to war, Eddie. War's a mug's game, unless you've got the cannon fire, and you ain't got it, friend; but I'll get on the phone to New York and try it on for size. The boys have played the casinos; they know the odds and how to play their cards. I'll call you back in an hour or two."

He got up and casually waved himself out. He kept his walk casual until he was certain he was out of sight; then he rushed from the office to his suite at the Ritz. He personally thought this was all a grand idea, an appealing idea; and if it called to him, he guessed it would appeal to the boys as well.

But what could he trade for it? C.D.R. was a Canadian icon, a treasure of the country. Union never would, never could, get complete control over it. One way or another, the government would find a way to block them. There just wasn't enough stock available at sensible prices, unless they could buy the syndicate's position, and putting business aside, James knew that Brandenbrooke would loathe being accused of selling out Canada to the Americans.

Especially when they stood to make more money, much more money, invisibly in the long run selling on the open market.

He dialed up Baruch and got through immediately, quickly relating good Sir Edward's proposal, together with his own view. "Winning a proxy battle would be a hollow victory at best. It would invite government intervention, among other less-than-desirable outcomes; however, with their current position secure and well-represented on the board, and with the prospect of substantial market appreciation, Union should go for it.

"What do they really give up? The choice is obvious, Bernie, old boy. A four-for-one stock split and dividend increase will add a minimum of 10% to the stock value immediately! And with earnings forecasted to be forty-eight million dollars next year, it's a win-win situation for all, and you can take that all the way to the bank, guaranteed. To repeat Sir Edward's remark, 'It's a Blackjack'."

Baruch was jubilant as he sized up the situation and related his own views. "What Harriman is likely to do is weigh the long-term gain of going along with the proposal against the political risks of going for the jugular now, with the risk of ending up with a minority position, with no representation, and facing hostile legislation to block future accumulation of voting power.

"Union could bid a large premium for stock and tempt the syndicate to sell out, but it's too late for that maneuver to be effective for the current meeting, and after the national election, they might find themselves stymied by an order in council disallowing foreign control and the prospect of expropriation."

James thanked the man and quickly dialed up Richard for his two-cents. The man answered immediately and listened calmly as James explained the situation. Finally, once James had stopped prattling and babbling in his ear, he let out a sigh of potent relief.

"Oh, wonderful. No more risk of a proxy battle in the middle of the election. Well done, James."

"Nasty things, aren't they?"

"Indubitably. It was the last thing any of us needed right now. Anyway, back to the proposal; it's certainly bullish for the stock. Of course, Union could get around the agreement if they wanted to, using Kuhn-Loeb or some other group to buy while they stayed out of the market. It would be a subterfuge, and hard to control; I'm sure those boys expect that possibility. What Eddie is really after is blocking the syndicate from selling out to Union. They all know there is no honor among buccaneers, not when big money is on the table. And maybe they're right," he laughed sardonically.

"Well, I'm not going to worry about that," James deflected. "They're big boys. They can take their chances. I think we'll either be taking the deal or renegotiating it, if Harriman is in agreement. It makes sense all around, and two years is a lot of time. Who knows what'll be happening two years from now? Maybe you'll be prime minister by then. What do you think of that for an idea?" He chuckled over the phone.

Baruch reported back within an hour. There was one counter-condition: "Harriman and his board will go for the deal, but only if the restriction is for one year. His chairman and his legal advisor, Jacob Manulson, will be in touch with Sir Edward in a few minutes with an amendment in drafting the agreement."

When James advised Sir Edward of the counter condition, you could cut the silence with a knife; until he exploded, "That proves what those bastards are after, goddamn it. We've smoked them out at last, now we know their real agenda. They want their big fat nose in my tent."

"A year is a long time, Eddie, let's go for it; it's your only way," responded James.

Clunk went the phone.

"Whoa, he's hit roof again, Elizabeth," exclaimed James, "He slammed the bloody phone down on me, but I know bloody well he'll be back." It wasn't very long before he was back on the line with fervor.

"My board says, 'No, god dammit, not one year, and not five directors'. We'll settle for eighteen months, and that's it, goddamn it, and only four new directors: that's our bottom line. Brandenbrooke, MacTavish, Harriman, and Baruch. You boys can sure as hell wait a year or two for the next annual meeting to elect your Frenchy!"

"Okay, Eddie, here's the deal: tell your board that I personally will accept eighteen month s on behalf of Union. Okay? Enough of this hair splitting; eighteen months, is that a deal? And the four directors?"

"Yes, goddamn it, that's a deal."

"Good, then we'll get Manulson to write it up."

When Baruch heard the details of the little charade, he burst out laughing. "You traded six months and the Frenchy for the deal, a mere bagatelle; you let him win at least one hand at the table to save face. I'm sure Harriman will go for it. Consider it done."

They congratulated each other, with James advising, "We'll all be appointed directors, and the stock split will be approved at their meeting. I'll keep you posted as soon as I hear from the big chief with confirmation."

In anticipation of everything going according to plan, James decided it was to host a grand celebration, a black tie dinner parry to take place after the meeting at the Saint James Club. Elizabeth took charge; she was better at party planning than he was.

She made arrangements for a private dining room to seat James's twenty-four guests as the list among their number many of the leading lights of Montreal's social and financial elite. Separately, he planned another private dinner for Baruch and Harriman with Sir Edward a few days later, after the dust had settled and passions ebbed, to allow for frank discussions and an opportunity for all of them to get to mow each other on a personal basis.

He fired off a quick cable to Ian, currently in London, alerting him to the day's happenings.

Directors meeting 2 p.m. today. Expect election and resolutions to be carried out as planned and to be ratified at shareholders meeting. Union has entered into certain agreements which are satisfactory to all. Will advise. Watch stock when 4 for 1 announced. Traded here today at $88.

Baruch called to say that Averell Harriman and Manulson had been in touch with Sir Edward and were the drafting the agreement. "We will bring the signed document with us by train."

"Excellent, excellent," said James. "I'll have a car to meet you on arrival, Bernie, and book you here at the Ritz."

"Thank you, James. Look forward to seeing you."

Elizabeth was surprised to discover how much she enjoyed planning the party. The menu was a particular joy. It started off with a caviar and iced vodka appetizer followed by a lovely Chateau Rothchild Lafite with a choice of beef Wellington or venison as the main dish, topped off with a meringue glacier dessert. It felt fulfilling, arranging the minutiae and details to ensure a pleasing evening, and it left her with her feet treading the clouds.

Meanwhile, James pursued details in preparation of the meeting. He was in almost constant contact with Gordon Howard, reviewing proxies and talking with shareholders who were planning to personally attend, trying to ensure their support for the motions. Despite how frantic and rushed everything felt, it did seem as though things were, or at least would be, going along without a hitch. Still, anxious energy built up inside him as he waited for a call to come through from his spy in the enemy camp following their directors' meeting.

Averell Harriman called from New York, confirming his discussion with Sir Edward. The lawyers had completed the agreement restricting share purchases for eighteen months.

"I found him quite agreeable under the circumstances, James. He was very businesslike, and he even said he looked forward to our first meeting. Can you believe it? He confirmed that Bernard and I would both be elected to the board, and he trusted it would be a long and constructive relationship."

"Wow!" enthused James, starry-eyed. "You certainly seem to have tamed the lion, at least for the time being. I'm delighted." He rubbed his jaw. He felt tired and though he made sure to keep impeccably shaven, he could feel prickly stubble under his fingers. Maybe he could take a bit of time and sleep in tomorrow.

"It sure was a drama," he sighed. He definitely needed to shave again. "We're looking forward to meeting you and Bernie on the night train in the morning. I think things have calmed down sufficiently, and you will enjoy meeting a cross-section of the Canadian establishment. They certainly will be interested in meeting you and hearing all about Union Pacific."

A few hours later, the call James had been waiting for came through: 6:30 p.m., from one Sir Edward himself.

"Hello, James. Eddie here. Just called to say we've finished our board meeting and passed all the resolutions that have been agreed upon. Everything is, of course, subject to receiving signed agreements tomorrow from Union Pacific."

"Perfect. He'll be here soon, with all relevant documents."

"Excellent. I'll have the necessary agreements ready and waiting before the meeting commences. You, Brandenbrooke, Harriman and Baruch were all appointed to the board today, subject to shareholder approval." He paused on the other side of the phone. James heard him draw breath before continuing in a surprisingly calm, pleasant, and overall respectful tone, "In spite of our past confrontations, I feel congratulations are in order."

James would ever deny how happy and proud he felt in that moment. "Thank you, Eddie. I'm glad this whole thing has worked out to everyone's satisfaction, in spite of our difficulties. I am extremely optimistic about my group's contribution to your board. You won't regret it. Harriman will be here tomorrow with Baruch, as you know. Perhaps we can all have a drink after the meeting."

"Sounds like a great idea. We'll see you then."

The date was July 22 in the year of our lord 1927. It would be now and forever etched in the mind of Sir James MacTavish. Today was his crowning achievement. Today was his coronation. Today the king arose and took his spot out in the sun. All his past achievements paled in comparison.

This was his victory. Not his alone but certainly primarily his and not Ian's or Richard's. It was a day, the day, he had worked for tirelessly towards since boyhood. He would soon be elected a director of the biggest corporation in Canada and he would vote the largest block of control stock at the annual meeting; larger than any other ever voted by a single shareholder in the company's forty-seven-year history. There would be no doubt about Sir James MacTavish's identity following the meeting. He was about to achieve celebrity status in the Canadian establishment.

Elizabeth joined him in their sitting room as he uncorked a bottle of Dom Perignon champagne and lit his favorite Cuban cigar. He put his arm around her and proposed a toast to their future together, as well as to his two great friends in absentia, Richard B. Benson and Ian Macleod.

It was a proud moment early the following morning when his two famous guests arrived at the Ritz from New York; Averell Harriman, the railroad heir, a man of considerable political and financial influence, together with the legendary Bernard Baruch. At breakfast, they reviewed and joked over some of the gory details of winning the battle royal while James regaled them with blow-by-blow descriptions of his encounters with Sir Edward and his board.

Following a sumptuous breakfast, they took off on a brisk walk from the Ritz to the head office of the Canada Dominion Railway Company. James had walked this path so often in the past few weeks he was sure imprints of his boots could be seen in the pavement.

As soon as they arrived, James and his stalwart partners were ushered into the company's large, four-hundred-seat amphitheatre. The press, who always covered important corporation shareholder meetings such as this one, immediately locked in on the two Americans as they identified themselves to the clerk. Photo flashes went off while they signed the shareholders' register, making it known that they were the well-publicized financial tycoons from Wall Street with the baronet from England rumored to be at the center of the control controversy.

As the directors filed in, Sir Edward, recognizing James and his two friends, greeted them civilly; and after being introduced to Averell Harriman and Bernard Baruch, asked them to join the board table, following their confirmation as directors.

"I presume you have been notified, Sir Edward," advised Harriman, "that Jacob Manulson, Union's attorney, has delivered the commitment documents to your attorneys this morning."

"Yes, yes, all is in order, thank you, Mr. Harriman; and we have circulated copies to all members of our board."

SHAREHOLDERS' PROXIES TAKE CONTROL

The chairman took his seat, and called the forty-seventh annual meeting of shareholders to order. His first order of business being to ask the scrutineers from the Royal Trust Company for their report on the number of shares represented in person, or by proxy, and qualified to vote at the meeting.

While the scrutineers' report was being prepared, the chairman took a moment to address the shareholders regarding the content of the annual report. He directed attention to the four resigning directors who would not be standing for re-election during the ensuing year, waving away any concerns the press might have, and to the four new directors recently proposed and appointed by a resolution of the board, subject to ratification by shareholders.

He handled it masterfully, painting the changing of the guard less as what it was, a concession, and more as something that had been in the works for some time now but had only recently come to fruition. He announced that their names, as well as a brief description of their professional status and personal qualifications, were being circulated to all shareholders present for consideration.

James glanced at Harriman and Baruch with a look of relief The decks had been cleared for confirmation of their election and the approval of the agreement with Union.

The scrutineers declared, they had completed their report and handed it to the chairman.

Sir Edward, reading from the report, stated that there were 8,634,000 shares represented at the meeting, in person or by proxy. Of these, 763,000 were represented in person with the rest being represented by proxy. Furthermore, a little over four million shares were in favor of management, which amounted to almost 49% of all the shares present at the meeting. The rest were in favor of Sir James MacTavish.

Harriman's expression as he eyeballed his partners was telling. "We've made it by a very thin margin, only one hundred ninety thousand votes, barely one and three quarters percent. I wonder what would have happened if they had gained those votes," he thought.

There followed a hushed silence, and then a flood of questions from surprised shareholders concerning the voting power of one new director. "Who is this man, MacTavish, Mr. Chairman?" asked a shareholder.

"Allow me to introduce Baruch and Harriman from the U.S.A.," he made a gesture prompting the two to stand, "and Sir James MacTavish, of course. They are three of the four new directors.

168

The fourth director, Lord Brandenbrooke of London, England, isn't currently present. They are all very welcome newcomers to the board, especially Sir MacTavish."

He proceeded to lay out a summary of James' professional history, drawing particular attention to his time in Canada and England as a financier for a number of well-known industrial enterprises. Baruch and Harriman exchanged discreet but telling looks behind his back. They supposed this would be just one of many slights they would have to deal with.

"Furthermore, Sir MacTavish will be casting his votes independently on each resolution on the agenda as the meeting proceeded, representing major shareholders in Canada, England, and the United States. Now, moving on to the next article of business, we need to pass a resolution ratifying all acts of the board of directors, including the board's resolution of July 19.

"For those of you who weren't present, that was the resolution altering the capitalization of the company by a division of the share capital on a basis of four new shares for each old share. It will also increase the dividends by 12.5% or up to $3.60 per share, pre-split; an equivalent of $0.90 per share, post split. Who would like to move?"

"I will."

"I second the motion."

"Moved by Mr. G. Watson and seconded by Mr. J.D. Kippen. All in favor?"

James jumped into his feet and facing the meeting, declared, "I hereby cast my proxy of 4,412,000 shares in favor of the resolutions." He gave a brief dissertation on the sound reasons for the resolutions and the benefits, which he felt would accrue to the company and its shareholders.

Following the chairman's address on the year's activities and his vision of the company's future, it was time to elect the new board of directors to hold office until the next annual meeting.

A resolution was moved and seconded. The secretary read out the names of fourteen nominees, including Lord Brandenbrooke of London England, Sir James MacTavish of London England, Mr. Bernard Baruch of New York, and Mr. Averell Harriman of New York. The chairman asked if there were any other names to be nominated. There being no motion for further nominations, he declared nominations closed.

"I therefore put the vote to the meeting."

Sir James was on his feet again in support of the slate of directors as presented, and again cast his proxy in favor of the resolution.

The chairman then asked, "All in favor- contrary minded? I declare the resolution passed unanimously."

After all other business of the meeting had been concluded, the chairman asked, "Is there any other business to come before this meeting?" As there were no further questions from the floor, he declared the meeting terminated, and reminded the shareholders that lunch would be served at 12:30.

The lunch that followed was a rare experience for Bernard Baruch and Averell Harriman, being in the company of leaders of Canadian industry and finance for the first time.

James made every effort, took every opportunity, to introduce himself and his partners to the many prominent shareholders present. There was Sir Herbert Holt, president of the Royal Bank of Canada and Sir Frederick Williams Taylor, president of the Bank of Montreal, as well as

W. BRUCE KIPPEN

Mr. T.B. Macaulay, the president of the Sun Life Assurance Company of Canada, all immensely important people who made a distinct impression on him.

And there were the presidents of Dominion Cement Corporation, of the Steel Company of Canada, and of the Consolidated Paper Corporation; names both old and familiar to the businessman. The list of Montreal's Anglo establishment was so long as to be called endless and it included among its number those anxious to both see and be seen at such an august assembly of self-styled elitists.

Sir Edward and his board made an effort to make their three new directors feel at home, in spite of the tensions and rancor that had preceded the final agreement, and expressed an interest in seeing Averell Harriman privately following the meeting. "Would four o'clock today be suitable, Mr. Harriman?" asked Sir Edward.

"Why certainly! I look forward to having a chat with you, Sir Edward."

"Excellent. Could we meet here in my office, then, at four p.m.?"

Harriman agreed with enthusiasm, and James was delighted to hear they were going to get together.

Following their lunch, they made their back to the hotel, stopping to pick up some of the afternoon newspapers. The Montreal Star's headline glared back at the two: C.D.R. Control Remains Canadian. The Herald's headline emphasized a change in the board: American Tycoons New Directors of C.D.R. It came complete with front page news concerning the details of the stock split and dividend increase.

The minute James was in his suite, the phone rang. It was Jack Kippen reporting the reaction to financial news on the street.

"The stock is active at eighty-nine dollars, James. The stock split and dividend news has been accepted bullishly, of course, and the street is talking of ninety-five dollars per share before year end, or twenty-four dollars for the new stock."

"Great, Jack. Looks like we're in the money, see you tonight at the dub. It's going to be a glorious evening."

CANADA IN THE LIMELIGHT

Harriman and Baruch, being the guests of honor at the dinner in a large private dining room of the Mount Royal Club reserved for the occasion, were introduced by James to the star-studded group of Montrealers, as two of Wall Street's modestly successful players, bringing down the room in a roar of laughter.

Before dessert was served, he stood to say a few words about the day's activities and the election to the board of Mr. Bernard Baruch, Mr. Averell Harriman of New York, and Lord Brandenbrooke of London, and making a particular reference to Ian Macleod and their thirty-year relationship.

He highlighted the forthcoming general election and proposed a toast and good wishes to his friend, Richard B. Benson, as the future Prime Minister of Canada, now campaigning in the riding of Calgary South in Alberta.

Bernard Baruch rose to thank James for the inspiring evening. He then turned to the other guests, saying, "Gentlemen. I can't tell you what a great honor it is for me to be here in Canada for the first time, for me to have been elected to the board of your illustrious Canada Dominion Railway Corporation. I can only imagine what an amazing experience this will be.

"We at Wall Street have often gazed northwards, envious of this vibrant young land, rife with beauty and unparalleled resources and potential. Our countries may be incredibly distinct one from the other, but there is much we have in common. We share the longest undefended border in the world. In the world! Nowhere else are two neighbours more trusting and at peace." James could probably say something about that, but he held his tongue. There was a time and a place for cheek, and this was neither.

Baruch continued, "The American capital looks at Canada as the outstanding country of opportunity for our foreign investments. That is why a small group of us have invested heavily in C.D.R. shares. We will grow with you as your country continues to expand, fulfilling its potential alongside your very friendly and ever admiring neighbor. Thank you again, Sir James, and good luck to you all."

He bowed low as the room filled with enthusiastic applause, returning to his chair soon after. Averell Harriman took to the floor in his absence. "I would just like to add something to Bernard Baruch's wonderful speech. It has always seemed to many of us in the United States that nature has so endowed our two countries that we share the same destiny, leading the world in the development of industrial technology, natural resources, and scientific discoveries. May I propose a toast to Canada, the emerging giant of the north. To Canada! And to peace and harmony between us forever more!"

Enthusiastic applause was followed by more brandy and some of James's favorite malt whisky, received by special shipment from Inverness, Scotland, only a few days earlier.

The dinner celebrations ran long and loud, easy chatter filling the room, the tension of trying times falling away. The trio were among the last to leave, strolling back to the Ritz for a roundup of the day's exciting activities.

"I must admit, being in Canada for the first time has been a revelation to me," confessed Averell Harriman. "You Canadians are both strange and familiar. You speak like us but act like Brits. In fact, I can detect a strong cultural bias to England. Some of the directors I met tonight seemed to emulate some of my friends in London clubs, especially the titled ones. In New York, we often hear about Canada being a British colony, but I never quite understood what that meant. Considering that only three hundred miles separates us, it's extremely interesting to observe how much our cultures seem to differ."

"You've put your finger on it, Averell; Canada and the United States could be certainly more alike than they are, but our histories happen to have run completely different courses. For one example, you've built your economy around the principles of Adam Smith and Thomas Reid, driven by individual self interest, common sense, and a desire for limited government direction. Canada meanwhile, being a British colony, was controlled and in many cases financed from the top down.

"We may no longer be a British colony, but the unfortunate truth about this country is that too many Canadians still harbor a colonial mentality. Indeed, some of our new merchant princes have a regretful tendency to become more English than the English," asserted James. "It's one thing to have a title as I have; it's good for business in England's class-based society, but I've gone to great lengths to make it clear that I'm a Canadian, goddamn it.

"I have no interest in pretending to be anything else. Canada made me what I am today and I am proud of that. Ian is much the same, in that regard. But to answer your query, the essential difference between our two cultures goes all the way back to 1776, when the Americans took on George III. You rejected everything British and as such you were set adrift to form a republic in your own image.

"We, on the other hand, never did nor had to do that. Instead, we voluntarily imported the British parliamentary system, the culture, the traditions, the system of law. As a colony, it's been a mixed blessing, but it's what's at the root of this great difference between our two cultures, divided by the 49th parallel."

"What's your take on Canadians, Bernie, from all your travels to England, Ireland, and Scotland?" asked James.

"The interesting thing to me," observed Baruch, "is that Canadians are as different from the Americans as the Scots are from the Irish or the Irish from the English. The paradox has often been cited: how is it that two great nations can who speak the same language, share similar religions, originate from similar countries, and yet be so different?

"England, Ireland, and Scotland, so similar and so dissimilar; founders of two of the world's greatest democracies. We are cousins and yet we have such difficulty understanding each other's cultures. How can this be? The answer, I believe, must lie in our diverse histories, and in the fact that Americans know precious little history of other countries.

"I think you really nailed the divergence point on the head earlier, James. If you recall, after that revolution some two centuries ago, almost 200,000 Americans rejected our republic, rebelled against our rebellion, and fled to Canada. We called them United Empire Loyalists; Monarchists. Isn't that precisely what tied Canadians to the British values which have persisted for over two hundred years?"

"That's exactly right, Bernie, and I think I can say, with some regret, that we have made a point in this country of being un-American."

"Getting back to business, and speaking of Canadians," interjected Harriman, "that fellow Montgomerie, Sir Edward, the president; seems to me he'd be more at home in London than New York. I suppose being knighted tends to influence your demeanor somewhat. Of course he was guarded about the railroad business, but I'm hopeful we'll be able to exchange useful data from time to time."

James happily sighed, "Well, it's been a long and bumpy ride, gentlemen, but it seems we've survived the stormy seas, the unexpected typhoons and whirlpools, and now have arrived safely at the harbor, carrying with us an impeccable bounty. To us!" he cheered, miming raising a glass. "To control of the largest transportation company in the world and a profit of over one hundred million dollars for the effort; not bad for a team of poor boys, eh?"

"I'll drink to that!" Harriman toasted.

"Just you wait till we get back to my hotel and then we'll drink. Now what's your forecast for the stock over the next six months, Bernie?"

"Well, I'd say we're in the grip of a very powerful bull market; not only in the U.S.A. but throughout the industrialized world. Judging by how things have been progressing, I'd be willing to bet on American corporate earnings expanding by 18% over the next several years."

"That's very specific."

"Could be more, could be less, but I have a good feeling about that 18%. The Dow Jones Industrial could reach the four hundred level. C.D.R., with the current year's earnings approaching fifty million dollars, could trade as high as a hundred dollars on the old stock, or twenty-five dollars per share, past the share split."

"Then you're recommending we hold our position and ride out the bullish trend."

"Absolutely, that's the way I see it," replied Baruch. "How does Lord Brandenbrooke view the situation?"

"I think he would share the same outlook as you do. The only thing that worries me is, if the Liberals win the election here, we may see a sell off; Richard is a bit apprehensive."

James poured each of them a nightcap of his highland malt whisky, toasted their good health, and bid them good night, returning to Elizabeth's suite with a smile on his lips.

"What a day!" he thought to himself "What a prize! And what will the future hold as the universe continues to unfold?"

The next morning saw Montreal's morning newspapers, English and French, carrying front-page articles on C.D.R.'s annual meeting. There was a list included with the names of prominent shareholders in attendance predominantly displayed, alongside a full report on the meeting, the resolutions passed, and the election of directors. There was special emphasis on the new directors from the United States and England.

The stock opened on New York, up a full two dollars, at ninety two, with an announcement that the new stock following, the four-for-one split, would be called for trading on August 4.

James decided to invite a small group for lunch at the club in honor of his prominent American guests. Conversations around the table were generally bullish, with predictions that the new stock would reach twenty-five dollars by the year's end based on projected earnings of one dollar and twenty-five cents per share, and a price-earning multiple of twenty.

Jack Kippen was quick to remind everyone that back in 1912 the old stock had traded as high as seventy dollars per share on earnings of a meager nineteen million dollars for a price earnings multiple of over twenty five.

The Montreal guests were extremely interested in the views of Mr. Harriman and Mr. Baruch on the American economy. Baruch expressed his optimism that Herbert Hoover might well be the next Republican president of the United States.

Before their departure on the night train to New York, James presented his summary of the syndicate's position. They had bought two million, eight hundred thousand shares, starting at twenty-five dollars per share and averaging thirty-five dollars per share, or ninety-eight million dollars.

Following the four-for-one split, their share position would total 11,200,000 shares, each share costing approximately $8.50 per. With a current market value of slightly over $246,000,000 and an unrealized profit of $148,000,000, before making adjustments for bank interest charges, dividends received, and shares optioned to friends for support in the crises; the numbers were enough to make James' head spin.

The syndicate had borrowed heavily to finance its position, putting up an equity of only $25,000,000 and borrowing approximately $73,600,000 against the value of the stock for an unrealized return on equity of over five hundred percent, if Baruch's forecast was close to the mark.

The syndicate was divided seventy percent between Lord Brandenbrooke, Sir James MacTavish, and Richard B. Benson, while twenty-five percent was divided between Baruch and his associates in New York, including Kuhn Loeb and secretary of commerce, Herbert Hoover.

Now each of the three frontier pioneers, or the Gold Dust Trio, as they had been nicknamed in 1901 in Calgary, had twenty-five percent of the syndicate with a profit at current market prices of approximately thirty-seven million dollars.

Based upon Baruch's forecast, an additional six million each was a distinct possibility, bringing their individual winnings for their risky and ingenious scheme to approximately forty million dollars.

That evening at dinner, James, his face aglow with pride, reviewed the numbers with Elizabeth, "Not bad for three poor boys from Atlantic Canada, and all in less than thirty years. What do we do for an encore?"

"You can marry me," she shot back, lifting her glass with tears of happiness in her twinkling blue eyes.

"Ah," smiled James, as he kissed her, "Of course, and that will be my ultimate reward."

The next morning, he received a telegram from Richard and his attention was once again magnetized on the remaining days of his election campaign. As he packed his bags in preparation for his return to England after so long in Montreal, he reread the missive in his head.

> The campaign gets more intense each day. I am traveling the prairies, making three speeches a day. Financial position of the party isn't bad but we're running close. Any contribution would be a great help. Have put in over three hundred thousand dollars of my own money as you know. Richard

It took him a little time to draw up a suitable response but he sent it off almost as soon as he had it.

> Forwarding check tomorrow to party headquarters, for $100,000. I have wired Ian for a similar amount, should I take the train west and join the campaign in Calgary? James

Richard replied he wouldn't be there that much, as he was campaigning across the provinces from Winnipeg to Edmonton, etc., for other candidates. "Just keep sending me your moral support. Nice to know that railroad issue is behind us. Could have been a nasty piece of business, politically."

PRICELESS HEADLINE

In London, Lord Brandenbrooke reveled in the prestigious headlines, stories, and editorials he had engineered through his papers, highlighting his election to the board of the Canada Dominion Railway, along with Sir James MacTavish and Baruch and Harriman. Of all, the many headlines to be found, Ian's favorite had to be: CANADIAN INDUSTRIALIST ELECTS BARUCH AND HARRIMAN TO BOARD OF C.D.R.

The dramatic headlines resulted in a timely invitation to dine at 10 Downing Street, allowing Ian to recount to the prime minister the tale of James's controlled drama in heading off American control of Canada's greatest enterprise, and of their combined support of the Conservative Party of Canada.

"I believe James will be in a position to enhance your party's financial coffers substantially as soon as he returns to London. It shouldn't be more than a few weeks from now."

"I'll be happy to see him. Tell me, I heard a rumor not long ago that both you and he had contributed to Canada's Conservative Party in support of a Mr. Richard Benson?"

"Indeed we have, sir, $100,000 each. He's liable to be prime minister before the end of the decade. I could introduce you, if you'd like? He's a good man, perfect for the job. He's also a dear friend of James'."

"Is he now?"

"Yes sir, a good friend and very proud. If you let him, he'll brag about James' contributions. Why, just the other day he sent me a wire bragging about how James was humbly helping to advance trade relations between the United Kingdom and Canada. He just went on and on about James was as stalwart as a knight in defense of both countries, how he was securing support for the Conservative Party wherever he went."

"Well, if he's done half of what Richard says he's done, he's more than earned a knighthood. We might have to give that some serious consideration. I look forward to seeing him upon his return to England. I heard he's been heading those Wall Street buccaneers off at the pass certainly deserves our attention." He chuckled heartily.

Pausing to think, he pondered, "As I'm sure you know, only five Canadians have ever been offered peerage. What I've always found interesting is that of those five, only one of them ever refused. Prime Minister Andrew Bonar Law declined any title he was offered, even an earldom, when he retired from politics. Frankly, I've never understood why."

Ian shrugged. "I'm afraid I wouldn't know. Law was many things, a friend, a mentor, an ally, but he was never particularly clear on that fact."

The National Telegraph, founded in 1894 and owned by the estate of the late Lord Wellstrom, had been a point of notice for James and Ian for several years. It was a prestigious politically-orientated paper with an impressive circulation. James was aware of several press barons, such as the Lords Northcliffe, Rothermere, and Camrose, who had taken a serious look into the paper when it was rumored to be for sale.

Luckily for James and Ian, Lady Wellstrom, at the time, had not responded to their overtures, for one simple reason: James, a long-standing friend and member of her advisory committee, had counseled her against selling, quoting his estimate of the paper's value and comparing it to the somewhat lacking offers from the press barons.

Now it seemed it might be time to renew that relationship. In a letter Ian had written him, summing up his conversations with the prime minister, he encouraged him to charm Lady Wellstrom once again into renewing discussions concerning the National when he returned.

> We'll go 50-50 on an acquisition deal. We could consolidate our printing presses in one plant, enhance our arsenal of public relations through increased circulation, and add leverage to our political influence, to the delight of the prime minister. We both know what that can mean.

CONSERVATIVES FALL

Election Day proved to be the busiest in Canadian history. Massive crowds of people turned out, casting more votes than ever before. And when the polling booths were closed and the votes were counted, the results came rolling in.

The Conservatives had outvoted the Liberals by exactly 83,050 votes.

The Liberals had won the election.

This was due to the constituency representation of the Canadian electoral system. It wasn't the individual votes that mattered but the seats. The Liberals won a hundred and twenty-five seats to the Conservatives' ninety-one. On the positive side, as much of one as there was, Richard won his seat in Calgary South, the only Conservative elected in the three prairie provinces of Western Canada.

The loss was a shattering blow to both the party leader, Arthur Meighen, who lost his own seat, and to Richard, who had never worked harder or longer in any past campaign. Alas, the Liberals swept the province of Quebec, which had never really forgiven the Conservative Party's wartime conscription issue of 1917.

Richard, depressed and disillusioned with his failure to gain support in the west, was confined to Ottawa, a member of the shadow cabinet of His Majesty's Loyal Opposition. He had to swallow his pride and contain his ego, biting down his contempt for his nemesis, Mackenzie King, all the while being compelled to observe him across the house

Arthur Meighen, leader of the party in spite of protests to the contrary, made a decision to resign. He appointed a committee to determine a new procedure for choosing a new leader.

Richard wrote to James; among the general news and chitchat of the letter, he penned down his thoughts on the political situation.

> It's time we elected a leader of this party from the grass roots, in a full fledged
> party convention. There are at least four or five party stalwarts in the running,
> but I will not declare myself until the caucus is convened and the method of
> election is determined.

James penned back a quick message, mostly about how Richard could count on him and Ian to contribute $200,000 each, should he decide to run. He also told his old friend about his plans to sail to London on August 28, meaning that instead of being in town for the convention, he'd be overseas trying to acquire a newspaper.

He also penned down a private idea he'd had to acquire the Central Canada Steel Corporation, which was for sale as a result of a financial crises in the family of the controlling British shareholder.

A couple of months later, in October, the Conservative Party caucus took place and made an important decision, a first in the history of Canada: they decided to convene a national convention of grassroots members to elect a new leader.

Richard fiddled with his tie and twiddled his thumbs, a well-dressed bundle of nervous energy; it was clear his time had come. He announced his candidacy to run against five other contenders, most of whom had equally strong claims to the throne.

Concurrent with preparing for the convention, he also engaged in negotiations for the sale of the Ottawa Valley Match Company to Ivar Kreuger, the world-famous Swedish Match King. The company was worth a little over three million dollars and Kreuger was perhaps the most famous international financier of the 1920s, reputed to control half of the world's match market.

They met in New York to finalize terms, but fortunately did not sign a deal. Over the course of their acquaintance, Richard had slowly become apprehensive and suspicious of Mr. Kreuger's grandiose scheme, eventually writing to Ian to call the whole thing off.

Ian,

There's something about Mr. Kreuger I'm unable to fathom; he troubles me. I'm pulling out.

Richard

A few years later, in 1932, Kreuger would commit suicide. In the aftermath of this startling event, it would become known that he was one of the world's most accomplished scoundrels. From Wall Street to England and most places in between, bankers and brokers and chartered accountants would come forth to announce what he had manage to finagle out from under their fingers: $500,000,000, by way of his sophisticated bookkeeping scams.

Richard's leadership campaign got off to a slow start. Canadian newspapers paid little attention at first, mesmerized by a hundred other stories from across the border: Charles Lindberg's solo flight across the Atlantic, Bill Tilden's tennis epics, Bobby Jones's pursuit of his second British open golf championship, Charles Chaplin's divorce from Lita Grey, and Babe Ruth's sixtieth home run in Yankee Stadium.

However, his speech in Winnipeg at the convention was dynamic, focusing on Canadian history and the building of the Canadian economy, with innovative fiscal and monetary policies to perpetuate the prosperity of the 1920s.

He pulled ahead on the first ballot and increased his percentage to win on the second, eventually emerging as the undisputed leader of the party. Once the votes were tallied and the results were in, he accepted the position with a rousing speech, stating, "It has been said that I am a man of great wealth; that is true. But I came by my wealth through my own tireless efforts in this great land. Thus, I see it as a solemn trust to enable me to serve my country objectively, without fear or regard for my future."

It would be three more years before his star would rise in a national election, and he was able to draw a bead on his nemesis, Mackenzie King, who he had studied for years; maintaining that he was one of the most accomplished Machiavellian politicians of the century, a master of compound sentences, the man he dubbed, "the most contemptible charlatan ever to darken the annals of Canadian politics."

BULLS OF NEW ERA

The Dow Jones Industrial Average topped two hundred in the third quarter of 1927, as did the Times Industrial Average. American corporate earnings were ahead each quarter, confirming the growing belief that a new era had dawned, with America leading the world with industrial innovations and the dynamics of a free-enterprise economy. In New York, the carousels of pleasure turned and ticked away as dozens of speakeasies enriched bootleggers and defied the law.

Will Rogers was often quoted as saying, "Prohibition is a sight better than no booze at all."

The three titans, fully invested in prominent Canadian industrial enterprises as they were, were well-positioned to ride the crest of the prosperity wave. As America boomed, so too did its neighbor to the north. The Montreal Stock Exchange led the charge to ever greater heights as the year 1927 came to a prosperous and enticing close, with stock-exchange averages up over 25%.

The capitalist world sailed blithely into 1928, seemingly without a cloud in the sky. It seemed to everyone that common stock prices were simply catching up to the steady increases in corporate earnings and productivity. In the month of March alone, the industrial exchange averages rose by twenty-five points, nearly 12%, catapulting reports of the boiling market into national headlines.

And as winter slowly gave way to spring, the nature of the boom changed, now a psychology of unfettered exuberance, a euphoria of speculation on the New York Stock Exchange. Many a skeptic likened it to other fleeting incidents throughout the history of humanity, from the tulip mania of the seventeenth century to the great speculative orgy of the South Sea bubble in the early eighteenth century.

Onboard a ship bound for Europe in the spring of 1928, John J. Roskob, a director of General Motors, was met with journalists. He was more than happy to tell them all about automobile sales, to tell them of General Motors' share of the market. He predicted that the earning prospects should command a share price of eighteen times earnings, approximately $225 per share. This would result in moving the stock immediately when published from 187 to 199, setting off a great burst of increased volume of trading across the board.

Likewise, the mighty knights of the automobile, steel, rail, and radio industries were all issuing forecasts of boundless optimism. And then, all of a sudden, it came to a screeching halt.

June 12. Over five million shares spontaneously changed hands. The market fell in a steep decline, the ticker now running two hours behind for the first time. A New York paper reported the collapse of 'Wall Street's bull market'; stating it went out with a detonation heard around the world.

This opinion was countered by a man named Andrew W Mellon of the Mellon Bank in Pittsburgh, a founder of Gulf Oil Corporation in Texas and former Secretary of Treasury, who stated publicly, "There is no cause for worry; the high tide of prosperity will continue."

PEERAGE, THE GOAL IS PRICELESS

In London, James met with his old friend, Lady Jane Wellstrom. She was a sweet older lady with a sharp mind for business and a great desire for peace of mind in her twilight years. It was an easy task, charming her into reconsidering the sale of her controlling interest in the National Telegraph Publication Company, which was experiencing a decline in daily circulation.

Lady Jane, recognizing her publication was in need of new blood with a more stimulating editorial policy, was willing to sell but quick to advise that her executors had put a value of seven hundred and fifty thousand pounds on the property. James' research had suggested that a more accurate appraisal value would be closer to six hundred and fifty thousand pounds. He told her he would get back to her with a firm offer.

"I can buy the National Telegraph from her ladyship for seven hundred and fifty thousand pounds, and have offered her six hundred and fifty thousand pounds," he informed Ian. "What do you think? And by the by, what's with the prime minister these days? That's also going to take a piece of change, no doubt!"

"Grab the paper, James!" Ian enthused. "It's a steal at her price; the savings of utilizing our presses at the Express alone will pay for bank interest costs, which is really what we need," he chortled. "And as for the prime minister, you'd better get your checkbook out, my boy, these jewels have gone up in price lately.

"I have it on good authority that the prime minister has been reviewing your accomplishments, including your Norwegian saga. And just the other night, he even casually suggested to me, with a merry little twinkle in his eye, 'Why doesn't Sir James follow your example and buy a newspaper? It's been know to sometimes help to gain membership into that exclusive dub he yearns for so adamantly.'

"That paper, James, the National, is a gem of a paper. It's priceless. You can't compare it to any other tabloid rag. Here, Oscar Wilde put it best. I don't remember the exact wording so just let me paraphrase here: journalists give us the opinions of the uneducated to keep us in touch with the ignorance of the community."

"That settles it," blurted James, "I'll do deal with Jane; you're dead right: it's cheap at the price."

If there was one thing James had learned from Ian, it was the subtle influences newspapers could bring to support or intimidate politicians. He could recognize that the greater the circulation, the greater the publishers' influence, power, and prestige. Ian's immense ego and drive for power had propelled him into journalism, where megalomania reigns supreme and is contagious; and James had caught the bug, and was ecstatic at the prospect.

"The question is most asked," continued Ian, "is what's the value of being a member of the peerage?" And then, with jovial sarcasm, he added, "Those chinless wonders, the fox hunters of the House of Lords, the tally-ho boys, the Brahmins of social capital; what do you gain by joining them and becoming a baron or a viscount?

"When you weigh the pros and costs, the conclusion becomes obvious: in the British structured society, the caste system, as I call it, the goal is priceless. And you know what they say about prices: if you have to ask the price, you can't afford it and shouldn't bother. And don't forget the expenses attached to a title; you have to live and act the part."

"By Jove, jolly good show, old boy!" James chuckled, pontificating in his best English accent, acting the part, "I say, what old chap; and all that sort of thing."

As their railroad investment continued enhancing their wealth, trading at over twenty-nine dollars per share, their acquisitive natures became greater than ever. With their friend Herbert Hoover now in sight of the White House and Richard on his way to becoming the next prime minister of Canada, the partners were caught amidst the throes of heady visions of grandeur.

Leading American blue-chip stocks continued their bull run through the summer of 1928. Radio Corporation had gained just a little over two hundred points, from eighty-five. Dupont, in the past two years, had risen from three hundred and ten to over four hundred and fifty dollars. Wright Aeronautics rose from sixty to a hundred and eighty-seven.

The year was making headlines as the 'get rich' year of the American dream, with the public, including shoeshine boys, flocking to the market like moths to a flame. Newspapers quoted pearls of wisdom from the financial gurus of the day.

One prominent observer, writing for an issue of World's Work was quoted as saying, "After reflecting on the wonders of the past markets, one must understand the difference between a gambler and an investor. A gambler wins only when someone else loses, whereas with an investor, all will gain. One investor buys General Motors at a hundred dollars, sells it to another at a hundred and twenty-five who sells it to a third at a hundred and fifty, and so on and so forth, with everyone making money."

As a sad statement of fact, relatively few Wall Street players recognized the absurdity of such a statement; there was no surer sign that vast illusions and the madness of mob mentality was taking hold as the market continued its merry rise with intermittent corrections.

Even the great sage Baruch was quoted as saying at a dinner meeting at the Waldorf Astoria, "The economic condition of the world seems to be on the verge of a great forward movement. After all, bears don't have mansions on Fifth Avenue, do they?"

And President Calvin Coolidge joked, "The secret of financial success is to buy a sound stock, wait until it goes up, and then sell it. If it doesn't go up, don't buy it."

Later that year, Bernard Baruch's close friend and confidant, Herbert Hoover, the former secretary of commerce in the Republican Party, was elected president of the United States. A 'victory boom' ensued, enhancing New York market indexes by ten to fifteen points, with record volume.

The next week, an astonishing number of shares changed hands, over six and a half million, far exceeding all previous records. During these heady days, Canada Dominion Railway shares traded heavily – over twenty-seven dollars following the four-for-one split, up from twenty-two dollars a month earlier.

James continued his negotiations with Lady Jane Wellstrom regarding the purchase of the National Telegram Publication Company, spurred on by the prime minister's encouraging remarks to Ian about journalism and peerage. At a club reception some weeks later, he was delighted to meet up with him, hearing once again his subtle reference, half in jest, to the benefits that can flow from a Fleet Street address. James seized the opportunity, advising that he was on the acquisition trail of a publishing company, and that the deal could close within a few weeks.

"Well, well, congratulations James, that seems interesting. We politicians, as you know, always enjoy having friends in Fleet Street; especially those on our team. Best of luck; do keep me posted."

It was an exciting summer and fall for Canada's Titans, as the year 1928 sped along, and their net worth continued expanding, allowing the liquidation of some holdings to fund the newspaper-and-steel-company acquisitions, but the syndicate remained intact, with its 11.2 million shares of C.D.R., following the four-for-one split.

In the late fall, Baruch wrote to the Titans, his letter full to the gills with concern.

James,

Please share this with Ian. There's something screwy going on. Hoover's made some comments about excessive stock market speculation, and I've been seeing a lot of credit-driven transactions on the stock exchanges. It might be prudent to start selling the shares. I think the syndicate should try to reduce its debt by at least twenty-five million dollars. Also, it might be a good idea to reduce your exposure to a possible severe market correction.

Baruch

MEGALOMANIA

It was a bright, sunny morning as James was chauffeured along Piccadilly and the Strand into Fleet Street to close his transaction to acquire one of England's oldest newspaper publications.

Two hours later, he emerged as the proud owner of the National Telegraph Publication Company. The company had a massive circulation, over two million. He rushed over to the offices of the Commonwealth Express to draft news releases announcing the deal. Included in the news releases would be a detailed review of his business career in Canada and England, including repeated references to his recent success in saving the Canada Dominion Railway Company from the clutches of American interlopers.

He quipped to Ian, "Seven hundred and fifty thousand pounds for international publicity like this; you were dead right: the ink is priceless. I love that line about the Canadian Dominion Railway epic." He exclaimed with exuberance, "It will go down beautifully with the prime minister, supporting his recommendation to the king."

The morning newspapers in London carried a variety of headlines: "Sir James MacTavish, Canadian Industrialist, buys National Telegraph." "Canadian Associate of Lord Brandenbrooke buys control of National Telegraph." "Millionaire Canadian industrialist and railway tycoon, Sir James MacTavish, buys National Telegraph."

The frontier boys were in their element and the headlines certainly confirmed their long-standing principle: When you own newspapers, you own your own public relations firm; your own self promotion is a free bonus.

James couldn't help his exuberance as he waved a number of headline copies. Messages of congratulation poured in from every center. He had developed celebrity status overnight, so much so, that he was in danger of being blinded by his own ego. It was a common failing among self-made tycoons, sometimes resulting in disastrous business decisions which reduced them to the status of their humble beginnings.

"Megalomania is an occupational hazard in our business; it's a narcotic," Ian wisely counseled as they wallowed in the heady prestige of newspaper barons, with fame and fortune enveloping their lives.

"Yes, indeed," confirmed James, "Who was the wise old sage that wrote: 'While all excesses are hurtful, the most dangerous and damaging is unlimited good fortune?'"

TRUST AND PEERAGE

At the same time these matters were proceeding, negotiations continued with the Dunbartan Trust for the purchase of control of Central Canada Steel. The reason behind the purchase was the eventual goal of either merging with or selling to one of the company's greatest competitors, the Canadian Steel Corporation, which Ian had financed in 1910.

The deal, if completed, would result in the largest steel company in Canada, and the fifth-largest in North America. James organized a syndicate to finance part of the financial commitment, retaining forty percent of the voting stock to control the board and elect himself chairman, preparatory to commencing negotiations for a profitable merger.

The last months of 1928 witnessed even greater stock market frenzy and appreciation. Companies like General Electric hit three hundred dollars per share. Meanwhile, brokers' loans in Wall Street rose to an all-time high of over six billion dollars.

Canada Dominion stock surpassed their objective of thirty dollars, trading in volume at thirty-two, and again Baruch advised that the syndicate sell up to 900,000 shares and reduce their loan position by at least twenty-five million dollars. He personally undertook the handling of an orderly distribution of this sizable block, and they all agreed, giving him the green light.

At a gathering of Conservatives at the Carleton Club, James, Ian, and other press lords all enjoyed being catered to by members of the party, whose political destinies would be influenced by their editorials during the forthcoming election campaign.

The prime minister advised James that his baronial title would be announced by the king in his New Year's honors list and that he must submit his name selection to Garter King of Arms immediately.

He had considered a number of suitable names from his home province in New Brunswick, Canada, including Stonehaven, Eastbrook, and Fredericton. But the name he chose in the end was Dungarven, in honor of the town he was born in. As such, he would be Baron Dungarven of Dungarven, New Brunswick, and Five Oaks, Surrey.

Between setting policy at the National Telegraph, financing his acquisition of the steel company, acting on behalf of the syndicate in reducing their stock position, and preparing for his baronial appointment, Sir James MacTavish was burning his unending energy with an exhilarating sense of achievement and optimism.

A cable from Richard in Ottawa was disturbing, however.

> Understand prime minister has been consulted regarding your peerage as a Canadian citizen, which runs contrary to a 1919 parliamentary resolution against titles for Canadians. You may have to give up your Canadian citizenship unless Baldwin will proceed without support of Prime Minister King.

Ian exploded in a blind rage upon receiving this news over the phone from James. "That obsequious son of a bitch!" he snarled. "James, you know my opinion of King. To quote an old sage, 'He has all the virtues I dislike and none of the vices I admire'. Where the hell does he think he'd coming from? The two of us already have titles already. He's playing silly buggers. It's his personal fixation; I'm sure it's not the attitude of the Conservative party."

James would never claim to be anywhere near as proficient in matters of law as Richard, but he was good when it came to research; and a short visit to the local library yielded fruit: there was no law against a Canadian being honored by Britain's monarch or by its government.

Incensed, he stormed down to 10 Downing Street to strongly plead his case to the prime minister. The man in question was well aware of the fact that much of James' political support and capital commitment was at stake; he agreed to let the recommendation stand, in spite of political interference from Canada.

The new year brought with it the official announcement of his elevation to the peerage. Some of his friends in the House of Lords decided to organize a black-tie dinner party to celebrate on the eve of the ceremony. Soon, he would cease to be a 'Sir' and become a 'Lord'. His friends congratulated him, calling him Lord even before he received the title. Such a potent word; he stood straighter the more they said it, puffed out his chest and squared his jaw.

Elizabeth, present at the ceremony, sat relishing the moment, peering down from her vantage point onto the illustrious Chamber of Lords. James, in all his finery, dressed resplendently in a red robe trimmed with ermine and ribbon, was escorted by his peers to the Lord Chancellor. Kneeling before him with all the grace deserving of his new title, he presented his Latiens patent, as the reading clerk pronounced the terms of his royal summons.

Licking his lips, he took the oath. "I, James, Baron of Dungarven, do swear to bear true allegiance to the king and his successors according to the law. So, help me God."

The Chamber of Peers gave an aristocratic and enthusiastic cheer.

The great moment had come, James MacTavish, with style and dignity had become a peer of the realm, joining the blue bloods of political influence. He beamed immodestly as he gazed at Elizabeth in the gallery and in typical candid fashion said to her following the ceremony, "It's been a long, long rough road from a barefoot boy in New Brunswick to a peer of the realm in England."

The barons wasted no time publicizing the event in their newspapers, ensuring that it was well-reported throughout Canada and the United States.

The new year advanced negotiations to buy control of the Central Canada Steel Company. James and Ian had discussed strategies for how best to combine the two companies for some time and Ian began negotiations with major shareholders from both companies, as well as investment bankers to determine relative values for an acceptable share exchange.

He exercised his influence as the Canadian company's original fiscal agent, director, and major shareholder everywhere he could. Ian loved a good challenge and this new challenge of financial engineering had lit a fire in his gut. What Ian wanted was a larger bite of the merged company, but how to get that without putting up additional capital and creating added value?

"We need an iron ore property," said James when Ian voiced his thoughts, "an asset we can sell to the company for shares we can exchange with shares from the consolidated company. Who do we know in Canada's mining world that we could consult?"

"If we can buy a property on a delayed payment or a future promise and sell it into the consolidated company at premium value, with stock reflecting the added value to the company's long-term ore reserves, we'll be able to leverage our stock position substantially."

Enquiries were sent out across Canada to mining associates advising of their interest in acquiring an iron ore property that was of proven tonnage, reasonably assessable, equipped with large ore reserves, and capable of producing an economic concentrate for smelting.

Ian cabled his former partners at Macleod and Company in Montreal to let them know that a merger with Central Canada Steel was now possible, as control had been acquired by Lord Dungarven. He suggested they structure a deal whereby Central Canada Steel would become a wholly owned subsidiary of the Canadian Steel Company through a stock swap based on independent valuations.

He personally advised them, "We can place a block of the consolidated company's common stock in New York for up to ten million dollars with a number of investment trusts."

Macleod and Company were bullish on the proposal. They put their deal partners to work, negotiating terms and preparing documentation for shareholders' meetings of both companies.

Time was of the essence; that is to say, time was of the essence if they wanted to complete this ambitious deal while the stock markets remained in full bloom. The shares of U.S. Steel Corporation, currently the largest steel producer in the world, were trading at two hundred and ten dollars, up over forty-five dollars in six months. It was a clear and powerful measure of the strong demand for steel products to feed in the expanding industrial base of the U.S. economy and export markets to the world.

INVESTMENT TRUST LEVERAGE CRAZE

The most exploited and speculative financial innovation of the late 20s was the development and promotion of investment trusts; in other words, the practice of buying shares in a wide variety of existing corporations on a leveraged basis and providing shareholders with exposure to a so-called diversified portfolio.

An estimated 186 trusts were organized and sold to eager investors throughout 1928, with investment banking houses, commercial banks, and brokerage firms giving birth to new issues of trusts, valued at over three billion dollars in the first six months of 1929. Sponsors ranged from the prestigious J.P. Morgan and Company all the way down to unscrupulous promoters who directed the trust funds into buying stock of designated corporations they controlled.

The trust craze became so prestigious that it carried the seeds of its own destruction, attracting economists and professors of economics as money managers and advisors. As 1929 wore on, many first-time investors relied on the judgment of these prestigious, self-styled gurus as trust managers who had discovered and endorsed the magic of leverage. They funded their trusts heavily with bonds, preferring share issues to leverage the common shares they held as founders at nominal prices.

Goldman Sachs and Company were only one of many companies to sponsor a trust; the most well-known, but still only one. It was the Goldman Sachs Trading Corporation, a typically leveraged trust, with an issue of one million shares, at a hundred dollars for a hundred million dollars.

Within a scant few months, the shares were selling at $136.50 per share. Soon after that, it jumped to $222.50 per share. The trust issued a hundred million dollars of preferred stock, providing leverage to the common stock holders. It proceeded to acquire a variety of shares from other New York Stock Exchange companies, funded through the issuance of additional debt securities, totaling over two hundred million dollars.

One thing built on top of another thing built on top of another thing; it was a pyramid of pyramids, architecturally dubious stacks of metaphorical buildings all balanced on a knife edge. It was impossible to fathom the wild imagination and gargantuan madness that prevailed on Wall Street, exploiting great Ponzi schemes, of pyramids built on pyramids during the last throes of the greatest bull market in stock market history.

In 1933, at a senate investigation hearing, Mr. Sachs was asked, "What was the high of Goldman Sachs Trading Corporation, sir?"

He replied, "Four hundred and eight dollars, before the split."

And when asked "What's the price today?", Mr. Sachs answered sheepishly, "A dollar and seventy-five cents."

Baruch watched the scene from afar, watching as things spiralled ever further out of control. He became increasingly defensive in his interactions with Ian and James and the syndicate, strongly repeating himself time and again, trying to get the lot of them to see sense.

He told them to exploit the greedy Wall Street trusts constantly, in search of companies with exciting stories of growth and market gain. Knowing many of the trust operators, the sponsoring investment banks, and their ferocious appetites, it was easy to attract buying support for new issues, or for liquidation of sizeable syndicate positions such as C.D.R. and Central Canada Steel.

He cautioned, by cable from Scotland, "Time is of the essence, do your deals now, boys; we are getting into the blow-off stage. Mass euphoria is becoming the driving force. Market heading for a nasty correction."

MARKET MANIA

As spring gave way to summer, the roar of the bull on Wall Street became louder. It rang out across the Atlantic to London and the capital centers of Europe; the great investment trust promotions drove up the blue chips on a daily basis.

In June, the Times Industrial Average rose nearly thirteen percent while the Dow Jones Industrial Average approached 325 points and U.S. Steel hit two hundred and twenty dollars per share, up eleven percent in twenty trading days.

In Canada, Central Canada Steel Corp. and the Canadian Steel Company each moved ahead, vigorously, while C.D.R., attracting buying in London, and New York, traded in volume at over thirty-nine dollars per share.

The orgy was escalating at an alarming rate, being fuelled by easy access to massive speculative credit. Broker loans were expanding by four hundred million dollars per month with interest rates soaring to fifteen percent, attracting capital from all over the world, fuelling the buying surge on thin margins, as low as ten percent.

When broker loan interest rates hit eighteen percent and outstanding loans topped seven billion dollars, Baruch knew the market was out of control. He cabled the boys again.

> Two plus two now equals about eight in the market. When it returns to four,
> there will be devastation. Baruch

Meanwhile, the board of directors of the Canadian Steel Company concluded their analysis of the Central Canada Steel Corporation. There were plenty of benefits to be gained by Canadian Steel shareholders as a result of the consolidation, such as emphasized anticipated economies of scale, enhanced cash flow, and net profits per unit of steel production, reduced competition, and expanded market share; all music to the bull market.

Ian's colleagues on the board sounded him out as to whether Lord Dungarven would consider out and out selling his 40% interest, as opposed to an amalgamation or merger, which would take several months to complete and involve the issuance of a large number of additional shares.

LORDS OF THE FRONTIER

The shares of Central Canada Steel Corporation were trading up, twenty-two percent over James's cost price. Ian's board was quick to inform him that they would consider a premium price if a deal could be made quickly; another indicator of the current market atmosphere. If a deal could be struck, Canadian Steel would buy out James's control block for cash, using bank lines of credit, and they would finance the loan repayment with an equity issue at enhanced market prices, which the board expected would result from the perceived benefits of the acquisition.

As one pundit, reflecting on the market behavior in the summer of 1929, wrote, "Stock market prices and new issues are being floated by on smoke, strings, and mirrors, with little attention being paid to the realities of value."

On July 10, 1929, Baruch distilled his thoughts on the market in a letter to Richard, James, and Ian. Much of the letter was simply analysis and paranoia, but there was a section near the end that really caught the boys' attention.

> You must always remember, and never forget, that all markets are driven, to some extent, by a fundamental perception or illusion. You must identify the illusion and its root cause, then judge when the illusion or mirage will fade and be replaced by a new illusion. The illusion driving force in Wall Street today is the concept of a 'NEW ERA OF PROSPERITY'. ALL ERAS ARE EPHEMERAL. I fear reality will break out. Then watch out.

The barons took heed of the sage's advice, reassessing their respective portfolio and debt positions, and continued reducing their holdings and debt, increasing their liquidity as quickly as possible.

The syndicate's position had already been reduced by three hundred thousand shares, and they cabled Baruch to proceed with the sale of a further seven hundred thousand shares, reducing debt by an additional twenty-five million.

He wired back soon after.

> Major trust has bid $38 for 200,000 C.D.R. Consider it sold. Proceeding with balance. B.B.

The market continued on its merry way, bounding ahead on a daily basis with only minor corrections. A well known Wall Street pundit, Paul W Warburg, of the International Acceptance Bank, called for a restrained federal reserve policy, arguing that if this juggernaut of unrestrained faulty economic principles were not brought promptly to a halt, there would ultimately be a disastrous collapse. He even went so far as to predict that should such a collapse occur, it would bring about a powerful general depression involving the entire country. He was described by Wall Street sages as 'obsolete', while others accused him of talking from a short position. As the market continued to rise, his warnings were recalled with contempt.

One other rare voice of sobriety was that of New York Times financial editor, Alexander Dana Noyes, who reiterated with regularity, "The day of reckoning is approaching."

In July, the board of the Canadian Steel Corporation, at Lord Brandenbrooke's suggestion, made a formal offer to James of nineteen dollars per share for eight hundred thousand shares of Central Canada Steel Corporation, for a total of fifteen million, two hundred thousand.

James, after being advised of the bid, balanced the possible gains he might benefit from as a major shareholder of the potentially consolidated company against the risks involved in such a venture. Ultimately, he decided to go for it. These were the good times, times of prosperity for all, and he saw no risk beyond the absolute bare minimum that was always involved in sales.

He conferred with Ian and advised his agent of a counter offer at $25 per share, plus an option to buy 100,000 Canadian Steel Corporation shares for one year, at $75 per share; one dollar over its current trading range. After some negotiation, the final agreement was drawn up: $21 per share, plus the 100,000-share option.

James accepted. They arranged to close on the deal at the BNW, the Bank of New Westminster, pending the shares being delivered and all relevant documents and legalities being exchanged and signed.

James could never have guessed how little time was left in this phenomenal stock market environment. He could never have known what would soon follow in its wake. He was navigating by instinct only, an instinct that would in the future be termed as 'uncommon common sense'.

No; instead, the Canadian Steel Company offer for Central Canada Steel was interpreted bullishly, as he had expected. Canadian Steel moved up to $89 per share, supported by research reports from several Montreal brokers that the earnings of the combined companies could reach five dollars per share, justifying a price of ninety to ninety-five, on a multiple of eighteen times earnings.

James offered 25,000 shares, at $92 or better, through Kippen and Company, Inc. The offering was snapped up at a slightly higher price within the next two days.

Baruch kept the barons and Richard Benson informed on a daily basis as they all continued selling into the boiling market. Being an avid student of history, in particular financial history, he cited famous events that had mirrored similar market psychology in the past. A favorite of his was recalling and quoting the famous South Sea Bubble of 1720 and its legacy.

"When it was observed that statesmen forgot their politics, lawyers their bar, merchants their traffic, physician their patients, tradesmen their shops, debtors of quality their creditors, divines the pulpit, and even women themselves their pride and vanity," read one excerpt. Baruch questioned whether they weren't observing a similar degree of madness.

A young Princeton economist, Joseph Stagg Lawrence, issued a classic and widely quoted comment that stunned Baruch so much he printed it as a warning to his clients. "The consensus of judgment of the millions whose valuations function on the New York Stock Exchange is that stocks are not at present overvalued. Where is that group of wise men with all-embracing wisdom which will entitle them to veto the judgment of this intelligent multitude?"

"This so-called intelligent multitude," he scoffed, quipping, "I'll be damned, that's what I'll be! Can you believe it? These fools are wearing rose-tinted glasses." He paused, noting, "Even love-song writers have joined the parade of clowns with some timely ditties. Have you heard 'I'm in the market for you, darling' or 'Blue Skies from now on'?"

TWILIGHT OF THE ERA

On August 17, the Leviathan and the Ile de France left New York with complete wireless facilities for speculators to use for trading even while on the high seas, going through established brokerage offices stationed on board.

Business on opening day was described as brisk; one of the first transactions was executed by song writer, Irving Berlin, selling 1,000 shares of Paramount-Famous-Lasky at $72 per share. The stock later dropped to zero when the company went into bankruptcy in 1932.

However, during the present time, this new way of doing business gave rise to very creative poetry which would be bounced back and forth between ships.

> We were crowded in the cabin,
> Watching figures on the board,
> It was midnight on the ocean,
> And a tempest loudly roared.
> 'We are lost,' the captain shouted,
> as he staggered down the stairs.
> 'I've got a tip,' he faltered,
> 'Straight by the wireless from the aunt
> of a fellow who's related
> to a cousin of Durant.'
>
> (Founder of General Motors)
> At these awful words we shuddered,
> And the stoutest bull grew sick,
> While the brokers cried more margin,
>
> And the ticker ceased to tick.
> But the captain's little daughter said,
> 'I do not understand,

Isn't Morgan on the ocean
just the same as on the land?'

Labor Day brought the historic summer of 1929 to its traditional end. And on September 3, the market opened firmly on what pundits termed good undertone.

It was, however, merely the high-water mark of this Great Bull Market.

The Dow Jones Industrials was sitting pretty at 401. Many of America's great companies were enjoying new heights, most sitting anywhere between two and four hundred dollars. The Radio Corporation of American, which had never before paid a dividend, was quoted at an astonishing $505. Broker loans were up another one hundred and thirty-seven million dollars in just one week, with the horrifying total now sitting at over eight billion dollars.

On September 5, Rodger Babson of the Babson Research Service observed, "Sooner or later, a crisis is coming. A crash is coming, and it may be terrific. The Dow Jones market averages could drop sixty to eighty points."

Wall Street promptly and soundly denounced him. An editorial in Barron's Publication on September 9 referred to him as the "Sage of Wellesley" who should not be taken seriously, owing to his notorious inaccuracies of bearish reports published in the latter half of 1928, and throughout 1929.

The Babson Break on September 5, as it was referred to, was followed by a rally on September 6 and 7. On September 11, in keeping with a regular practice, the Wall Street Journal printed its thought for the day, a quote from Mark Twain. "Don't part with your illusions; if they're gone, you may still exist, but you have ceased to live."

Baruch continued to report sales of C.D.R., which had topped forty-one dollars on September 5, liquidating over five hundred thousand shares during the summer months, and negotiating a sale of two hundred thousand shares with the Goldman Sachs Investment Trust at forty-two dollars per share.

James's option on 100,00 shares of the Canadian Steel Corporation, priced at $75 a piece, was easily worth $1,200,000, even with the stock selling at $87 instead of $92. He cabled J.D. Kippen his company in Montreal with a simple request to sell 75,000 Canadian Steels shares at the best price he could.

The frontier entrepreneurs were exposed to the vicissitudes of the boiling market with frayed nerves. The market stank of time running out. They could finally sense what Baruch had been pointing to from the very beginning: the hour of the speculative orgy was late, rife with whisky talk.

A wire from Richard spurred them into action.

When the inmates of the nuthouse have bought all the stock, to whom do they sell?

They felt the urge to continue cashing in their chips, to sit back and watch the parade of speculators from the sidelines as they marched forward in lockstep, like lemmings to a cliff, until the bubble burst.

They had other priorities to occupy their time. There was a British election in the near future and Richard had a lot of work to do reorganizing the Conservative Party before the next election, expected sometime in 1930. What's more, James had some decisions to make concerning his relationship with Elizabeth.

Prime Minister Baldwin called his election for September 28, with Ramsey MacDonald, leader of the Labor Party, as his major adversary, and the Liberals running a distant third.

The Conservative Party began its fund-raising campaign with the usual support of right-wing aristocrats and the business establishment, kicked off by James, with a sizable personal contribution of a hundred thousand pounds and the organizing of campaign headquarters in Saint James Square.

The barons directed their newspaper editors in full support of Baldwin and his policies. In reality, they became the propaganda machine for the party. It was the least they could do in return for the honors which had been bestowed upon them by the party's hierarchy.

Several prominent candidates in the campaign were proteges of Stanley Baldwin, including two future prime ministers, Winston Churchill and Harold Macmillan.

IAN SEES THE LIGHT

Ian, now legally separated from his wife, had no intention of marrying again, so long as he could handpick his mistresses. He fully intended to exploit what he had once named 'the age-old female aphrodisiacs, power, and money'.

His long sequence of mistresses, married or single, was by now well known. His current dilemma was the many splendored Sylvia. Sylvia the lady, Sylvia the lover, Sylvia the actress, Sylvia the mistress, Sylvia the courtesan; he didn't quite know what to make of her.

James urged him often to terminate the relationship, but without success. "She's got you by the balls, old boy. Trade her in for a new one. You're the first one to preach of the blinding illusions of sex, yet you let your libido rule," he asserted. "Don't you think it's time to cut and run?"

"Quite so, quite so, old boy, but I have to admit she has that femme-fatale quality. Perhaps I've become addicted, which just goes to prove that old adage: 'that sex exploited with skill by a beautiful woman, is her lethal weapon'," joked James. And when exercised has often influenced history."

Some weeks later, however, James was amazed when Ian confided, "I've taken your advice. I've cut Sylvia loose. She's too bloody dangerous and expensive, so I made her a fair deal."

"Well done, you old roué! Was it expensive?"

"Well," chortled Ian, "I was very fair. I asked her to put a value on the relationship and handed her a signed, blank check. I said, 'Whatever you think is fair, my dear. But don't take advantage of my generosity. I'm not the richest sugar daddy in London, but I do wish you well.'"

"My God!" exclaimed James. "Have you got a guilt complex or something? That bitch will take you to the cleaners."

Ian looked at him quizzically and roared with laughter. "Well, not quite, old boy, you know me better than that. You see, Sylvia, poor dear, doesn't know how much money is in that particular account. If she proves too greedy, the check will bounce, and she's lost her bet. I said to her, 'My dear, use your best judgment, but just remember, I'm not as rich as many believe.'"

James doubled up with laughter. "That's a class act, Ian. Foxy, foxy, that cunning bitch. She was never my type, as you know. I wonder what she will do?"

"I wouldn't be surprised if she hightailed it to Montreal," grunted Ian. "You know, that

Frenchy De Rolland fellow is still hopeful. But I'm glad to be off the carousel. It's been some ride, and we have to admit, she was invaluable, being a double agent in the end."

"That's something only time is going to tell," remarked James. "I've always had my suspicions. Perhaps some day, the truth will come out!"

The two spent much of their time involved in the election campaign; in fact, they seemed to grow ever more involved as time passed. They attended meetings very frequently, usually in support of candidates, particularly the prime minister.

James observed to Ian one day, "Convincing fellow. Well, the best politicians can certainly convince themselves, and others at times, that they are going to win, against all odds." This was said in response to one of Winston Churchill's famous addresses to his constituents, "Victory is in the air."

Two evenings later, on election night, he was proven dead wrong as he joined with his party leader Stanley Baldwin, a man he had in the past described with Churchillian flair: "Occasionally he stumbled over the truth, but hastily picked himself up as if nothing had ever happened."

They met at 10 Downing Street to follow the returns, and were stunned by the results. By the following afternoon, when the final count was in, Labor had won 288 seats to the Conservatives' 260 and the Liberals' 59. Winston Churchill had been re-elected, while Harold Macmillan had been defeated. The only way the Conservatives could form a government would be with the support of the Liberal Party, who held the balance of power.

Baldwin refused to even consider the prospect and resigned. The Labor Party formed the government under Ramsay MacDonald, the Socialist leader. Here was another man Churchill had in the past described with characteristic flair as a man who had "the gift of compressing the largest number of words into the smallest amount of thought."

And with that, the country entered a tenuous period of political instability. Ian had held hopes of the two Conservative parties reaching out across the Atlantic and joining together in a trade pact; hopes now gone up in smoke.

ALL GALE NO ANCHOR

As September came to an end, the roaring bull in Wall Street was at last showing signs of exhaustion. Baruch, returning from his annual grouse-shooting sojourn in the highlands of Scotland, met with Ian and James at Claridges Hotel prior to sailing for New York.

He advised the immediate sale of a further five hundred thousand shares of the syndicate's stock already down from its high of forty-two and a quarter to the thirty-six dollar level; declaring that he was selling daily and advising his largest clients in New York to continue liquidating their positions. He recounted with disbelief a recent report received from a prominent Wall Street pundit, whose market opinions he had, at one time, respected. The report described market averages being "like weathervanes pointing into a gale of prosperity." It stunned Baruch.

"It's pointing into a gale all right," he declared, "a tornado that could destroy everything in its path. In my view, the market is all gale and no anchor. Greed has eclipsed caution and fear. The 'great-new-era' illusion will evaporate like a mirage on the shifting sands of the Sahara."

Their lordships didn't need further persuasion to continue taking whopping market profits. They had the wind up, and informed Richard, in Ottawa, of their concerns. He confirmed that he, too, had liquidated portions of his holdings in Alberta Light, Dominion Cement Corporation, and the Canadian Steel Company.

In September, new Wall Street issues of investment trusts continued to appear at an even greater rate than in August, commanding premiums over their offering prices. On September 20, the Times reported, "The stock of the recently launched Lehman Corporation Trust, offered at 104 in August, was trading at 136."

Other signs indicated that the gods of the new era were still in their temples, waving their magic wands. The young Time Magazine, founded in 1922 by Henry Luce upon his graduation from Yale University, had recently featured Ivar Kreuger, the promoter and international financier, the great match kind, who Richard had shunned a few years earlier, on its cover page, with the comment: "A general admirer of Cecil Rhodes."

The October 12 issue of the Saturday Evening Post also carried a lead story on Kreuger, where he was quoted in their interview as saying, "Whatever success I have had may perhaps be attributable to three things: one is silence, the second is more silence, while the third is still more silence."

Here, for once, he was telling the truth. His suicide a few years later revealed his aversion to divulging information. He had kept even his intimate associates in ignorance of his monstrous fraud, one of the greatest in financial history, totaling over five hundred million dollars.

Traveling in Germany, Charles E. Mitchell, chairman of the National Bank of New York, stated, "The industrial condition of the United States is absolutely sound. Too much attention is being paid to brokers' loans, and nothing can arrest the upward movement."

On October 15, as he sailed for home, Mitchell elaborated on the point, "The markets are now generally in a healthy condition. Values have a sound basis in the general prosperity of our country."

That same evening, Professor Irving Fisher of Yale University, one of many investment trust advisors, made his historic, and unfortunately untimely, prediction about the permanently high economic plateau, adding, "I expect to see the stock market a good deal higher than it is today within a few months."

The timing of these two profound forecasts were indeed most unfortunate for Mr. Mitchell and Mr. Fisher, and for other prominent financial pundits. While the Times averages and the Dow Jones Industrials began drifting downward, leading stocks, such as U.S. Steel, lost anywhere between 6 and 12 points on October 19. The blue chips were seriously off, and speculative favorites had gone into a nose dive. J.I. Case, for example, had fallen a full forty points, one of the biggest losses to date.

Baruch, while on the high seas returning to New York, sent his office a cable containing a single word repeated over and over again: Sell!

October 20, 1929, a beautiful Sunday; the Sunday news reported a Wall Street consensus claiming that the worst of the correction was over. In their words, there were prominent investors and rumored heavy buyers who would soon make right the situation. Unfortunately, Monday proved contrary to these expectations.

A staggering volume of shares tore through the market, disrupting the system come noontime. In times to come, Professor Fisher would be quoted as saying on the subject, "The decline only represented a shaking out of the lunatic fringe. The market has not yet reflected the beneficent effects of prohibition, which has made the American worker more productive and dependable."

Wednesday witnessed further erosion, with the Times Industrial Average falling thirty points. American Telephone and Telegraph was off another fifteen points, Westinghouse was off twenty-five, and J.I. Case was off by forty-six points. Again, the ticker fell behind.

Thursday, October 24, 1929, made history as the day the market crashed, with 12,894,650 shares changing hands in steep, vertical declines across the board, at prices shattering the dreams and hopes of thousands of naive speculators, as nine billion dollars in paper value evaporated in two hours.

The infamous stock market crash of history had begun.

At 12:20 p.m., the officials of the New York Stock Exchange dosed the visitor's gallery, which viewed the wild scenes below. One of the last visitors to leave was none other than Mr. Winston Churchill, former Chancellor of the Exchequer in England, on a speaking tour of the U.S.A., and a guest of Bernard Baruch's. He was also a victim, literally witnessing the meltdown of his own portfolio from the gallery.

THE CRASH — BLACK TUESDAY, OCT. 24

On Black Tuesday, October 29, the second tidal wave struck, with sixteen million shares, or forty billion dollars of market value, vaporizing; indelibly recording the end of the great era of illusion in stock market history, and the beginning of the longest and deepest depression on record in the industrialized world.

The Times Industrial Average, down a further forty-three points, had eclipsed all the gains of the preceding twelve euphoric months, ending the illusionary dreams of wealth in a long and sustaining nightmare.

By mid-November, stock markets everywhere were crashing. The Dow Jones for example was down nearly forty-three percent. Analysts everywhere watched in dismay. The Harvard Economic Society in particular has this to report, "In spite of market declines, a serious depression seems improbable."

And Andrew Mellon, who was Secretary of the Treasury come December 31 of that year, announced, "I see nothing in the present situation that is either menacing or that warrants pessimism."

The Atlantic Syndicate had not escaped the avalanche entirely, but thanks to Baruch's foresight, had liquidated over forty-eight million of its seventy-three million debts through the sale of approximately one and a half million shares, resulting in a reasonable debt-equity ratio.

While the city of London had not experienced the same panic as New York, it had suffered devastating declines in leading stocks and stock exchange averages.

It was a subdued Winston Churchill who returned from his speaking tour in Canada and the United States as a victim of the crash, facing serious financial losses and liabilities, to take his seat in the opposition of the House of Commons.

While the barons basked in the comfort of being out of danger, Ian was suddenly confronted with an embarrassing conundrum.

A letter arrived at his office soon after, marked 'personal and confidential' by its author. He opened it impatiently and was somewhat surprised to discover it was from Sylvia. It was a very short note but no man alive would have called it short and sweet. Instead, it was packed with dynamite.

Ian, my dear, I'm pregnant and being sued by my broker for 238,000 pounds. They want my house in Eton Square. I'm desperate. I must see you. Please call me, Ian dear.

Your former lover,
Sylvia

When James popped in for their morning chat, he found his partner subdued and in a foul mood as he tossed the note to him with a quip, "Here. Read this. Bloody hell, she wants to trap me with the oldest goddamned game on earth."

James, in good humor, reacted with his usual objectivity. "Well if I were in your position, my lord, I'd pay up and shut up, it's a no-win situation; she can trump you. If she's really preggers, you'll have to ante up. It's not the end of the world, and besides, maybe you are the papa," he suggested with a chuckle.

Ian, in an uncharacteristic state of anxiety, went into his usual form, striding about the office, cursing under his breath, and blowing up great clouds of smoke.

"What the hell is this all about, James?" he growled, gesticulating with his hands. "Who got her into the bloody stock market? Not me. And who got her knock up? Not me, somebody's trying to set me up. Damn it to hell! She can't hang this on me!"

"I think we should do a little checking on who Sylvia's been with lately. She moves in a pretty well-known circle here in London," responded James calmly. "I'll check it out, but if she's as desperate as she says, maybe you ought to give her a break for old time's sake."

His social network in London soon reported that Sylvia had been seen at the Drury Lane theater with a handsome American escort, though further investigation yielded somewhat contradictory results, as many of her friends thought she'd been off with a distinguished-looking Canadian instead.

When they chatted that evening, James expressed his curiosity about Sylvia's alleged escorts, "My god, I wonder if it could have been De Rolland after all. We all know she was constantly in touch with that little French turkey during the boom."

Ian's eyes widened in realization and he leapt from his chair, snapping his fingers and hollering irritably, "Of course, it's Frenchy! I'll bet that turkey's the one what knocked her up and I'll bet you again they want me to bail them out. My God, Sylvia really is a class act, isn't she?" he scoffed scornfully. "I have to hand it to her. She's a piece of work. I guess I'd better give her a call and listen to the whole bloody tale of woe!"

The stock markets continued their plunge through November and December, taking their toll; not only in the meltdown of capital, but in human lives as well. Newspapers reported tragic stories of men plunging from office buildings and hotels to certain death, as they were confronted with unbearable debt loads incurred by the extravagant and speculative purchase of shares on credit.

Baruch called them up one day out of the blue to tell them the sad story of Sir Winston Churchill. The two had been friends since their first meeting shortly after the war and they had always striven to stay in contact. It seemed Churchill was in serious financial trouble. He'd invested heavily in severely companies that were heavy on marge and had been force-liquidated, leaving him with debit balances of unmanageable proportions.

It was a depressing Christmas atmosphere that pervaded the homes and offices of the capitalist societies of London and New York, with so many reports of acquaintances and friends in serious trouble, and many facing bankruptcy.

But the season, with its annual wave of introspection and generosity of spirit, provoked Ian to suggest, "Perhaps the time has come to put together a fund to assist some of our friends. Maybe I'm getting old, James, but we've been so bloody lucky to escape this financial inferno, we could afford to give a little back. What do you think? And perhaps Bernie will join us."

"We are ahead of the game all right but we still hold a hell of a lot of C.D.R. stock; it's down to twenty-seven dollars, and looks lower," responded James. "But, yes, I think Bernie would contribute, and Richard as well. What the hell, it's only money," he laughed, in a generous Christmas mood. "Perhaps we are becoming a little philosophical in our old age. I really thank our lucky stars when realizing how dangerously exposed we've been."

"And maybe it's about time," replied Ian. "I'll write to Bernie immediately about Winston. We'll start with him. I understand and he's in so deep he'll never get out without help. 'That man must be preserved,' Bernie has often said, 'He's destined for greater things.'"

THE FEMALE TRAP

Ian's rendezvous with Sylvia in her familiar library in Eaton Square was at first somewhat chilly, as the estranged couple sipped their martinis; but her vibrant and seductive charm had its usual mellowing effect, allowing him to converse calmly about her brokerage debts and pregnancy.

"When I got your note, Sylvia, I was knocked over. How in the world did you get so heavily into the stock market? I never heard you discuss it. You never asked me about stocks. And what's this about being pregnant?"

"Well, my dear Ian, which of these shall we deal with first? It's quite a long story, and I'm so grateful to you for calling me. I just had to tell you everything. We've known each other so well these past years."

He lit a cigar and sat back, slightly nervous, wondering what was coming next.

Sylvia continued. "After our last night together last summer, I realized that I couldn't keep up my lifestyle on my alimony. I heard all sorts of amazing stories going around about fortunes being made in New York off the market. I was tempted in. I took out a mortgage on this house for some extra money and a broker friend of mine here in London persuaded me to open an account with him.

"He took all my savings and started investing it for me. I wasn't worried at the time. I expected that your check would tide me over for a while, but alas, we both know what happened there. I don't know who's to blame, but that's water under the bridge now.

"Not to long after I opened an account, back in July, my broker bought U.S. Steel and Westinghouse. And in August, stock in a movie company called Famous Players. All in all, about two hundred and fifty thousand pounds, on margin of forty-five thousand pounds. He even bought me two thousand shares of Canada Dominion at forty-one dollars a share."

Ian, visibly shocked, jumped up, exclaiming impatiently, "Who was this bloody fool who loaded you up with these stocks, just when James and I were getting out while New York was boiling over? So, what's the damage? How deep are you in the quicksand?"

"It's an awful lot – at least for me," she said softly. Then after a quiet moment, she added. "It's about one hundred and twenty-thousand pounds, plus my mortgage."

He sat back in silence for a moment before commenting, "Well, my dear, it may not be the end of the world. I've heard of cases a lot worse. Now tell me about your really big problem. Is it true?"

"Yes, my dear Ian, it's true. You remember our last night together? Well, I guess that was it. I thought that I was safe, but we both know these things can happen."

Standing again in silence, he very quietly responded, "You're saying I'm responsible! Come, come, my dear, you've got many other admirers."

"But I've been alone since our split," she murmured. "You must believe me."

"I wish I could, my dear, it's pretty hard to imagine you being alone for very long. Who in London knows about this?" he inquired rather sheepishly.

"Very few of my friends," Sylvia responded. "I've made every effort to hide it to date."

"Very few of your friends, my God, it only takes one cackling gossip," he quipped, pacing about the library and drawing heavily on a fresh cigar, asking bluntly, Now, Sylvia, who's the handsome Canadian I understand you've been seen with. Somebody said it was that Frenchy senator from Montreal."

The remark broke the tension as Sylvia broke into laughter. "My god, Ian! I haven't seen Olivier for ages, even years; he never comes to London, but I'll tell you who has been here a few times: Sir Edward Montgomerie. I saw a play with him on his last trip."

Ian was aghast, standing frozen for a moment. "What! I can't believe it! No, not Montgomerie, it's too much! Will I ever be free of the man?" He threw his hands in the air dramatically. He scoffed and shook his head quizzically, with a flicker of a smile on his lips, saying, "You know, it seems to me that you and I and Sir Edward have been playing blind man's bluff for quite a few years, ever since our fateful ocean voyage in 1922.

"We've been the most delightful three-ring circus, it seems, but the question here, I think, is who's the clown?" he laughed. "I always suspected you had a secret passion for him, even when you were romancing Frenchy. Well, my dear, what do we do now? Why don't you lasso him? It's time he got married, and you'd be an ideal president's wife. You'd be a natural at corporate politics."

"I have considered it, but everybody says he's a consummate bachelor, the type who's married to his work," responded Sylvia with a sigh. "And now that I know it's your child, Ian dear, I want to bear the child in England."

The remark hit a nerve as he felt trapped. He reacted abruptly, blurting out, "Great balls of fire – No! No! You can't hang this on me! My god, I can't be father to a bastard son in this town!" And then he composed himself, "I must say, you've got yourself into a king-sized mess for someone so young and talented. What about your ex, Sir Gifford Fox? Get him on your case; after all, you are still Lady Fox."

"Not a chance, my dear, I'm afraid he's always been jealous of you ever since he learned about us, and besides I hear he's about to remarry."

"Hell, no, it's too bloody much," replied Ian testily, with a deep frown. Then, after a moment of reflecting, he said, "You know, my dear, I'll have to think about all this, I still think Eddie boy is your best bet. Or even Frenchy De Rolland. I really can't keep track of all your suitors. I know, and you know bloody well that I'm not the only one! The irony is, we philanderers often get caught in the crossfire."

As he left, he kissed her forehead. "My dear, it's been a long road for the both of us, a long, strange road of twists and turns. If you want my support, I am willing to provide it, but for God's sake, don't let the London gossipmongers link me to all this. You know how this town is: it doesn't care about how things are, just how they look.

"Did you know that it has been said that the Brits have developed adultery to an art form, an art form based in hypocrisy and discretion. Well, for once I agree with them! Some of my newspaper enemies would love to exploit a juicy scandal in their tabloids. I shudder to think of the headlines: 'Lord's secret bastard' comes to mind as a potential title. God knows I have enough problems with my ex-wife as it is."

ELECTION IN THE MIDST OF GLOOM

Canada's financial markets paralleled New York's, and with its decline of approximately 45% by year's end, the seeds of depression were in the wind. Prices around the business world were collapsing, particularly those related to agricultural products, natural resources, and factory orders. Pockets of unemployment sprang up across the economic globe, at first small and mostly inconsequential but quickly growing larger and more worrying until what had been an unnerving turn of events turned into a serious employment crisis.

It was particularly bad in the Maritime provinces and in Western Canada, the places where such businesses had been thriving up to that point. The Conservative Party repeatedly appealed to the federal government for loans or grants that might be able to help the provincial governments relieve and address the unemployment crisis.

Alas, it was in vain as Prime Minister King responded to their pleas with a single comment, soon to be infamous: "I would not give a single cent supporting recommendations of the Tory party."

The economic crisis did pave the way for Richard to sweep the Liberals from office in the 1930 election. He strode through the campaign like a colossus to reach his lifetime goal, becoming Canada's tenth and richest prime minister with a strong majority.

His partners celebrated with prominent Conservatives in London and gave Richard the newspaper headlines he had always dreamed of: "Benson, Canadian Industrialist, Canadian Prime Minister" and "Millionaire Canadian becomes prime minister".

Ian's celebratory cable was the most nostalgic and welcoming of all.

> Your integrity has carried you far since the day we first met, when I was but 10 years of age, and you, a grown up of 18. Your counsel to me when I arrived in an impecunious state in Calgary at the age of 19, and the friendship we welded together will always be an inspiration to me, and something I will always cherish. We have prospered together, and with you at the helm of our native land, it will continue to grow and prosper, becoming one of the great nations of the world in the 20th century. James joins me in wishing you every good wish. Godspeed. Ian

THE GREAT BEAR TRAP

While the bullish exuberance that had dominated the markets from the year of 1923 through to 1929 had evaporated, stock markets rallied vigorously in the early months of 1930, recovering over one-half of their steep 1929 decline. C.D.R., which had dropped by nearly fifty percent to $20.50, managed to rally back to $28 per share; this proved a true blessing to the syndicate as it allowed them to sell a further 940,000 shares. At an average price of $27 per, they managed to retake a little over twenty-five million dollars.

By June 1930, the syndicate was in a positive position, holding 7.16 million shares, before adjustments, for options granted to third parties.

President Hoover, wealthy in his own right, had benefited greatly from the syndicate and from the liquidation of his own investments, having constantly consulted Baruch as the economy continued to take its toll.

However, it was not to be. The 1930 rally began losing its momentum in June and was almost dead come July. The faceless monster of the market marched forth, a relentless beast sweeping aside all in its path. It passed out bloodless verdicts and sallied forth unimpeded. The market cared for nothing save wealth.

And it was these bloodless verdicts that cut off President Hoover at the knees. Each day brought forth further proof of the blatant delusions and untruths exhibited in his frequent political pronouncements. For example, in March, he was quoted as saying, "The worst effect of the crash upon unemployment will end in sixty days." And in May, the ill-informed Mr. Hoover had two laughably false proclamations to declare: "We have now passed the worst, and with continued unity of effort, shall rapidly recover," a joke if ever there was one, and "Business will be normal by the fall."

Many pundits advised that the shattering correction was complete, claiming the markets would continue recovering and would even eventually surpass their old highs.

Baruch, in a phone call to Ian, described it as "nothing more than a great bear rally trap, Ian! And I'm not the only one who sees it. Take this chance to liquidate any shares you've got, but by God, don't you dare try to buy anything."

It was obvious to him that the grand illusion and emotion of the twenties had been spent. Now the ebb tide was turning the euphoric, unbridled optimism into a nightmare of apprehension and fear the likes of which would trigger massive debt liquidation and contracting credit.

In actuality, no one had a crystal ball revealing what laid ahead, not even Baruch or other market gurus who had seen the crash corning. Many who had sold out at the high were caught in the famous 1930 'bear trap'; something even more devastating than the 1929 debacle.

The Dow Jones industrials, at 401 on September 3, 1929, had dropped nearly in half by December, rallying to over three hundred in May of 1930, and then proceeded to decline for the next two years in Titanic fashion, plunging by eighty percent to a bottom of forty-two in July of 1932.

For the year end of 1929, the Canada Dominion Railroad Corporation reported its highest earnings in company history. Alas, freight traffic as well as steamship and hotel revenues were all in steep down trends in the first and second quarters of 1930.

Ian set sail with James and Elizabeth on September 16 aboard the Empress of Japan. It was an easy, pleasant, and uneventful trip. They arrived in Montreal on schedule, on September 23, with plenty of time until the C.D.R.'s annual meeting on September 30.

Ian's first priority upon arrival was to sort out his Sylvia dilemma. As he told James emphatically, "I must meet with Sir Edward and that damned De Rolland fellow. I've got to get this damned Sylvia situation straightened out. You'll have to arrange the meetings, James."

"Me?" He seemed surprised.

"Of course! You know these two high-wire actors better than I do. I wonder if they know how much I paid to bail out Sylvia." He shook his head. "Oh the things I do for people. I've saved her house and set up a trust fund for the child, relieving them of any responsibility and possible embarrassing rumors concerning the child's father. To give Sylvia credit, I think she has kept her commitment not to identify the child's father. Not that it matters any. Most of London suspects it's me. Frankly, I'm damn sure it was Sir Edward."

The city was nothing like the optimistic, dynamic center of financial activity they had left in 1928. The crash had taken its toll, on everyone, but their lordships were well received as they dined with friends who had so far managed to still cling to their mansions, though some of those were now mortgaged to the hilt. The famous square mile on the side of Mount Royal had been hard hit.

The railroad's revenues were down somewhat in the first half of 1930, but not out of line with rail traffic in the U.S.A. Sir Edward seemed optimistic that the year would be reasonably good. Of course, it was still early in what would soon be known as the Great Depression. Very few people had yet to realize the scope of the crisis, how it would shrink international trade and global Gross National Product in Canada and the U.S.A. by almost thirty-three percent over the next year or two.

The barons' net worth on paper had diminished from the dizzying heights of September 1929, but the trio had liquidated a large proportion of their portfolios, as had Baruch, and had since built up a veritable war chest of cash of enviable levels.

"The big question," Baruch said over the course of one call from New York, "has to be what is our policy with regards to the syndicate's seven million C.D.R. shares? It is still the largest single block of outstanding stock, roughly 17% or 18% of the company."

Richard's outlook was pessimistic when they all met at the Chateau Laurier in Ottawa. He foresaw western Canadian grain and commodity traffic falling, as world markets began contracting, and tariff barriers were being erected, inflicting significant declines on corporate earnings.

Baruch also remained apprehensive as he advised them over cable.

> How long will it be before the great forces of the American economy reassert themselves? From time to time, over the past year since the crash, I've thought the bottom had been reached, but as the months go by, my confidence that the country will right itself is waning. The economic indices are telling a story.

C.D.R. shares were down roughly 40% from their pre-Depression high. Still, they weren't beat yet. They'd managed to reach moderate stability at the current price, $23, and they were still above their post-crash low by a few dollars. It wasn't much of a security net but a security net it was. For now, at least.

Baruch favored further sales. He shared with his friends a mild scheme he was working on to generate serious interest among the born-again bulls who, rightly or wrongly, saw the market in a recovery trend. It would be difficult to move a large block without breaking the market, but he had a plan to talk to the greedy investment trusts. A few of them were still kicking, with liquid funds to spend and a great need for depressed and oversold issues. "We'll sell into that bear trap," he counseled with a chuckle and a vicious grin.

They departed from the Canadian capital in agreement to liquidate a further five hundred thousand shares at the twenty to twenty-three-dollar level, in the full knowledge that it might take months in the prevailing environment of diminished-trading volume.

With Prime Minister Benson scheduled to attend the Commonwealth Trade Conference in London later in the fall, they expected to reconvene again to review their decisions and the economic outlook.

Ian returned to Montreal for several directors' meetings, prior to their planned departure from New York with James and Elizabeth on October 28, onboard the Duchess of Athlone.

James, as irrepressible as ever, was off to Toronto in pursuit of control of yet another potentially great industrial enterprise: the defunct, debt-burdened Northern Algoma Iron and Steel Corporation. The company's steel plant had a capacity of two million tons a year and immense ore reserves. However, with the crash, the furnaces were cold, the works were silent, and the company's shares traded for a dollar or less. The Bank of Montreal was pressing for a reorganization to reduce company loans and debt by at least fifty percent.

James was in a strong cash position and his credentials were at a record high, making it easy to accumulate a substantial share position. In turn, this was sufficient for controlling the board of directors and effecting the capital reorganization and equity financing necessary for moving forward.

He firmly believed the company had immense potential, in spite of its thirty-year-long checkered history of dismal performance. It had been founded by a wide-eyed American optimist from Michigan who had ventured north to Ontario and discovered the great iron ore reserves of the Algoma district. While he hadn't know the exact nature of what he had discovered, ore reserves totaling over one billion tons, he had known enough to try for this territory.

However, things had not gone well for him. Optimism is no substitute for the likes of experience, knowledge, or funds. Rather than rise to its full potential, it had fallen nearly into bankruptcy from the go, getting by by supplying coke to the great Canadian nickel smelters at Sudbury and producing steel rails for C.D.R. and the Canadian National Railway Company.

It had grown into an important producer of alloy steel for Canada's emerging automobile industry in competition with the Canadian Steel Company. Incidentally, James had recently sold his control of Central Canada Steel Corporation to them not long before the crash. With his vision of the company's potential and some moderate encouragement from the Ontario's Premier and some of London's brokers, James was sure the company would not only recover but grow into an amazing company.

To that end, he committed large sums of his own personal capital funds to the reorganization and refinancing of the enterprise, buying the company's defaulted bonds at deep discounts to strengthen his negotiating position.

When he left Toronto, the die was cast. As he emphasized to Elizabeth, "Life is like an express train, shovel all the coal in, gotta keep a rollin'." His future had taken on a new direction, which would absorb his energies for the next twenty years. They spent a few days in Montreal before leaving with Ian by train for New York to board the Duchess of Athlone.

Ian revealed a little surprise as they checked into the Waldorf Astoria on Park Avenue: they would be setting sail in two days' time with none other than their dear friend and partner, Richard. He had already checked in with them, claiming he would be in London a few weeks ahead of his scheduled Prime Ministers' Commonwealth trade conference. However, his was not the only surprise, for Baruch had arranged a dinner with President Hoover and his wife at the White House. James in particular was delighted, as he knew just how thrilled Elizabeth would be to meet the president.

THE WHITE HOUSE

As they were chauffeured from the Union Station in Washington to the east security gate of the White House on Pennsylvania Avenue, Elizabeth silently mused to herself, her thoughts colored with the awe she felt towards her companions and their impressive spheres of influence, 'Here am I, off to dinner with two British press lords and industrialists, the President of the United States, the Prime Minister of Canada, and Bernard Baruch, a legend of Wall Street, a great investment banker and presidential confident. I must say, I love it.'

They were ushered in to the president's private quarters in the east wing of the White House and received by their charming host, who was delighted to meet the Prime Minister of Canada for the first time, and to see James again after so many years, following their successful joint venture investment in C.D.R.

The conversation at dinner ranged from the British political situation, with its new Labor government, to Canadian-American trade relations, the ever-intensifying unemployment crisis, the growing power of labor unions, and the outlook for their respective economies and stock markets.

"The market hasn't stopped spiralling since mid-June. I tell you, it has to be because of the continued liquidation of excessive margin positions! Add to that the way brokers' loans are being squeezed at an alarming rate, by contracting the banks' lines of credit, and you yourself one messy situation," he ranted.

"You're probably right," Ian agreed, "but what can be done about it?"

"I don't know," he admitted. "I'm afraid there is more to this bear market than is generally recognized. I've been continuing to liquidate positions myself, when it's possible. I've managed to move another 350,000 C.D.R. shares to an investment trust, at $22.50. Some of these trust boys are taking the bait and falling for the bear trap illusion," he sneered sarcastically, "and I mean to let them have it! I hope I'm right."

Baruch was a businessman and as such he was a master of balancing subtlety with drama. The glare he sent Hoover's way lacked both of these and was mostly just baleful.

"Come now, Bernie, you know how I feel about my predictions. I admit I was more optimistic than events called for and I realize the markets have yet to recover. I can admit when I'm wrong, but you know a president has to maintain a positive view. We can't go around predicting gloom and doom; we have to convey optimism, while conserving credit and government expenditure. We continue to work intensely with the Federal Reserve in this regard, moving to a conservative posture of fiscal and monetary restraint."

"The heart of the problem," advised Baruch, "is that we've gone from a period of wild excess credit to the very opposite; shrinking the money supply and bank credit. We may have overreacted to the market crash, doing more harm than good."

Neither of these worldly men, dining in the White House on October 27, 1930, could possibly have foreseen the economic devastation that would manifest itself in 1931 and 1932. Hoover would be driven from office in the aftermath which would lay the groundwork for a whole new political and social order to be conceived by Franklin D. Roosevelt, which would be known as the New Deal.

But that is then and this is now. James and Ian proposed toasts to the president, who in turn toasted Prime Minister Benson and the great relationship between their two countries. That night, they told tales of younger days and business adventures long passed until late into the evening. When it was time to retire, the president's limousine was called to meet them at the east gate entrance. President and Mrs. Hoover wished them all luck and escorted them personally to the private exit.

The following day, they boarded the Washington Express for New York, dubbed the 'Congress on Wheels' whose club car had transported so many senators, congressmen, and lobbyists who commuted between the two great power centers of the nation.

Baruch convened a dinner party at his Fifth Avenue mansion for his British and Canadian friends on the eve of their departure for England, with guests including Averell Harriman, Franklin D. Roosevelt, New York Governor John D. Rockefeller Junior, and Richard Whittney, the president of the New York Stock Exchange.

There was vigorous discussion centered around Maynard Keyne's most recent book, The Economic Consequences of the Peace, which revealed the alarming terms and severe reparation demands of the Versailles Peace Treaty. It also focused on the disturbing warnings cited in a recent publication, Mein Kampf, by the jailed rebel, Adolf Hitler. Baruch was in complete agreement with Winston Churchill's dire concerns of the peace treaty backing Germany into an economic straitjacket, a fact he shared with any who would listen, frequently adding that he feared this could severely unravel the Europe's hard-won peace.

"Winston maintains that Mein Kampf is a candid blueprint to war, and yet no one is taking him or it seriously. He's a voice in the wilderness, while the British hierarchy and the peers of the realm, even some press lords, led by Rothermere and Beaverbrooke, pay court to the newly-elected chancellor Hitler. They visit him in Berlin and make publications praising his leadership and hard stance against Communism."

Franklin Roosevelt questioned the table about Keynes's foreboding. "Weren't his predictions overly pessimistic? Why shouldn't Germany pay up? Didn't they start the bloody war?" he asked.

"I'm not qualified to judge," responded Baruch, "but I know that Winston is watching political developments in Germany like a hawk, and that fellow Hitler, particularly with apprehension. I guess we all should take a damn good look at Mein Kampf. It sounds like a bloody depressing forecast."

"Canada paid a hell of a price over there from '14 to '18: 60,000 of our boys killed and a further 140,000 wounded, and for what?" exclaimed Richard in disgust. "I say, put the bloody Huns back in their cage and watch them like a hawk! They're a goddamn warring race; always have been, always will be."

Bernard Baruch picked them up at the Waldorf at noon the following day and saw them safely to the Duchess of Athlone, docked at Pier Five in the Hudson River.

As they arrived alongside the vessel, the band was playing "Happy Days are Here Again," while confetti and streamers showered from the decks over the dock.

Onboard the beautiful, twenty-thousand-ton Duchess, owned by the Canada Dominion Railroad Corporation, they enjoyed the finest staterooms on the upper deck, as directors of the company traveling with the prime minister.

SAILING ON THE *DUCHESS*
WITH THE DUCHESS

At four p.m., the Duchess of Athlone weighed anchor, casting off amid a host of well-wishers on the dock, with passengers lining the decks, waving and throwing streamers to their friends.

As the ship slid out into the Hudson River towards the Statue of Liberty to the sound of 'Happy Days are Here Again', James stood at the rail with his arm around Elizabeth. As they watched the New York skyline fading into the distance, he kissed her gently, commenting, "Well, my darling duchess, this may be the last time you'll sail on a Duchess as a duchess."

She laughed, saying, "You're a darling, James. It sounds to me like you want to make a lady of me. Won't that be fun?"

Their three staterooms were filled with flowers, baskets of fruit, and Dom Perignon champagne, together with a personal note from the captain inviting each of them to visit the bridge, and to join him at the captain's table that evening.

Once settled in their luxury quarters, they strolled the decks, familiarizing themselves with the ship. Richard observed, "It is great to be with a couple of company directors, the service is superb."

Ian, laughed, replying, "Nonsense, Richard! It's traveling with the Prime Minister of Canada that gets the attention; but I guess owning a few shares of the company doesn't hurt either."

As the sun set that evening, they gathered on deck, at the stern of the ship to view the New York skyline, silhouetted against a crimson sky, and chatted about their North American trip. They even reminisced as far back as their early school days in New Brunswick in the 1890s, and about early entrepreneurial adventures on the prairies of western Canada at the turn of the century.

Ian, in a thoughtful mood, confessed, "In recent years, I've found myself reflecting on my boyhood days in Chatham. It was never something I thought too deeply on. I didn't enjoy my time there. I didn't have an easy time in school and the austere environment all along the Atlantic seaboard was never my style." He sighed wistfully. "Maybe I'm getting old, James, but I think it's time to do something for that area, that province. They need better schools, better hospitals – maybe even a historic museum or some other feature – we could put a fund together and make a difference, like we did last year after the crash."

"I never thought I'd see the day," Richard confessed to Ian, looking at him through fresh eyes, "when you two boys would become sentimental philanthropists. Have you, by any chance, been reading that recent biography on Andrew Carnegie? He's quoted as saying: 'America would have been a poor show had it not been for the Scots.' Apparently, he's also revealed a personal philosophy of his, that it's a sin to die rich and he's been working for the last twenty years of his life at giving his money away."

James laughed, "I can't say I've read it but I can say I want to. I am aware of his philosophy. I was always of a fan of his. The man had the right of it. He came to America barefoot and penniless, worked a week just for $1.20. He left behind poverty back home and struck big here. I think he was right to give a lot back, but perhaps there was an element of guilt there in his case. You can see it when you read about how he busted the famous union strike with machinegun fire at the Allegany River steel plant back in 1896."

DISCUSSION RE: CHILDREN AND WEALTH

"Well, we're not Carnegies, lads. At least, not yet," Ian chuckled. "But you're right, there's a lot we could do and a lot we should do. Just remember: even the footprints of a great colossus striding across the desert sands of the Sahara disappear before sunrise."

"Are you quoting my own sayings back at me?"

"Well you said it best, Richard! Nobody will know or even care what you've said, or how rich or poor you were. Those footprints will disappear. You'll only be remembered for what you've left as a lasting benefit to your country or mankind; the rest will be buried in the ever shifting sands of time."

"I might offer my own view," added James. "There is no immortality, except through one's children, and that's the only lasting oasis you can create to outlast the shifting sands of life."

"I must say, James, old boy," confessed Ian, "I've always suspected you had a well-concealed poetic side to your nature. Yes, indeed, whatever we do should be designed and financed to withstand the vicissitudes of time and tide, as was the Carnegie Foundation."

Their conversation turned to their children, as it often had in the past. Ian's son, Blair, was now twenty-four years old; and James's two children, Sheila and Matthew, were seventeen and fifteen.

"How's that handsome, headstrong, young stag, Blair?" asked James in warm admiration. "Is he still giving the old man a run for his money?"

Ian, smiling with pride, responded, "He most certainly is. We've had a battle royal going on ever since he came down from Oxford and took up flying. Wait until that young fellow of yours, Matthew, gets into his early twenties. They get the bit in their teeth, and by God, you can't rein them in." He laughed heartily. "These boys have never had to struggle for a goddamned thing, not even women.

"Blair's too bloody good-looking, and although I make him work for every nickel, he still thinks he's bloody rich. Of course, he will be, in time, but he's not yet and he should keep that in mind, the damned kid. There is some truth in the saying about being privileged to be underprivileged and not to have been dealt a royal flush at birth like us, but I love him dearly." He chuckled, "I'm afraid he's a chip off the old block."

James laughed, poking fun at Ian. "I wonder how you would have been at age twenty-four with a rich pop."

"That's what worries me, James. Probably impossible. Like father like son; but the saving grace is that Blair's got a head on his shoulders. It's just that, at times, he forgets to use it, especially when he's chasing women around Europe when he should be in the office, learning his trade as a publisher."

"You know how I've always felt about Blair," said James, "He's really very solid. Just let him sow his wild oats; he'll straighten out, you'll see. I don't worry about my boy, Matthew; but that Sheila, she's a femme fatale in the making; she'll find it hard to find a man strong enough to keep her from jumping the traces."

"You're dead right, old boy," replied Ian. "She's a beautiful piece of work; we'll have to guide her a bit when the pot hunters come around. You know the young bloodhounds around London sell romance for fortune. They can smell an heiress a mile off, especially those young impecunious bastards who think they can trade a title for a dowry."

"Of course they think that; plenty of them succeed!"

"Bah! Maybe we can encourage Blair to take a good look at her in a few years. Now what's this about Blair taking up flying?"

"Well anything for excitement, I guess," replied Ian. "He's joined a flying club in Surrey. He's there on most weekends, and often even on weekdays. They fly these damned little Tiger Moths, and I hear he's soloed. It's one hell of a distraction from business, and of course, the girls love it when they are taken for a flip."

"You know damn well we would have been up there if there had been such things as Tiger Moths around in our day, and if our pops could afford lessons," suggested James. "And as for the girls, can you think of anything more seductive than air flips for a young girl? Don't knock it, old boy. I'm even envious hearing about it."

"Yes, but I tell you, James, it worries me, especially when he talks about training with the Royal Air Force."

CAPTAIN'S TABLE

That evening's dinner party was set to start at 8:15. The hall was beautifully assembled, done up in elegant whites and golds. The captain's table, the largest and most elaborate there, had been set with place cards for the honored guests. Firstly, the prime minister was seated on the captain's right with Elizabeth on his left.

Lord Brandenbrooke was next to a well-known and moderately popular Hollywood star, Norma Shearer, who a Canadian actress originally hailing from Montreal. She left home for Hollywood in 1926 and won one of the first Academy Awards in 1929 for her lead in 'The Divorcee'.

Next to her was Mary Pickford who was chatting with her neighbour, Lord Dungarven. Mary, better known as 'America's Sweetheart', was another Canadian actress. She'd some time ago married the swashbuckling Douglas Fairbanks and the two were living at Pickfair, in Beverly Hills, Hollywood.

The guests savored their ice-cold vodka and caviar; chose between Chateau Lafite Rothchild and Dom Perignon champagne from the wine steward. The evening progressed as most such events did, with drink and song and pleasant conversation. The Canadians stole the show with their charm and their stories, tall tales of acting misadventures and light gossip poking fun at directors and actors alike. The captain interrupted at some point with a short but heartfelt, and slightly tipsy, speech about how honored he was to have such a star-studded cast of passengers onboard.

As the night carried on, it developed into a hilarious dinner party, with even the prime minister getting into the swing of things. He was on his feet several times, usually proposing half-serious toasts to the Canadian Hollywood stars.

Following dinner in an adjourning salon over coffee and liqueurs, the captain, a gregarious personality with a red, weather-bitten face and a keen sense of humor, persuaded Norma Shearer and Mary Pickford to do one of their pet skits from Idiots Delight with a talented guest at the piano, to everyone's amusement.

LOVE À LA KAMA SUTRA

When James and Elizabeth returned to their suite in high spirits, they sipped more champagne, while James recounted Norma Shearer's interesting comments about her husband, Irvine Thalberg, Louis B. Meyer's brilliant director. He chuckled over Mary Pickford's stories about her husband, Douglas Fairbanks, in his swashbuckling movies, Robin Hood and The Thief of Baghdad.

When they slid under the sheets, slightly tipsy, he quipped, "Is my duchess in the mood for her Beverly Hills lover, a la Rudolph Valentino?"

Elizabeth, throwing her arms around him, kissed him passionately, giggling, "My Lord, you may take me as you will. You are my Valentino."

It was always the same when they embraced; a sort of explosion of passion and sensuality. It was only seconds before they were in each other's arms in rapturous anticipation of the ecstasies to follow. The night was young, and they had never felt younger. James murmured, "We mustn't rush the moment, my love. It is so fleeting, even between passionate lovers."

"Yes, yes," she said, "but it is such bliss. I wish it could go on forever."

"I'll teach you some of the oldest erotic techniques from the oriental world when we're married, Duchie."

"Who cares about being married?" she laughed. "What's wrong with right now?"

"Duchie, my darling," he sighed, almost out of breath. "You remember when I explained Kama Sutra to you one night?"

Elizabeth let out a sigh of passion and longing remembrance. "Oh my, yes! What ecstasy! Are you going to teach me more?" she asked with an impish, sensual grin. "To think that the maharajahs practiced it for so long while we stuffy Brits in England maintained our dismally unimaginative sexual prejudices." She rolled her eyes. "The Victorian era must have been dreadfully boring sexually. Imagine, young apprehensive virgins being advised by their mothers before their wedding nights to just close their eyes and think of England. It seems ridiculous and yet, it's true. It even happened to me."

They slumbered to the salty scent of the sea air and the rhythm of waves lapping against the ship as she cut through the sea into the night.

When the trio met at breakfast following their morning promenade on deck and a review of morning radiograms, James reported Baruch's confirmation of the sale of a further hundred and fifty thousand shares of C.D.R. at twenty-one and a half, down nearly four dollars in the last ten days.

The headline news that morning, October 31, announced Hoover's request to Congress for a program to combat unemployment, which had grown to over four million.

They returned to one of the many salons for coffee and continued their chat. Richard Benson, discussing James's involvement with Northern Algoma Steel. Corporation, inquired how much labor the operations would employ at varying levels of production.

James explained, "The ore bodies in the Algoma district are enormous. The challenge is the smelting of the ore economically. The reserves are composed of hematite and siderite ores, typically very complex. I've ordered a technical analysis in search of an improved process to produce an economic concentrate."

"Do you think you're up for this challenge? It strikes me as a bit more involved than the last few."

James laughed. "Richie, my old son, when I have full control of this company, I assure you nothing will stop me from developing this mine and mill into one of the largest steel-producing operations in Canada. As soon as I have a bit more capital at my disposal, I'm going to buy out a few of our British and American shareholder peers and reorganize the debt structure." Richard didn't look completely convinced so James clapped him on the shoulder, saying, "Don't you worry about me, old boy. I am completely confident in my ability to do this.

"I've committed over a million dollars to this endeavor, buying stock at these distress levels of seventy-five cents per share, and the deeply discounted defaulted bonds," asserted James.

"If you can see your way to joining me, Richard, let me know. I'm confident we'll have a winner when this damned economy recovers."

"I'll go for five hundred thousand bucks," responded Richard. "Let me know when you want my commitment."

"Look, boys," interjected Ian, "our share of the C.D.R. deal is going to net the lot of us a profit in excess of sixty-five million dollars, depending upon the markets. Richard, I'll go in with you for $500,000. We'll follow the developments as James gets the company turned around. God knows where this depression is going to end, but when the economy turns, steel production will be one of the first things to lead the recovery."

As the captain's guests gathered in the salon for cocktails on the fourth evening of their journey, it was abundantly clear that the relaxing charms of ocean travel had taken hold, as the evening got off to a lively start with a choice of Russian vodkas, golden Caspian caviar, and Dom Perignon champagne.

Elizabeth was well in her element, beaming happily and dripping charm as she mingled. She spent a great deal of time with the Hollywood contingent, who were being entertained by Sir Thomas Lipton, a man well-known in the tea world, who had invited them to join his group as he regaled the ladies with many exciting tales.

His current story revolved around sailing escapades at Newport, Rhode Island, where he'd been unsuccessfully racing his boat, Shamrock, in his fifth attempt to recover the America's Cup. He was a great addition to the party; as a gregarious Scot from Glasgow and a self-made grocery boy who had put his famous tea on the world map through innovative advertising methods, he had many anecdotes to share.

The ship's orchestra was also in fine tune with the latest from the Broadway Musicals Girl Crazy, as well as songs such as George Gershwin's 'I Got Rhythm' and Fats Waller's 'Ain't Misbehavin''.

Richard, recognized as the pre-eminent passenger by the crew, was not a man generally known for his sense of humor. While Ian and James had seen him relaxed and playful before, no one would call him the life of the party. But in the here and now, out at sea, he was rapidly letting his hair down, drinking champagne and even dancing with the starlets.

Ian and James had never seen him in such high spirits – he was usually serious even in light-hearted moments and whenever the trio did party, Ian and James were almost always the wild ones – but it was a nice, if unexpected, change of pace. They could now finally focus on celebrating the culmination of the C.D.R. adventure and Richard's election as prime minister, a celebration which had been pushed back by political problems and the onset of the Great Depression.

There would, of course, be more challenges ahead, more accolades to be won, but for the moment, it was a time to rejoice, a time to reminisce; they could relax, withdraw and let the world go by, if only for a few brief moments. It was the perfect setting for James and Elizabeth to behave as honeymooners, retiring to their stateroom at odd times through the day, Elizabeth reminding James, with giggles, "You may regret having taught me about Kama Sutra, darling, but I never will."

The days and nights continued to be filled with sports activities and entertainment, until they docked at Southampton and said their bittersweet goodbyes to their many shipboard friends, with whom they had shared the Journey.

During their drive to London, Ian brought up the subject of funding worthy causes in his home province of New Brunswick. Richard listened carefully, smiling proudly and remarking, "Well, I am delighted to hear these altruistic thoughts. You two frontier adventurers have always been such Philistines," he joked. Ian laughed quietly. "It sounds to me like you've seen the light. Well, I'll support you both if you get things going. We've been damned lucky so far to have escaped a great financial calamity, and from what I hear, there aren't very many of us."

LONDON

In the late fall of 1930, the London market, while not as devastated as New York, had suffered deep declines. Between the election of the Labor government and a steadily declining Financial Times index, the city was withdrawn amidst depressing and gloomy forecasts.

Ian and James took their former prime minister to dinner at the Carleton Club. They were joined by many interesting and notable political figures, most of them Conservatives, and were delighted with the presented opportunity. Some of the more interesting of these included former prime minister and now-distant friend, Andrew Bonar Law, and the irrepressible Winston Churchill, now an M.P in the opposition.

As one might expect in such a crowd, discussion was heavily centered around political, specifically the great political event of this decade, the Great Depression and Wall Street's rather dismal performance, as it had given up over fifty percent of its early 1930 rally.

The New York market continued its chilling decline, proving most of the great bullish pundits wrong. In particular, attention was being drawn to one John D. Rockefeller, who had made a now classic, and erroneous, remark, "Believing that fundamental conditions in the country are sound, my sons and I have, for some days, been purchasing sound common stocks."

Alas, he was not the only one under financial pressure. Eddie Cantor, a radio comedian, cracked, "Sure, who else has any money?"

Meanwhile the president of General Motors, Alfred P. Sloan, was on record as stating, "Business is sound." The Ford Motor Company seemed to feel similarly and, as proof of their conviction, announced a general reduction in prices, lowering the price of the Roadster $15 and the price of the Tudor Sedan $25. It wasn't a great difference – the Roadster was still over $400 and the Tudor was now $500 even – but it did help. The vice president of sales would soon go on the explain, "We feel such a step can be made to assure continuation of a good business practice."

The Harvard Economic Society Report on September 30, 1930, was a classic: "The present depression has about spent its force." On November 15, they declared, "We are now near the end of the declining phase of this business cycle."

However, the true highlight of discussion was the agenda of the forthcoming Commonwealth Conference. There were reports of depressed conditions in all the countries of the empire, collectively accounting for a significant proportion of world trade. Richard explained to the group that Canada was particularly vulnerable, as it was more dependent on exports than most other countries, with exports accounting for over thirty percent of the country's gross national product.

THE CLANDESTINE RENDEZVOUS

Later that evening, Richard and the two roués wandered over to Ian's after-midnight club to share a laugh and swap yarns. The Clandestine Rendezvous was a neat mix between cozy, elegant, and just a little bit sleazy. The boys ordered drinks and Richard let himself be entertained by the other two's stories.

Ian shared the entire sordid tale of his dalliance with Sylvia for the first time, as well as explaining the role it wound up playing in the whole Atlantic saga. James, meanwhile, decided to elaborate on the series of events which eventually culminated in his meeting and romance with Elizabeth.

Richard, who was a long-time teetotaler, set down his fizzy water and ordered a double brandy, to the complete shock of his partners. The drink arrived by the time both stories were finished and he downed half the glass in an instant, remarking, "You two play women the way we play politics with our fellow caucus members. I'm damned if I know which is more dangerous or unscrupulous. I have to say, planting an informer in the inner sanctum is a high-wire act, but no stranger to what goes on in Ottawa, I'm afraid."

His friends lapsed into thoughtful silence before James, with a grunt, moved into a new tale, this one relating to a different member of Sir Edward's private team of secretaries, a beautiful bilingual Parisian girl named Jacqueline De Laporte. She had been living in Montreal for about ten years by that point. She had a nine-year-old son and a Canadian ex-husband, and lived on the lakefront close to Montreal.

"I was introduced to her on one of my visits with Sir Edward at C.D.R.'s head office," James explained. "Then one day, completely by chance, I happened to run into her at the newsstand in the lobby of the Ritz Carlton Hotel. Now, let me set the scene: stunning gal, all ebony-black hair and cobalt blue eyes. She had flashing eyes and a wicked set to her lips. Well, I just couldn't resist engaging her in conversation. She wasn't in any particular rush so we got to talking about Montreal and her job in the president's office.

"She told me it was pretty much a dead-end job, not much upward mobility even after several years of good hard work. At around four p.m., I asked her to join me for tea and she jumped at it, admitting to me, 'I have considered contacting you, Sir James, for some months; yes of course, I'm

227

227

delighted, but the Palm Court is a little too public, don't you think, n'est-ce pas? But anywhere else, I would love to.'

"As Elizabeth was out for the afternoon, I invited her to my suite for tea," continued James. "And what followed next . . . well, it was like something out of a Hollywood script! At first, I was very suspicious of her motives. I'm afraid I must confess to being rather rough and rude with her, but she held up and insisted that I understand what was going on. So I listened attentively to a tale of unrequited love and bitter vindictiveness.

"She was surprisingly familiar with every detail of the 'Atlantic' from the very beginning, as she happened to be privy to every one of Sylvia's communications with Senator De Rolland and the president. Can you imagine what a great help she was to me in the act of separating rumor from fact and in assessing our leverage with Sir Edward and his rebellious board of directors?

"Jacqueline, as it turns out, had been romantically involved with De Rolland before he met Sylvia. When he jilted her for Sylvia, he apparently used his influence to get her into Sir Edward's office and onto his personal staff, as a sort of consolation gesture. There, she became extremely familiar with all pf his business activities and even his social life. She's the one who warned me about Sylvia's designs, past and present, on Sir Eddie.

"She openly admitted to me that she had gradually become infatuated with the president and that she was aware of his past relationship with Sylvia. Her attitude was that, since she'd been eclipsed once already by Sylvia in her relationship with De Rolland, she was determined to make sure it didn't happen again between her and the president; but when she discovered that Sylvia continued getting all of Sir Edward's attention in her double-game with Lord Brandenbrooke, her secret passion for him began to wane. Even though he encouraged her in many ways, she suspected he was only playing with her emotions, and she became vindictive."

"James, I think we can all safely say this is beyond the fiction of a Hollywood movie," exclaimed Ian in fascination, relishing every aspect of the intrigue. "The great charade becomes more incredible with every word. Why doesn't one of us write a novel about all these characters, or maybe even a movie script?"

Richard chirped sarcastically, "A grade A or a grade C, old boy?"

James then continued to explain how he probed her about what was really going on between Sylvia and the president. She responded that Sylvia was wild about Sir Edward, and was constantly advising him, concerning Ian and the syndicate's activities through their go-between, Senator De Rolland.

"To get to the point," said James, "I asked her how she felt about us and Atlantic. Did she want to help? She answered, 'If Sylvia can play this game, why can't I?'"

Richard remarked again in jest, "This little charade goes to prove how women have sometimes changed the course of history. Is it a case of 'Hell hath no rage like a woman scorned?'"

"You're right, Richard, but about the movie script, I'm still not sure yet whether it's a grade A, B, or C, or who are the villains or heroes. When I've finished, you tell me."

"I was stunned at first," he continued, "but I sensed I had struck gold and went straight to the point. 'Can we do business, Jacqueline? That's the long and the short of it. If so, we'll set up a code name, Atlantic II, and I'll set up a trust fund for your son's education."

James grinned. "As it turned out, boys, it was worth every nickel, and a lot more."

As they listened intently to the tale of convoluted espionage and intrigue in silence, Ian became visibly incensed and perplexed, as he heard details of what he had suspected for some time. He exclaimed, "I never would have guessed Sylvia was that smart! I knew she was a piece of work, of course; and your gal, Jacqueline, how did you get her to play such a treacherous game?" Knowing James as he did, as well as having a low opinion of women, Ian suspected there was more to it than James was saying. Giving in to his suspicion, he fired off a personal question in jest, as he ordered more brandy, "She must have fallen for you, James, old boy. You old dog, how long was it before you took her to bed?"

"None of your goddamned business, my lord," James replied with a hefty laugh. "Remember, it's absolutely between us, and only us, forever. All is fair in love, war, and corporate raiding; but some confidences are sacrosanct. You set up Sylvia for reasons best known to you, and I set up Jacqueline; and I must admit she played fair and square."

"Well, boys," interrupted Richard, "you're quite a pair when it comes to the ladies. I couldn't bat in your leagues if my life depended on it. It took me forty-seven years to secure one relationship, and I hope it's the one and only."

The mellowing environment of the "clandestine rendezvous" brought on further discussion concerning their long term missions. Richard remarked, "This depression and growing unemployment calls for greater imaginative initiatives from governments, and from the lucky few who have survived this financial catastrophe."

"We could help out in Atlantic Canada with some specific projects," said Ian, "but, Richard, do you think we can do this? Turn government thinking into increased spending, instead of focusing on balanced budgets and contracting bank credit? All we've read in the press in England, the States, Canada, all the grim news you hear these days, it's all about 'cut spending', 'contract credit', and 'balance budgets'. It's the tortoise withdrawing into his shell in terror. It won't do anything other than drive this Depression even deeper."

"You're dead right, Ian. And what's worse is that it's getting worse," Richard confessed. "These 'economists' seem to be even more adrift than usual." He scoffed before adding drily, "You know, I've come to the conclusion that being an economist must be a marvelous profession; it's certainly the only one I know of in which you can be consistently wrong and continue to get paid instead of sued for malpractice. I can assure you that fiscal and monetary policies are high on everyone's agenda at the Commonwealth Conference in a few days."

The next morning, he called Ian at the Commonwealth from the Connaught Hotel in Mayfair. "I see New York was off again yesterday, my boy. Where did C.D.R. close?"

Ian, always up to date on all markets, reported, "C.D.R. closed at seventeen and a half. Bernie cabled to confirm the sale of another 132,000, at eighteen dollars a piece. Good old Bernie, he never misses. He must have socked it to one of those thirsty trusts. The Dow Jones closed off again at two hundred and sixteen, with the Industrial Index at two hundred and twenty." His face twisted into a dark, unhappy expression. He raised his glass and downed the last of his drink. "It's a grim market. God knows where the bottom is. I think we should continue liquidating what we can. Let's meet at Claridges for lunch. Say about 12:15?"

"See you then," said Richard.

SPORT OF KINGS

At twelve o'clock, Ian strolled out of the Connaught Hotel and turned onto Booke Street for a brief walk to Claridges. It was a lovely day. The air had a fresh, pleasant scent to it, though he could spy storm clouds on the distance. Looking all around him, he was forced to do a double take when his eyes alighted upon someone he could swear was Sir Edward Montgomerie!

It was hard to tell. The streets were relatively full of people and they blocked his view. And he was off in the distance. Still, he thought it might be Sir Edward. He was getting into a limousine in front of the hotel, accompanied by three people, two of whom Ian was certain were women.

They drove off before he could be certain who it was. However, there was an easy way to find out. He entered the hotel directly through the large foyer, where the usual string quartet was playing quietly in the corner, and he inquired at the reception desk of Sir Edward Montgomerie.

"Yes, sir," said the room clerk. "Sir Edward Montgomerie is registered."

"And do you, by any chance, have a Senator Olivier De Rolland in the house?" asked Richard on a hunch.

"Yes, sir, the senator is with us."

When James arrived and they had been escorted to their table, each ordered a glass of sherry, and Richard burst out with the news. "James, you'll never guess who's in the hotel suites on the first floor just up that elegant sweeping staircase. A couple of your old pals from Canada," chortled Richard. "Sir Edward and that French fellow, De Rolland, with a couple of gales, I think."

"Are you serious? I don't believe it!"

"Oh, yes, they're registered, I checked with the desk," said Richard.

"I'll be goddamned, those two operators are still going strong. Shacking up a long way from home," responded James, "I've never met Frenchy, as Ian calls him, but it would be fun to meet Sylvia's messenger. What did the girls look like?"

"I couldn't tell, really. One was blond, I think. The other looked tall and dark," replied Richard.

"Tall and dark, oh my God, not Jacqueline; no, it couldn't be," exclaimed James in astonishment, "but wait until Ian hears about De Rolland. My God, he'll be astounded. He'll go berserk with curiosity." Then as an afterthought, he said, "Maybe we ought to invite them to the House of Lords for lunch. That Frenchy fellow really goes for the lords and ladies stuff, I'm sure."

The following morning, Richard was picked up at the Connaught Hotel by his driver from the Canadian High Commissioner's office and chauffeured to Cartier's, on Bond Street, to pick up a diamond and emerald necklace for his bride in Ottawa.

"Just wait here, driver," he said as he stepped out of the car at the famous jeweler's front door. "I'll only be a few minutes."

As he approached the entrance, several clients were leaving, and a familiar voice called out, "Good morning, Prime Minister."

Looking up, he was amazed to see Sir Edward Montgomerie.

"Well, good morning, Edward, what a surprise, glad to see you here in England. How long are you here?" asked Richard.

"Oh, for several days. I'm at Claridges, but if you have a minute, let me introduce Lady Sylvia Fox, Mrs. Jacqueline De Laporte, and Senator Olivier De Rolland." Vividly recalling his introduction to the nefarious activities of these actors at Ian's Clandestine Rendezvous Club the night before, the surprise meeting caught Richard off guard; it was a bombshell, to say the least.

"Good morning, ladies. Good morning, Senator. Nice to see you all," stammered Richard as he fumbled for words. "What a coincidence, us all meeting at Cartier's," he chuckled. "Hope it's a good omen for this depressing bear market."

While settling his account for the necklace, he reflected on the Hollywood script that James had revealed at Ian's hideaway nightclub in SoHo. Having now met the female players of the great railroad saga, he was provoked to wonder, "Who's won who? Who was Sir Edward with, Jacqueline or Sylvia? And what about that De Rolland fellow?"

Pondering the answer to this riddle, if indeed there was one, he rang James immediately from a private phone at Cartier's. Upon hearing the news, there was a deadly, crackling silence at the end of the phone, then a gasp. "Hell, James, are you there?" asked Richard impatiently.

"Yes, yes, of course, sorry. I was just talking to Ian. We can't believe it. Well, ain't that one for the books? It sounds like the continuation of the movie script we talked about last night. You say they're all at Claridges, shacked up together? Are you sure? I can't believe it! How do I get in touch with Jacqueline? She'll give me the scoop. Ian says he'll be goddamned if he'll contact Sylvia, especially if she's with Sir Edward."

"Well, Sir Edward suggested we get together," said Richard. "I expect he'll call me at the Connaught. I'll check out the situation."

"But Richard," interrupted James, "I must see Jacqueline alone, and soon; if he calls, get a message to her to call me." "I understand completely, James. Let's see what I can do."

"These revelations are the strangest twists of fate," ruminated James, pacing the floor in Ian's office. "I mean, who's in bed with who? What do Eddie or Senator De Rolland know about the role these girls played in making our deal?" He turned to Ian, visibly excited. "My God, this is T.N.T., Ian, genuine corporate dynamite! The sport of kings! I can't wait for my clandestine meeting with Jacqueline. It will be just like old times," he exclaimed. "We understand each other so well. Why don't I just slip over to the hotel and see if she is registered? You know, she might even be around the grand salon at tea time."

"No, no, no!" Ian emphasized, but James was already long gone, practically sprinting away.

Ian hurried to catch up with him, barely keeping pace with James' brisk walk along Fleet Street. "You had better keep away from Claridges, my friend. I'll call up some of Sylvia's friends and discretely find out what's going on, and I'll ask them to get a message to Jacqueline to call you."

James slowed his pace and reluctantly agreed. The two men split, with James heading to lunch to get his mind off things while Ian rushed off to make the promised inquiries. When he returned to his office afterwards, his secretary handed him a list of calls. He thumbed through them impatiently. There were calls from bankers and brokers and lawyers and so on; nothing interesting until the very last slip jumped out at him.

Please call Jacqueline D. at 452-1010 before 3:15 p.m.

He grabbed the phone, putting the call in instantly.

"Good afternoon, Gainsbourgh Gallery. Jameson here," said a voice.

"Do you by any chance have a Mrs. Jacqueline De Laporte there?" asked James.

"Yes, sir," came the reply. "Just one moment, please."

She answered in a few seconds. "Is that you, James?"

"Yes, yes, my dear, it's me all right. How are you? I'm so glad to hear from you. I was delighted to hear from the prime minister that you were in London; it was so lucky you ran into him."

"Oh yes, wonderful," she replied.

"I hoped after our meeting that you might be here with him in London; it was so exciting to get your message. Can we meet somewhere quietly and soon?"

"My office, my dear. That's the most private place I can think of. Can you come this afternoon? about four o'clock? Take a cab to the city and tell the driver you want 56 Gresham Street."

"C'est bien, James. At four o'clock. Merci, cheri. I'll be there. *À bientot.*"

His secretary was able to keep him distracted for several hours while he impatiently awaited Jacqueline's arrival, filled with curiosity. She arrived promptly at four p.m. and was ushered into his large sitting room off his office suite.

"Jackie, my dear girl, how wonderful to see you; you're looking marvelous. Come and make yourself comfortable while we have tea," said James as he arranged the pillows of the sofa for her.

"My, it was exciting to meet the prime minister this morning," she enthused, "and then to get your message, James. So much has happened since I last saw you: the stock market crash, the Conservative election victory, your appointment to the House of Lords, and . . . my marriage."

"Your marriage? My dear, how exciting! To whom?" exclaimed James, do I know him?"

"Well yes, you do know of him; Olivier De Rolland."

"Do you mean Frenchy!?" he asked in astonishment, "I'm flabbergasted, no c'est impossible, I don't believe it! Are you serious? I thought you told me that romance was jinxed! My God, when?"

"Oh, just a few months ago, chéri," she said, all smiles. "It's a long story but we're very happy. Nobody knows that I know you or that you know all about Sylvia's game with Sir Edward through me. If they did, it would be une grande cause célèbre, or a donnybrook, as you say in Ireland."

"Nobody ever will, my dear, not from me, remember our deal. You have my word," said James emphatically. "Now what can you tell me about Sir Edward and Sylvia?"

"Well, first I have to tell you that Sylvia managed to make quite a lot of money in the C.D.R. shares, with the help of Olivier. They had a very simple plan and they stuck to it: buy when you buy and sell when you sell. As such, they really did quite well for themselves. Additionally, Olivier thought Sylvia was estranged from Lord Brandenbrooke and I guess his lordship thought, for a while at least, that she was estranged from the senator. So she got information from both sides.

"While I was on the inside helping you, I remained in touch with my old friend, Olivier, who helped me make money trading in a joint account he set up for us. All I had to do was keep him up on the activities of the inner sanctum and what was going on between you and the president."

"Good Lord!" chortled James. "With you two femme fatales at work, poor old Eddie boy didn't stand a chance, now did he? Not that I would have given him any more wiggle room."

Jacqueline continued with an airy laugh, "I always suspected Sylvia's secret passion was Sir Edward. I presumed that was why she kept him well advised of Atlantic's activities through my dear Olivier and why she came back to Canada after Ian threw her out. Is it true he gave her a check and it bounced?"

"Oh my god, you've heard about that?

"Yes, Ian has related the story to me. I really can't get over the turn of events; they're astonishing, my dear. But what you may not know is that Sylvia went broke in the market crash, and Ian bailed her out."

"Ah mon dieu! She never told me. Are you sure? It must have happened without Olivier knowing, but your syndicate, it made beaucoup d'argent, non? And you know Sir Edward, he made beaucoup aussi."

"Sir Edward did what? No, it's impossible! Not my nemesis!" James shouted melodramatically, throwing his arms in the air. "It boggles the mind, how?"

"Je ne sais pas quoi vous dire, chéri! That man, even when he was fighting you and Union Pacific, he was buying stock for himself and Sylvia. I can't tell you what they made, but c'est beaucoup." She nodded in emphasis. "He did what Olivier did, bought when you and Ian were buying, and sold when you were selling. Once, I overheard him say to a few confidants in the boardroom," she tittered and giggled at the memory before mimicking Sir Edward's voice and mannerisms, "'If we can't beat those sons of whores, we had better join them. I don't like that son of a bitch Brandenbrooke, but he and Baruch sure know how to make money.'"

"Well, my dear," laughed James, wiping tears of mirth from his eyes, "that really is a staggering, yet fitting, finale to the whole 'great railroad charade'." He leaned back in his seat, almost wishing he had a cigar. It felt like a cigar moment. "You can't deny it was a great time to be alive.

"Let me tell you, if you heard this story in a play in Drury Lane or even in a Hollywood movie, you wouldn't believe a word of it. You'd leave the theatre at the end scratching your head and wondering what addled mind came up with such a crazy plot. Well, it's pretty much over and done with now? So what do say we should do now, my dear? Perhaps Ian and I ought to accidentally meet you all at tea time at Claridges for the last hurrah. We could put on a pretty good act, don't you think?"

"Ah, non, non, chéri. Mon Dieu, c'est trop difficile. Your friend Ian might explode. You see, Sylvia has a very young son who some people say is Sir Edwards', but he says it's Monsieur Brandenbrooke's, and Sylvia won't say."

Upon hearing this revelation, James was startled again. He was sorely tempted to reveal Ian's side of the story, but restrained himself.

"We know neither of them wanted marriage or scandal," she continued, "So I understand they are both contributing to her high lifestyle to keep her quiet. But James, I have the grand secret. Sir Edward still doesn't know anything about the strategy and intrigue played by Ian through Sylvia, and I certainly have never disclosed anything to my husband about our communications. My secret remains my secret and your secret."

"These revelations are so bizarre, my dear," exclaimed James as he continued in a state of amazement. "Are you saying we should just let sleeping dogs lie? Why stir the cauldron of intrigue? Let them figure it out for themselves?"

"Mais oui. Exactement, James. C'est mieux comme ça, n'est ce pas?"

"Well my dear, you're probably right. I'm quite sure Ian wouldn't want to get involved again. And if the boy isn't his, well, it wouldn't be the first time he's been tricked by a huntress. I know he's always suspected Sylvia of having a secret passion for Sir Edward–"

"As secret as the Eiffel Tower," Jacqueline interrupted slyly. James dissolved into barks of laughter.

"Well, you have the truth of it right there! Anyway, seeing them together here in London is just confirmation. And yet, in spite of everything, I'm sure he will see to it that the boy has every advantage in life. If there's just one thing I know about his lordship, it's his unswerving commitment to young boys and their education."

Tea was the last thing he wanted following this tale of surprise and intrigue from Jacqueline. It was whisky he sought for relaxation, reaching for his decanter as he said au revoir to Jacqueline and wished her luck.

Provisional Ending (ignores most of the previous chapters)

To say that Ian's world ended with a whimper rather than a bang would be highly inaccurate, though the reverse would be even more so. After C.D.R., everything went five ways to hell.

The event, or rather series of events, later known as the Great Depression, happened in accordance with Baruch's predictions. It was a slow beast, full of false starts. For a time, there was hope it would not be as terrible as it seemed.

False hope, in the end. For all that it started much slower than history would later recall, it was no less inevitable.

Most of the syndicate managed to avoid the immediate fallout, entirely thanks to Baruch. But as time carried on, even they felt the pressure. Ian and James survived largely unscathed. They were both spending most of their time in London at that time and London was not affected quite to the same level as New York or the rest of the States.

But Richard, Richard suffered. Not financially; even if he had, Ian and James would have bailed him out. No, Richard suffered politically. He was Prime Minister only a scant while before the people ousted him.

He was not a bad prime minister but his rise to power coincided with the advent of the Great

Depression. People like to blame politicians for all their problems. Sometimes they are right to do so. Sometimes, they are not.

Richard was innocent but he paid the price. Ian could still remember the devastated look on Richard's face the next time he saw him.

In truth, Richard never fully recovered from the loss. He retired from politics and spent the rest of his relatively short life with his wife and young son. Of the trio, he was the first to go.

Ian maintained he regained some happiness in his latter years, perhaps even a happiness he'd lost long ago or maybe never even had to begin with: the simple happiness of a family.

The years of the Great Depression marked the end of an era Ian had thought immortal in every sense and it did so with a quiet, devastating insistence.

But then, not so long afterwards, the second end of Ian's worldview came with the slow, insidious march of war, specifically World War II.

Ian had been done with war after the first one and, it seemed, so had the rest of the world. But not Germany. Specifically, not one Mr. Adolf Hitler.

Even on his deathbed, Ian's fists would clench in rage at the thought of Adolf Hitler. The man was brilliant, a brilliant orator and a brilliant judge of political climate.

The Nazi war machine would have never gotten anywhere near as far along as it did if it weren't for the complacency of war-weary politicians and Hitler's unapologetic abuse of their incompetence.

The only politician to see through him was Winston Churchill. Winston did good for himself, during and after the war. But Ian could sometimes scarcely remember the days that came after.

Sometimes, the war was the only part of his silver years that felt real. He played his part, as did most people at the time. He designed planes and his planes turned the tide of battle.

He would always take pride in that. But the war weighed heavy on his bones, his and James' both. They'd both been semi-active businessmen up until that point but both had retired after the war.

James and Elizabeth were happy together, with their two sons and their adorable young daughter. Sometimes Ian was jealous of what James and Richard had.

But he knew he'd brought this upon himself. He never fully reconnected with either his wife or son, though not for lack of trying.

Most days, he was over at James' place or visiting Richard's grave. He knew his time was fast approaching. James was older than him, yes, but Ian felt older. There was a weight to his bones he could tell James lacked.

Death used to be so scary. It used to terrify him out of his wits. But age brings . . . not necessarily wisdom but perspective. Everything dies. He could feel the Reaper creeping closer.

At this stage, he was no longer afraid, merely . . . waiting.

And, he supposed, that was quite alright.

Printed in the United States
by Baker & Taylor Publisher Services